Evorath: The Rise of Yezurkstal

ISBN 978-0-9978838-2-4

Free Dragon Press, LLC

www.freedragonpress.com

https://www.evorath.com

Book II of the Evorath trilogy. Immerse yourself in a world of fantasy adventure with the Legacy of Evorath family of books.

Read free stories online and keep up with future releases.

www.evorath.com

Please see the end of this novel for an appendices section, which provides a reference for Evorath, a map, and presents additional information within the world.

Chapter 1

Somewhere in the Runeturk Mountains
21 Zerrum, 1087 MT

The sun reached up over the mountains, light trickling down through the cliffs and crevasses. A putrid odor wafted out from a large cave, the stench tainting the entire area. Yezurkstal stood just inside the entrance, his black garb tattered and torn, from his work over the past week.

A griffin lay lifeless in the back of the cave, the sunlight only barely exposing the wounds Yezurkstal had inflicted. The cave floor was red, dried blood surrounding the once regal creature. Flies and other insects circled around it, feeding on the open wound. Maggots had already hatched from the beast's wounds and a cockroach crawled down its side, scurrying off further into the cave.

Yezurkstal was finally getting close to figuring out the secret to accessing the other realms, but no matter what progress he made he always fell short. It came naturally for him to reach into the plane of demons. But no matter how hard he tried, breaking through the barriers between other worlds seemed an insurmountable task. If he could reach into another plane, he might be able to find what he needed to save Evorath's people from themselves. After all, if he could summon forth demons with such ease, only the gods could say what other wonders were out there to discover.

Clutching a small stone in his hand, the rough edges jabbing into his skin, he looked outside and cursed. Letting out a grunt he threw his arm forward, propelling the stone out and off into the distance. With his acute sense of hearing, he listened until it landed and rolled off somewhere unseen.

Frustration. It was an unfamiliar sensation for him.

This was the third sunrise he had witnessed from within the cave, which meant it had been over three days since he had eaten. Bringing his mind to this fact, he could feel the void inside his stomach calling out for sustenance. Hunger was a weakness, and after he solved his current dilemma perhaps, he would explore putting an end to his need for food.

Yes, that would have to happen.

Unfortunately, he had more pressing concerns at the moment. His wives and children had been left back with Verandas at their poor excuse for a home. Though Verandas was a competent General, it was past time Yezurkstal checked to make sure that everything was still alright.

He looked back into the cave before departing, debating whether to take its previous inhabitant with him for food. Though he had never eaten a griffin himself, he knew the meat was edible, and some considered it to be quite delicious. With a simple spell, he could transport it with relative ease, so perhaps it was best to just go ahead and take it. Or perhaps he could rectify all this failed time experimenting and try out another spell he had been working on.

Considering the corpse, he gathered up his magical reserves, pulling from the cave moss and the putrid air around him. Refocusing this energy, he channeled it throughout his body, mixing it around with his own life energy. He drew the energy close until it coalesced in his hands, palms emanating a dark gray aura as he approached the griffin. In his mind, he focused on the creature's flesh, willing it to move once again.

With a low hum, Yezurkstal placed his hands on the beast's side, passing the energy into the creature. Over the past few months, he had toyed with the idea of reanimating his enemies, but this was his first actual attempt. In theory, it would be like the mind control magic he had been using for a few years now but bringing back something from the dead brought in a new aspect, which was why he tied it into his own life force. He remained focused, intent on making this new experiment work out.

The energy drain was more than he had expected, even for a first-time spell, but he felt the magic flowing through the beast. The griffin jerked its head up with a shriek, wings flapping as the magic spread. Yezurkstal backpedaled and watched the creature struggle for a moment before pulling itself up onto its four legs.

It spread its eagle wings out wide, giving them a single flap and swinging its lion-tail around with a jolt. Taking a couple steps back, the griffin kneaded the ground, its talons digging into the dirt and displacing some small rocks. The creature appeared to be alive, but its empty eyes and silent heart said otherwise. Neither living nor dead, this creature would serve its new master loyally.

Yezurkstal couldn't quite describe the sensation he felt. It was as if the creature had become a part of him, like a phantom limb detached from his body.

Testing out his influence, Yezurkstal willed the griffin to take a few steps forward. Though griffins were said to be stubborn and proud creatures, it seemed like this one had lost all will of its own. It moved forward with no hesitation, looking at its master with emotionless, dead eyes.

Yezurkstal smiled a sinister grin, pleased to see he could get one of his spells right on the first try. Still, it had required much of his magical reserves, and the cave was all but bare of its latent magic as well. This made it that much more important that he head back home and check on his family. Grabbing a day of rest couldn't hurt either.

Once again, Yezurkstal willed his new pet into action, this time instructing it to step outside the cave. Following the beast outside, he regarded his own black cloak, which had been torn and tattered over the past few days. Unlatching it from his shoulder guards, he let it fall on the cave floor and continued forward with a certain spring in his step.

Failing to find a new plane over the past few days may have been discouraging, but this new spell could prove quite useful. Once he perfected this new spell, he could make sure that any fallen enemies became part of his army, a welcoming concept. It was the first magic of its kind -true necromancy.

The griffin stood silently outside the cave, looking forward with a blank stare. Yezurkstal considered the creature's wounds. Its side was sliced open, muscle tissue and tendons exposed. Beyond that, Yezurkstal had penetrated its underbelly and impaled the creature's heart with his sword, yet somehow this magic kept it moving as if it was in peak shape.

Kneeling down for Yezurkstal to mount, the griffin lowered its wings. Without regard to the open wounds, Yezurkstal proceed to climb onto its back, grabbing hold of its feathers and digging in his heels. He'd have to hold on tight this time around, but when he returned home, he would furnish this new pet with proper riding gear.

How had he not thought of doing this before?

With a mental nudge, the griffin spread its wings wide and pushed off the ground. Yezurkstal felt a light gust from his mount's wings, tightening his legs around its side to ensure he was not displaced. From his vantage point, Yezurkstal was able to appreciate the mountains more than he ever had before, the rock faces forming unique works of art. The tall peaks reached up in the morning sky, the sun reflecting off and glimmering as it hits the trees below.

As he soared down towards the lower peaks, he felt the cool breeze created by his momentum. The griffin flapped its wings, and the wind stung Yezurkstal's eyes. His mission often left him unable to appreciate the joys that life had to offer but soaring through the sky made Yezurkstal wonder what else he was missing.

Anticipating the thrill, Yezurkstal willed his mount to increase speed. The more he commanded it, the easier it became to do so, like the creature was simply becoming an extension of his will. The griffin dived down and threw its wings back, the force propelling them towards the lower peaks and the caves that Yezurkstal now called home.

After acquiring his wives last year and making a move on Erathal City, Yezurkstal had exposed his childhood home, which had left him homeless. Fortunately, he devised a divining spell to look for a suitable cave and stumbled upon his current home, which was more than two hundred kilometers to the east of his previous dwelling, and a few hundred meters higher. Unfortunately, it was still just a cave, and certainly not suitable for raising his people.

Soon, it would all change.

Yezurkstal looked ahead and noticed he was nearing the cave system. The hike up to the griffins' cave had taken him an entire afternoon, but this undead mount got him home in a matter of minutes. Willing the griffin to slow its decent, he prepared to dismount and thought of what he would tell his family. Once again, he had been unsuccessful, which meant they would still be unable to claim a legitimate home.

As the griffin set down just a few meters away from his home, Yezurkstal loosened his grip and slid off to the side. He paused for a moment, making sure his legs were steady after hitching a ride for the first time. Willing the griffin to wait outside, Yezurkstal strode towards the entrance.

Thanks to some warding and illusion magic, the outside of the cave appeared to be a sheer rock formation. It was one of

Yezurkstal's more creative works, and even if one were to lean against the imagined rock front, he would find it to be quite solid. Even if someone knew what they were looking for, no one would be able to enter without Yezurkstal's permission. He had made sure of that much.

Passing through the barrier, Yezurkstal immediately found himself accosted by the sound of crying babies and some muddled yells from further within the cave. Verandas greeted him only a moment later, stepping out from behind a sheer rock wall with a look of relief.

"Sir, we are glad that you have returned," he stated plainly.

"It does not sound like anyone is glad around here," Yezurkstal spat with contempt.

He had hoped that the children would all be sleeping when he returned so he could go over his plans without interruption. Now he would have to calm all the disgruntled children before he could accomplish anything. Sometimes, he wished the responsibility of purifying Evorath did not involve breeding a future generation.

"Sir, I think you should speak with Valkyrie about that. She says the children are getting too big for this arrangement." Verandas seemed timid as he spoke, a hint of fear in his voice.

"I will do that. But first, Any news from our minions in the east?"

Verandas nodded.

"Yes, sir. We got word just yesterday that they have reached the Marta Plains and the plan is in motion."

"Good," Yezurkstal spat, trying to ignore the incessant racket from the other room. Perhaps Valkyrie needed a reminder of her position.

It was strange. He had chosen each of his mates due to their aptitude for breeding, but when he transformed them into hájje they had lost most of their independent thought. For some reason, Valkyrie had kept more than the others and acted as a matriarch, representing the interests of all his wives. Fortunately for her, she did a good job, so Yezurkstal figured there was no harm in letting her continue.

Over the past year, she was the only wife that seemed to fully comprehend what he was trying to accomplish. Still, it was unexpected that it worked out that way. As he dismissed Verandas and strode back further into the cave, he pondered how it happened. This magic came without practice, so he did not understand much about it. Why did the spell he used eliminate free will in the first place?

As he moved closer to his crying children, he focused on the task at hand, affirming in his own mind that people were better off with diminished independence. After all, this proved to keep them more obedient, which made for a very orderly society. Without the evil of free will, he could ensure that everyone would live life as they should.

Entering the opened area of the cave that Valkyrie had named 'the nursery,' Yezurkstal shook his head in disbelief. Out of his fifteen children, only three of them were in their cribs. His eleven wives were chasing the others around the cave, the children all moving at different speeds and levels of success. Two of them were even taking a few steps prior to stumbling.

"Yezurkstal, we are glad you have finally decided to return," yelled Valkyrie over the cries of babies. Though her voice was usually controlled and rhythmic, it now sounded exasperated, with a definite hint of underlying anger.

She was stepping over the line.

With a flick of his wrist, Yezurkstal propelled a bolt of dark magic towards his counterpart. Having no time to react, Valkyrie cried out in pain as the energy hit her stomach, pulsing around and forcing her to drop to the ground. Her body convulsed for a few seconds, her screams of pain drowning out the noise of the babies. Releasing his hold, Yezurkstal approached his wife and looked down at her.

From his vantage point, he noticed that for the first time he felt no pleasure over inflicting pain. She looked pathetic.

"I will not be spoken to in such a tone ever again. If you do not mind your tongue, I will remove it." His tone left no room for doubt, and his ten other wives all looked at him with utter obedience, their faces flushed with fear.

Rising to her knees, Valkyrie wiped a few tears from her eyes and bowed her head.

"I beg your forgiveness. It will never happen again." She sounded pathetic.

Yezurkstal remained unwavering, glaring down on her without pity.

"Rise."

Without another word, Valkyrie looked up towards her master, a mixed expression of fear and sadness glued to her face. As she came up to her feet, Yezurkstal realized that all the babies had stopped crying.

Chapter 2

Erathal News Article 101:79
Writer's Addendum
By, Cyboral Cabal

It is my unique privilege to announce that tomorrow I will be attending the wedding of two very important people in the city of Erathal: Artimus Atyrmirid and Savannah Sylvanas.

A year ago, these two individuals lead our armies against the evil that ravaged our lands and kidnapped eleven young girls. They were also an integral part in the shift of leadership that has occurred over this past year. Most importantly, they are my friends.

To help us commemorate their journey of life together, I ask that any citizens who can attend be present at this momentous event. Appropriately enough, this event will be held near the center of the city, just outside where the recently closed food proctor building is located. The celebrant for this union shall be none other than high priestess Yojomein.

After the wedding ceremony, all guests are welcome to return and enjoy a reception within the old food proctor, where there will be wine and food for all to enjoy.

I hope to see you all there and am privileged to be able to provide this announcement on behalf of all Erathal.

Thank you both for your contribution to this great city, and we all wish you the most happy, productive, and prosperous future of your desire.

-=-=-=-=-=-=-=-=-

Erathal, Elvish City
21 Zerrum, 1087 MT

Today would mark the beginning of a new life for
Artimus. The smell of sweet incense filling the air, the sound of
harps playing a gentle melody and the sight of Savannah's
gorgeous face; these things added up to bring him into a state of
complete happiness. For the first time in his life, Artimus felt
truly connected with another elf, and today he would be joined to
her in the most holy matrimony.

Choosing the old Food Proctor as the location was
brilliant, leaving an open field where all witnesses and
participants could gather. Rays of sunlight danced upon his skin,
the gentle breeze offering a cool respite. With clear skies and
temperate weather, Artimus could not have wished for a better
day.

He stood facing Savannah within a circle of flowers, red
and blue blossoms mixed in with the green lilies. The flowers
were only a few centimeters away from them, surrounding them
and the priestess they chose to officiate this blessed day. The ring
of flowers was left unbroken, meticulously arranged in a perfect
circle to signify the united journey Artimus and Savannah were
embarking upon.

According to tradition, the families would stand just
outside the circle, but with no families to speak of, this space was
empty. A bard sat two meters to the east and another to the west
of the circle, both plucking their harp strings to produce a placid

and calming melody. To the north and south, an acolyte stood, each holding a thurible with incense pouring forth to the beat.

Around these officials, much of the city had gathered to witness this event. Artimus was still somewhat confused as to why so many had gathered, but he attributed it to the note Cabal had included at the end of his article yesterday. It all seemed too grandiose.

People from all walks of life were in the crowd. There were farmers and gardeners, blacksmiths and carpenters, hunters and fishers, and of course many fellow rangers. Most of those gathered wore their normal clothes, but he noted some of his closer associates wore special attire for this occasion. Among the crowd, he also recognized many of Savannah's fellow revolutionaries, each wearing a white gown to signify the solemnity of this day.

As was traditional for an elvish wedding, Artimus wore an unadorned, forest green robe with a simple hemp rope to keep it secured. With pressure from Savannah and some of her friends, he had it made from silk, which he admittedly found to be quite comfortable. Savannah also wore simple attire —a dress colored in the traditional soil brown and sewn from silk. It wasn't her best color and it didn't show off her figure like the usual attire, but it was tradition.

Artimus squeezed Savannah's hands, gazing adoringly into her sweet eyes as the priestess spoke.

"…And after this day, these two shall no longer be separate individuals, but instead are to be united as one. As they embark on their journey and enter into a new life, they must learn to act as one. Evorath has blessed us with all that we could desire, and now these two shall become one and bless one another with all they have…"

Some of the smoke from the incense crept past his nose, causing Artimus to turn his gaze downward and squelch a cough. The smell of pine filled his nostrils as he cleared his throat and returned his attention to Savannah.

"…Like a seed planted in fertile ground, the connection that is established today will still need to be nurtured and cared for. Love must act like water. Trust, like sunlight. Commitment, like compost. Only by truly accepting one another can these two spirits be joined in matrimony."

Artimus noticed Savannah's smile expand, her eyes glimmering with excitement. He could not help but reciprocate, a foolish grin coming over his face.

"So, Artimus Atyrmirid, will you devote yourself wholly to this woman, protect her, love her, and provide for her?"

"It is Evorath's will and mine as well. She shall be of my own flesh." Artimus felt as if he was observing himself as he incanted these words, a tangible excitement running down his spine and filling him with energy.

"And Savannah Sylvanas, now to be Savannah Atyrmirid, will you devote yourself wholly to this man, support him, love him, and bare his children?"

"It is Evorath's will and mine as well. He shall be of my own flesh." Savannah looked as if she might burst with excitement as she spoke, her voice higher pitched than usual.

"And so it is, and ever shall be. Once Evorath has willed it, it cannot be unwilled." The priestess spoke with force now, her voice booming throughout the clearing.

"Henceforth, Artimus and Savannah Atyrmirid shall be united as one. Through times of abundance and times of scarcity, they will have a bond beyond the physical realm. Their spirits are intertwined and shall remain as such for all eternity. Let everyone bow their heads now and observe the song of Evorath."

The bard in the east continued playing the harp, the melody of his tune slowing to a modest rhythm. He played four consecutive notes in a simple meter, progressively moving from a low pitch to a higher one. This simple melody continued for a few measures before the western bard pulled out a wooden recorder and joined in.

Tapping his foot to the rhythm of the first bard, the woodwind player started with a soft and calming melody. Each note worked to propagate the romantic atmosphere. Like most aspects of the ceremony, this traditional song was simple but effective, the soothing melody instilling a palpable feeling of love and commitment.

Artimus stood cradling Savannah's hands, peering deep into her eyes. The entire crowd stood listening in silence, affected by the contagious feeling of bliss. Artimus could feel his skin tingling as if he was being influenced by magic as the music rose in intensity, the recorder playing louder and more pronounced notes.

After the crescendo, the music lulled back into a soothing tone, a feeling of completeness overcoming him. Artimus was not a musician, but as he stood watching tears of joy well up in Savannah's eyes, he felt a connection to the music. Though he had heard this wedding song a few times in the past, it was different experiencing it from the center. This was a day he had been awaiting, and this song signified that the wait was over.

After what seemed like only a moment, the music faded, and the entire gathering was left in complete silence. This moment seemed to last for eternity, and Artimus held Savannah's gaze, he felt the fire fanned within him. He knew exactly what she was feeling as the priestess broke the silence.

"Now that you are joined in spirit, in mind, in soul, you shall also be joined in body. Go forth now and consummate this union in the name of Evorath and all her creation. Life must beget life, and by entering this union you have opened yourself up to the grace of Evorath.

"All of you gathered as witness today, bow your heads and leave room for the betrothed to enter their new dwelling. Artimus and Savannah Atyrmirid: accept the grace of Evorath and let it lead you to a fruitful and productive future. Go now and commence your life as one."

The married couple turned to face the south, where the crowd was stepping aside to make a clear walkway. Both bards began playing their harps again, also turning to the south to keep up with the married couple. Squeezing Savannah's hand, Artimus wore a large grin on his face as they walked. He noted again the familiar faces in the crowd, as well the unfamiliar ones. Everyone wore a smile.

Artimus kept his focus ahead, but out of his peripherals he watched as the crowd followed, keeping formation around the newly married couple. As was tradition, this crowd would follow him and Savannah to their new home. These witnesses would not disperse until the couple broke the barrier of their home, a symbolic ritual that showed Evorath's support.

Like any new marriage in Erathal, it was traditional for a couple to abandon their separate dwellings and immediately start a new life in a brand-new home. With the recent changes in governmental structure, they were no longer just assigned a home based on their professions. Fortunately, Cabal and some of Savannah's other friends had all pitched in and had this house built; they even helped Savannah move her Yggdril tree. Tonight would be the first night anyone slept in the home.

Artimus was just happy the house was built close to where Savannah had insisted they get married. As he and Savannah walked barefoot through the crowd of people, he couldn't help but wish for a change in the wedding tradition. The dirt road would have been fine on his bare feet, but as they walked through grass, he kept stepping on unseen pebbles and sticks.

Savannah faltered a couple of times as they walked, wincing slightly each time she did. Artimus just kept her hand held tightly, focused on moving with haste towards his new home. He was certain they were supposed to move at a slower pace, but now the anticipation was getting to him.

They hustled from the field and into the residential area of town. The crowd kept pace with them in silence, the bards continuing their gentle melody as everyone approached the new Atyrmirid home. Like most homes on the edge of the residential district, this one was larger than the average, but modest nonetheless.

It was crafted like a typical cabin, the outside walls made from unfinished hemlock to provide for a strong foundation. There were two windows at the front of the home, both covered by brown shutters, and an unassuming oak door in between. Leading up to the door, three stones provided for a short walkway.

Savannah let out a sigh of relief as they stepped onto the first stone, and Artimus noted that the bards had quieted their tune. If there was one thing Artimus hated, it was being the center of attention. Having these people follow him made him uncomfortable, so as he reached the front door he was overcome with relief.

Quite certain he was supposed to acknowledged those gathered before entering the home, Artimus turned around and held up his right hand, a nervous smile replacing his otherwise happy demeanor. With a gentle wave, he opened the door with his left and held it wide for Savannah.

Flashing him a look of disapproval, Savannah turned towards the crowd and gave a slight bow.

"Thank you all for coming, each and every one. We appreciate your support and look forward to sharing our joy with you all." Her speech sounded rehearsed, and as she finished Artimus realized that she had asked him to say something as well.

"Yes," he stammered. "Thank you all for coming." It wasn't much, but at least she could not accuse him of saying nothing.

Still, he noticed Savannah roll her eyes as she stepped through the doorway. Without wasting a moment, Artimus stepped through after her, promptly closing it behind and latching it shut.

Finally, he could be alone with his new bride.

"Well, Mrs. Atyrmirid, shall we explore our new home?" he asked the question with an emphasis on their last name, a satisfied grin coming back over his face as he moved in behind her and held her by the waist.

"I believe tradition calls for us to explore the bed chambers first," said Savannah, gently laying her hands on Artimus's own and slowly pushing them down to her thighs.

"In this case, I think I will agree with tradition," whispered Artimus, grabbing onto Savannah's thighs and spinning her around to face him.

"Lead the way," whispered his wife with a smile.

"I'll do you one better," exclaimed Artimus lowering himself and grabbing her around the knees. Standing back up, he lifted her over his shoulder and began walking towards the bed chambers to the right.

She let out a squeal and laughed as they passed the fireplace. Artimus tried to ignore the faint squeak of a loose floorboard as he approached the doorway to the bedroom, which had been left ajar. Holding out his left arm, he pushed the oak door inward and stepped inside, going to one knee and letting Savannah back down.

He had actually been looking forward to showing Savannah the house, but he could not argue with her on this. If he was honest with himself, he had really been looking forward to this for a long time anyways. Savannah giggled some more as she stepped backwards towards the bed, and Artimus crept forward towards her.

The bed chambers were decently large, with two dressers against the far wall, the large bed, and a wardrobe wide enough to store more equipment than Artimus could imagine them needing. Right now though, his only concern was with his new wife and the absurdly large bed behind her.

Savannah seemed just as eager, for as she backed against the bed she grabbed a hold of her dress and wrenched it over her head, leaving her with only her undergarments. Artimus admired her pale, slender figure for a moment before moving in and kissing her.

Chapter 3

"If we leave the caves of Jyrimoore, it is much more likely this pesky Avatar will find us. Remember what happened three months ago when I ventured into the forest?"

Yezurkstal sat on a smooth stone, looking across his makeshift, stone table at General Verandas. The general stood at full height, looking back with an inquisitive expression. To his right, Valkyrie listened obediently, still seemingly worried to speak up.

"What about the spell you use on this cave? Wouldn't that shield us from him?" Verandas asked.

"Perhaps. The issue would be moving all of you there and setting up the proper enchantments though. My wives would also have to make sure not to let our children wander outside of the protected area. Could you handle that Valkyrie?" Yezurkstal turned to his matriarch, whose face became pale at mention of her name.

"Yes, sir. I will make sure all your children stay within the enchantments." Despite her flushed cheeks and apprehensive expression, her voice remained strong and confident.

Still, Yezurkstal was not sure it was wise to bring his people back into Erathal forest. Though he possessed tremendous power, Yezurkstal had been reminded on more than one occasion that he was no match for the avatar. That evil creature held powers straight from Evorath herself, and without some more development of his magic there was no way Yezurkstal could best it. Waiting for an update from the Marta Plains might make more sense than venturing out now.

"We will make our move, but only after I finish mastering this spell that I am working on. It will give me access to the armies we need to stand on our own. I can't always be around to protect everyone after all." Yezurkstal looked to Valkyrie and then Verandas, waiting for their responses.

Valkyrie responded first.

"As you will it. Still, I must remind you that your children need more room, so the sooner we can make the transition, the better." As she spoke, she kept her glance cast downward as a sign of submission, her tone betraying her bold words.

"I will do as you instruct," added Verandas in a monotone.

"Good, because I am going to ask more from both of you then I normally would. Verandas, I am going to get some fresh air and think over our next move. When I return, I need you to head out to the outskirts of the forest for reconnaissance. We will want to find a suitable place to build a village. Hiding may be useful but hiding in plain sight gives us a unique advantage."

"Yes, sir," replied his underling mechanically.

"As for you, Valkyrie, I am going to leave you completely in charge. With the cloaking field around the cave, you shouldn't have any trouble. Just keep the children in check for a few more days. I am on the brink of figuring this spell out, and once I do, I will return with an army."

"If that is what you wish, I will obey," answered Valkyrie a hint of aggression creeping into her voice. Fortunately for her, it was not so much that it was obvious, so Yezurkstal let it slide.

Rising from his uncomfortable seat, Yezurkstal looked to Valkyrie and Verandas in turn.

"You both do a great service to me and to all our people. That service will not soon be forgotten. Remember what we are working for in these coming years, for it will take time to achieve our goals."

Not expecting a response, Yezurkstal turned and marched towards the cave exit.

-=-=-=-=-=-=-=-=-

Yezurkstal strode through the mountain pass. Shuffling through some loose dirt and stray pebbles, working to keep his balance, he thought back to the conversation with his family. Living in the mountains was not what his people were meant to do. It was beneath them. In fact, any creature that could tolerate such a place as home would have to be eliminated to assure Evorath could truly reach its full potential.

This would present a particular problem with the dwarves, who had a substantial city established in the northwestern part of the Runeturk Mountains. With their advanced weaponry, inherent fighting spirit, and superior tactical positioning, they would be all but impossible for any traditional army to defeat. Luckily, they had been isolated from the forest since before Yezurkstal was born, so they would be there unsuspecting when it came time for their elimination.

There must have been some magical influence on his thoughts, for as Yezurkstal continued forward he could hear some movement from within a cave up ahead. Estimating it to be about five meters away, he immediately channeled some energy into his boots, ensuring a silent approach. With his enhanced hearing, he could discern two -no, three voices- from within the opening in the cliff face.

As he crept towards the cave, their harsh notes and raised tones suggested they were having a heated exchange. Reaching the mouth of the cave, Yezurkstal remained outside and listened for a few moments.

"I don't care what you consider 'pure!' This does not live up to Dwarven standards! I will not pay you ten gold pieces for such an inferior product!" This voice was gruff and low pitched, probably belonging to an older dwarf. The volume of his voice raised as he spoke, becoming more and more agitated.

"We will not accept anything less than ten pieces!" insisted another voice, this one feminine and discordant.

"Yes, so we suggest you reconsider," added another female, this one sounding younger and less sure of herself.

Judging by their shrill voices, Yezurkstal guessed they were harpies.

Done with his little game, he turned the corner and stood in the entrance, his right hand resting on the hilt of his sword.

"I'm afraid that none of you have need for gold any longer, or for whatever inferior goods you are peddling," interjected Yezurkstal. He stood in place, waiting for one of the fools to make a move.

The dwarf looked over Yezurkstal head to toe, disregarding him in turn.

"Who in the name of Kelgen's beard do you think you are you daft, albino elf?" the elderly dwarf inquired.

Yezurkstal considered the little creature. The dwarf had a long beard, the colors ranging between brown, gray, and white. For clothing, he wore a simple brown tunic and green pants supported by a brown, leather belt. His boots appeared well-worn, but expensive, the buckles somewhat more garnisheed than Yezurkstal had expected.

Though he was clearly a merchant, the dwarf also had a rather sizable hatchet at his side. A simple, wooden cart rested just beside him, some empty burlap sacks placed inside. He would present little threat.

Before making his move, Yezurkstal regarded the harpy sisters. They appeared to be twins, both ugly and undernourished, with eyes full of hate and desperation. Their bodies were frail, ribs showing through the thin layer of feathers. These feathers looked thin as well, some exposed area of skin due to a lack of proper care, the natural purples and blues fading to a dull gray in many areas.

There was perhaps a few centimeters difference between the two in height, the taller of the two probably a half meter shorter than Yezurkstal. Though neither of them had weapons, it was well known that these carnivorous flyers could do considerable damage unarmed. If Verandas had been faced with such a threat, he might be in trouble, but for Yezurkstal they were no more a threat than the old midget.

"I am not an inferior elf," replied Yezurkstal with his attention turned back to the dwarf. "I am a hájje."

With his proclamation, he threw his hand forward and propelled a bolt of dark energy. Normally, he would have considered making the dwarf one of his own, but since he planned on building a more perfect army to work with, there was no need for a short little peddler such as this. Instead, his spell was intended to kill.

The dwarf was much quicker than he appeared however, and much sharper in his reaction time. Without hesitation, he dove away from the blast and behind his cart. The magic passed overhead and dissipated against the cave wall.

Impressive.

With a smile on his face, Yezurkstal pulled out his sword and advanced towards the dwarf. Though the two harpies had been arguing with this little creature just moments before, they sided with him for this skirmish, both lunging towards Yezurkstal on the offensive. Their talons spread wide as they neared the dark elf, sharp teeth showing through demented scowls. They were making this too easy.

With one swing of his sword, Yezurkstal sliced clear through the taller sister's neck, decapitating her effortlessly and following through to dig the blade deep into the other harpy's shoulder, dismembering her arm. The body of the first sister continued its flight through the air, but Yezurkstal avoided it with a simple step to the right, using his left arm to guide it harmlessly away and to the floor.

The surviving sister shrieked in pain, wailing like a banshee as she grabbed for her dismembered arm. Blood poured from the wound, and the harpy began crying tears of pain as she fell to her knees. Swinging the blade back around with a figure eight, Yezurkstal continued his momentum and brought his weapon overhead before dropping it and instantly ending her life.

The dwarf was cleverer than Yezurkstal would have predicted, jumping to take advantage of the hájje's turned back. He threw his hatchet with full force, the blade spinning over itself towards the dark elf's back. Yezurkstal pivoted around just in time to intercept the projectile, throwing his free hand up and catching the weapon by its handle. Ignoring how close he had just gotten to being hit by this axe, Yezurkstal focused on the dwarf who had thrown it and smiled from ear to ear.

"You have some real spirit for a mountain dweller," he laughed cynically, casting the axe aside and slowly moving towards the dwarf like a lion stalking its prey.

"If you wanna see real spirit mate, then fight me like the animal you are." The dwarf spat on the ground in front of him. "Face me without that weapon of yers."

Yezurkstal chuckled, carelessly dropping his sword on the ground by his side.

Once again, the dwarf demonstrated surprising speed, springing forward and spinning around to deliver a powerful punch aimed for Yezurkstal's groin. As surprising as it was, Yezurkstal was quicker, putting forth only marginal effort to deflect the blow and counter with a hammer fist to the dwarf's skull. Yezurkstal winced slightly as his fist landed; the dwarf had a harder head than any creature he had encountered before.

Still, the blow was enough to leave the dwarf dazed. The small merchant took a step back and his eyes rolled in his head as he struggled to focus on Yezurkstal. With one last laugh, Yezurkstal took the opportunity and grabbed the creature's throat, squeezing with all his might to crush its windpipe. As he let go, the dwarf dropped motionless to the ground, letting out one final breath as the life escaped its body.

Gently rubbing the bottom of his hand, Yezurkstal turned to retrieve his sword. Though his initial thought was to leave the bodies as they were, curiosity got the better of him. Replacing his blade in its sheath, he turned back to the dwarf and knelt, placing his hand on the merchant's head and searching through recent memories.

Normally, Yezurkstal took the memories and knowledge of those he transformed, but with no desire to expose his children to a dirty creature such as a dwarf, he was left sifting through them manually. It was a bit trickier but required very little energy. Most of the information this dwarf possessed was worthless, including exchange rates, market values, and other financial concepts. Eventually, Yezurkstal would eradicate the concept of currency from Evorath entirely. It was an evil construct and there was no need for it in his perfect world.

After sorting through some of this worthless information, Yezurkstal found what he was looking for. He saw himself from the dwarf's perspective, inspecting tobacco leaves the harpy sisters were looking to sell. He rummaged through the bag, pulling out one of the leaves and taking an exaggerated smell. It was not low quality, but it was certainly not as impressive as the sisters had said it was.

Yezurkstal shook his head, pulling himself out of the dwarf's memories. What a waste of time.

Kicking the corpse in anger, Yezurkstal rose to his feet and walked towards the mouth of the cave. He had work to do.

Chapter 4

Erathal News Article 101:82
Remembering Our True Leader
By, High Wizard Guildpac

In three weeks' time, every elf around Erathal will be faced with a potentially life-altering decision. Since this is to be the first ever election to occur among elves, it is important to remember the real issues for which we are voting. We must all remember the history of Erathal and keep this in mind as we move forward.

This new concept of a republic to replace our long-standing monarchy may certainly have merit, but as intelligent and independent citizens, we must vote for the elf who can ensure our continued survival as a kingdom. Keeping this in mind, remember who has been there for you in your times of greatest struggle. Even just last year, when our kingdom was threatened by a powerful hájje, remember who sent out an army of our finest warriors to keep us safe.

Also, remember whose ancestor was responsible for killing the arch demon in this very city. Remember Ulagret, the king who united all elves under the flag of Erathal and brought us from disorganized and scared nomads to a cohesive and united society, organized for the greater good of all. As our ancient history tells us, he made a promise that all elves would be united and safe from future invasions, and he and his bloodline have kept that promise for three generations.

There are two candidates in this election for Chancellor, but only one elf has a history of providing for us in the way that we need to be provided for. There is only one elf who has shown time and time again that he understands what the people need and is able to make the hard choices to ensure everyone is taken care of.

On the other hand, there is an elf who has shown he is not above convoluted lies and deceit to advance his goals. Faking his own death to escape his duties as a senator and then using his position to usurp authority from the true ruler. No one really knows what he has been up to all these years, and it is safe to say that he hasn't been doing anything to help the average citizen.

As for me, I can assure you that I will not be taken by these false promises. I will be casting my vote for the elf who has shown time and time again that he is looking out for the good of all. My vote will be cast for Ulagret III.

-=-=-=-=-=-=-=-=-

Erathal City, Castle Meeting Hall
24 Zerrum, 1087 MT

For nearly twenty years, Artimus had been wholly content with his role in life. Each day brought with it new crimes, and each day he would solve those crimes. For many, it might have seemed like a boring routine, but to Artimus it meant structure, which meant predictability —an important facet of an otherwise unpredictable existence.

Waiting in the central meeting hall of Erathal castle, he almost wished to return to those simpler times and resume his role as head investigator. Though he agreed with most of the long-term objectives of this new republic, he wished the transition could be smoother. Somehow, the resistance had pulled off a non-violent revolution, but the time it was taking to organize a system people could accept was nothing short of exhausting. This left many citizens in a rough position when it came to finding work, and Artimus was one of them.

A year ago, he would have never imagined himself wearing an uncomfortable, ceremonious purple robe while standing guard for Cyboral Cabal. He also would not have imaged that anyone outside of Ulagret and his wizard puppet Guildpac would have been involved in a meeting of this importance. Then again, a year ago he didn't even know that Cabal was still alive and Erathal was still a monarchy.

Yet, now he shifted uncomfortably as he waited for the guests to arrive, resting his right hand on the hilt of his bastard sword, and going over every detail in the room to better understand his surroundings.

The room was small compared to most in the castle, fifteen meters long by ten meters wide according to the figures Artimus had been given. They seemed accurate. A decorative chandelier sat centered in the room, hanging about three meters down from the unnecessarily high ceiling; ten meters according to specifications. Either way, the chandelier was gaudy and gigantic, made from bright gold with sixteen diamond encrusted candle holders. Each of these holders contained one of the most lavish, obnoxious purple candles Artimus had seen in his life.

The ceiling itself was decorated in an extravagant fashion as well, a bronze star pattern demonstrating a precise attention to detail. This intricate, raised pattern ran throughout the entire room and melded into the walls, where decorative bronze buttresses merged with the pattern every meter and a half. Artimus guessed there was a practical reason for these buttresses, but the flashy adornment felt distasteful to him.

Like the rest of the castle, the floors were constructed of the finest marble, a sheer white with only minor imperfections, which most people would never notice. A long, rectangular table was centered underneath the chandelier, made from stained red oak. It ran four meters long and just under two meters wide, and matching chairs were placed around the table for a large gathering – there were twelve chairs in total.

Another, identical table was positioned behind this first one with no visible differences from what Artimus observed. Beyond this table was the far wall, most of which was composed of a large, exterior window, the glass stained in various colors for aesthetic purposes. From Artimus's observations, there was no real pattern to the work, but it did have a certain, unexplainable visual appeal. The window was about five meters tall and three meters wide, tapering up at the top in a crescent with a flat bottom.

His attention remained on the first table though; for that was where today's meeting would be taking place. Chancellor Cabal sat in the center of the nearest side, and General Zeidrich sat directly to his right (when Artimus had found out that Zeidrich was part of the revolutionary movement, he had been somewhat less than surprised).

The two of them were sorting through a few parchments, discussing various changes the felite delegation might suggest.

"Artimus," Cabal piped up turning to look at the Lieutenant. "You've become fairly familiar with felite culture, right?"

Artimus turned his attention to his leaders, considering the question for a moment before responding.

"I don't know about that. Savannah and I have kept in touch with one of the felite warriors that fought alongside us against Yezurkstal." Artimus did not want to be asked anything about policy. He was not a politician.

"You're being coy," Cabal replied tongue-in-cheek. The weathered old man was perceptive, perhaps not in the same sense as Artimus, but he could certainly read people well. Somehow, he must have known Artimus was holding back.

"I really think you and Zeidrich are better qualified. After all, you two have been working on this treaty for the last few months," continued Artimus uneasy.

"That may be true," countered Cabal, "but I value your insight. It's a simple question really. Do you think we should place any garnishments on the table prior to their arrival? Zeidrich here seems to think they might appreciate a centerpiece of some sort, but I'm thinking they would appreciate a simpler presentation."

Artimus sighed in relief. He thought it would involve some detail to do with the treaty.

"From my experience, no. Leave the room as it is. This is already much more 'garnished' than any felite structure I have seen."

"As I thought. Thank you, Artimus."

"My pleasure."

Zeidrich brushed it off, returning to the more pertinent details.

"Decorations aside," he began dismissively, "I think that we are skirting around the most likely objection. Felite are generally withdrawn and don't easily trust outsiders. Though you have developed some rapport with their elder, we have an election coming up. They might be worried about you losing. If Ulagret returns to power, will he uphold the treaty?"

Zeidrich had a point. Though there was no doubt in Artimus's mind that the new Erathal Republic would help all elvish kind, there was the simple reality that people feared change. Even many of those who had gathered to back the proposed constitution had started to falter in their backing of Cabal. After all, adapting to the newfound independence was difficult for many elves. If Ulagret used this to regain power, what was to stop him from undermining the progress thus far?

Apparently, the Chancellor did not share these fears.

"That's a moot argument Zeidrich. Even if Ulagret somehow gets elected Chancellor, the treaty is specifically worded to avoid violations. He would be destroying elf-felite relationships if he even tried to violate it. Besides, every treaty must be entered into with some amount of good faith. It's not like the only reason for this treaty is to expand trade. We are obligating ourselves to come to their aide if they requested it. There isn't much they could do if we violated those terms."

That reasoning seemed somewhat flawed to Artimus, but he knew the Chancellor was right.

"Alright, but what if they bring up the concern. I don't much think that answer will make them happy," said Zeidrich, his face scrunched and eyes severe.

Before Cabal could answer, the large, wooden door to the chamber creaked open and an attendant poked his head through.

"Chancellor, the felite delegation has arrived. Shall I send them in?" he asked sheepishly.

The Chancellor turned to Artimus. "Lieutenant, stall them for a minute and then lead them in."

Without a response, which was definitely a breach of etiquette, Artimus complied. Pulling the door ajar only enough to slip out, he guided his sword through the opening and put on his most diplomatic smile. This was not what he signed up for.

His leather boots clacked as he walked behind the attendant down the narrow hallway. Most of the hallways were rather plain in contrast with the rooms, the walls made simply from smoothed stone. As he approached the end of the hall, he focused his energy to be as diplomatic as possible. To his surprise, he felt a bit of a boost in his morality as the attendant opened the double doors to the next chamber.

Tau Lu, the top felite elder was at the head of the delegation and beside him were two female elders, both wizened and leaning on their staves. All three elders wore matching robes, a simple design with a solid green hue. As usual, they were accompanied by two guards one of them an unknown male, light warrior and the other a friend of Artimus's -Tel' Shira.

After the conflict last year with Yezurkstal, Tel' Shira and Savannah had kept in close contact and through that relationship Artimus had come to think of her as his friend as well. They had spent weeks together planning for different contingencies should signs of Yezurkstal surface and she had been a gracious host on various occasions when Artimus had accompanied the Chancellor to the felite village for some of the initial peace talks.

Artimus could count on one hand the number of people he truly trusted and she was one of them. Still, he was here to welcome the delegation and not to distract himself with personal friendships. Ignoring the urge to greet her first, he took a deep, elongated bow.

"On behalf of Chancellor Cabal, I would like to welcome you to Castle Erathal," Artimus recited, his voice full of exuberance.

He took his time standing upright, making eye contact with Tau Lu before continuing.

"I am Lieutenant Artimus Atyrmirid of the Erathal Rangers, head of investigations and personal guard to the Chancellor. I am honored to be the first to welcome you to our castle."

Even though he had accompanied Cabal to the felite confederacy on several occasions, he had never actually met any of the elders or even entered any of the discussion chambers. This helped make for the perfect delay tactic, but it hadn't quite been a minute yet.

Tau Lu returned the bow and indicated to his left and then right as he spoke.

"Mine, the honor is, Lieutenant. Two of our most esteemed elders, these are, Kel' Mora and Reg' Nira. That felite interests are adequately represented, they are here to ensure. To the discussion hall, shall we proceed if no objections, you have?" His voice was raspy and dry, but as with most of his kind there was very little emotional inflection.

"Of course, revered Elder, I would be honored to lead you on. Will your aides be joining us as well, or shall I have an attendant show them to a more comfortable waiting area?" Artimus asked, hoping to stall for just a few more seconds. He took care to remain perfectly still, making one final effort to slow them down.

"Accompany us, they shall. Onward, you can lead." The elder replied.

That would have to do for stalling.

"Please, follow me," Artimus instructed, stretching his hand out and motioning towards the meeting hall.

The attendant stepped aside allowing Artimus to lead the delegation forward. Like his speech, he took his time walking, exaggerating his steps in a way that he hoped was not obvious to anyone other than Tel' Shira —she would undoubtedly see through his delay tactics.

Reaching the oversized door for the meeting hall, he grabbed hold of the brass handle and paused. Turning back to the delegation, he took a slight bow and held it for a few seconds. If this was not enough of a delay, he would not take the blame for it. With a friendly grin, he pulled the door open wide and motioned for them to step inside.

The delegation continued forward and as Tel' Shira passed the threshold she shook her head slightly and shot Artimus a disapproving glare. With a subtle shrug, Artimus followed behind and pulled the door closed. General Zeidrich was already standing behind his chair.

"Revered elder!" began Chancellor Cabal as they entered, rising from his seat at the table and spreading his arms wide in greeting.

"It is an honor to host you here. I speak for everyone in this Republic when I say it is long past due that you visit our great hall." The Chancellor took a slight bow and motioned to the side of the table where he'd been seated.

"Please, take a seat," he continued. "I am sorry for the delay. I instructed the Lieutenant here to hold you up while I finished talking with the good General. I hope he did not bore you too much."

Artimus wasn't sure what kind of strategy this was and found himself looking at the only friendly face in the room. His eyes met with Tel' Shira's and she returned his look with a subtle tightening of the cheek, a silent way to communicate she agreed this was unusual.

"Figured you wanted us delayed, we had. Necessary, your apology is not. Understand, we do," replied Tau Lu smugly.

Artimus felt he was in some sort of strange dream, but he was admittedly no diplomat. He'd have to remember this strategy for future situations. In the meantime, he merely stood by the entrance, his hands resting by his side.

The felite delegation all proceeded forward. The male warrior pulled out the first two chairs at the table and Tel' Shira circled around to pull out the third. All three elders took positions in front of the chairs and sat down at the same time, perhaps a sort of ceremonious gesture. Both Tel' Shira and the other warrior took a few steps back and kept their hands trained at their sides.

Chancellor Cabal continued around to stand next to the General and both took their seats at the table.

"Well, I assume you would like to get straight to business?" Cabal asked, motioning to the parchment in front of him.

"A correct assumption, that would be." Tau Lu nodded.

"Excellent. Would you like to read the latest draft first? You can bring up any questions as you read." Cabal picked up the treaty and passed it across the table.

Taking the parchment from the Chancellor, Tau Lu nodded and began reading.

Artimus waited in his place, staying as still as he could and merely staring out towards the window. He did his best to keep his mind on the present moment, ignoring the fleeting thoughts that plagued him. Thoughts of Savannah kept entering his head, wondering what she was doing at this moment. They had been married only three days ago, and part of him wished he could have taken her away to escape from all of this. Still, his focus remained on the present moment, for though his heart was not here, his mind was always attentive.

As Tau Lu read through the document, he would nod from time to time and occasionally even lean over to one of the other elders and exchange words. Artimus wished he could hear what they were saying, but even his sensitive elvish ears could distinguish naught but mumbles.

Turning his attention to Cabal, Artimus was surprised to see how calmly the Chancellor waited. If it had been Artimus in this position, he would not have maintained such an emotionless demeanor. After all, the Chancellor had spent a good deal of time these last six months developing this agreement and had traveled to the felite confederacy more than a few times to iron out the details. It had to be nerve racking.

After a handful of side conversations with his other elders, Tau Lu finally put the treaty back down on the table and looked over to the Chancellor. His expression was unreadable, even for Artimus.

"Satisfactory, this treaty appears. But, some questions, we do have," stated Tau Lu plainly. "Kel' Mora, your concerns, please voice."

Cabal remained silent and still, waiting for elder to speak. Artimus noticed a hint of discomfort from Zeidrich, who shifted his position a few millimeters.

"The size of your army, we question. Never would we have considered, under your monarchy, a treaty of this magnitude. The stability of your Republic, we still question. A new government, you are in these lands, and, the true strength of the elves, we question." Kel' Mora spoke directly, her tone seemingly neutral. But, Artimus could tell her words were laced with genuine concern, an almost imperceptible oscillation of her voice relaying a level of distrust.

For many other races on Evorath, the syntax of the felite language was difficult to grasp, and Artimus had admittedly found it challenging to follow initially. Since he had become friendly with Tel' Shira, it was much easier to understand. Cabal seemed to grasp it with similar ease, but Artimus noted Zeidrich's slack jaw, and calculating eyes.

"I certainly do understand your concern," began the Chancellor carefully. "The truth is that our army is smaller than it was under the rule of a king, but our troops now serve by choice, and not out of a false sense of devotion. I believe this leads to a stronger army and a much more capable defense force. If you would like specific figures though, I believe General Zeidrich could explain the situation of our forces better than I could. General?"

Zeidrich expanded his chest, sitting up as tall as he could and shifting his position. He leaned forward and steepled his fingers.

"Yes, I would be happy to elaborate. As the Chancellor indicated, our numbers are somewhat diminished since the introduction of a constitution, but I can personally guarantee that we are stronger than ever. Our active military presence still stands at nearly 1,000 elves strong with more than one third of which are trained extensively in both archery and swordplay. And that is not including those citizens who have signed up to be part of our militia force should the need arise. More importantly, those 1,000 elves are all well-qualified and devoted to their profession. This was simply not the case before the formation of the Republic.

In fact, we have recently instituted much more stringent standards for our soldiers. This means weekly battle drills and tougher testing on both strategy and combat proficiency. Furthermore, we have expanded our military so that every unit includes a magical component. We believe this improves the effectiveness of our soldiers significantly and offers a much more diverse fighting force should we encounter an enemy like the one we found last year with Yezurkstal."

Zeidrich sat back a little in his chair, keeping his hands on the table and maintaining stern eye contact with Kel' Mora.

"On this matter, satisfactory, your answer is," Kel' Mora offered a faint nod before continuing. "Another concern, however, I do have. A more efficient communication method, the felite have developed. To trust this treaty, faster mobilization, we would require."

Artimus caught a momentary glimpse of doubt from Cabal. He hadn't expected this concern.

"I thought we had cleared up these details last month on my visit to your village. The road we have jointly worked on will allow us to quickly get across the continent. Our mounted units will be able to arrive within 36 hours or less. Also, last time we discussed communication we agreed that the fastest method was the use of a strategic scouting net where signals could be relayed in only minutes. Is this a new development?"

"New development, it is not," Tau Lu replied. "Consulted our mages, however, we now have. Authorized to teach, we now are; a powerful spell, they have. To communicate across the land, we can now."

Cabal nodded as he took in the new information.

"That will be desirable on both sides. The faster we know about the need for reinforcements the faster they can be dispatched. Does this also cover your doubts about mobilization time?" asked the Chancellor pointedly.

"Cover that, it does not," interjected Kel' Mora again. "Ready and dispatched, our troops can be, in one hour. Promise, you do, no less than 200 troops. Specify how quickly they will depart, you do not. Hold up for 36 hours, our walls can. Longer than that, we cannot be sure of anything."

Cabal nodded again and responded. "Of course. We will gladly put in that we must have troops mobilized within one hour of receiving word from you. That can be accomplished, correct General?"

"Urgo," replied Zeidrich, a slight grin on his face as he nodded in confidence. "Should the need arise, we should be able to do it in less. We definitely can deploy no later than one hour's notice."

"Satisfactory, that also is," said Kel' Mora with a gentle nod. "All of my concerns, that covers."

Cabal waited for a full five seconds at least before speaking to ensure that Tau Lu did not have anything to add.

"Excellent. If those are the only revisions, let us make the changes and get everything in writing," he proclaimed with joy.

Tau Lu shook his head. "More concerns, we still have. Sign the treaty now, we still cannot."

Moving back in his chair a few millimeters Cabal grinned through his teeth. "Of course. How many more points concern you?" he asked, his voice laced with honey.

"Many concerns, we still have," began Tau Lu. "Confident, we are, that by nightfall, an agreement we can reach."

Artimus resisted the urge to moan. Cabal had spent so much time on this treaty and today was meant to be a formality; simply meet, make some final wording adjustments, and sign the treaty. Now, it was going to be an all-day project.

This was not what Artimus had signed up for.

Chapter 5

Somewhere in Eastern Runeturk Mountains
25 Zerrum, 1087 MT

Drip.

Drip.

Drip.

Yezurkstal braced his left hand over a small stone, tilting
it slightly over to let the blood drip down freely. Once he was
satisfied there was enough, he ran his right hand over the wound,
instantly sealing it with dark magic. Wiping the remaining blood
on his pants, he focused and lifted the stone.

Yezurkstal's blood coated the entire rock and using his
right, pinky fingernail he carefully started to form a shape in the
palm-sized stone. He had already done this with four others, so
by this point he had gotten the technique down perfectly.

Starting in the bottom left corner, he moved up to make a
sharp angle, then after tracing down a fraction created an even
higher point before moving towards the bottom right part of the
stone. Tracing up once more, he formed a third peak as if
drawing a mountain and then moving back down. Starting
precisely at the center of the first peak, he drew an arched line to
the right, which passed slightly below the halfway point of this
peak. Finally, he continued the curvature of the line to form a
rounded shape that intersected the tallest peak about a quarter of
the way down.

In truth, he was not entirely sure how he decided upon this specific symbol, but the idea of using magically imbued stones had come from that dwarf he had executed a few days earlier. Though he was much more accustomed to using magic he could immediately cast, Yezurkstal believed these rune stones would help focus his magic and bring his efforts to fruition.

The morning was yet young, the sun still resting somewhere over the horizon. Yezurkstal had been working for the last few hours trying to perfect his method. Now that he was satisfied he had four stones to work with, it was time to get started.

He walked to the northern end of his little plateau and placed the stone in its place. Precision was important to this extra focusing, so to make sure he had placed the stones properly he placed the heel of his left boot directly in front of this last stone and measured his steps as he walked in a perfectly straight line to the stone at his west. Next, he moved south, and then finally east. As usual, he had estimated perfectly, each of the stones sitting eleven steps apart.

The more he thought about what he was hoping to accomplish, the more he realized the need to put a little more time and energy into this than he had ever done before. Since he had the natural ability to pull demons into this realm, he had always believed he could access the ether in a similar fashion. With recent failures and some contemplation, he knew that it was time to re-strategize.

Every creature Yezurkstal encountered had some knowledge of the Demon Wars. According to common knowledge, these demons were servants of the goddess Frogatha. And by instinct, Yezurkstal knew his mission was appointed by the goddess Frogatha. By this same instinct, he knew this world and that of the demons was somehow connected. This made his previous efforts an instinctual act.

Though his knowledge of Evorath's history was somewhat limited by his own experiences, he had still absorbed enough information to feel confident the magic he was attempting had never been accessed before in all the world's history. So, while accessing the realm of demons was instinctual, this was something completely new. If he could refocus his energy, he was sure he could create a gateway to access another realm.

Taking his place in the center of the ritual square, he took a moment to focus. He felt a somber sense of satisfaction that he had solved this challenge. Evorath had created him to cleanse the world of its problems and here he was ready to reach out and bring in the tools he needed. Once he figured out how to access the ether, it would only be a matter of time before he had complete control of the forest and eventually the entire world.

Elves, centaur, felite, barghest, dwarf, lizock: none of them could ever understand his purpose on this world, but he did. One day, the hájje would outnumber all these inferior races. He would eliminate disease, pain, and suffering, building a world that was truly worthy of Evorath's blessings.

It would all begin today.

Standing erect, Yezurkstal closed his eyes and spread his arms wide. He channeled magic into his core, centering himself and grounding his feet in the earth. He felt the energy swelling inside and pushed it around to engulf his body. Feeling the energy coat his skin, he held his eyes shut tight before releasing the energy to the northern rune stone.

The dark magic enveloped him, a tingling sensation filling him with vigor. A stream of magic poured out and impacted the first stone, causing it to glow with his black energy. The magic continued to pour forth, branching out to both the eastern and western stones. They both began to glow as well and simultaneously shoot out beams of magic towards the southern stone.

As the square was complete, the ground around Yezurkstal started to shake and the rune stones began humming at a low frequency. They lifted off the ground, floating rhythmically around their creator. The magical energies intensified, a black veil surrounding Yezurkstal.

It was euphoria like none he could have ever imagined.

His body seemed ethereal, his consciousness reaching towards the heavens. Suddenly, he felt omniscient, aware of everything in Evorath. Images from around the world flashed through his head. He felt a strange familiarity as pictures of tundra and desolate arctic lands to the north filled his head. There was a castle located on an island, the greatest fortress ever conceived; constructed in his honor.

There was power in this ritual square. Even more power than he had imagined.

Yezurkstal opened his eyes.

The magical veil around him was like a reflection of his inner thoughts. Images of faraway lands flashed before him: great deserts to the west, unexplored mountains on a southern continent, a strange and wondrous city to the east.

This must have been what it felt like to be a god, or so Yezurkstal thought. There would never be another creature that would understand this feeling of power he now had. But this was not what he was looking for. No, these images were all coming from Evorath.

With a maniacal smile that stretched from ear to ear, Yezurkstal refocused his energy, willing his mind to home in on the space beyond his realm, allowing himself to get lost in the sheer thrill of the magic.

His looking glass seemed to shift focus, the dark energy fluctuating and changing pitch. The visions went completely blank, nothing but an empty darkness stretching for as far as the mind could fathom. As his visions shifted, Yezurkstal could feel a pit in his stomach, a feeling of complete emptiness and isolation.

He was accessing the ether. Now he just needed to reach one step further.

Testing the limitations of his mind and body, he pushed further, a stream of dark energy shooting forward in the shape of his silhouette. As it hit the energy field, it shattered the darkness and light began creeping through. The area was filled with fog, but he could immediately feel that he was accessing a realm not so different from his own.

Fog began to clear, and he focused on the images. He was witnessing some sort of great battle, two armies clashing with one another in an open field. It was hard to tell them apart among the chaos, both sides wearing very restrictive, heavy army. Their weapons seemed very similar to the ones found in Evorath, an assortment of maces, swords, shields, hammers, and bows.

Some of the creatures even rode horses, which appeared identical to the ones found in Erathal. As Yezurkstal watched the battle, he felt a strange thrill, somewhat different than the thrill he got from his own experiences in battle. It was refreshing to see others engaged in such a vigorous conflict. Still, this battle seemed somewhat peculiar for two reasons.

First, it appeared that all these creatures were from the same race, each of them with a body much like an elf. Their ears were deformed though, rounded instead of pointy. Most of them also had facial hair like a dwarf, many of their beards long and unkempt. Though it was strange to see one species battling so ferociously amongst itself, the second factor was even stranger.

No one was using magic.

Yezurkstal scanned the battlefield repeatedly, watching these creatures destroy one another with their weapons, bashing with their shields and hacking with their swords. Within the melee though, not one of them seemed to have the ability to cast a spell.

What luck that he would find such a world on his first try?

These creatures would make perfect pawns in his war to control Erathal. If they were fighting their own people with such aggression, they had to be a disorganized lot, which would make ruling them easy. Not to mention, a species without magic would not only be terrified by Yezurkstal's power, but they would also be easy to control. To add to the equation, there had to be thousands of them.

Now, Yezurkstal just needed to figure out how to pull them into his world. If this was the demon realm, he would simply enter and bring the demons of his choosing out with him. However, that method would be terribly ineffective if he hoped to pull in such a large group and right now his efforts to focus on an individual soldier didn't appear to be yielding any results.

It was as if he found the perfect way to witness another realm, but he was unable to do anything about it. What if this was all he could do? His mind filled with rage at the notion, his blood boiling hot with anger.

The ground around Yezurkstal began to shake violently, the humming of the rune stones rising in pitch to an almost deafening squeal. His body felt like it might explode, waves of power shooting out and impacting the magical field around him. The images became distorted and once again Yezurkstal felt empty, like he was passing back through the ether. Clenching his fists and yelling at the top of his lungs, he closed his eyes and slammed his arms down to his side.

His eyes shot back open.

The magic around him exploded outward, sending a shockwave of dark energy out for as far as his eyes could see. Each of the four stones exploded as the high he felt turned into a feeling of loss and complete emptiness, his magical reserves exhausted like never before.

In fact, he was so exhausted that he was not sure what magic he would be able to cast, which was unfortunate, considering his efforts had worked.

Stepping forth to the edge of the plateau, he looked down and there they were. Hundreds of the creatures from his spell were scattered around the mountains below, spread out randomly and in a disorganized fashion. Most of them had stopped fighting and were now looking around with expressions of fear and confusion.

Yezurkstal took a moment to gather his thoughts, wondering how he had pulled it off. Well, at least with some degree of success. There was only a small fraction of the creatures within sight. Perhaps some more were in lower areas of the mountain. Either way, Yezurkstal needed to act immediately.

His reserves may have been tapped, but there was still latent energy in the mountains. Gathering what little magic remained in his vicinity, he stepped forward and amplified his voice.

"Welcome to Evorath," he exclaimed looking down at these confused creatures.

"My name is Yezurkstal, and I have brought you here to serve me," Yezurkstal continued with confidence. Unfortunately, they didn't seem to think this was acceptable.

One of the nearby soldiers pulled his helmet off and stepped forward, revealing a long mane of amber hair and a matching red beard that reached down to his chest. He held a great sword in his right hand, the design somewhat different than any Yezurkstal had seen before. It looked like a claymore but had a different blade and hilt configuration.

"Ye tink we'll jist geave in an' serve some strange deamon loch ye?" he yelled up from below, his voice deep and demanding.

It was thrilling to hear. The creature had such a peculiar accent something completely unique and different than any Yezurkstal had heard before. And he had those deformed ears. He was really from another world.

"I assure you, I am no demon," Yezurkstal retorted.

"But," he continued, "I also assure you that you will serve me. That is why I have brought you here."

"Ah dunnae wat kinna strange witchcraft ye used tae brin' us haur, but thare is nae way we gonnae serve ye," the creature shouted angrily.

The other soldiers all seemed to agree with this strange-accented creature, joining together and walking towards him. For each second that passed, Yezurkstal had been able to continue gathering magic. Though his energy was still extremely limited, he still had enough power to make an example of this loudmouth. At this point, it was his only option.

If only he had more energy, he could just take over them all in bunches. Once he converted this one though, the others would hopefully fall into line, at least for now. They could then all be led back to his family, and he could convert them in masses.

Throwing his hand forward, he let loose most of his stored energy. The black bolt hit the loudmouth directly in the chest, pushing through the creature's armor and knocking him onto his rear.

Yezurkstal felt a swift pain and clutched his chest. Visions and memories flashed through his head, knowledge from the other world and an abridged history of this creature -this man. It was different than it had been with any other race, and as soon as the momentary pain dissipated Yezurkstal knew he had made a mistake.

The man doubled over and let out of a shout as his life slipped away. These creatures came from a world without magic and the sudden shock of such powerful energy had destroyed his life force. To make matter worse, the death of their fellow man seemed to intensify the fear of these other warriors.

They belonged to two warring nations, one fighting for independence against the other, but for some reason, fear of the unknown seemed to pull them together quicker than any force Yezurkstal could have imagined. It was time for a temporary retreat.

With a quick thought, he re-aligned his mind with his pet griffin, willing the creature to come out of its nearby cave and collect him. A few of the men below were preparing arrows, aiming up towards Yezurkstal while their cohorts closed in on foot.

Pulling in as much magical energy as he could, Yezurkstal waited for his mount to arrive. Just as a handful of the men below released their arrows, the undead beast ascended from the plateau behind Yezurkstal and let out a shriek.

Yezurkstal waved his hand and deflected the incoming projectiles before spinning around and grabbing hold of his pet's saddle. Without a second thought, he pulled himself up and willed the griffin to fly out. He wasn't sure how long it would take him to gather up enough energy to rectify this situation, but for now he needed to rethink his approach.

There had to be some way he could use these men to serve his purpose, but as he lifted off and flew away from the scene, he could not help but feel he had failed again. Perhaps he would have to look elsewhere if he wanted to build his army.

Chapter 6

Northern Coast of Erathal
25 Zerrum, 1087 MT

Sitting to the east of the Runeturk mountains, lying just along the northern coast of the Erathal forest, there sat a peaceful village. Since anyone could remember, this village had remained separate from the turmoil of the continent, its inhabitants living in tranquil seclusion. The concepts of conflict, war, and discord were far removed from the residents of this peaceful village.

Its citizens had never directly interacted with any outsiders, avoiding every major event on the continent. Even during the ancient Demon Wars, these unique residents of Erathal had avoided confrontation, using their innate abilities to escape the conflict altogether. Though some outsiders spoke of a mysterious species to the north, most merely assumed it was a myth.

These residents called themselves the Preajin, and they valued their isolation.

Unlike all the other creatures in Evorath, Preajin were blessed with a natural resilience to the effects of aging. They were immune to illness, hunger, thirst, or natural death of any kind. These creatures were made from pure magic, so magic had little effect on them. More importantly, they were blessed with the ability to mimic the world around them, allowing them to transform into any creature they interacted with extensively enough.

And so they had existed, part of Evorath but separate from her strife. Strong and powerful, but independent and illusive, they continued.

This day began the same as any other. The sun slowly crept up over the horizon, majestically reflecting off the waves as they lapped upon the shore and casting a serene light on the unassuming village. Gophers popped their heads up from the soil. Trees uprooted themselves, changing into all manner of wildlife; wolves, lions, deer, and even some elves, and felite.

Each of these creatures was Preajin, all of them wearing different forms, but all of them united by a common cause. Among these residents, there were two creatures of interest. One had spent the night in the form of a rock and the other as a neighboring bush.

When the sun hit its foliage, the small bush began to move, its branches crackling as they came together and transformed. The green leaves melted away and were replaced with a leathery flesh, losing much of their vibrancy as the skin hardened and expanded into a gray mass. A grouping of branches took their place at the front of this creature, forming a trunk and two tusks and its legs and feet expanded downward as it began to assume a new form. In a matter of seconds, the once small bush now resembled a fully-grown elephant.

The rock started changing as well, expanding outward as its light gray hue began to darken. Its surface stretched out over a meter and then began expanding upwards about half that length. Slowly, this formless blob began to smooth out, four legs expanding downward. Bones cracked and spread as the legs stretched out. Both a tail and head started to take form. The stone's surface began to split apart, changing to sleek but dirty hair. This was a younger Preajin, and its transformation was taking longer than the other.

Any spectator might have looked on in complete fascination as this stone slowly made its change. Upon closer inspection, however, hearing the bones push into place and sinews snap, they might have cringed in pain. In fact, this young Preajin was in excruciating pain. But this was just part of mastery.

Willing the bones to form and the hair to grow, it pushed itself as it had yesterday, the day before, and the day before that. This was the quickest time it had made so far, which is what helped push it through the especially painful formation of ribs and internal organs. As the claws and teeth began to grow in, it prepared itself for the completion, ready to talk to its progenitor about its progress.

Taking on the full form of a dingo, it panted a little and turned up towards the elephant.

"I was fast? Faster anyways."

The dingo's jaws did not move, but its thoughts were transmitted to the elephant. Its voice, or the thought of its voice, was like a small child seeking the approval of its parents.

"Insomuch as I could perceive, your transformation has improved indeed." The elephant's voice was wizened, like an old sage talking to his pupil.

"Will you help me today? I want to get faster still!" Thought the dingo, his voice booming.

The elephant swung its trunk up and shook its head slightly.

"Zelag, my beautiful off-spring, always looking to move onto the next thing. Allow yourself the gift of time if you ever hope to be sublime. First you must review, before you can hope to learn anything new."

Zelag barked with impatience.

"Why?" he asked defiantly.

"Zelag, oh young and unaware, I-" his progenitor's thoughts were cut short as the sounds of growls, roars, barks, and squeals filled the air. Both Zelag and his progenitor shuddered as the thoughts of their fellow villagers rushed in.

"HELP."

"What vile creatures!"

"Get out of here!"

"Where did they come from?"

The rest of the thoughts were a disorganized buzz.

Through all the confusion, Zelag did his best to block out the other voices and focus on his progenitor.

"Hide away quickly now, I do not care where or how."

His progenitor did not wait for him to act or respond, immediately charging away with abandon.

Zelag was not sure how to process what was happening. He had only become conscious of this world a few decades earlier, and during that time he had never experienced this sensation. As a dingo, he found his tail instinctually tucked between his legs and his heart pounded. There was this strange discomfort in his stomach and his consciousness found it difficult to settle on any one course of action.

His body began to involuntarily change, his bones cracking and reforming to revert to something simpler. Somehow, he focused on one of the trees, willing himself to climb it and take on its form. Just like a rock, he had mastered the transformation into a tree years ago, but this time he wanted to use it to get a better vantage point.

Each of his organs pushed in on one another, causing intense pain as his body warped around the stump. While his skin transformed to match the rough bark, he began scaling the side in a state of flux. Between the pain and the unusual movement, everything was fuzzy for the next few minutes. He heard both strange voices and horrendous cries as he slithered up the side, high enough that he could see out around the village. Finally, his body began to stiffen, pushing out from the tree as he latched on and completed his transformation into a branch.

Though he did not have eyes or ears, Zelag, like all his people, was still aware of his surroundings in this form. Images, sounds, and even smells were processed in a surreal hallucination. From his vantage point high above the village, he could experience everything.

The village was being invaded by strange, bipedal creatures. Most of these mysterious invaders wore heavy armor, somewhat like the type crafted by elvish and dwarfish smiths, but with unfamiliar markings. There was something strange about their life energy, an unfamiliar aura emanating from these barbaric creatures.

There was too much to keep track of, so Zelag focused on his progenitor, who charged towards a grouping of four bipeds that had just slaughtered a tiger Preajin. The unsuspecting invaders turned too slowly, three of them getting trampled under the elephant's massive legs. The other one managed to jump aside just in time, but while he struggled to get back to his feet Zelag's progenitor turned around and impaled him with one of its tusks.

Zelag allowed his focus to shift slightly as a Preajin just to the north of his progenitor began shifting. It was one of the Originators, and with its developed powers it began transforming from its shape as a horse. Its chestnut fur turned bronze and its body began contorting in all different directions. The hind legs expanded outwards while the front legs began shifting up on its torso. Though he had never seen this before, Zelag knew exactly what the Originator was shifting into.

Its hooves exploded into claws, its fur hardening and changing into scales. The bushy tail on its hindquarters warped in on itself and shot outward like a giant serpent. Its snout stretched forward and became more rigid, razor like teeth jutting out as it let out a sound halfway between a great bellow and a distressed neighing.

It appeared to be about halfway into its transformation when the bipedal invaders took notice. A couple of them charged forward with their greatswords held high, but Zelag's progenitor had a different idea in mind. With a violent spin, it used its trunk to sweep out the attackers' legs and followed up by trampling them both.

Zelag lost all focus.

He was petrified.

As his progenitor went to take a defensive position in front of the Originator, a single, large biped took his axe and with a wide arch dug deep into the elephant's left hind leg. The elephant let out a painful trumpet, shrieking in agony as it struggled to turn towards its attacker. With such limited mobility, it was unable to do so before the attacker took another swing, and then another. Blood began pouring out of the injured leg, and the elephant lost its balance, tumbling over onto its side.

The evil biped was about the size of an average elf, but it was built much stronger. It wore some sort of leather armor, studded with pieces of metal, presumably for added protection. The axe it wielded was crude compared to both elf and dwarf smithing, at least from Zelag's understanding. As he watched the creature hack away, he felt a completely unfamiliar sensation, one that his progenitor had never taught him about.

His body felt hot, his mind racing for some reason amidst the apparent chaos. It was as if a swarm of bees were racing around inside him, stinging him everywhere. He focused his full attention on this single creature, capturing the essence of its life energy and anchoring it within himself. He took in all its features: the blue eyes, short brown hair, wild beard, two ears, prominent nose, toned figure, and yellow teeth. He could see within the creature: its heart, ribs, lungs, spine, brain, each and every muscle and neuron.

Zelag wanted to jump from his place in the tree, let go of his hold and transform back into a dingo to attack.

But he couldn't.

A new feeling took over his body, a cold and empty feeling. It was like he had been left alone in some barren tundra and there was no sign of any rescue.

He felt frozen in place, this unexplainable sensation keeping his body completely unable to change or to even move in the slightest.

It was a fear like none he had felt before.

He remained fixed in place, unable to act and unable to move, an overwhelming feeling of despair taking over as he watched two more creatures charge towards his progenitor and hack away. Blood was everywhere. His progenitor's shrieks died down to a weak rumble and then ceased altogether.

Zelag's own life force seemed to diminish somewhat as he watched his progenitor's slip away.

Meanwhile, the Originator had just about completed its transformation. Zelag didn't care.

The alien creatures swarmed the now grand dragon, stabbing it with their swords, hacking it with their axes, and smashing it with their hammers and maces. Zelag didn't care.

His entire race could be exterminated right before his eyes, but to him, his whole world was already lost.

He wished for the means to act, for the means to move, for the means to eliminate this inexplicable feeling. His progenitor had been with him since his first memories, and now there was nothing left.

Nothing.

Never again would he feel the presence of his creator.

Never again.

As the life force left the Originator, Zelag lost consciousness.

Or so it seemed.

Zelag didn't know how much time had passed, but before he knew it, the fight was over. The invading creatures had moved on past the village, leaving only slaughtered corpses in their wake. The young Preajin was still in his place on the tree, but the fear and anguish dulled.

With enough willpower, he let go of the tree, his body falling helplessly to the forest floor. There was still an empty feeling in his body, and as he searched for any life energy that might remain, he was only met with more despair. The only life around him came from the forest itself.

His people were gone.

His progenitor was gone.

He was alone.

As the reality of his situation sunk in, he began transforming, his mind locked in on the figure of that evil creature that had slain his progenitor. That creature needed to be punished. His progenitor needed to be avenged.

The brown of his bark started to lighten slightly, imitating the bronze, leathery skin of his progenitor's murderer. His body expanded, stretching out to form arms and legs to fit on his torso. His insides felt like they might explode as the solid composition of his wooden core separated to form a skeletal system. His internal organs took shape as well, and immediately upon gaining use of his vocal cords he howled in pain.

His skin began to take shape next, the bronze of his bark diminishing to a light tan. Across his chest the wood changed in substance to form armor, the same studded leather that his progenitor's killer had worn. Every detail appeared to match perfectly, except that he lacked any kind of weapon. In truth, the armor was an inseparable part of his new form, and a weapon was simply not possible, a limitation to his transformative abilities.

Completing his transformation, he slowly pulled himself up to his feet, his hands shaking slightly as he got used to the strange new form. His face felt itchy, the hair above his lip brushing against his nose as the wind blew. The armor felt very heavy and unwieldy, causing an uncomfortable itch between his legs. Overall, this form seemed much less effective than that of the dingo he had been practicing lately.

Holding his hands out in front of his face, he moved his fingers about independently, a task he had never actually done before. This new form felt some strange sensations and noticing his itchy throat he found himself making a strange, guttural sound somewhat like a growl. Realizing that his vocal cords were capable of so much more, he opened his mouth, trying to find the right word for the occasion.

His scream reached out across the remains of the once peaceful village.

"REVENGE."

Chapter 7

Preajin Village
25 Zerrum, 1087 MT

Zelag walked through the aftermath of his village's destruction, searching every Preajin corpse in hopes of finding survivors. Though his sense for life told him there was no one left alive, his heart would not let him accept it without visual confirmation. His knees buckled as he approached his once proud progenitor forever stuck in the form of an elephant.

In this body, Zelag felt sensations differently than he ever had before. His life among the village had been sheltered, and though he had experienced his fair share of physical pain through shapeshifting, his emotions were not very well-developed. With this strange, bipedal form, he was experiencing so much more than he previously thought possible.

Pushing through the apparent weakness in his knees, he trudged forward. It felt like a pit was forming in his stomach, but not like the hunger he had experienced as any other animal. No, this was like a palpable feeling of sadness, an extraordinarily painful reminder of his loss. His lower lip quivered as he looked on at all the blood, and his eyes began to water.

In all his life, he had never experienced anything like this.

His hands began to shake as he neared the fallen elephant, his lip trembling. The moisture in his eyes intensified, pouring freely forth. He couldn't control himself.

With less than a meter to go, he fell on his knees, covered his face and began to weep. No word in his vocabulary could describe the anguish he was feeling. He kept trying to tell himself this was not real, that someone else had survived.

But they had not.

Now, kneeling before his lifeless progenitor, the reality hit him like a stampeding herd.

What was the point of living anymore?

He fell to his side, his muscular body and heavy armor causing him extreme discomfort in this awkward position. It did not matter. No physical pain could ever compare to what he was feeling inside.

His voice was hoarse as he wept, his tears running down his face faster than he could wipe them away. Breathing became difficult, as he gasped for air between exacerbated fits of crying.

Zelag felt as if the world around him faded away and he remained like this for hours before finally being interrupted.

"My troubled son, I am sorry that I did not arrive sooner."

The voice came from behind, a deep and confident speaker uttering the words.

Though it startled Zelag, he turned slowly, still shaking in anguish, trying in vain to squelch his crying as he turned and beheld the creature.

It was another biped, one that very closely resembled the invaders. Its face and head were both perfectly bald though, and instead of armor and weapons it only wore a simple, brown tunic. Though it stood with an unassuming posture, it was a good third of a meter taller than Zelag, and much larger in stature.

After overcoming the initial shock, his despair was almost immediately redirected into rage. It was as if some magical force overtook him, and his body burned red hot with energy. Zelag felt as if he could move as fast as a lynx and had the strength of a centaur.

Using this rage, he lunged up and charged towards the strange creature with abandon. As if anticipating the attack, the creature nimbly stepped to the side, leaving one foot out and tripping Zelag, causing him to fall flat on his face.

"Please, calm yourself child. Look at my life force and you will see I am not one of the men who attacked your village."

Zelag moved as fast as he could, but his bulky armor made it difficult. Pushing off the ground, he pivoted around, his anger still boiling. With all his aggression, he lunged forward again, but this time was stopped as vines shot out of the ground and wrapped around his wrists, holding him steady in place.

Struggling to get free from these unexpected bindings, Zelag cursed.

"DAMN YOU! RELEASE!" he yelled angrily, his voice so loud and deep that it seemed to shake the forest.

The strange figure remained completely still, controlled by an unusual calm.

"Not until you calm yourself. What is your name young Preajin? Look at ME and see that I am one with Evorath. Those men who attacked you are gone. I am here to help." The creature sounded sincere, its powerful voice somehow gentle and serene.

Zelag fought against the vines for a good minute, spit flying from his mouth as he yelled incoherently. His limited vocabulary left him to simply "arrghs," "graaahs," and "damns." Finally, his mettle gave out and he collapsed back to his knees crying.

The vines immediately loosed around his wrists and returned to the ground. Zelag used his now free hands to wipe the newly flowing tears from his face.

The strange biped stepped forward and extended its hand, resting it gently on Zelag's shoulder. It was a bizarre sensation, but somehow this physical contact passed on some sort of solace. Though his despair was still intense, he felt he had someone to share his burden. Of course, this only made him cry that much more freely.

This large biped knelt before Zelag, putting both of its arms out and embracing the young shapeshifter in a hug. The mysterious creature took his time and lifted Zelag up to his feet, holding him closely. Zelag's head only just reached its chest.

Zelag sniffled and wiped his eyes, looking up towards the creature's face. Who was this creature to take an interest in Zelag? Did it know what he was? It had called him a "young Preajin," so it must have. But no outsiders knew his people. Was this creature a Preajin?

Still sniffling, Zelag pushed away and looked closely at this creature, looking beyond its physical appearance, and taking in its life force. It took him a moment to focus through his anguish, but as he pulled it into focus, he gasped and stumbled back.

Like his own people, the life force of this creature was quite unique. It was a being of pure and focused magic, no internal organs, blood, or skeletal system to speak of. Though it didn't seem to have the same transformative qualities of the Preajin, it held a immeasurable power within it, a vibrant life energy that seemed to shoot out and brighten the world around it.

"WHAT ARE YOU?" asked Zelag as he took a couple more steps away from the creature.

"I am the physical manifestation of Evorath's might, an avatar of this world," answered the creature confidently.

"NAME?"

"My name? I am afraid I do not have one, nor do I see the need for one. What is your name?" asked the avatar gently.

"ZELAG."

"Zelag. The death of your family leaves a scar on Evorath that will never fully heal. But your legacy will not end here, even though you now feel alone. I cannot replace your family, but if you will allow it, I can be a friend."

The young shapeshifter listened, but his emotions in this form were still unfamiliar, and he found it difficult to focus on anything other than the new manifestations of anguish. His experience with sadness was limited by the fact that he had never felt loss before, but even when he found himself upset it had never felt like this. No matter what form he took, he also took on the inherent feelings of that creature. For some reason, this body processed not only the ethereal feelings, but also took on physical discomfort.

His stomach ached and his muscles felt constricted. His heart pattered in his chest, and these tears that streamed from his eyes left him utterly dumbfounded. How could any creature endure this sort of pain?

Zelag wished he didn't have to. He wished that he had ignored his progenitor and died alongside his family. Instead, he was stuck on Evorath to endure these unbearable sensations. And this creature? How could it be a friend? No, he didn't want a friend. He just wanted to end his pain.

"PAIN MUST CEASE!" he yelled angrily through stifled tears.

The avatar took a step forward and laid his hand upon Zelag's shoulder once again.

"*What if we communicate in this fashion? This is what you are more accustomed to, isn't it?*" thought the avatar.

Zelag was taken aback, pulling away from the avatar and for a moment -a very brief moment- forgetting his pain. This creature could communicate like him.

"*But you are no Preajin. How?*" asked Zelag in his head.

"*I am part of Evorath herself. I am blessed with many gifts. You, Zelag, are also blessed with many gifts that you have yet to realize. If you will allow me, I can guide you along the path you are meant to walk. Like me, your people are meant to be guardians of these lands. Unfortunately, these creatures that destroyed your people -these humans- were not meant to exist in our world. But it would be easier to show you than to explain."*

As the avatar finished this thought, Zelag's consciousness was immediately barraged with images. He witnessed a dark and cloudy world; dust being thrown into the air and magma flowing out along the surface. He saw trees sprout out from the ground and expand to form a forest. He watched water surge from the ground, filling the land with a great flood.

Then he got images from all around the world, and his perspective shifted from the outward world to the ethereal. He saw the outline of the universe, like how he witnessed the life force of creatures around him. These lines were torn asunder, spilling out a variety of creatures throughout Evorath.

Humans started appearing all around the world, from the mountains to the west, the forest to the south, and across different continents Zelag had never learned of -deserts, tundra, and strange wooded lands with unfamiliar trees. Then Zelag saw the avatar, working to patch these holes in the multiverse, trying to ensure that all of them were sealed up.

He understood.

"What caused this?" asked Zelag with an unexpected calm as the images ceased.

"Over twenty years ago, a misguided elf committed a great atrocity. An evil from outside of this world used that atrocity to create a grave threat to Evorath and all her creations.

This calamity, named Yezurkstal by his mother, will do everything in his power to reshape our world.

"One year ago, I was summoned forth and manifest to combat this evil, but even I underestimated his power. He fled, and since then has been avoiding me while working on a way to rise to power more rapidly. I am afraid his latest endeavor reached beyond the scope of any magic the world of Evorath has seen before, reaching through the ether and pulling in these humans from another realm."

The avatar stood there in a stoic pose, his arms hanging by his side. His face belayed his body language, a pensive look keeping his eyes downcast as he spoke.

"So, we must eliminate these humans?" inquired Zelag, his thoughts returning to the sadness and anger he had felt only minutes before.

Revenge was all he had left.

"Zelag," started the avatar, his voice trailing off for a moment before continuing. "Revenge is an empty endeavor, and it will not fill the hole you feel in your heart. No, I am afraid I will not help you satisfy your revenge. I can continue your education in shapeshifting and help ensure you reach your maximum potential.

"As for the humans, they are already rooting themselves in as part of Evorath. Their impact has been made, so the only option now is to make sure they end up on the right side of the battle. Yezurkstal will try to make them his pawns. We must not allow that to happen."

"If they were dead, they would not be pawns," retorted Zelag immediately.

"Allow me to show you more of the world. Let me help you to master yourself. After one decade as my student, then you can decide. Should you still seek revenge, I will not stop you." The avatar responded with authority, a certain resolve implying this was not a request, but rather an explanation of how things would be.

"Why do you care? Are you not busy dealing with these humans?" Zelag spoke with contempt, his anger for the humans more focused now that he understood what they were. They did not belong here.

"I will not force you to do anything, because that is not the will of Evorath. However, I believe you understand as well as I that you cannot hope to get revenge in your current state. It would be suicide, and you would be destroying the last trace of your people."

"So, what if I do? I don't want to live any longer," shouted Zelag defiantly. His pain was still too fresh to allow him clarity of thought.

"What did your progenitor ask of you just before he died? Did he not wish you to survive? Will you really dishonor his memory by disobeying his last request?"

This struck a nerve with Zelag and for a moment his vision blurred, and he felt an intense heat well up inside of him. The next moment, this sensation subsided; he knew it was true.

He needed to live. His progenitor would want him to. That was it. From now on, he would live just as his progenitor would have wished.

"Fine," Zelag started, his voice laced with determination. "What would you have me do?"

"We start by sealing the remaining breaches. But first we must make one stop."

The avatar extended his hand, inviting Zelag to take it.

Zelag hesitated for a moment, looking back around him at his people's devastation. He sniffled, trying in vain to prevent more tears from leaving his eyes. There was nothing left for him here.

He reached out and clasped the Avatar's hand.

Chapter 8

Erathal Forest - Dumner Village
25 Zerrum, 1087 MT

A shadow was cast over Dumner Village, the sun slipping below the horizon and obscuring the splendor of the central mound. Over the last year, the village had undergone some significant changes, and other than this hallowed mound, the village was virtually unrecognizable. From the new residents who had joined the tribe to the updated structures, it hardly resembled the village Irontail had been raised in.

Log cabins had taken the place of the poorly constructed lean-tos, most of which had been destroyed during last year's demon attack. More prominent than this, the mound was no longer at the center of the village, the borders having expanded since they opened trade with the neighboring city of Erathal. Aside from the visible changes, the tribe itself had also experienced a fair deal of change.

As Irontail trotted through the peaceful village, he could not help but think of all these changes that had occurred. Reconstruction of the village had been taxing, but by keeping open communication with the neighboring elvish kingdom, they were able to draw in wayward centaur from around the continent. After such great tragedy, they had shown unique strength and rallied behind a united banner.

Of course, Irontail still could not get used to the most significant change in his life.

The foliage at the eastern end of the village rustled and Irontail heard one of the city guards approaching. A few moments later, Woodenbrow pushed through wearing a look of concern.

Though only a few years younger than Irontail, Woodenbrow did not ever show much initiative within the tribe, but since he seemed to be good at keeping guard, there was really no sense in pushing him to do more. Still, as the younger guard approached Irontail, he could not help but feel that this was another instance of overzealous behavior.

"Chief Irontail," started Woodenbrow, his voice relaying even more uncertainty than usual. "I am not sure what is happening, but there are strange people approaching our village."

"What sort of strange people?" asked Irontail dismissing the concern off hand. Just because Woodenbrow was more on edge than usual didn't mean it was cause for alarm.

"They wear unusual armor, with strange crests. Maybe elves, but not from Erathal, and they seem larger in stature. Most also have hairy faces. It's…strange." Woodenbrow squinted, his lips pursed tightly and brows raised.

"That does sound somewhat unusual. Did Tungstenhand have any ideas as to what it might be?"

Ever since Irontail had taken over as chieftain, guards always worked in pairs to ensure a more efficient watch system.

"He thought it strange too." Stated Woodenbrow simply. Irontail waited for a few seconds, thinking there was more. Why he expected such, he could not say.

"Alright, how many of these mysterious soldiers are coming towards our village?"

"Uhh-" Woodenbrow gazed off to the east. "I didn't count. Some were going other ways too. They seemed much disorganized."

Irontail sighed.

"I will go to Tungstenhand and determine whether we need to be alarmed. Go to Silvertoe and make sure he is prepared to sound the alarm. Make sure to WAIT for my word though, understood?"

"Yes."

"Yes, what?" pressed Irontail.

"I will go to Silvertoe and tell him to sound the alarm."

"NO!" shouted Irontail impatiently. "You will tell him to WAIT for my word. Repeat what you are to say."

"Irontail wants you to wait for him to sound the alarm," responded Woodenbrow staring off dumbly.

Irontail wanted to pummel the incompetent guard.

"I suppose that is good enough."

Irontail turned and started towards the eastern guard post. Silvertoe was a bright warrior. When Woodenbrow conveyed the message, he would ask enough questions to get to the bottom of things.

Meanwhile, Irontail needed to determine what these foreign forces might be up to. The guards were due to rotate in the next few hours, which made it a convenient time to defend the village. Still, he prayed that would not be necessary.

Most likely, it was just a case of Woodenbrow overreacting. After all, unless these strange people had been to the village before, none of them would be able to see it. Still, there was a certain fear sitting in the back of Irontail's mind.

What if Yezurkstal was readying for another campaign?

Dashing through the narrow path towards the eastern guard post, Irontail started considering the implications.

It had been almost a year since he first revealed himself to the forest. After kidnapping a bunch of elf girls to make his wives, Yezurkstal started eliminating many of the small villages in Erathal forest, including Dumner. If he was behind these strange soldiers, it was likely that Irontail would not be able to defend his people.

His heart weighed heavy as he dwelled on this thought, picking up his pace and rushing to the guard post. As he rounded a small willow, he slowed down and beheld Tungstenhand, who was standing attentively between two large oaks.

"Report!" barked Irontail.

"There is strange troop movement outside the village sir," replied Tungstenhand. He was sharper than his partner, which was why Irontail assigned them together.

"Move aside so I may assess," commanded Irontail.

"Yes, sir."

Tungstenhand stepped back and to the side, bowing to let Irontail between the two trees.

Since before Irontail had been born, the spell that protected the tribe from outside eyes also provided some sort of enhanced viewing from designated guard areas. The two oak trees at this spot provided a 180 of the eastern side of the village, giving whoever stood between them the ability to see all manner of movement for a good kilometer out. Like most magic, Irontail did not fully understand the mechanics, but he did understand it was quite useful for guard duty.

As he focused his attention outward, his field of vision expanded, passing over the many different trees and small critters that lived nearby. He did not like what he saw.

There were dozens of strange people trekking through the forest. Like his scouts had reported, they wore unfamiliar armor and many of these also wielded strange weapons, the designs completely unfamiliar to Irontail. Though he was no expert on elvish blacksmithing, he had spent enough time with soldiers from Erathal to know they were not affiliated with that kingdom.

Furthermore, these people had strange ears, much smoother than the normal elf. Their features were, for the most part, much harsher as well and many of them had long beards upon their faces. If these were elves, they were not native to this forest.

Irontail attempted to get a count of how many of these people there were, but they seemed to be disorganized. Some of them traveled together, but many were in smaller groups. The

nearest group consisted of nine soldiers, the shortest of whom
was taller than any elf he had met before. They all wore leather
armor, some of them simple and broken while a couple had
studded vests to add additional protection. Their tallest member
wore a large, two-handed sword slung over his shoulder, the
design quite unique. It was a sword fit for a centaur's hand and
seemed unnecessarily large for someone of his build.

Still, Irontail was not here to assess whether these men
were outfitted for war -after all, it was clear they were. Instead,
he needed to assess if they were a danger to the village. To his
relief, the answer appeared to be 'no'.

Taking a step back, Irontail looked to his sentry.

"Tungstenhand, I want you to keep an eye on their
movement. They are much too disorganized to be an attacking
army, but I want you to observe everything you can about them.
Some of them may pass through our village. When they do, listen
to anything they say. It is important that you pay close attention
to everything. Do you understand how important this is?"

"Yes, sir. I will not disappoint you," replied
Tungstenhand, standing upright and proud. He puffed out his
chest, giving a slight nod as he turned back to observe.

Returning the nod, Irontail turned and started on his way
back to the village. He approached at a fast trot, trying to sort
through the situation rationally as he went. Their lack of
organization made them little as far as a threat now, but who
were these strange people?

Irontail had heard tales of unusual people who lived in the northern continent, but since none of his people had ever left the forest, he assumed they were legends. If they had come from overseas, they would not seem so scattered in the center of Erathal. Where else could they have come from though?

The only civilized people in the mountains were the dwarves and though his tribe stayed in the forest he heard from others that the hills and plains to the south were home only to barghest, lizock, and some elvish nomads. That didn't describe these peculiar invaders.

As he rounded the path back into the village, he came to an abrupt halt. His instinct was to yell out to warn his people, but he paused just long enough to realize that would be a mistake.

One of the strange wanderers stood before him, its beard long and unkempt. It had tan skin, shoulder length hair, and wore studded leather armor. Of course, the creature that stood next to this male came as even more of a surprise.

"Avatar," started Irontail in shock, his words slipping out before he even knew what to say. "What is going on?"

Irontail pointed to the strange person in the leather armor. "And who is he?"

-=-=-=-=-=-=-=-=-

Zelag felt as if his new stomach dropped all the way to the floor as the world around him went into a state of flux. It was as if the avatar was forcing him to transform as their hands touched, but somehow there was no pain involved. Just as before, his consciousness briefly connected with the avatar, and he could see a quaint village in his mind.

The village was surrounded by a magical field of energy, and it was comprised on a couple dozen small cabins. A small mound pulsating with magical energy made for the focal point of the village. Zelag felt invigorated by the magical energy and before he knew it, he was flying towards it.

His physical form coalesced with the Avatar's, and they shot through the very soil of Evorath, flying at an unimaginable speed towards the village center. Though his experience transforming was somewhat limited, he still had imagined and experienced a great many sensations.

This was unlike any of them.

It was like his body had become incorporeal and he was simply flying along the magical lines of energy that ran throughout the planet. Unlike any of his other transformations, this required no effort on his part, but seemed a matter of will. Was this something he was capable of on his own?

The experience ended as soon as it began, his body phasing out of the ground and into the village he had seen in his mind. He was once again in his human form and the avatar stood beside him.

"Where are we?" asked Zelag, still trying to make sense of the strange experience.

Before the avatar could answer, a centaur trotted in from the east and looked at them dumbfounded. He stopped in his tracks and pointed at Zelag.

"What is going on? And who is he?"

Zelag opened his mouth to answer, but the avatar stepped in front of him and spoke first.

"His name is Zelag, but he is not with the men outside of your village," answered the avatar.

"What are men? And what do you have to do with this?" questioned the centaur. It started forward in a show of aggression, its voice raised, holding undertones of anger.

"Time is of the essence. Please, gather your council and come with me and my pupil to the meeting hall. We will explain everything there."

The centaur stood almost perfectly still, rubbing his hands together before his chest in some strange thinking ritual. Zelag could tell the centaur was trying to discern how to respond. Though it was obviously familiar with the Avatar, it seemed a bit hesitant to trust him.

"Alright," it said after a considerable pause. "Follow me."

Chapter 9

Erathal Forest - Dumner Village
25 Zerrum, 1087 MT

Irontail listened as the Avatar completed his story. He and his two most trusted elders were gathered in a small meeting room within the mound, standing around a simple wooden table with the Avatar and his friend, Zelag. Both Nickelear and Stonehair (the eldest member of Dumner) stood to his left. The young chieftain's mind raced, trying to put together the different pieces and make sense of everything.

Though Irontail had claimed his position in the aftermath of Yezurkstal's last attack, he was still younger than many of his tribesman, which made it necessary to stay sharp. He worked to put together his words carefully, trying to ensure he would not sound foolish in front of his subordinates.

"So, these humans come from a plane where they are the only sentient species? And there is no magic? How are we supposed to approach them peacefully? From what you have said, they are a savage people."

Irontail scanned the room quickly, ensuring everyone was following him. Both the elders diverted their gaze to the Avatar, as if awaiting his response.

"It will be no simple task, but you must attempt to open communication. If Yezurkstal succeeds in controlling these men, your tribe will be one of the first to fall." The Avatar's face was unwavering, his eyes resolute, leaving no room for questioning his absolute certainty.

"How do you know this? And what do you mean by 'one of the first'?" asked Irontail. He noticed Zelag was looking at him quite quizzically, his features contorted and head askew.

"I am no oracle, so I cannot know the future. Despite this, I can make predictions based on the facts we have. Dumner is not only closer to the mountains, but it is also smaller than most of the other likely targets. I would guess he will test his new strength on some of the smaller tribes around Erathal and then focus on eliminating Dumner. After all, he failed to eliminate you last time. He will undoubtedly make another attempt."

Irontail thought about this for a moment. Though centaur were not the best at teaching military strategy, he had enough experience to know this line of reasoning made sense. Dumner was small compared to the other major communities scattered about, but it held a strategic position.

If Yezurkstal could take over this land, he would have a front to muster his forces for an invasion of the Erathal Republic. After that, he could easily wipe out the lizock to the west, leaving nothing but the Felite Confederacy to defend the forest. Without any aid, they would fall in no time and the entire continent would be Yezurkstal's.

Irontail was about to respond when the Avatar suddenly backpedaled from the table, his eyes wide.

"I apologize, but Zelag and I must take our leave. There is much for me to do in light of this incursion, and Evorath is calling for me elsewhere. Confer amongst yourselves and go to the elves. You must parlay with the humans if you wish to maintain peace."

Giving Irontail no time to object, the Avatar reached out and grabbed hold of Zelag. The ground opened beneath them, the dirt shifting up around and swallowing them whole. They were gone the next instant, whisked off to some unknown destination. Irontail had seen the Avatar do this before, but how was it that he could take another with him?

No matter.

"I never did trust that one," started Stonehair after a few moments, his voice hoarse.

"I've said it from the start; something went wrong with the ritual that brought that abomination into this world. How does he expect us to talk peace with some savage race that he suggests will react violently to us? Back in my day, we would have just gone out in force and eliminated these hue-mans before they could pose a threat."

Nickelear nodded, curling his lips, and narrowing his eyes.

"I concur. It sounds like negotiation with these people would be more difficult than just eliminating them." Though his words suggested a certain finality, his tone seemed to indicate he was not quite convinced.

This was common. Nickelear was a good twenty years younger than Stonehair and what Irontail had gathered in his tenure was that he always tended to side with his elder. It was a sign of respect and reverence, no doubt from the fact that

Stonehair had been an elder for so long. Irontail needed to convince them otherwise.

"If there is one thing I have learned as a warrior, it is that violence is a normal fear response. I certainly mean no disrespect to either of you but going out in a show of force against these humans would just cause more trouble. They will be more afraid of us than we are of them, and that fear will make them a violent and fearsome adversary.

"The Avatar proved his worth a year ago in the battle against Yezurkstal and was called forth in a ritual planned by our deceased Goldenchest and supported by a dryad of Evorath herself. It is past time that we accept he shares our interests. He indicated that these humans had appeared all over Evorath, with hundreds or maybe even thousands right here in Erathal. Fighting would not seem like a prudent choice."

Irontail looked to Nickelear as he made this point. Though he didn't have an impressive service record, Nickelear was a warrior as well and he understood enough to know that even with superior strength and magic, Dumner could not hope to overcome the number advantage.

"Irontail does have a point," started Nickelear after a few seconds of silence. "Open conflict does not sound like a reasonable military strategy and if He -if Yezurkstal does get to control them, we will really be in dire straits."

"Yes," continued Irontail straight away, "and remember what happens when Yezurkstal does get control. Whatever magic he wields makes his troops quite formidable. Not to mention, if we were to attack these humans without provocation, who would be the savages then?"

"I suppose that is one way to look at it," answered Stonehair, his eyes downcast. Irontail had learned this response was about as close as this elder got to admitting he was wrong. "You are the Chieftain, so naturally I will support your decision."

"As will I," affirmed Nickelear.

"Good. It is settled then. I will leave the two of you in charge while I make my way to Erathal to warn them of this development. With our protective barrier, I do not foresee any challenges while I am away, but if trouble should find the village send word immediately. Any other concerns?"

Irontail finished with a sense of urgency, his hurried tone suggesting that he had little interest in discussing anything else.

"Nothing that can't wait," Stonehair whined.

Nickelear nodded in confirmation.

Without further delay, Irontail turned from his fellow elders and trotted to the exit. The vines barring the entrance quickly separated as he approached, allowing him to continue without slowing down. Now in the mound's main corridor, he continued his pace, slowly ascending the gradual slope. Since assuming his role as the village chieftain, he had gained a newfound respect for this mound.

Though all the elder druids had died during last year's battle against Yezurkstal, the Avatar had been kind enough to explain some of the workings to Irontail. While it might appear like a simple underground tunnel, he now respected the magic that made it possible. As he reached the top, he willed it to open, the earth splitting apart and dirt shifting to the side. It crackled as it opened fully and let him pass through, closing once he cleared the threshold.

Turning to the north, he galloped to the guard hut. It was a simple construct consisting of 4 oak beams and a thatched roof. There were no walls around the structure, but its position within the village made it ideal for coordinating guard shifts and dispatching orders during a combat engagement. Irontail himself came up with the idea a few months back, and so far, it was doing the job quite nicely. As he approached, he noted his club was leaned up against the nearest post, just where he had left it.

Silvertoe stood waiting within the hut, his stance rigid as Irontail approached.

"Orders sir?" he barked before Irontail could even come to a complete stop.

"I will be traveling to Erathal to deliver a very sensitive and urgent message." Irontail explained. "While I am making this journey alone, I have left Stonehair and Nickelear to tend to matters in the village. If any defensive actions become necessary in my absence, I entrust you to handle them appropriately."

"I shall do as you have instructed, sir."

Silvertoe was one of his best.

Having alerted his main subordinates, Irontail was ready to depart. Truth be told, he felt excitement welling up within him. Since taking on his role within the tribe, he had very little opportunity to travel outside of the village. Though he wished for less extreme circumstances, he was eager to depart for Erathal. He hadn't had a good gallop in some time, and now seemed like the perfect excuse.

He grasped his club in his right, heaving it up over his shoulder. Though it was made from the trunk of an oak tree, he had made sure it was a weapon more fit for leader since becoming chieftain. It had been shaved down along the handle, tapering off to provide a lighter weight. Furthermore, he had the weapon enchanted, making it tougher than most steel blades. Of course, the elvish city was a couple hours away, even if he galloped at full speed. This meant he wouldn't be able to maintain his speed the whole way, especially while carrying his club.

Keeping this in mind, he had one stop to make before setting off. Without delay, he turned south at a fast trot, heading towards the edge of the village. Though his people mostly ate whatever vegetables or fruits they found around, sustaining a growing population meant having some organized agriculture. While it was nothing compared to the larger farms the elves had developed, Dumner had a modest little field of its own.

Fortunately, the village garden was more or less on the way, sitting to the southwest of the village right at the borders of the protective field. He trotted down the dirt path, walking past a couple of huts and arriving at the wooden fence, which marked the garden entrance. The fence was made from a single hickory tree, cut with such precision that it did not waste one centimeter yet crudely constructed so that it left many gaps. In truth, it wasn't designed to keep anyone out so much as to mark the borders and avoid any confusion.

Half a meter to the right of the fence's center was a small opening, which Irontail used to enter. Slowing his trot, he took care not to step on any of the rows that had been arranged and proceeded in. Up ahead, he spotted one of the garden caretakers.

Her name was Silkhair, chosen because her fur was unusually smooth after birth. She was one of three centaur who were tasked with tending the garden and out of the three she was Irontail's favorite. Of course, it was not for the reason many suspected.

Yes, she was a young and decently built centaur, her fur smooth and a pleasing light brown in color. By any other centaur's standards, she would have been called beautiful, but the truth was that Irontail had never grown to have much interest in such things. Instead, it was her intellect that attracted the young chieftain and more than that her work ethic that accompanied it. She was exceptional at her job, which was not something he could easily duplicate.

As he approached, she was tilling the bare soil, presumably preparing to sow some new seeds. Seeing Irontail approach, she stopped what she was doing and leaned slightly on the rake.

"Good morning Chief Irontail," she greeted him kindly as he approached, her voice gentle and calm.

"Good morning Silkhair. I require a full day's worth of rations. Perhaps just some carrots and greens to help me make a journey to Erathal and back."

She smiled and turned her gaze towards a nearby wheelbarrow.

"I believe I have what you need there," she said with a nod. "Please allow me to fetch a satchel so you might have something to carry it in."

Irontail returned the smile. "Thank you. I will gather what I need while you do so."

As she trotted further into the garden towards the supply hut, Irontail proceeded to the wheelbarrow. It was over three quarters full, comprised mostly of heads of lettuce and cabbage. He put down his club and leaned it against the wheelbarrow, shifting some of these vegetables aside to also discover a healthy supply of carrots. He grabbed a handful of these carrots and could already hear Silkhair returning.

Looking up, he saw she had a simple satchel with her. It was just the right size to carry his rations. She approached and held it out to him.

"Here you are sir," she said casting her eyes down.

"Thank you," he responded in earnest. He grabbed the bag and stuffed the handful of carrots inside. Keeping it held open, he proceeded to grab some lettuce and cabbage, adding those to the bag as well. He only needed some light food for the road, so that would do nicely. Stuffing in a couple more carrots for good measure, he slung the back over his shoulder and grabbed his club.

"Keep up the great work Silkhair and thank you again."

She blushed and cast her gaze down yet again. "It is my pleasure sir."

Irontail had still not quite gotten used to dealing with his position in informal situations like this. Though it felt a bit awkward, he offered a slight nod and turned away.

He took his time navigating to the garden exit and once he was sure he was out of sight picked up his pace. Brushing aside some out-hanging foliage, he made his way towards the road with haste. Since last year, Irontail and his tribe had worked on better clearing a path towards Erathal, which served as the foundation for opening trade channels. Irontail only wished he had more time to open serious diplomatic talks.

Kicking aside a few stray stones, he arrived at the road. This first stretch was cleared as far as his eyes could see, the trees chopped down and overgrowth maintained by some of the village guards. Knowing this, he took off at a gallop.

The wind felt good on his face, giving him some solace from the late spring heat. His satchel of rations fit tightly against his body, flapping only gently as he ran. Though his club was quite heavy, he hardly felt the strain at this point. Considering all the potential threats along the way, he felt it was a worthwhile burden.

A few minutes into his journey, the thought occurred to him that he had not been able to get such a great run in a long time. Even during his time on guard duty, he rarely had the opportunity to let go like this. Sure, he spent some time transporting logs and even running some messages, but the last time he really exerted himself like this it was to become a warrior of Dumner. Since taking on the mantel of Chieftain, he had hardly done anything to compare.

Of course, he had a lot of other duties to tend to now that he was in charge of an entire village, and he missed the opportunity to just get away. It was kind of ironic, or so he thought, that he had spent so much time as a mere warrior constantly lost in thought, wondering what was right and what was wrong. Now that he had such a higher responsibility, he missed the time in his own head. Being able to just run like this was relaxing and helped to relieve some of that tension.

For the next thirty minutes or so -Irontail wasn't sure about timing- he continued to run, but after this time he started to feel the weight of his club encumbering him. His heart was pounding hard in his chest, sweat flowing freely from his pores. It was time to slow down.

He allowed himself to take a deeper breath, slowing his legs and letting his momentum taper off. After about three or four hundred meters, he had slowed to a steady trot. His chest heaved in an out as he continued forward at this slower pace. As the road took a very slight curve to the east, he adjusted his club, swinging it around and taking it in his left instead. Resting it upon this shoulder, he concentrated on slowing his breathing.

The road was still clear of debris, but he had reached a particularly dense area of the forest. Foliage was thick on both sides of the road, branches reaching out to form a complete canopy overhead. With extra shade, he felt the temperature was even easier to handle, but the reduced visibility also made it difficult to know if there might be a threat lurking in the bush. After all, he had no idea how many humans might be between him and Erathal and the last thing he wanted was to stumble upon one of them.

Fortunately, the forest seemed quiet, perhaps uncharacteristically so. As his breath settled down and his heart took its place resting in his chest, he said a silent prayer to Evorath that the rest of his journey would go smoothly. Without much additional thought, he started pumping his legs harder again, building up into a gallop and focused again on the path ahead.

Chapter 10

Erathal, Elvish City
25 Zerrum, 1087 MT

Artimus squeezed Savannah's hand under the table, quickly casting a glance to convey his eagerness to leave. She lowered her own gaze and shook her head, gently squeezing his hand in return.

"Well, it did take longer than expected, but I am just grateful that we have concluded the talks. It is nice to be sitting at this table united."

The speaker of these words, Cabal, sat at the head of the table to the left of Artimus and Savannah. Immediately to his right, Zeidrich nodded in support of this sentiment, a look of relief on his face as he did. Artimus sat next in line, then Savannah, with plenty of space around them. Tel' Shira was seated to the right of Savannah to close off this side.

Tau Lu was situated next in line, seated at the head of the table opposite Cabal. To his immediate right, around the other side, sat the male guard who had still not said a single word since arriving and whose name Artimus had yet to learn. The other two felite elders sat opposite Artimus and Savannah, finishing off that side of the table with even more space to spare.

In total, the table could have seated more guests, the long oak piece easily able to accommodate three or more guests per side. Despite this, the felite delegation only consisted of five members, so Cabal made it easy by keeping his own members to a minimum. If the castle had any, he would have likely opted for a smaller table, but this was the smallest dining table available.

Of course, while the others seemed to be enjoying the occasion, Artimus just wanted to escape from the castle and get some more quality time with his new wife. Still, he knew what her head shake meant, and he took in a deep breath and put on a fake smile to fit in with the others.

"The first step, only this is. For more agreeable arrangements, we certainly hope," replied Tau Lu as he raised his goblet.

Everyone else at the table followed suit, including Artimus after Savannah nudged his leg under the table. He grabbed the golden goblet before him, the burgundy wine swooshing about as he lifted it up for a moment and took a sip. It was much too dry for his palate.

Placing it back down on the table, which was covered in a simple red cloth, Artimus waited uncomfortably for someone else to speak. In truth, he was not sure why he, Savannah, or the two felite guards were even there. He would have much preferred a quiet evening alone with Savannah or even spending time with Savannah, Tel' Shira, and the other felite guards down at the mead hall.

Unfortunately, no one really seemed to want to break the silence. More surprising than this, Artimus scanned the other faces and it seemed that no one else felt the same awkward tension in the air. Perhaps he was even less socially inclined than he believed. Turning his glance downward, he wished for the food to arrive so he would have a good reason to be quiet. Of course, he knew that was a fool's wish.

"Putting aside matters of state" started Cabal, "I hear that your confederacy has introduced a new sport of sorts. If I have been told correctly, your guard Tel' Shira is one of the leading athletes. Would you allow her to explain it to us?"

Tau Lu merely nodded to Tel' Shira, a definitive way of approving her to speak.

"Honored I am, to hear have reached you, my feats" she began humbly. "Participate in this new sport, I do."

Finally, something that would keep Artimus interested. He had spoken to Tel' Shira previously about this new sport, so he was more than happy to hear an update.

"Capabolo it is called. Different than most sports, it is. Rather than individually, as teams, we participate. To hone skills for battle, the game is intended. A bolo and a spike, each player wields on the field. Consist of three players, each team does. In each game, three teams participate.

Claim three trees, the winning team must do. The top of the tree, a player must go to, if to claim it she is. Into the tree, she stabs the spike, and protect it she must. Keeping a claimed tree, the real challenge is."

Artimus heard footsteps approaching as she neared the end of her explanation. His shoulders perked up and he glanced towards the door. Just as those final words escaped her mouth, the door creaked open, but it wasn't the food. Artimus sighed and cast his glance downward in disappointment.

A single elf slunk into the room, but he wasn't even coming from the kitchen. He wore a purple robe adorned with the crest of Erathal, which happened to be the standard attire for a castle courier. In truth, Artimus was a bit confused as to why this position still existed, as it seemed to fit in much better with the traditional feudal system than with the Republic they were supposed to be building.

The courier approached Cabal and bowed.

"Please excuse the interruption," said the Chancellor as he signaled the courier to approach.

Conveying his message, the courier got right next to Cabal and whispered. Artimus was interested now. Cabal appeared to be surprised. His face held tight, but his eyes darted around the room; yes, it was definitely a look of confusion.

"Zeidrich," he said as the courier backed away. "It seems that we have an uninvited guest. Please inform the chef that we need another place setting and accompany our courier to greet him."

Zeidrich was clearly not pleased, but he got up without hesitation. Pushing in his chair, he took a slight bow. "Please, excuse me," he uttered gruffly. Adjusting his leather tunic, he turned around and followed the courier out to the hall.

Now Artimus was really curious. There was a brief silence, and then Chancellor Cabal spoke.

"I apologize for the interruption. It seems that the Chieftain of Dumner has arrived at our gates with some important news. If you do not object, I would like him to join in our meal. From what he informed our courier, it concerns Yezurkstal."

Artimus shot his gaze over to the felite elder, looking to catch the leader's response. He remained somewhat calmer than Artimus would have expected, only a slight twitch of his whiskers conveying any sign of concern.

"Troubling, this news is" started the elder. "To join us, I certainly welcome him."

The Chieftain of Dumner, Irontail, was another individual who Artimus had learned to call 'friend' since Yezurkstal's attack last year. He was extremely intelligent, especially for a centaur warrior. This intelligence showed through in the work he did, restoring his village in a matter of months and since then even welcoming in new members to create a respectable town in its own right. If he kept it up, Dumner would surely become the largest centaur tribe in all Erathal.

A few weeks ago, Artimus had even met with him to discuss opening serious diplomatic channels, which could mean another ally. With the way things were these days, that could be an important step to ensuring the continued survival of Erathal City and Dumner alike. Of course, Artimus had heard nothing of talks between the centaur and felite, so he was pleasantly surprised to hear how accepting Tau Lu was willing to be.

No one spoke for the next few moments. Artimus listened carefully for the sound of hooves and eagerly watched the door in anticipation. There was a palpable discomfort in the room, everyone presumably feeling anxious about news to do with

Yezurkstal. Last year, this hájje had caused considerable mayhem and, according to the avatar of Evorath, he would only continue to get more powerful.

After much too long a wait, Artimus could hear Irontail's approach. He shifted in his chair, sitting upright while continuing to focus on the doors. The servant pushed open the door and Irontail walked through, followed by Zeidrich.

Artimus noticed his attire had changed a bit since last he had seen the Chieftain; well, the limited attire he had anyways. He wore a necklace this time, small bronze strips hanging down around his neck. There was a smooth stone in the center –a pearl. In addition to this new accessory, he also had a simple sack slung over his left shoulder. It appeared to hold a few light items, but Artimus could not quite make out what.

"Chieftain Irontail," began Cabal standing up. Zeidrich proceeded to stand behind his chair and the Chancellor stepped out to indicate for Irontail to stand over by the two felite elders.

"Please, join us for dinner. We would love to hear of your journey as we wait." He continued.

Irontail plodded along to his place at the table, his barrel chest expanding outward as he walked. He appeared to be out of breath.

"Thank you," he gasped arriving in his appointed spot. He took an audible breath, pushing the air back out and closing his eyes for a moment.

"I apologize -for my appearance. I ran, most of the way here, to make good time, but I am afraid, my duties as Chieftain have, left me in less-than-ideal, shape for such a journey."

Artimus could attest that he was adapting well to his leadership role. Even since Artimus had last seen him, Irontail appeared to be getting more and more comfortable with his formal tone. Then again, his labored breathing might have also been covering his discomfort.

"Please, take your time," insisted Cabal. "While you catch your breath, let me formally introduce our other guests. You already know General Zeidrich, and I believe you are also familiar with Lieutenant Atyrmirid, his wife, Savannah, and one of the felite guards, Tel' Shira. Also, you might remember her counterpart, Ger' Jula, who also fought in the campaign against Yezurkstal. Finally, these three are elders Kel' Mora and Reg' Nira and the most esteemed elder Tau Lu."

Cabal motioned to everyone in turn, and as he ended on Tau Lu the felite elder took the opportunity to speak.

"Finally honored, we are, to meet you," he declared with a slight bow. "Grown, has Dumner, since taking over, have you. Responsible, your great leadership is. To begin diplomatic talks, we soon hope."

After the introductions, Irontail seemed to have caught his breath a little more. His chest continued to heave, but his face showed a bit less distress, the red giving way to his usual bronze skin tone.

"The honor is mine," Irontail responded with a lower bow. "I too hope we can open up serious diplomatic talks in the near future."

He split his gaze between Cabal and Tau Lu before continuing, his face hardening. Whatever news he had, it appeared vital.

"For now though, I would like to apologize for interrupting your talks. I understand that I am intruding upon a celebration, so for that, I am sorry. Unfortunately, the news I bare could not wait."

Artimus detected a hint of fear in Irontail's voice; but only a hint. He was masking it well and spoke with real authority.

"Your apologies are unnecessary," replied the Chancellor in earnest. "I must admit though, you are beginning to worry me. What news is it you bring?"

"I am afraid the news is worth worrying over," started Irontail. "Yezurkstal has made a serious transgression, one serious enough that it has the Avatar flying across Evorath to correct. I admittedly don't understand the details, but from what I am told, he tore open a rift between our world and another. With it, he has pulled in a species not native to our world. The Avatar called them 'humans,' and tells me that they are from a world without magic. He warns that if we do not open communication first, Yezurkstal will undoubtedly turn them to his purposes. We cannot allow this."

Artimus listened with intent, trying to process this all. He ran through it in his head, but he couldn't grasp how this could happen. According to the legends, demons came from another realm, but since they had naturally found their way to Evorath, it made sense that Yezurkstal had been able to use them as his allies. On the other hand, tapping into a world without magic would require a force unlike any dreamt of before.

It was unprecedented.

"I'm sorry," blurted Cabal a bit frustrated. "When did the Avatar visit you? Why did he deign to share this information with you only? Could he not take the time to visit my castle and inform us as well?"

Turning sharply towards the Chancellor, Artimus did his best to hide his surprise. This was not only an undiplomatic response, but also uncharacteristic of everything he had heard from the statesman thus far. Flashing his eyes to Zeidrich, it seemed the General agreed as well.

"Sir, if I may," interrupted the General. "I believe it makes perfect sense. The Avatar has demonstrated the ability in the past to move through Evorath herself. Our palace has marble and stone floors, so he would be unable to come to us directly, at least in a prompt manner. If the incursion is as serious as Irontail makes it sound, the most tactical move would have been to inform him first."

That was some impressively quick thinking, and it might have been correct. If the Avatar was perceptive enough to see these humans being brought in all around Evorath, he would be able to know the felite elders were here. Visiting Dumner meant getting the message out to all relevant parties as quickly as possible while allowing him to then move onto other matters.

"Irrelevant, these questions are," added Tau Lu after a few seconds of silence. "To approach these humans, our goal must be."

Irontail nodded, speaking again with authority.

"I completely agree. In appearance and stature, these humans are quite similar to elves. This is why I believe that your Republic has the best chance of reaching them. But the Avatar warned it would be difficult. They come from hilly lands without magic and transitioning to the wilds of this forest might be tough. Not to mention, he pointed out that they are already scattered around Evorath."

A voice to Artimus's right interrupted, her beautiful tone unmistakable. He placed his elbow on the table and planted his face in his palm.

"It sounds like we need to take some time to really consider the implications of this," started Savannah. "I apologize for speaking out of turn. I understand that I hold no authority in diplomacy, but I must interject. This is no simple matter. Imagine being plucked out of your home and then quite suddenly appearing in an unknown land. Even if we might look similar, our clothing is sure to be strange, and our language. People fear the unknown and unfamiliar. How are we supposed to reach these humans without causing a panic?"

Artimus kept his eyes shut, not even wanting to see the reactions of those gathered. Savannah held no proper position and if she had spoken in such a manner to King Ulagret, she would have surely been thrown out of the room, if not imprisoned. Fortunately, both Cabal and Tau Lu were a bit less traditional. Even more fortunate, Irontail spoke next.

"You certainly make a good point Savannah. The Avatar did indicate that they spoke with a strange accent, but like all species of the forest they do understand the common tongue. He also informed me that these men come from a war-torn land. Apparently, one is a powerful nation and the other feels subjugated as a result. If we ally with one, we may not be able to find favor with the other."

Not giving him a chance to continue, Zeidrich chimed in. "Our next course of action sounds simple then: ally with the powerful nation."

Artimus wasn't sure whether to be relieved that no one seemed bothered by Savannah's contribution or to feel disturbed by Zeidrich's short-sighted thinking. He chose the latter.

"I apologize General, but you are ignoring some important details. To begin, how do we know which is the large nation and which is the subjugated people? Are they not both geared up for battle? More than this, are we to assume that those who are from the larger nation are, by default, better allies than those of the smaller?"

Artimus continued with passion. "Perhaps this smaller people are really subjugated and would make a more trust-worthy ally. Not to mention, there may be more of them than there are of the large nation. You are making entirely too many assumptions."

"And what would you have us do?" argued Zeidrich, stepping forward into his chair. "You always seem so eager to sit around and think, but now is not the time for that. We need elves of action, and I am merely suggesting a direction for that action to take."

"And you always seem eager to draw your sword and forget about potential repercussions" countered Artimus, planting his feet and grabbing hold of the table.

"Enough!" shouted Cabal. "You are both officers of the Republic and I will not tolerate such flagrant disrespect in these halls. Both of you keep your opinions to yourselves until I ask for them."

Artimus felt a bit embarrassed. He didn't usually let emotions get in the way of reasoning, but the premise of this development had him on edge. Trying to wrap his mind around a magic that could pull people from another plane left him vulnerable. At least the little disagreement pulled attention away from Savannah's indiscretion, or so he mistakenly thought. After a brief pause, Cabal spoke again.

"Savannah, I would like to hear more of your thoughts on the matter. For instance, what kind of magic would be required to pull off such a feat as this?"

For a fleeting moment, Artimus let worry flash through his mind. How could Savannah possibly know anything of this? But then he reminded himself of the main reason he had been so attracted to his wife in the first place. She was likely the most qualified person in the room to conjecture on the matter.

"In all honesty, I cannot even begin to imagine how he pulled it off, but the magic he used for this should be fundamentally similar to how he would call demons from the ether. Prior to Yezurkstal, such feats were reserved for cults of summoners. As you recall Chancellor, I already shared a story from my own past where my former village inadvertently meddled with such magic. Since we know he can reach into the ether already, it follows that he has figured out a way to reach even further.

"According to all accounts of history I know, the realm of demons is just a stone's throw away in the cosmos. Similarly, this realm that Yezurkstal has pulled the humans from is likely on the other end. If I were to guess, reminding everyone that this is conjecture, I would demonstrate it like a coin. Evorath is on one side of the coin and the world of humans sits on the other side. The demon realm lies somewhere between the two. Yezurkstal has simply figured out a way to reach through the demon realm and into that other side."

Artimus couldn't help but smile as Savannah finished her explanation. He always loved listening to her talk, and it made him proud to know he had married someone with such a brilliant mind.

"Agree with this, I do," started Tau Lu after a brief silence. "A dream, I had, just two nights ago. Before a lake, I stood. Into the depths, I gazed. In the lake, shadows I saw, but no reflection. Different, the trees were, in this land of shadows. From the sky, a strange stone flew. Into the lake, it crashed. Out the shadows came, as the water settled down. In the distance, welcomed the shadows, a strange figure did. Helpless, I was, as consumed the land around me, the shadows did."

Tau Lu finished her story abruptly and glanced around the room as if to make sure everyone was listening.

"Dismiss this vision, I did. Unable to make sense of it, I was. Great destruction, this incursion could bring, if befriend these humans, we do not."

Artimus could feel the dense air surround him as everyone considered the elder's words. While Tau Lu didn't have a reputation that compared to his predecessor, the reality was that any felite elder in his position needed some degree of clairvoyance. And, while Artimus wasn't one to prescribe to fate, he couldn't help the feeling of dread welling up as he considered another confrontation with Yezurkstal.

Chapter 11

Erathal, Elvish City
26 Zerrum, 1087 MT

Irontail had come to appreciate the perks associated with being Chieftain of Dumner, but after spending an unbearable number of hours standing within this meeting hall, he was being painfully reminded why he never had much interest in political leadership.

He was tired, hungry, and his legs ached from being crammed in one place for so long. Still, it seemed there was finally an end in sight, so as Chancellor Cabal droned on about his strategic approach to the situation, he did his best to pay attention.

"…which is why I think we ought to wait for word from the scouts as to how many we include in the convoy. And, despite your concerns General, I do intend to lead the convoy. I also intend to have you, Artimus, and Savannah accompany me. I trust all three of you to keep me safe, and if you recall, I am not helpless myself."

The Chancellor seemed to be repeating himself a bit, but at least that annoying felite elder had finally agreed to trust the elves to open communication. After all, the Avatar had explained quite clearly where these humans came from -there was no way they would be accepting of a felite or centaur.

In fact, Irontail was quite sure these invaders would be unlikely to have any sort of diplomatic talks with a centaur or felite anytime soon. More likely, the elves would find them difficult neighbors at best. After all, they were fighting one another prior to being pulled into this world. If they couldn't have peace within their own race, how could they possibly be peaceful to those of another?

Still, the Avatar had suggested they try to broker a peace, so if the elves wanted to do the leg work, Irontail was more than happy to pledge his support.

"The idea is to ensure that they realize we mean them no harm. We are to avoid using magic at all costs, even if they do react violently. Savannah, that means you are there as a last resort. If necessary, I trust your magic is strong enough to help us get out of there alive. Tau Lu, Irontail, do either of you have anything to add?"

Without giving Tau Lu a chance to speak first, Irontail jumped in.

"That sounds like a good plan to me. I think it is best that I return to Dumner and discuss this with my elders. I must prepare contingencies in case things do not proceed as planned. So, if you would please excuse me, I'll be on my way."

Irontail was careful not to phrase this as a question, making it quite clear he was leaving, but doing so as politely as he possibly could. Since no one raised an objection, he started towards the door.

"Thanks, we give," interrupted Tau Lu just as he reached the door. "For your report, we are grateful. Our best wishes, we give your tribe."

Whipping around and giving a slight bow, Irontail smiled.

"It was in all our best interest for me to share this. I wish you the best as well and hope we can meet under less alarming circumstances next time," Irontail proclaimed sincerely.

"Share this hope, we do," replied Tau Lu with a nod. "In our own council hall, next time, perhaps we will meet. Longtime overdue, a treaty between our people is."

"I very much look forward to that discussion." Irontail said with a bow.

He really was interested in creating a more formal relationship with the felite confederacy. After all, they were one of the most powerful people in all Erathal forest, so having them as an ally would really help ensure Dumner's growth and long-term survival. Despite this, he felt a cramp forming in his left hind leg, and he just wanted to get out of this room now.

"Elder, Chancellor," he continued after letting these thoughts pass through his head. "I bid you both farewell. If you need my aid, you know where to find me. Until then, I look forward to news about progress with the humans."

Hoping no one else would interrupt, Irontail turned and pushed the door outward, quickly trotting out to get some relief.

-=-=-=-=-=-=-=-

Savannah listened as the Chancellor continued to explain his plan for opening discussions with the humans. It had been many hours since they first sat down for dinner last night, and she could tell Artimus was done with the entire process. Unlike her husband though, she found this sort of discussion fascinating.

Though she lacked the observational acuity of her husband, she could tell she was in the minority. Zeidrich was visibly upset with this development and seemed to have trouble listening, his eyes continuing to stray off as if lost in thought. Similarly, Tel' Shira appeared to have zoned out hours ago, just sitting and staring blankly into the distance as if she might nod off at any moment. Of course, she didn't realize Irontail was so uncomfortable until now.

"That sounds like a good plan to me." Gushed Irontail as soon as the Chancellor finished speaking. "I think it is best that I return to Dumner and discuss this with my elders. I must prepare contingencies in case things do not proceed as planned. So, if you would please excuse me, I'll be on my way."

He was so clearly annoyed with everything that Savannah felt a bit disappointed she hadn't noticed it before. As Irontail reached the door, Tau Lu spoke up.

"Thanks, we give. For your report, we are grateful. Our best wishes, we give your tribe."

Irontail wrenched around uncomfortably, pouring out his words much too quickly.

"It was in all our best interest for me to share this. I wish you all the best as well and hope we can meet under less peculiar circumstances next time."

"Share this hope, we do," responded Tau Lu without breaking composure. "In our own council hall, next time perhaps we will meet. Longtime overdue, a treaty between our people is."

"I very much look forward to that discussion." Irontail answered with a half-hearted bow. He looked to be in physical pain.

"Elder, Chancellor, I bid you both farewell. If you need my aide, you know where to find me. Until then, I look forward to news about progress with the humans."

With these words, Irontail rushed out the room, leaving everyone in an awkward silence. There was no way Savannah was the only one who noticed how impolite and generally tactless that was. Still, Tau Lu did not seem to be bothered by it.

"But one concern, I have," he stated calmly. "How to handle their violence, you have explained, but vague, the future still is. If to them first, Yezurkstal gets, what do we do?"

This was Savannah's concern as well. While everyone seemed to offer some great ideas on how to approach the humans and strategies to ensure they could adapt to life in Evorath, no one seemed willing to discuss the worst-case scenario. It was a bit refreshing to see this elder felite was considering this important reality.

"I'm afraid I don't have a contingency for that," answered the Chancellor plainly. "The truth is, if we can't protect most of these humans and keep them away from Yezurkstal, then we have little choice but to prepare for war. This was the reason for our discussions all these months though, was it not? What I mean to say is, if we do have to go to war, you know you have the full support of my Republic.”

Savannah tried not to dwell on the phrasing. What did he mean *his* republic? It was a Republic for the people, not for Cabal. Still, she had known the Chancellor for some time, so she allowed herself to disregard this wording and take the statement at face value. Apparently, Tau Lu was willing to do the same.

“Unfortunate, this is, but accept it, we must. Like Irontail, your leave we must take. To my people, I must go. Prepare for the worst, we will. With you, Tel’ Shira we will leave. To us, she will report, after discussions, you have had.”

As Savannah turned back, intent for the Chancellor’s response, she caught a glimpse of her husband, who shifted with excitement, his back straightening and eyes darting towards the door. The Chancellor, on the other hand, looked a little less delighted with the conclusion of this discussion. Or maybe he was just apprehensive about moving forward from here; she couldn’t really tell.

“I understand,” started the Chancellor rising from his chair. “If you would like, I can send some of my soldiers to escort you back home and ensure you arrive safely. I would hate for you to run across a threat without enough support.”

“Misplaced, your concern is. Old, we might be, but nimble, we still are. Safely home, we will arrive.” Tau Lu wore a hint of a smile on his face as he stood.

The other felite, including Tel’ Shira, all rose with him. Tau Lu glided across the room, showing that even in his old age he still had great grace. His two elders followed right behind, and the guard formed up the rear quickly. Tel' Shira merely turned towards her elder and bowed her head as the party passed.

Seeing Zeidrich and the Chancellor rise, Savannah also decided it appropriate to stand. Of course, Artimus seemed a bit slow on the uptake, so she nudged him as she did. He quickly scanned the room and followed suit. Seemingly catching on, he even took the opportunity to continue around and stand next to his chair as the felite elders passed. Savanah, of course, did the same.

She wore a friendly smile and made sure to extend an appreciative look to the elders as they passed. As Tau Lu reached the Chancellor, he stopped and took a low bow.

"An honor, it has been. To reach an accord, I am delighted. Unfortunate, this threat may be, but facing with you, we are glad to be," he spoke with sincerity and calm.

The Chancellor bowed his head as well.

"The honor has been mine. Knowing that you are by our side makes me certain our two people can deal with whatever rocks might fall into our path."

Both the Chancellor and Tau Lu stood upright again. Without delay, Tau Lu turned and walked towards the door. Savannah hadn't even noticed it, but the attendant must have slipped in after Irontail had left. He, Falahar was his name, opened the door and held it wide for the felite party to leave.

As he shut the door behind them, the Chancellor and Zeidrich both took their seats again. They exchanged a brief glance before turning towards Tel' Shira, their faces expressionless. Savannah wished she could discern what they might be thinking.

"Tel' Shira. We will have one of the attendants prepare quarters for you here at the castle. Since the General and myself will be taking both Artimus and Savannah with us to greet these humans, I am afraid you might not know anyone else in the city. If you need to get out and stretch your legs, the attendant will be more than happy to show you around. Once we return, we will have you summoned to debrief you on the trip. Do you have any questions?"

The Chancellor asked this question as a bit of an afterthought. This time, Savannah was quite sure that her leader was a bit annoyed by the entire situation. Whether it was just the news about Yezurkstal, or it was simply because Tau Lu had unilaterally elected to leave a member of his delegation behind, Cabal was clearly not happy.

Probably feeling no more thrilled about the situation than anyone else, Tel' Shira merely shook her head and responded with a simple "No."

Looking over to the attendant at the door, Chancellor commanded "Please take our guest to some sleeping quarters and provide her with whatever she might need."

"Yes, sir," replied Falahar sheepishly.

Savannah took a moment and considered how she knew Falahar from before the coup last year. He was actually a very intelligent young elf if you engaged him in conversation, but he lacked confidence. Though it was widely a secret, Falahar really wished to be a bard rather than remain a simple servant in the palace. During the past few months, he had even picked up a lyre and started learning how to play during his free time. So far, he was still too shy to let her hear anything he was working on.

Still, he did his job well at the palace and as he led Tel' Shira out of the room, Savannah offered them both a warm smile.

As he shut the door, Savannah heard Artimus clear his throat. She turned around and it occurred to her that she was the only one who had yet to take her seat. She dropped right back into place and pivoted towards the Chancellor.

"Alright," he began with a sigh. "I realize this is not ideal, but we cannot take time to plan this one out anymore. Artimus and Savannah, you can return to your home to get whatever limited rest you might. Once the scouts return with word on any concentration of these humans, I will have a courier fetch you. So, be prepared. You'll have at least an hour, but perhaps no more than this. Zeidrich and I are going to the barracks to brief an infantry unit on the situation. The courier will tell you where to meet us. Any questions?"

"Just a suggestion, sir," interrupted Zeidrich. "We should take a unit of archers as well and have them stay back from the troops. If things go south, we could use the ranged support, and no offense to Artimus, but even his quick shooting won't be enough alone."

"Fine, but I think half a unit will do. We don't need twenty extra bodies when we are trying to show we come in peace. The idea is to approach them under the flag of friendship. Like our ancient ancestors meeting dwarves for the first time, it is important that we are very careful if we want to avoid open war. The last thing we need is to provoke them directly; then Yezurkstal won't have to do much to get them on his side."

"You won't hear an argument from me," answered Zeidrich, seemingly satisfied.

"Anything else?" asked the Chancellor.

Without even asking Savannah, Artimus stood up and spoke.

"No, sir. I will make sure both my wife and I are properly prepared to accompany you."

While Savannah was a little peeved that he wouldn't even take a moment to look at her for confirmation, she couldn't say she blamed him. After all, he had spent most of the last three days in the castle standing guard for these negotiations. She had only come with him tonight for the dinner celebrating the treaty. He needed some rest and was tired of all the politics.

Forcing a smile, Savannah followed her husband's lead and stood up.

"Good. You two are dismissed."

Artimus was to the door quicker than Savannah could even register it. He pushed it open and held it wide for her to follow. Giving him a smile, she took his hand as they walked out and let the door shut behind them.

"I'm sorry we have to be involved in all of this," said Savannah without hesitation. "I know this is not what you want to be doing right now, but you know there is no one better for the job."

They walked down the hallway at a brisk pace for a few moments before reaching the end. There were double doors as this point, and Artimus stopped and looked at Savannah. There were bags under his eyes and a hefty weight on his shoulders.

"It's times like this that I really wish there was."

Chapter 12

Outside Yezurkstal's Cave
27 Zerrum, 1087 MT

Yezurkstal stood just outside his poor excuse of a home, the stone entrance sealed to ensure he would not be disturbed. Removing his sword from its sheath, he inspected the blade with a sharp eye. Taking a deep breath, he calmed his mind, focused on drawing magical energy with each inhale. Though he had just rested, he still felt drained from the earlier ritual. The magic he intended to use would not be easy, but with enough concentration he knew it would work.

The sword was magically forged of adamantium, a special gift he had created for himself just last year. Taking a moment to admire his own craftsmanship, he could not help but feel proud of his work. It was an ideal bastard sword, the blade precision sharpened to a 35-degree angle. This afforded a superior cutting ability without sacrificing the strength. Of course, the adamantium construction and magical process used to create it also provided for an indestructible body.

While dwarves were known for producing exceptional, full tang adamantium blades, he had taken the art a step further. Using his tremendous magical might, he created the sword from a single piece of adamantium, the pommel and cross-guard even part of the blade itself. After shaping the weapon, he also placed some strategic enchantments upon it and wrapped the grip in black leather for comfort. To add an accent, and to reinforce the magical potency of the weapon, he included a large, black moonstone in the pummel. Yezurkstal believed it created a nice contrast with the greenish hue of the adamantium.

Focusing on this allowed him to calm his mind, bringing it to the singular details of a creation he always kept at his side. Having traveled back to his home, the moonstone had been able to absorb enough latent magic to help him focus his energy. This, added to the rest he had taken, would give him more than enough energy to accomplish the feat at hand.

Closing his eyes, he took the sword in both hand and flipped it, so the tip faced the ground. Resting the blade vertically so it just penetrated the dirt, he concentrated on the magical energy around him. Thanks to his enchantment, his cave was protected from drawing energy, but the area around him was filled with other magical sources. He could feel the snakes hiding under rocks, the bug borrowing into the ground, and even the birds flying overhead. He also drew from the primal energy of the mountains and reached deep into Evorath to pull from the volcanic activity beneath.

Summoning all this energy forth, he could feel an aura forming around his body. The familiar feeling of darkness filled his soul as he reached into the fold between worlds and traveled to the demon realm. It was difficult to describe how he felt in this moment, his soul leaving his body and traveling into the darkness. While everything around him was distorted, his vision blurred and feelings dulled, he could see himself traveling into the darkness. With a brief flash of red, he passed through the threshold to his destination.

The world around him was dark and damp, a new vigor overtaking him as he tapped into the abundant dark energy. It had been months since he last visited, and he almost forgot just how much vigor and purpose this world gave him. As he arrived, he looked around for any signs of company.

There was a river to his left, the water black as coal and bubbling over as it snaked by. He could hear strange gurgling from the water and noted occasional bones floating to the surface. Black trees surrounded this river, some of the branches burning with an unquenchable fire but never consuming the trees beneath. Off in the distance, he spotted the mountains, smoke rising as meteors sailed through the heavens above.

Having lived on Evorath his entire life, he recognized that most people would not feel comfortable in such a place, but to him it felt familiar. Even though he was only able to travel to this world in spirit, he felt at home whenever he was here.

"I have returned," he shouted towards the mountains.

"There is an important mission on Evorath, and I am prepared to bring back all who are ready. Our time has come to take back the world, so join me." His voice echoed out, using all his magical might to make sure it reached far and wide.

It seemed he was missed, for as he finished his last statement, he could feel the ground beneath him trembling, the red sands quaking as the world responded. The last time he had come here, he needed to search around just to find some participants for his cause. Now, it appeared many were willing.

The river to his left burst open, a spray of black tar narrowly missing him as a large claw emerged.

This was a new one.

Reaching up from the depths, the demon extended its sinewy arm from the murky waters, its other large claw grasping the ground and pulling itself up. A single hand alone was larger than Yezurkstal was tall, and for a fraction of a second, he felt what must have been fear.

The creatures head appeared next, breaking the surface, and releasing a terrible roar. It had large brown horns, each curved around its head like a goat's. The creature's face was scaley, somewhat resembling a serpent as it ascended and opened its jaws. Jagged teeth jutted from its mouth, each larger than Yezurkstal's sword and likely just as sharp. Its face was disproportionately small, and spikes crowned the creature's head. Most terrifying of all, its eyes burned like fire.

As the demon pulled itself from the depths, Yezurkstal realized it also had a set of wings ready to deploy. Its strong chest was like the side of a mountain and its abdomen like jagged peaks. Both arms were also lined with large spikes and as its torso cleared the waters it spread its wings wide. Its wingspan had to be the size of a fully grown tree, stretching out more than thrice the width of its body. The wings resembled those of a bat, but they were riddled with holes, the flesh torn away as if it had fought something just as fierce as itself.

Finally, it cleared the river, lifting its legs from the depths and laying its massive feet on the ground. The entire plane shook as it landed in place, looking down on the spirit of Yezurkstal with its burning eyes. Despite its massive size and terrifying features, it appeared submissive.

"Are you the only one who answers my call?" asked Yezurkstal without flinching.

Speaking in the ancient demon tongue, the creature responded.

"I offer my army to serve." Its voice was deep and booming, garbled like it had something stuffed in its throat. As it spoke, smoke poured from its mouth, a faint flame burning from within.

Before Yezurkstal could open his mouth to reply, he noticed something in the distance. At first, he thought it was a simple cloud, but as it neared, he realized it was something much more. It was a swarm of winged demons approaching, dozens – perhaps hundreds in number.

Never had he found so many demons ready to leave at once. In fact, their numbers were usually capped at a dozen or two before he needed to return to his body. As this legion approached, he could not help but think about how his presumed failure with the humans had led to this most fortuitous circumstance.

The great demon shrugged its shoulders and stretched its arms wide, letting out a deep grumble. It knelt before Yezurkstal, looking him square in the face. Despite the fire in its eyes, Yezurkstal could see that it intended complete obedience.

"You are the one we have been awaiting. She told us you would be arriving in our world. My legion is here to serve."

She? Had Yezurkstal caught the attention of some otherworld spirit? Was "she" just another demon who was part of the ranks? His curiosity was piqued.

These demons alone would surely help him tip the scales and give him the power he needed to overcome the Avatar. Still, he would move forward as planned and continue to build his army when he returned.

"Who told you of my arrival? How many of you are there?" Yezurkstal asked with caution.

The demon's eyes flared at the first question. A small eruption of flames accompanied his response.

"She is our creator, Frogatha. After your absence, She called us to organize. We are over 200 in number and all prepared to die in battle."

Frogatha was blessing his crusade. He knew it had to be so.

"And you are the commander of this legion? What shall I call you?"

The demon clenched its right hand and pushed its fist firmly into the ground. "I am. You may call me Naberius."

By this point, the rest of the legion had almost arrived. Yezurkstal could feel their life energies and worked to link them with his own. He had never before tried to take so many back, and, considering the size of his new commander, he was a bit concerned about generating sufficient magic to make the trip. As usual, he had a method in mind to ensure the trip would go without issue.

"Naberius, are you or any of your legion versed in the arcane arts? The sheer number of you requires that I have some extra support in making the journey successfully back to Evorath."

"Magic is no use to a demon like me," responded Naberius quickly. "But there are sorcerers in our ranks."

Standing upright, Naberius cast a long shadow over Yezustal and into the rugged fields beyond. He was colossal.

"Sorcerers!" Naberius yelled with force. "Form up around our master!"

While his senses were limited mostly to sight, sound, and ephemeral feelings, he could almost feel a squall form around him as the demons came in for a landing. Though most continued to circle overhead, a good two dozen or so flapped down like a tornado and quickly surrounded Yezurkstal, leaving him in awe.

This would be more than sufficient.

"I will handle the spell to bring us back to my world, but to ensure I can pull you all back with me I need you to focus all of your magic energy into my spirit. Simply channel your energy into me."

Yezurkstal closed his eyes and braced for the influx of power. It was slow at first, a small boost compared to the power he was accustomed to. But then it began to well up inside him and exploded. A tremendous force built up, giving him access to more power than he had ever tapped into before; it was even greater than his ritual to summon the humans. His spirit pulsated with all the arcane energy, and he knew he could bring ten times this number back to Evorath if he had to.

A limitless void opened around him and his legion, black energy pulsing into the sky. Once again, his senses dulled, and his vision distorted. His spirit lifted from the ground and pushed through the barrier between worlds. With another flash of red, he opened his eyes and caught sight of his lifeless body.

It looked so helpless without him. In an instant, he snapped back into place, gasping in a breath of air.

The ground shook and he felt the new magic energy from the demon realm pulsing through his veins. A void opened in the chasm before him, a black cloud forming overhead. Yezurkstal waited for what seemed like an eternity.

In a rush, the demons began flocking out of the portal, swarming into the world. Dozens of them flew through in an instant, surging into the sky and lining up in a crude formation. It took nearly thirty seconds for the last of them to emerge and Naberius to follow.

Just like his emergence from the black river, the giant commander seemed unable to fit through the portal properly. He reached one arm out and then the next, pulling forward to get himself through the entry. For a moment, he paused with his torso stuck filling up the entry into Evorath, his enormous muscle pulsating as they worked him through. His wings spread out as he breached the gap and flapped vigorously, sending out a gust of wind. With this extra push, he was through the portal, rising above to join the ranks.

Yezurkstal looked up in wonder at his demonic army, a force that was finally worthy of his command. Still, if his mistakes last year had taught him anything it was that he should never underestimate his enemy. Looking from Naberius and through the ranks of demons, he began formulating his next move.

"My generous servants; as you already know, my name is Yezurkstal, and I will be leading you into glorious battle. Before we prepare for an attack against the disease that plagues this forest, we must build our ranks further and prepare an advanced camp. Naberius, I want you and your sorcerers to land in the chasm below. You will accompany me on an important mission. The rest of you; I want you to do something more immediate."

Yezurkstal extended his arms into the sky, channeling magical energy up through his body and out towards his demonic legion. He focused his thoughts on the humans he had released into the world. Reversing the same magic he often used to see into other's thoughts, he projected these thoughts onto his minions.

"These are humans," he continued with his arms still upraised. "I want you to split into groups of no more than six to twelve and scour the continent for them. You must avoid cities and large settlements at all costs. The last thing I need is to reveal our hand, so stealth is important. They are not native to this world, so you will not likely find them well-organized yet.

"Instead, stick to the forests and search within natural clearings for these magicless creatures. If possible, leave them alive, but if they resist, do not hesitate to kill them. I want you to bring them back here dead, or alive. By the time you return, we will have a secure prison established to hold them. Do not report back until you have gathered up at least one for everyone in your party. Once you return, you will receive additional orders from one of your sorcerers? Is this understood?"

There was a clamor among the demons in the sky, many of them yelling out cheers, others merely shrieking incoherently and a few articulating a responsive "yes." Upholding his mental connection with the creatures a moment more, he could tell they were all on board.

Confident his order would be followed, he dropped his arms.

"The day will wait no longer! Go forth!"

It was a tremendous sight watching the winged creatures all disperse. Even though he had just welcomed them into his ranks, he knew he could trust these demons. Last time, he had gone about this all wrong. This time, he would bide his time and prepare for an assault the right way.

While the many minions dispersed in every direction, the giant Naberius slowly began lowering himself into the chasm below. His sorcerers remained behind until the other demons had cleared and then followed suit, quickly diving down to join their commander. This was the first time Yezurkstal had anyone magical working on his side, which he knew would be a tremendous asset going forward.

He had waited in hiding far too long. It was time that his children leave the cave and make a proper home somewhere away from these wretched mountains. To do this, he would need to get all his resources on the same page.

Turning away from his soldiers, he swept his hand to the right. Releasing a jolt of magic, he lifted the seal on the cave and moved the stone barrier aside.

"Verandas!" he shouted into the opening.

He waited only a few seconds before his general arrived.

"Yes, sir," came the expectant response.

"Any new updates from our troops in the field?" Yezurkstal asked.

"I received word from our spy this morning indicating things were progressing well. Our minions in the Marta Plains should be ready by the end of the month."

"Excellent. I need you to prepare my wives and children to travel. We are going to be flying to our new home shortly, so they must secure the infants for the journey. Tell them to take only what they need and leave all else behind. We are establishing a permanent home to the south. Stay mindful, there are demons below preparing another project for me, so remain within the cave until my return."

Verandas nodded without hesitation. "Urgo."

He spun around and marched back into the cave. It was nice to have someone who obeyed orders so well.

Not bothering to reseal the entrance, Yezurkstal turned back towards his troops. All of them had either left in the search for humans or were awaiting their orders below. With a mental nudge, he summoned his pet griffin from its perch up above, where it had been waiting.

Responding to its master's mental command, the creature swooped down and landed gracefully in front of Yezurkstal. It lowered itself to the ground and let him mount. Holding onto some of the feathers around its neck, he commanded the creature to descend into the chasm.

Naberius and the demon sorcerers had all landed on a large plateau less than one hundred meters below. Focusing on an open spot before them, he urged his mount to land. The undead griffin set down on the plateau softly and lowered itself to the ground once again, allowing Yezurkstal to dismount. Turning towards his soldiers, he began once again.

"Alright; your jobs are essential to the success of our campaign. I need half of you sorcerers to remain here and erect a prison of sorts. I want a space big enough to herd at least one thousand humans around this plateau. If the plateau isn't big enough, use the space below. Whatever you do, make sure the area is secure and that none of these humans will be able to escape. Any demons who return with prisoners before I get back are to go back out and search for more.

"For the rest of you, I want you and Naberius to accompany me south. You are to follow my flight path and land just behind me. There is a lake somewhere to the south. It lies just southeast of a major elvish city, so make sure to remain well above the tree line to reduce the risk of being seen. Just south of this larger lake is a slightly smaller one. I will set down there, where the forest meets the hills. This is where we shall land and once there, I will give further instruction."

Pointing straight ahead, Yezurkstal continued. "Those to the left stay here. Those to the right follow me. Any questions?"

He realized his commands were somewhat simplistic, but demons were not the brightest creatures in creation. In fact, while he found their might impressive, he very much thought of them as inferior beings. Still, they were loyal enough and that was all he needed right now. In a few decades, his children would be matured and many more would have joined them. Once the hájje were strong enough, he would no longer need foul creatures like these to do his bidding. Until then, they served a purpose.

Hearing no questions from his underlings, he tightened his legs and pulled back on the reins.

"Good. We depart immediately."

Chapter 13

Somewhere in Central Erathal Forest
27 Zerrum, 1087 MT

Zelag looked with intent as the strange snake-woman used her magic to start a fire. It seemed as if he had learned more in this last day than in the entire previous decade. Witnessing a power like this was something he had never been able to imagine before. While most of his time was still spent dwelling on the death of his people, namely his progenitor, for a brief moment, he could almost forget the pain.

It was…fascinating -yes, that was the feeling. It was fascinating to see such magic firsthand. While magic was a part of his people, no one he had ever known was able to use magic outside itself in such a fashion. To see the red energy welling up within this strange creature's hands and then watch it fly out with such speed and light up the firewood was an entirely unfamiliar experience. He never would have imaged such powers existing.

"That is very good," said the Avatar. "I am proud of your progress Casandra."

The snake woman smiled at the mention of her name, or perhaps at the words of encouragement. In all truth, Zelag was still adapting to the feelings of these complex creatures. He was seeing the world in a new light, and his powers of observation and empathy were the two features most impacted. This left him unsure of most things.

The Avatar turned to Zelag.

"You see Zelag, most citizens of Evorath do not wield magic as you do. Your very essence is magic, which is why you will discover that most magic you encounter does not affect you. Instead, you are a being of pure magic, so while Casandra here is able to manipulate the elements through her geomancy, you can manipulate your very form. Do you clearly see the magic she is wielding?"

Zelag nodded.

"Yes teacher, I do. I can see the energy as she gathers it and as she releases it to create the fire."

"And when you look at the fire now, what do you see?" asked the Avatar.

Zelag turned back towards the fire and looked through towards its essence. Once again, he was distracted from his pain as he realized; even after alighting the wood, the fire was still magic in nature. He could see the red magical energy coating the log and pulsing with life. Its waves flowed forth and continued to hold itself fast to the material world.

"I see magic," said Zelag in awe.

"Good. You too are making fast progress. Eventually, you will be able to see that magic is as much a part of Evorath as the air most creatures breathe. Seeing through the fire and into the magic may not seem important now, but it is essential that you learn to spot when magic is at play and when it is not."

Zelag nodded. In all truth, he was hoping to work on his shapeshifting, but the more he learned, the easier it was to imagine a future without pain.

"I will learn."

The Avatar responded with a gentle smile. "I know you will. Now, speaking of the nature of magic, can you explain to me Casandra; how it is you tap into these different magics so easily? What is the root of your geomancy?"

Casandra cast her eyes towards the ground, her barbed tongue darting out between red lips. She reached up and fiddled with her silver necklace, rubbing the sapphire stone gently. Zelag assumed it was some sort of thinking ritual. Of course, he could also detect a hint of sadness in her matching, blue eyes.

"My mother always taught me that magic was all around uss. While mosst might just see the verdant energy of the foresst, growing up I was instructed that all magic is interchangeable. So, while a druid normally drawss straight from the energy of the treess to manipulate nature, geomancers learn to accesss this same energy and form it to their will."

She sounded unsure of her response. Zelag turned towards the Avatar to gauge whether this was correct response.

"Alright, but what exactly makes geomancy different from other disciplines? Like druidic magic for example? How do you form that magic and change it from the verdant, life-giving force to a volatile and aggressive magic like fire?"

Casandra continued to play with her necklace. She shifted her torso, slouching down and coiling her lower body. The blue scales glimmered in the faint sunlight that made its way through the trees.

"I am not ssure," she answered after some fidgeting. "It- I have alwayss been able to through focus."

The Avatar reached out and touched Casandra's shoulder. It must have been a method of comforting, for she relaxed slightly and loosed her posture as he did.

"You are not wrong, my child," he said with a note of sympathy. "You were born with the gift of geomancy, and you have the innate ability within you to convert the magic around you and bend it to your will. This is the true nature of magic that many mages never really understand. You do not choose what you excel at, Evorath does. She blesses all her children with unique gifts and yours just happens to be geomancy. With time and practice, you will find that your current abilities are just touching the surface of what you are capable of. In fact, you will realize that the necklace your mother gave you can help you more than you might think."

Casandra pulled away and grasped the necklace. She scrunched her face and tightened her eyebrows, her eyes becoming dark like a storm over the ocean. Her face turned red, as if the pigment from her lips shifted around to cover her. The next moment, she returned to before, her features softening and her face lightening.

"What do you mean?" she asked with urgency.

"Your tribe was quite knowledgeable in the ways of magic, and that necklace you wear is more than just a pretty way to complement your eyes. All gemstones hold great deposits of magic and that one in particular is quite impressive. I cannot reveal the secrets it contains, but if you continue your tutelage with me, you will understand that power sooner than you think."

"Why can't you just tell me now?" Casandra questioned, her face darkening again.

"If there is one thing I have stressed in these past months, it is that you must have patience," started the Avatar. But he turned away as he spoke, holding up his hand with palm open and facing outside the clearing.

"Someone is approaching," he continued.

Zelag swung his head around, looking in all directions and listening to see what the Avatar might mean. He couldn't hear or see anything. Curious if Casandra could, he turned towards her. She stood at the ready, her body angled to the side and her hands held up defensively. With his unique sense of sight, Zelag could see her gathering magical energy, a light green aura emanating from her chest into her hands.

Turning back towards where the Avatar was facing, he focused this gift to try and detect life. Beyond the Avatar, Casandra, and himself, he could sense no one. Yes, there were some small animals scurrying about, but nothing substantial. Maybe he just wasn't focusing enough.

Looking back to the Avatar, he tracked his teacher's eyes, which he realized were facing towards the ground. Zelag could feel another unfamiliar feeling welling up inside him. His fingertips tingled and he felt energized; it must have been excitement.

He saw it, a figure of pure magic approaching from…beneath the ground? It -or she- was just ahead, rising up through the foliage and out of the grass.

Her figure broke the surface, wild hair resembling the moss of the trees both in appearance and in color. As her face emerged, Zelag felt yet another sensation, but he was not at all familiar with this one -not even in concept.

She was gorgeous, more beautiful than any of the flowers in the forest, mountains on the land, or clouds in the sky. She was a glowing shade of green, most closely resembling the leaves of a flowering plant. Her eyes shown like the moonlight, emitting a faint green glow as she looked up. Her lips were perfectly symmetrical, a natural shade of brown. Completely without blemish, her face must have been the most beautiful thing in creation.

Her neck was strong but small, her shoulders powerful, and her breasts perfectly symmetrical. She was completely nude, baring her body without hesitation as she rose from the ground. Her slender figure was complemented by a flat stomach, and toned legs; her entire body matched the green hue of her face. Overall, she couldn't be more than a meter and a half tall. Despite her slender figure, Zelag could see through to the energy inside her.

Of course, he couldn't explain why but in this body he was completely drawn to this mysterious women. The rest of his senses were dulled and he was overcome with the desire to be close to her and embrace her. In fact, he didn't realize it as first, but he was walking towards her.

He felt someone trying to pull him away, but he shrugged it off without turning around. Nothing else mattered in this moment but her.

Just as he was a few paces away, the Avatar stepped in front and grabbed Zelag, breaking his focus. The feeling faded ever so slightly, and he could sense his teacher sending magic into his form.

Suddenly, this desire turned into pain, and he felt his body crumbling in on itself. His skin began to grow more hair, his legs shrinking down in an instant and his hands turning to paws. Before he could even figure out what had happened, he was looking up at the Avatar from the ground, his eyes just barely above his teacher's ankles.

Zelag hadn't ever imagined shifting so quickly, but somehow, he had; he was a squirrel.

"Zelag," started the Avatar sternly. "You will remain in that form until our guest leaves. Your human form is not suitable for this meeting."

What had happened?

How had he even transformed? A moment ago, he was looking at this beautiful creature and felt absolute bliss. Now, his feelings had become limited again, his mind unable to contemplate what was going on. Still, he took comfort in the sound of the Avatar's voice, and he trusted that everything would be alright.

"You should not come here without warning," said the Avatar addressing the new arrival.

"This was too urgent to delay," responded the mysterious woman, her voice peaceful and melodic.

"And what is this about?" asked the Avatar, his voice forceful.

"Yezurkstal has been busy. He has traveled to the demon realm yet again and has returned with an entire army. According to my sister of the pine, he brought back at least two hundred demons."

Zelag attempted to transform back into his human form, his mind focused on that unexplainable connection he felt just moments ago. For some reason, he simply couldn't move.

The woman paused and cast her glance down towards Zelag. In this form, he felt a strange obedience towards this woman; her gaze made him feel completely docile and content. After a moment, she looked back to the Avatar.

"It is more serious than this though. My sister also indicated that he brought something more sinister back with him. It is an archdemon of old, the likes of which Evorath hasn't seen in millennia."

In his current form, Zelag could not quite distinguish facial expressions as well, but judging by the way the Avatar tensed up he assumed there was some level of apprehension.

"Alright, daughter Willow. You were correct in coming to me straight away. I need you to find all the sisters you can and spread the word of this development. You must all remain vigilante. If Yezurkstal can command these demons, there is no telling how powerful he has become. I want you to all start traveling in pairs.”

“You know that not all of my sisters will heed-” the woman started before being interrupted.

“I know. You worry about doing your part. I will worry about them.” Even in this feeble form, Zelag could feel the authority in the Avatar’s voice.

“Very well,” replied the woman softly.

She turned around and glided towards the dense coverage. Her form began to sink into the earth, her body phasing out as the ground opened to consume her. She faded away into Evorath, and without his transformative properties, Zelag was unable to keep track of her.

He looked up towards the Avatar, once again willing himself to transform.

Nothing.

The Avatar just stood there, looking towards the horizon with a stone face. Hearing rustling from his right, Zelag turned and saw Casandra approaching. She slithered up behind the Avatar, stopping less than a meter away.

“I can help fight,” she exclaimed.

The Avatar turned towards Casandra and shook his head. “No, my child. This is not your battle to fight. The forest must defend itself against this threat.”

“But what is all of this training for if not to fight in defense of the forest?” asked Casandra clenching her fists.

Kneeling, the Avatar reached out and grabbed for Zelag. Zelag's first instinct was to dart away, but he stood there without objection. As the Avatar lifted him up, he could feel magic surge through his body.

Once again, he began transforming against his will, his bones expanding and reforming. His paws thickened and became fingers, the hair retracting into his body. He could feel his heart and lungs expanding, his ribs stretching out. With only a hint of pain, he was human again. Before he could open his mouth to ask a question, the Avatar replied to Casandra.

"You are right; I am training you to defend the forest. But you are not yet ready for a threat like this. My vision for you and Zelag reaches far beyond today, but if you try to engage with a demon like this, I cannot assure your survival."

"I do not understand," interjected Zelag. "Why can we not help? If this demon is so terrifying, you could use all the help you can get. If you are training us to fight, why not let us fight?"

In all truth, Zelag didn't care much about any demons, but if Yezurkstal was there, Zelag had a reason to go. After all, he was the hájje that had brought humans into Evorath, which ultimately meant he was responsible for the death of Zelag's people. He would face his end.

"Zelag is right," added Casandra with haste. "How are we supposed to learn how to properly defend the forest if you never actually let us fight?"

The Avatar sighed and cast his gaze to the ground.

"First of all, this is not the battle for you to test your training on. Casandra, I understand you have faced Yezurkstal before, but you are fortunate to have survived that encounter. This time around, you may not be so fortunate. Zelag, your training only just began today. Two days ago, you couldn't have even imagined the horror of a battlefield. Your recent loss leaves you unable to think objectively."

Zelag felt a sting at this statement. He thought about the horror he witnessed just days before and the pain he had experience. His stomach felt empty, a deep pain tearing away at him as he pictured his progenitor lying dead on the ground. Then it happened again; his eyes moistened and began to leak. Trying to shield his pain, he looked down and covered his face.

"It's known as crying," said the Avatar as if anticipating Zelag's thoughts. "It is a normal response in your current form for the pain and loss you feel. It also demonstrates that you are not ready to fight this battle. Casandra, I need you and Zelag to stay here together. Watch out for each other and stay on guard in case anyone shows up."

Zelag wiped away some of the moisture from his eyes, but it continued to come forth -rather, he continued to cry. With a sniffle, he began to object, but was interrupted by Casandra.

"I understand master," she said defeated.

She placed her hand on Zelag's shoulder, rubbing his back and slithering up right next to him. Like the embrace the Avatar had given when they first met, Zelag felt some relief from this contact.

"Thank you," responded the Avatar. "I will need to go scout out this situation myself and I may not return for a few days. While I am gone, I trust that the two of you can take care of yourselves. If you need anything, just pray to Evorath and word will reach me."

"We will be fine," reassured Casandra.

Zelag wiped his face again and looked up, his crying slowed to a halt as he attempted to focus on the present.

"Yes, we will be here when you return," he agreed.

The Avatar nodded and without another word sunk into the ground.

Chapter 14

Hills to the South of Erathal Forest
27 Zerrum, 1087 MT

Yezurkstal slid off his griffin, landing with a thud on the uneven ground. Though the magic he used to reanimate the amalgamated creature preserved its body, he made a mental note to be more careful when riding in the future. His pants were stained in red by the wound on the creature's side. While it was barely visible on the black leather, it still felt unfitting for someone in his position.

Giving the undead creature a mental nudge, he ordered it to perch in one of the hills to the south. Meanwhile, he looked back to the north, where his allies were approaching. Naberius was in the lead and the thirteen sorcerers followed closely behind.

Though Yezurkstal had never actually ventured this far south himself, somewhere along the line he had found a memory of this place. It seemed that the memory was accurate; this would make for the perfect location for a more permanent settlement.

The larger of the two lakes, Lake Algarath, would make for the northern border, offering a natural obstacle to deter invaders from entering his kingdom. West of this clearing was a small river followed by another lake, offering additional protection on this side. To his understanding, the hills to the south were uninhabited, and one in particular would make for a perfect spot to place a watch tower, ensuring he could keep an eye over the land around his new home. There would be a small opening to the east where he could erect defensible walls, creating a large enough city that his children could live in while he waged war for the future of the continent.

No longer would he be forced to live in the mountains like some gnome. Instead, this would mark a new beginning for his people and a real opportunity for the hájje. The rise of Yezurkstal was upon Evorath and his kingdom would serve as a testament to his unending might. No longer would creatures have to worry about hunger, disease, or strife. The impure would be cleansed and the hájje would inherit Evorath.

As he started to make some mental notes of his surroundings, Naberius touched down just next to the lake. His demon sorcerers followed right behind, landing one by one in front of their commander. It was amazing to Yezurkstal how thirteen different demons could look so alike. From tallest to shortest, there could not have been more than a couple centimeters difference in height. Each was unusually skinny for a demon, offering a lean profile that was perhaps telling of their magical nature. Their black skin was streaked with nondescript red patches and their eyes glowed yellow. None of them wore more than a primitive garb around their waist and they did not carry any magical implements; their bat-like wings tucked neatly in as they landed, adding to their already sleek profile.

"What are your orders?" asked Naberius as the last of the demons landed. Yezurkstal appreciated his ability to be direct.

"I intend to transform this area into a suitable home. While the full plans to fortify the area will take time, I want to begin setting out borders. What I need from you, Naberius, is to harvest trees from the edge of the forest. Stick to oak, cedar, and pine for building purposes. Bring back as much as you can at once and I will instruct as you go on how much we ultimately need.

"I need six sorcerers to pair off and head south. Scout out the hills below us and look for any spots where we might establish a suitable quarry. We will need a healthy supply of stones to build a proper watch tower on the highest hill and we will also want to build a wall blocking entry to the east. Meanwhile, you other seven demons will stay with me and begin placing the necessary magical enchantments on the land. We will establish a border and ensure that the lakes around us are also secure."

Sensing that the demons -Naberius in particular- were not very thrilled with these orders, Yezurkstal continued.

"Before we go on the offense, we need to make sure that we have a defensible position here. I can better coordinate efforts from here than from the mountains. I know you demons are bred for war, but before we fight, my people need someplace to call home."

Naberius grunted and spread out his wings. "Very well," he said before taking off into the air towards the tree line.

The sorcerers still stood their unmoving. Perhaps they needed some more direction.

"You and you, you and you, you and you," Yezurkstal said pointing to three pairs of the demons in turn; "you all scout out the land for stone deposits."

Without hesitation, the half dozen demons took to the sky and flew off towards the hills to the south. They had to be some of the dumbest mages he had ever encountered, but they seemed obedient enough.

"Alright," said Yezurkstal looking at the remaining demons. "Let's see what you are capable of."

-=-=-=-=-=-=-=-=-

Just North of Lake Algarath
27 Zerrum, 1087 MT

Artimus was glad that he convinced Cabal to allow him to act as the advanced scout for the group. While part of him didn't like leaving Savannah alone with the rest of the convoy, he was just thrilled to be away from the crowd. It was peaceful here in the forest and while he knew a small army waited for him through the dense brush of the trees, being this much ahead of them really made a difference.

Fortunately, his skills as a ranger were considerable, so it was easy enough convince them. After all, there were only a handful of other elves in the entire forest who had tracking abilities to rival Artimus, and that was to say nothing about his quiet movement and keen observational skills. Yes, Artimus realized he was perhaps a bit biased in this assessment of himself, but in his years serving the crown there was never an indication he could be wrong.

Of course, now was not the time to dwell on his abilities and qualifications. Instead, he needed to focus on the task at hand. According to the information received from scouting parties, a group of humans had begun gathering near Lake Algarath, so Artimus was slowly creeping his way east towards the northern end of the lake. Though the ground he walked on was relatively smooth, he noted the path narrowed ahead. He was entering dense bush, which meant staying quiet would become nearly impossible.

Fortunately, or perhaps unfortunately if he did not locate the camp soon, the sun was dipping down from its spot high in the sky. This meant that it was time for evening feedings for many local creatures, which would help mask any sounds Artimus did produce. Still, he crept up towards the bush slowly, staying low to the ground and scanning with wide eyes. It reminded him of his time as a hunter.

For this task, he had left most of his gear behind. His quiver and bow were both back with Thoron, his trusty steed that was without a doubt keeping Savannah good company. He also left his sword behind, leaving him primarily armed with his mythril dagger. Of course, he always held some other knives as well. Wearing his trusty green tunic and simple, leather shoes, he was well-dressed for a stealthy approach.

He spotted some deer tracks to his left, perhaps from a doe and two or three of her young. Though part of him wanted to inspect closer, he pushed the notion away. The plants here were all familiar, simple oak, pine, and maple trees mostly. Many wildflowers grew along the ground as well, but Artimus had not learned the name of many of them. He did recognize some lambs quarter growing in the clearing at his feet, some nasturtium just to his side, and even some alyssum spread out sporadically. The vibrant mix of their blooms complemented the rich green of the forest, while also allowing Artimus to breathe in a calming fragrance.

As he reached the thick bush ahead, Artimus pushed some branches aside, inching forward and keeping his breath calm. If these humans had any sense of bushcraft they would know not to try and hold up in such a dense section of the forest. On the other hand, there was a perfect clearing not far ahead and Artimus knew it could make the perfect spot for an impromptu camp, especially considering the quick water access with the lake just meters away.

Artimus could hear the scurrying of creatures both in the trees above and in the foliage around him. Most of the noise up top was likely from squirrels, but the noise on the ground could have been any number of species. Whatever it was, he listened carefully; at least he could be sure it wasn't the humans. Bipedal creatures sounded much different as they moved.

Edging around some rather sturdy oak branches, he strained to keep himself from stomping down too hard on some fallen leaves. He maneuvered himself around the obstacle with care, ensuring he put his feet on the ground toes first to avoid excess noise. He could still hear a distinct crunch as he stepped, but hopefully it was quiet enough that it wouldn't alert anyone to his presence.

Continuing forward, the path became a little easier to manage. While he had to brush aside some overgrown branches and tiptoe around roots and flowers, there was nothing else substantial in his path. This allowed him to concentrate more on the sounds around him. After a few meters navigating this narrow path, he stopped dead in his tracks.

His potent sense of hearing allowed him to pick up an unusual sound ahead. There was a faint clack up in the distance the dull sound of something biting into wood. At first, he thought it might be a woodpecker, but now that he was standing still, he could identify with confidence that it was something else. If Artimus were to venture a guess, he would attribute the sound to an axe chopping up firewood.

Resuming his approach, Artimus took special care to balance himself on any roots he could, avoiding any leaf buildups to ensure he could make his way forward with minimal noise. The path was expanding at this point, opening to allow for more relaxed movement. Just as he predicted, there were less sounds of wildlife the closer he got to the source of the chopping. Any animals that heard it were skittering away in fright. As he continued forward and the volume of the chopping increased, he began to make out other faint noises.

Continuing at a cautious pace, he could hear some voices up ahead. Though they were muffled, he could tell that he was getting close. It sounded like the speakers were trying to whisper, or at least speak in hushed tones. Fortunately, Artimus's hearing was almost as good as his vision, so he was able to listen in. Of course, he could only hear bits and pieces.

"They are no longer our concern… What strange land…we in? Did we die…battlefield?"

Artimus assumed he could fill in the missed words, but before returning to Cabal and telling him of his findings, he needed to find out how many of these humans were gathered. As he crept closer, he continued to listen in.

"…hath the women and children died too?" This was a different voice, one that was a bit more weathered with age.

"How else would ye explain this land?" asked the first voice again. "This land is full of strange creatures, more than just those horned demons we slew."

Artimus wondered if they had really encountered a demon after their arrival on Evorath. If they had, it meant he was fighting a serious battle against time. Yezurkstal could have already sent out demons to help round up the humans. Still, he had to focus on staying hidden.

He stepped with care, slowing down even more as he neared the human camp. His legs were tight from crouching low and his soft stepping was causing a stiffness in his back. Still, he moved forward carefully, minding every twig and pile of leaves to ensure he remained as quiet as possible.

The humans continued debating back and forth, apparently going through some spiritual crisis. They knew they were no longer in their realm, a land called "Ingland." One even questioned if they were "still on Earth."

Artimus could tell he was getting close, as the hushed tones become more distinct. As he approached, he could even hear some other footsteps around the camp and the crackling of a fire. It was time he really got to work.

Picking out a suitable oak, Artimus stood up straight and stretched out his legs. He could feel some tension leaving his neck and back as he extended his arms overhead. Grabbing hold of some sturdy branches, he took care and pulled himself up slowly. He strained a bit from the pressure, not used to pulling up his entire weight at such a pace. But he couldn't afford any extra noise, so he had to do it this way. After the initial pull, he was able to plant his feet on the trunk with care.

Switching his gaze between the tree and ahead towards the human camp, he continued climbing. It took a good couple of minutes of this slow climbing, his muscles on fire from the strain. As he reached the peak, the tension leaving his muscles, he looked down upon the encampment.

From up above, he was able to look down and see the two humans whom he had heard. Though he could no longer hear them, he guessed the closer of the two was the older one. This man had brown and gray hair, his face a bit worn by the sun. He wore a strange battle uniform, including a bastard sword at his side. Though the style of the armor was a bit unfamiliar to Artimus, the sword was surprisingly like elvish smithing.

The other man was a bit taller than the first, his hair a darker brown and without hint of fading. His skin also showed less signs of aging, only a couple of wrinkles under his eyes. From the way he was standing, Artimus could even make out his hazel eyes.

Beyond these two men, he could see further into the clearing. While bits were blocked out by other tree branches, he spotted the fire, which was in the middle of the camp, or thereabouts. Three children huddled around the fire, two males and one female, at least judging by what Artimus could tell. Two adult females were also with them at the fire

A handful of other males roamed the camp, a couple of them simply walking around with weapons draw and others working to clear the ground or forage for food -again, Artimus could only guess. Finally, he spotted the person who was chopping wood. Of course, he was not using a standard lumber axe, but rather a battle axe; likely the tool he had when Yezurkstal had pulled him onto Evorath.

Wanting to make sure he was not missing out on anyone, Artimus held himself in place for a few minutes, simply observing them as they moved. The axe wielder stopped about thirty seconds in and put his weapon down to rest. After a minute leaning against a tree, he continued to chop away. Meanwhile, the two males who had been arguing joined the party around the fire, going back and speaking to one of the females.

While he would have waited longer under different circumstances, Artimus felt at this point he had observed enough. It appeared these dozen humans were all they really needed to account for, so there should not be any challenge with opening communications.

Before descending the tree, Artimus traced a path from the campfire and out in the bush. He spotted an opening just to the north that will allow for easier entry for he and the rest of the convoy. Since none of the humans had a bow or arrows that he could see, there would be very little risk in this approach, and it would allow for the best presentation upon arrival. Doing one last scan, Artimus looked down and slowly began to lower himself from the tree.

-=-=-=-=-=-=-=-=-

Savannah continued watching in the direction Artimus had left, doing her best to hide her feelings. While Artimus had made a convincing argument as to why he should be the one to scout ahead, he wasn't fooling his wife. The only reason he wanted to get out ahead at all was so he could be away from the rest of the convoy for a while. Just because he was a good hunter didn't mean he should start volunteering to be a scout too.

Still, Savannah knew he could take care of himself, so she tried not to get too upset with him. Instead, she was more upset with the fact that she had to stand by Thoron.

Though she didn't have the heart to tell Artimus, she had never really cared for horses, this one in particular. Sure, Artimus took good care of him, but despite the attention he received, Thoron always seemed to smell extra…horsey. Of course, being left with Thoron wasn't enough by itself. It also happened that Artimus left her with his random accessories.

She had rested his quiver up against the nearest tree and his bow with it but seeing as his stupid bastard sword wouldn't lean properly, she had to hold it in her hands. Though Artimus had tried to explain how the blade was well-balanced and therefore suitable for close-range combat, she couldn't see it as anything more than a clumsy weapon. It was heavy and long, and while it was supposedly possible to use it in one hand, it couldn't be effectively wielded without two. Not to mention, the idea of her husband having to engage in combat at such close range was unappealing to say the least. Magic was so much more helpful in a battle than any elf-made weapon.

Of course, Savannah knew it did her no good to contemplate these things. Despite that, it felt like a welcome distraction compared to the current situation.

"It's getting late in the day," offered Zeidrich from his position a few meters away. "If the scouts were correct, Artimus should be back any minute with a report."

"I trust the information was accurate," replied the Chancellor from his position atop a lightly armored, chestnut destrier.

Savannah turned to look at the pair, trying to hide her feelings of annoyance. She paused and took a deep breath before responding, remember that it was often better to hold her tongue. Still, she felt it appropriate to speak up in this case. On the other hand, maybe fate had other ideas.

As she opened her mouth to question the Chancellor, she heard rustling from the trees up ahead. Turning back around, she caught sight of Artimus coming through the underbrush. In hindsight, it was for the best.

"Ah, you have returned," spoke the Chancellor, his voice rising in pitch ever so slightly.

Artimus continued forward, flashing Savannah a brief smile before moving towards the Chancellor.

"Yes, and I have good news. It seems only a couple of new members have joined their party, putting their numbers at exactly a dozen. I waited around for a few minutes to try and see if anyone else would show, but it seems that is the lot of them for now."

"Good," replied the Chancellor with a nod. "And your recommended approach?"

"I suggest we head north just a little and loop around. There is a large enough clearing that you and Zeidrich can proceed forward and still have backup nearby. Naturally, it affords a good enough line of sight that the archers and I can keep ourselves ready in case the situation demands force. Right now, the humans are tending a fire and looking for food. They are confused, unsure of where they are or how to approach the situation." Though Artimus stopped here, Savannah could tell he had something more he wanted to say.

"Very good," exclaimed the Chancellor. "Let us proceed."

Artimus took a slight bow and turned towards Savannah, walking to her side looking her over with his eyes. His face softened as he looked upon her figure. With a smile, he approached her and outstretched his hands.

"Thank you for tending to my gear and to Thoron."

Savannah returned the smile. Though she was still unhappy with the situation, she wasn't going to let it impact her relationship with Artimus.

"I still don't know why you insist on having this sword," she sniped. "Compared to your proficiency with a bow, you aren't really much good with it anyways."

"Hey!" Artimus shot back. "I take offense to that."

He grabbed the sword from her hands, unwrapping the belt and tying it around his waist with ease. Though she stood by her statement, there was definitely nothing lacking in her husband's dexterity. Without delay, he hopped over to the tree and retrieved his bow and arrows as well. Securing these about his person, he proceeded back to Savannah's side.

While he was retrieving his gear, Savannah noted Zeidrich and the infantry had already mounted their horses. Everyone was lining up and preparing to depart for the human camp.

"You best ride Thoron from here," suggested Artimus, laying his hand on the small of her back.

"Why would I ride your horse?" she asked.

"I need to be on foot to lead the archers. You notice none of them brought horses, right? Riding and shooting doesn't work that well."

"You would know, wouldn't you," riposted Savannah with a smirk.

Artimus just stared at her in response, his face stern. He was right.

"Okay, if you would be so kind-" Savannah placed her left hand on Thoron's saddle and extended her right towards her husband. Artimus didn't hesitate, taking her hand and providing the extra support she needed. Pulling herself onto the saddle, she adjusted her dress and took the reins.

"Thank you."

Artimus just nodded and turned towards the Chancellor. Savannah hadn't realized it, but the Chancellor appeared to be waiting on him.

"Well, Artimus. Are you going to lead the way?" he asked impatiently.

Artimus looked up to Savannah and then back to the Chancellor.

"I figured you and Zeidrich would do the honors. I can stay back with the other archers in case there is an incident."

"No, I want you up front with Zeidrich and me. You have a trustworthy face, and I want you to be our third representative," insisted the Chancellor.

When was that part of the plan? If he had shared this before, Savannah would have objected to coming in the first place. Artimus shot her a glance, as if he knew what she was thinking.

"I really don't think that-"

"It is decided, Artimus. Lead the way."

That was the last straw. Savannah couldn't hold her tongue any longer.

"What do you mean 'it is decided'?" she shouted, her voice coming out a bit more forceful than she intended. "You are our Chancellor, not our king -or have you forgotten?"

From the corner of her eye, she saw Artimus slowly turn back towards her, his mouth agape. He wasn't the only one in shock either. General Zeidrich looked like the color was drained from his face, and Cabal wore an eerie expression of discontent.

No one spoke for what seemed like a full minute until Cabal broke the silence.

"Alright, Artimus. Do I not pay for your service?"

"Yes, sir," replied Artimus right away. "You do."

"Then, I believe it is reasonable to ask that you do this. It's for the greater good."

Savannah fought her inner voice asking to object more. In truth, she realized the Chancellor wasn't wrong about his authority, but that didn't mean he was going about it the right way either. And what was the rhetorical nonsense about "the greater good?" How would Artimus leading the Chancellor help them?

"When you put it that way, sir, I would be happy to oblige," responded Artimus.

He looked up to Savannah again and winked.

Considering the situation, that was likely the best support she was going to get.

Chapter 15

Human Camp Near Algarath
27 Zerrum, 1087 MT

If Artimus had realized this mission would result in him being face-to-face with these humans, he would have objected from the beginning. Savannah was already upset with the situation before, but now that he was leading both Cabal and Zeidrich forward into the camp, he couldn't imagine how much angrier she must be.

He marched to the left of Cabal's horse, guiding the destrier forward into the clearing. Zeidrich followed his pace on the right, keeping his hands free and ready to reach for his own longsword.

Though the mission was peace, Zeidrich was exceptionally well-armed for the situation. He wore full plate-armor up to his shoulders, leaving only his head exposed. With his mythril longsword ready at his side, he could no doubt handle himself should the humans respond violently.

Cabal was a bit less armored, wearing a hybrid armor of sorts. Most of his body was covered in leather and studded with mythril, but he wore a chest plate of steel to help bolster his torso. Naturally, all this armor was enchanted for additional protection benefits. Sitting atop his steed, he kept his hands clear of the bastard sword at his side. In fact, he appeared much more relaxed than Artimus.

One of the humans on patrol spotted them first just before they entered the clearing. He wore polished armor himself, made of steel by the looks of it. The style was somewhat similar what a light infantry soldier might wear. He also had a bastard sword of his own and a matching dagger on his left. Drawing his sword, he ran towards the elves and yelled.

"Intruders!"

Artimus was impressed at how quickly the other humans responded, but he was careful not to make any sudden movements. As they mobilized, he simply stopped and lifted his hands up, keeping his palms faced forward.

The other guard quickly joined his cohort, running forward and drawing his blade. This one's armor was not quite as shiny as the first, but his sword looked just as sharp. Meanwhile, the men who were clearing the ground each grabbed their tools and held them up defensively. None of them charged forward though, likely because their simple wool tunics indicated they were not soldiers, but likely farmers. Further away, the tree-chopper picked up his axe and strode forward with great intent. Though he didn't wear full armor, he did have a chainmail shirt on, confirming Artimus's assumption that his axe was made for war.

Next, the women and children all ran behind the fire, huddling together and staying low. Finally, both the older and younger man who had been arguing earlier ran towards the clamor. Up close, Artimus could see that the older one also wore chainmail, but over that mail he wore a fancy tunic with a symbol of some kind, likely a family crest. The younger man had the same crest on his tunic, but he had no mail underneath for defense. In any case, each wielded a bastard sword.

Stopping about seven meters away, the humans lined up in a row, keeping themselves ready in a defensive position.

"What is your business 'ere?" asked the older human, his hand shaking.

"We mean you no harm," replied Cabal without delay. "Please, lower your arms and allow me to introduce myself. I know you are far from home, and likely confused about where you are. It is my intention to help welcome you to our land and make the transition as easy as possible."

"And what land is that?" asked the younger human, lowering his blade ever so slightly.

"This forest you are in is known as Erathal. My name is Chancellor Cabal, and I am the leader of the Republic of Erathal."

"A Republic? We couldn't possibly..." started the older human, his face scrunched tight, and eyes squinted. The other humans looked around in confusion as well, their defensive formation faltering slightly.

"I implore you, please. The answers you seek may not seem believable. You are far from home, but if you lower your weapons, we will gladly discuss our current situation."

It was a bit unsettling to hear Cabal talk in such a setting. His voice was almost soothing, calm and even toned. While there was a palpable tension in the air, it seemed that his words could cut right through it. In fact, it appeared that these humans were receptive -which didn't really make sense on the surface.

Artimus kept his eyes trained on the humans. The older human's eyelids shot up for a moment and his eyes widened, perhaps a sign of fear.

"Well, where are we? Did you bring us here?" he asked with trepidation.

"Just lower your weapons and we will happily talk. We come offering our friendship and hope that you will accept it," assured Cabal with confidence.

After a brief hesitation, the older human listened, lowering his sword, and standing upright. The others followed closely behind, the two armored soldiers hesitating for only a moment before returning their swords to their sheaths. Of all the camp though, the axe-bearer seemed most at-ease, his shoulders lowering and chest deflating. It seemed like an almost relaxed posture.

Artimus wasn't afraid to admit that he came into this interaction with few expectations, but this was going much better than he could have imaged. Were these humans so trusting of complete strangers?

"Thank you," continued Cabal without breaking stride. "I am afraid I have never been in a situation quite like this, so I don't know where to begin. First, let me again introduce myself. I am Chancellor Cabal of the Erathal Republic. To my right is General Zeidrich, the mind behind our nation's military power.

To my left is Artimus, a trusted adviser, and Lieutenant in our Ranger's Division. Who among you is the leader?"

"I am the leader," replied the older human without hesitation. "I am Lord Edward, and this is my son John." he said motioning to the younger human.

"Edward, John, it is a pleasure to meet you both." Cabal took a slight bow from atop his steed. "If you would please, I am going to get off my horse, so I am not sitting above you. Please do not mistake my intentions as hostile."

Edward nodded.

Cabal put one leg over his horse and grabbing hold of the saddle slowly lowered himself to the ground. Brushing himself off, he took a step forward. Artimus watched Zeidrich for a clue on whether he should follow suit. Since the General didn't move, neither did he.

"Now, I believe the best way to explain your situation is to just come out with it. I'm afraid this world is not what you are familiar with. From what I understand it, you come from a land called Earth. You have been forced into our world, Evorath, by an unsavory force."

John snapped his head between Cabal and his father, his eyes tight and deliberate. He was not happy with this explanation.

"What do you mean we are not on Earth? That is a preposterous notion. This is not a tasteful jest, not tasteful at all," his voice was uneasy, his tone fluctuating just enough that it was noticeable to Artimus. He continued looking to those around him, as if hoping for some support.

"As I said, the answers may not sound believable, but I give you my word as Chancellor, I am telling you only the truth - no more and no less. Our land is called Evorath, and from how it was explained to me we are a sort of mirror image of your world. You are the first humans in our land."

Edward spoke up this time.

"No humans? Do you realize what you are suggesting? Why...you are humans yourselves!"

Artimus felt pity for these humans. They really had no idea what was going on and coming from a land like Irontail had described, he wondered if they could really survive on Evorath.

"We are not humans," replied Cabal in a solemn tone. "We are elves. Despite this, I would like to stress that we have more similarities than we do differences."

John let out a laugh, snorting a little as he stepped back.

"I beg your pardon. You jest! You mean to tell us that you are some sort of fairy?"

Edward looked at his son, his face hard and eyes harder. Before he could say anything, Cabal responded.

"I assure you, we are not fairies" he said with some urgency in his voice. "I'm not sure what resemblance you could find between us and those meddlesome little monsters. Though, I must admit, I am a bit surprised. Are there fairies in your land? If you are familiar with magic, perhaps your integration into Evorath won't be such a shock."

"Now I must agree with my son," started Edward shaking his head. "What is this nonsense about fairies and magic? Please excuse my insensitivity, but I do see that deformity around your ears. If you think that is enough to make us believe you are some mythical creatures, then I must ask that you take your friendship and leave. We will figure out how to get home on our own."

Cabal offered a polite smile. "I think you would prefer to hear me out. Put aside your skepticism for just a few minutes and look around you. If this was a mere deformity, would both my General and Lieutenant share it? If you think you can find your way home, are there any forests like this one near you? Again, I implore you: hear what I have to offer you."

The two armored soldiers hadn't moved much during the conversation, but for some reason they chose this moment to lean in. It appeared that they were just as relaxed as the axe-bearer and willing to listen. Behind the lineup of soldiers, Artimus also noticed that the farmers (or foragers) had moved in closer to listen. They held their tools loosely at their side.

"You have my ears," replied Edward after only a moment.

Artimus looked around in confusion, trying to see if Zeidrich might understand what was going on. As usual for a situation like this, the General just kept looking ahead with a stoic look on his face.

"Artimus, please go fetch Savannah. I *think* the only way to help our new friends is to show them what kind of magic really exists in our land."

Without questioning, Artimus turned and started walking away from the group. A show of magic would certainly help to give these humans some perspective on their situation. Perhaps it would be the push they needed to convince these humans to return to Erathal and help gather as many of their cohorts as possible. After all, the more humans they could get to the city, the less potential soldiers Yezurkstal had for his army.

Artimus continued through the clearing, admiring the natural funnel the trees created. Willow trees lined this natural funnel, moss hanging from their branches to create a foreboding atmosphere. It was a fine testament to the inherent beauty of Evorath and her powers of creation. Savannah was another testament to how much beauty was in the world. But...why was this relevant to Artimus right now?

The Chancellor asked him to fetch Savannah because magic would help. So, he was fetching Savannah.

As he caught sight of Thoron and Savannah just around the corner, he paused to think for another moment. He looked upon them, standing peacefully by a small oak. His wife looked beautiful leaning against the tree, her lithe figure completely relaxed and at ease. She was enjoying nature, taking in the world around her and getting some real peace for a change. Though he wasn't a druid himself, seeing her standing there like that made him think she must be at home.

Savannah caught sight of him as he approached, standing upright and walking towards him. Her strides were rhythmic and metered, a certain enthusiasm in her step.

"How are things going?" she asked.

"Better than I expected," replied Artimus. "Though, the humans are not entirely receptive to their situation. They seem to have trouble grasping onto where they are. We believe that a little demonstration of magic might help show them that they are, in fact, in a different land."

Savannah appeared troubled. "And you want me to give them a glimpse of what Evorath has in store? Are you sure showing them magic is the best idea? After all, aren't they from a land that doesn't have any magic? Aren't you worried that this sort of show might make them fearful of us?"

"We think it is the only way to help our new friends. If we can show them magic, they will have to believe us." Artimus answered without hesitation.

"Sure, it might help them realize that they are no longer at home, but is this the way to really earn their trust? What have you discussed with them thus far?" asked Savannah.

Her eyes pierced into Artimus, the deep green drawing him in and helping him focus. Maybe she had a point.

"Well, the Chancellor is expecting us back there right away," said Artimus dismissively. "So, I think we should head back and just get on with it."

"If you really believe that it is the right move, then I will help. Lead the way."

Artimus nodded and walked over to Thoron. "Just wait here for us to return," he said patting his trusted horse on its head.

Spinning back around, he began marching back towards the clearing. He glanced back after taking a few steps to make sure Savannah was following close behind. She was.

They walked in silence back to the camp and as Cabal, Zeidrich, and the humans came into sight, Artimus slowed his pace. Turning back to Savannah once again, he motioned her to come to his side. She appeared uncomfortable, her pupils smaller than usual and her eyebrows pulled back. She also rubbed the tips of her fingers together -all her usual signs of nervousness.

Still, she pushed through it like she always did, proceeding forward with Artimus at her side. Edward was just finishing a story as they returned.

"What we couldn't figure out is how these women and children ended up so close by. According to their stories, they were in their homes one moment and then outside in the forest the next. Since that demon was in the north, we figured heading south was the best course of action."

"You made the right choice," replied Cabal with a nod. "Now, let's return to my explanation of where you are. I understand your skepticism, but I know you all will believe me when you see this. You are no longer on Earth, and right now our best move is to bring you back to Erathal so we can help keep you safe from the demon that brought you here. So, please remain silent and observe."

Cabal tilted his head back and looked at Savannah.

"Savannah, if you would please. I want them to understand the magnitude of magic in Evorath. Show us something profound." Cabal commanded, his voice rising in pitch at that last word.

Artimus was unsure of what Savannah had in mind, but he was certain it would do the trick. Still, a little voice in the back of his mind was scratching away. Why was he so confident in this plan in the first place? Pushing this question away, he watched as Savannah began. It started in her hands. She was gathering forth the energy she needed, an aura of green forming in her palms. Though her magic often took different forms, Artimus had seen this kind before. Like last time, she had closed her eyes, assuming an upright posture and breathing in through her nose and out through her mouth. Her breath maintained a rhythmic pattern as the glow of magical energy proceeded to encompass her hands.

Artimus took a moment to look up and observe the humans. Edward looked calmer than expected and so did the rest of the soldiers, but John was uneasy. The civilians behind had started to approach as well, looking on with curiosity. Returning his attention to Savannah, Artimus watched in anticipation.

Savannah was still focusing her energy, preparing for something much more significant than usual. Opening her eyes, she extended her hands forward. She propelled the green energy forward and it quickly wrapped around the humans, just missing them on the right as it continued its path. Edward, John, and the three soldiers all snapped around to watch as the energy coated the ground. In a moment, it sunk into Evorath, leaving no trace.

A few seconds passed, and the earth shook. What was just a small patch of grass and dirt before erupted with life. Green leaves rose from the ground, expanding out to encompass about two square meters. These leaves began to sprout up all around, growing from tiny sprouts to full-grown vegetables in a matter of seconds. As the teardrop-shaped leaves took form, Artimus realized what they were.

It was purslane, a common edible green that grew around these parts. There must have been seeds ready to sprout in the soil. With her connection to Evorath, Savannah was able to accelerate the process.

"You can eat those if you like," said Savannah as she finished. The magic was almost completely faded from her hands. Despite the impressive feat of magic, her eyes still appeared energized, a vibrant, youthful energy lying in wait within pools of green. She wore an accomplished smile on her face, but her breathing was a bit heavy considering that she had not moved from the spot.

Artimus looked back to the humans, hoping to see a receptive response. Somehow, even John's concern seemed to fade with this demonstration. Everyone looked on dumbfounded, Edward's mouth left agape.

"As you can see," said Cabal smugly, "you will need to make a new home here on Evorath."

Edward regarded the purslane for a moment before looking back to Cabal. He turned and looked at the purslane again, and then back to Cabal.

"Alright," he conceded. "Now you have our attention."

Chapter 16

Hills to the South of Erathal Forest
28 Zerrum, 1087 MT

Yezurkstal rubbed his hands together in front of his chest, massaging his palms as he regarded the progress so far. Naberius was exceeding expectations, bringing back two or three full trees every time he returned. In fact, the speed at which he was bringing back the trees was making it difficult for Yezurkstal and his sorcerers to process it all.

It did help that he had all thirteen of the demons since late morning. Knowing that a viable supply of stone was just a few kilometers to the southeast was a comforting thought, but having the extra help was even more comforting. After all, Yezurkstal had never quite used his magic like this.

Sure, he had used it to forge weapons before, and even to extract the adamantium he used in his own sword, but this was different. Yezurkstal was working off his own observations of the buildings he had seen in Erathal, and from those buildings he was trying to figure out just how much wood he would need to build structures for his own people. He wouldn't admit it, but he needed more technical knowledge to do the job right.

Despite this, he was proceeding to generate the raw materials as planned. Every time Naberius returned with more trees, his sorcerers would go to work. He watched in admiration as Naberius dropped down his final oak of this batch. Three of the sorcerers went to work straight away. The first used his magic to lift the tree up, levitating it parallel to the ground for easy access. The other two worked together and focused their magic. Shooting out streams of energy, they directed it forward in a condensed fashion. This condensed energy narrowed into a barely visible blade.

Using their magic in this fashion, they directed the energy to cut through the roots first. It seemed Naberius found the easiest way to remove these trees was to pull them straight out of Evorath. By removing the bottom in this fashion, they let the stump fall carelessly to the ground. Next, they moved up the sides of the tree, working their magic to flow around and individually cut away at the branches extending outward. It was an imaginative way to process a tree for sure, and Yezurkstal wished he could take full credit for it. The demons were the ones who suggested this system.

Naberius took off again while they worked, flying back towards the forest to the east. His wings let out squalls as he ascended, sending some of the loose branches flying around. The leaves and twigs effectively blocked Yezurkstal's sight for a moment, but as it cleared, he could see his sorcerers still hard at work. They were slowly catching up, but there was still a good dozen untouched trees to process.

As this trio of demons finished their oak, the levitating sorcerer sent it quickly flying south, where he lowered it and dropped it carefully next to the other finished trunks. At this point, the lumber was not perfectly smooth, but it was all free of roots or branches, which was enough to get things started. In total, the demons had processed twenty oaks, fifteen pines, and twelve cedars. Turning back to the unprocessed trees, he counted another twelve cedars, nine pines, and eight oaks.

Judging by the position of the sun in the sky, he still had a good five hours or so until sunset. If his minions continued to work at this pace, they could finish above their goal. The goal was to get fifty of each tree in total. His limited understanding was that all three of these could be used in the construction of sturdy buildings, so even if this were superfluous, he wanted to have more on hand.

Though he was just out of eyesight, Yezurkstal could hear Naberius as he uprooted another tree. The large, unknown tree crashing down in the distance. It was a faint sound, but he had quickly identified it as the only possible source of that sound. He waited for another and then another. So far, the archdemon had been bringing the trees back in threes, so he expected this pattern to continue.

Continuing to watch the sorcerers complete their work, he waited for Naberius to return. Another trio of demons completed work on a pine, the levitating demon quickly moving the bare trunk aside and dropping it with the other lumber. Without any hesitation, they continued to start on the next one.

Yezurkstal smiled in approval, but he did have other pressing matters to attend to. Closing his eyes to focus, he gave his undead griffin a mental nudge to return. Now he just needed his archdemon to return. Fortunately, Naberius appeared in sight over the horizon only a moment later. The demon's massive wings quickly flapped through the air with one tree held tight in either hand.

As the archdemon came close enough that Yezurkstal could feel the force from his wings, he yelled out.

"Naberius!"

The demon tilted his head down towards Yezurkstal as he landed. Dropping the trees at his side, he gave his master a blank stare.

"I want you and these sorcerers to continue at this pace until you have fifty of each tree. I must return to the mountains and supervise the rest of our operation. Once you have collected and processed all the trees, I leave you in charge. Take the time to rest as needed, but once you have the energy, resume operations by collecting stones from the south. Stockpile all the stones you can and await my return."

Yezurkstal could feel his ride approaching, so he hurried to finish.

"Do you understand these orders?" he asked.

"I do." Said Naberius without moving. His voice was deep and unwavering, as if this endeavor were boring him.

Of course, Yezurkstal didn't really care how he felt.

His griffin landed a few moments later, touching down in the dirt without making a sound. Yezurkstal hesitated for a moment, debating whether to say anything else to his soldiers. Deciding against it, he pulled himself up over the back of his ride and willed it to take off.

With the light mental nudge, the griffin spread its decaying wings and took off into the air. Willing the amalgamated creature to proceed north, Yezurkstal glanced back to see the progress one more time. With the wind rushing around his body as he ascended, he saw Naberius take off once more and fly to the east.

While he knew he could never fully put his faith in an inferior creature like Naberius, he did take some comfort knowing that this demon was being left in charge. Aside from Verandas and Valkyrie, there wasn't really anyone else he could trust. Sure, his other wives were preferable to the rabble that inhabited most of Evorath, but they were hardly adequate when it came to anything truly important. It was the children they cared for that were the real future.

Naturally, Yezurkstal would continue to take more wives and have more children with his existing wives, but these children were really the key. In a couple of decades, he would make sure they all had spouses of their own. Within a century, he could ensure that hájje were the most abundant species in Erathal. In the meantime, it wouldn't hurt to start thinning out the herd, starting with the most inferior species first.

Thinking about his family back home, he let himself get distracted from the world outside. He didn't really feel the wind rushing against his face. He couldn't really hear his griffin's wings as they flapped furiously through the sky. He didn't even smell the clear fragrance of the open air. He nearly failed to spot the strange figure approaching on an intercept course.

Opening his eyes at the last second, he nudged his griffin to ascend, hoping he could avoid an impact with this ephemeral creature. It was a female from what Yezurkstal could tell, but he was unfamiliar with the species. She had long, flowing brown locks and wore a flower crown on her head. Her ears were pointed, lying back even more than most of his elvish brethren. While he didn't catch a clear look, it appeared her skin was pale - almost translucent.

Her dress was modest, a deep green and covering her from the shoulders down. In fact, it covered her so well that Yezurkstal was not sure she had any legs. She did have wings, large and colorful ones that resembled those of a butterfly. They were a vibrant purple with black spots, flapping furiously as she maneuvered about and grabbed onto Yezurkstal's griffin. Without any experience fighting from the sky, Yezurkstal merely held on tight as the inevitable occurred.

The creature grasped on and spun around, sending his griffin plummeting towards the treetops. Bringing himself tight to the creature, he willed it to escape. The creature was much quicker than he could have anticipated though, quickly strafing around and slamming his mount in the side. He felt this impact, a focused pain running through his left leg as the griffin tumbled over itself and through the tops of the canopy.

The trees spun around him too quickly to process his fall. Without any other option, he began to gather magical energy from the tree around him, using it to form a barrier around himself. Expanding this field of energy to include his griffin, he let his fall continue, tearing through branches and bouncing off the sides of trees with considerable force. Of course, his magic was strong enough to take it, but his ego might not be.

After what felt like half an hour (which he figured must have been a solid minute or more), he finally crashed to the ground. Thanks to his magical cushion, he landed with a single thud, sinking into the dirt and leaving a small crater around him and his griffin. Though he could still feel the connection, it felt that the magic was leaving his pet.

Expecting the mysterious female to follow quickly, Yezurkstal pulled himself away from his fallen pet and stood up. It felt as if his face would erupt in flames as he clenched his fists and got his bearings.

How could anyone have the audacity to attack him mid-flight? Who would be foolish enough to challenge him?

The creature glided through the tree and levitated about six meters away from him. She floated in front of a large Erath, her slim figure revealing that she did, in fact, lack any legs.

"What are you and how dare you challenge me?" demanded Yezurkstal as she took her place there.

Yezurkstal's vision blurred, his face hot with the hatred he felt for this insolent creature. She waited to respond, almost long enough that Yezurkstal charged in impatience. But, just as he placed his hand on the hilt of his sword and shifted his weight, she replied.

"Many would just mistake me for the wind. Those who I reveal myself to, might call me many names. The most common of these is a Sylphid." her voice was irritating, so high pitched and peaceful. It was complete mismatched for a creature powerful enough to take Yezurkstal from the sky.

"This is your last day you worthless Sylphid," spat Yezurkstal.

He grabbed the hilt of his sword and charged forward, pulling it from the sheath.

Lifting the sword overhead, he swung down with considerable force. The blade went straight through the creature - but something was wrong. Instead of cutting into muscle or bone, it simply passed through the air. Using such force, Yezurkstal's momentum pulled him through after the blade, causing him to stumble and nearly fall.

It was incorporeal.

In a flash of anger, Yezurkstal stood up straight and slammed the sword into the ground. It sunk more than half-way into the soil.

Twisting back around towards the sylphid, Yezurkstal summoned forth some of his magical energy, a black aura enveloping his hands. Just as he pulled back to launch the energy, a new figure entered the field.

"You aren't killing anyone else," shouted the voice from his right.

This one was also feminine, but it held an unmistakable power. He knew what type of creature this was before he even turned.

Redirecting his dark magic, Yezurkstal turned and shot a stream of energy towards the creature.

A wall of vines immediately shot out from the ground, shielding her and forcing Yezurkstal's magic to dissipate around it. As he stopped his assault, she lowered the wall, revealing her figure.

She was a dryad; which one, Yezurkstal did not know -in truth, he didn't much care either. Like all her kind she was bare naked. Her skin was green and her hair more like twigs in a tree than anything else. Though he was aware of the affect she had on most creatures, it didn't faze Yezurkstal in the least. These vile harlots were the epitome of how flawed the goddess Evorath really was.

"Is this your doing?" Yezurkstal asked. He averted his gaze downward as he asked, trying to make it clear how much he loathed this vile creature.

"My sisters and I have been searching for you for some time now," she replied in a monotone.

"And are there any more of you hiding behind one of these precious trees?" asked Yezurkstal without pause.

"Just me and a few of my friends," answered the dryad. "And it will be I who show that foolish Avatar how it is done."

Intriguing. Was she not acting on the will of the Avatar?

Of course, Yezurkstal didn't have time to delay, so he would have to ignore the intrigue for now.

"It's a pity that none of your sisters are around. I hate for them to miss what comes next."

Assuming this whore wasn't lying, Yezurkstal knew the quickest way to win would be drawing out the other "friends" of hers and prioritizing from there. Once he knew what he was up against, he could devise the best plan of attack. To accomplish this, he needed to go for the weaker target first. Since the sylph was still floating in the same spot, it made this all much easier.

Turning around to retrieve his blade, Yezurkstal began gathering the necessary magical energy. He grasped the hilt of his sword firmly and yanked it from the ground, dirt flying up as he did. Funneling some magic into his sword, he twisted around and threw the blade towards the dryad.

In the same moment, he lunged towards the sylph. Using some of his extra magic, he sent a surge into his hand, causing it to fade into an ephemeral state. Matching the incorporeal nature of his enemy, he reached out and grasped her throat.

The sylph's mouth was left agape, her eyes wide in shock. She grabbed onto his wrist and yanked down. Her strength was nowhere near adequate to stop him, so Yezurkstal tightened his grasp, smiling with joy at the sight of her writhing body.

With his peripherals, Yezurkstal was able to also witness the dryad, who was currently dealing with troubles of her own. His simple enchantment left the sword cutting away at the dryad, relentlessly attempting to find a weakness and get through her defenses. As he expected, the dryad was quick to respond, tossing out spheres of green energy, sending vines to step in its path, and weaving away as the sword continued to advance. The magic would last for a good couple of minutes if she didn't figure out how to stop it, which would give him the opportunity to handle this sylph.

Getting a bit more spirited, the sylph made a more violent attempt to escape, casting forceful gust of wind right at Yezurkstal's chest. And it hurt.

Backpedaling a few steps, Yezurkstal pulled back his other hand and balled it into a fist, filling it with magic for the finishing blow. That's when he realized the dryad had not been lying about her other friend.

A lynx darted from behind a nearby tree. As this new opponent registered with Yezurkstal, he knew there was only a split second to respond. Rather than throw the punch, he refocused the energy into a different spell.

The lynx pounced, only milliliters away from tackling Yezurkstal to the ground. Yezurkstal unleashed the spell, a void black sphere flattening and expanding outward. As the lynx impacted the sphere, it vanished, disappearing into the void.

Of course, this wasn't the last he would see this creature, or apparently its family. As was common with these unusual cat-like creatures, there were more to come. Three more lynx charged from the trees, gnashing their teeth as they ran to get revenge. Taking advantage of the distraction, the sylph launched another attack, this one focused at Yezurkstal's arm.

He was unable to hold on as the wind energy cut into his arm like a dagger, pushing him away and forcing him to become fully corporeal again. This creature was becoming a nuisance.

Without realizing it, Yezurkstal shouted in anger, stomping his foot on the ground in front of him. This motion released an overflow of dark magic, the energy coating his body and releasing a black mist from the point of impact. Everything around him went black, even his keen night vision unable to see through the magical fog. Calming his mind, he cleared it away.

The sylph was nowhere in sight and searching for her energy revealed no life. All three lynx lay motionless on the forest floor, their bodies petrified. In fact, it seemed that nothing around him was left alive.

Yezurkstal turned his head, examining the forest. The ground was barren, all green sucked away and replaced with a dead brown. The trees were completely dried up, leaved stripped away leaving nothing but grayed, empty branches. There were no sounds of life, no energies but darkness. Whatever he did had affected an area of at least 10 meters around him.

Scanning the area, Yezurkstal caught sight of the dryad. She was outside the blighted circle, his blade penetrating her chest and pinning her to a half-dead ceder. Yezurkstal was filled with joy, his eyes bright and lips curled into a giddy smile.

Walking slowly over to the dead strumpet, he regarded her body and scowled. "You whores disgust me."

He grabbed the hilt of the sword, jerking it around with a sharp twist. The dryad screamed in pain, her verdant eyes draining of all life and filling with darkness. Yanking his sword from her dead corpse, he watched her fall to the ground.

No one could stand against his might.

Chapter 17

Erathal News Article 101:87
Unknown Visitors in Erathal
By, High Wizard Guildpac

If you had business around town late last night, you likely noticed the strange company that marched into our great city. General Zeidrich, accompanied by our Chancellor Cabal, led a sizable contingent to march out on an undisclosed mission. Upon their return, they also brought along some unknown visitors.

According to eye-witness reports, there were around a dozen of these strange visitors, and many indicate that some of these unknowns were armed and ready for battle. Additionally, many of the visual reports suggest that these strange companions had deformed ears, adding to the list of unanswered questions.

Right now, many citizens are worrying about whether these unknown visitors are friend or foe. Were they engaged in a battle outside of the city? Is this a strange troupe of bandits that might present a threat to the safety of the city? Could they be an advanced scouting force sent by Yezurkstal to prepare for a more serious attack?

Unfortunately, there is not official news from the Chancellor and neither he nor General Zeidrich have ventured outside the castle to offer a comment.

It is important for readers to note that this is not the first time the Chancellor has left you uninformed. He has a history of conducting business in secret and many wonder if he really had the best interest of the Republic in mind.

Bringing in potentially dangerous strangers like this without even consulting the people that he is supposed to represent is absolutely unacceptable. As the voting approaches for our new Chancellor, it is important that you keep this in mind and vote for the greater good of all Erathal.

-=-=-=-=-=-=-=-=-

Erathal City, Atyrmirid Home
29 Zerrum, 1087 MT

The sun trickled in through the window, its rays dancing across Savannah's face. She shifted onto her side, shielding her face to block out the brightness. Though her hands offered little respite, it was better than using the wool blanket -that would cause her face to itch.

Spreading her fingers apart, she peered out to allow some of the light in. This was the first time in over a year she slept in past sunrise, and she intended to make the most of it. Keeping her right hand over her face, she reached over with her left to see if her husband had stirred yet. Finding nothing but air, she touched around the empty bed, pushing down on the straw and groaning. After getting in so late last night, she was happy to accept Artimus's offer to sleep in, so she was more than a little disappointed that he had not joined her.

What was the point of sleeping in later if he was going to get up without her?

Rolling over onto her back, she reached above her head and stretched. Taking a yawn, she extended her arms up as far as she could. The blanket slipped down to her waist as she sat up in bed. She took another big yawn and tilted her head to the side. Her hair was all over the place, shooting out in all directions as she stretched her neck. Much of it was in her face, obscuring her view as she stood up.

The wood floor was cool on her bare feet, a welcome feeling she had come to look forward to every morning. Brushing the excess hair out of her face, she looked around the bedchambers. Both dressers appeared untouched and Artimus's quiver, bow, and sword were all resting in the closest. At least he hadn't left for the castle yet.

Trudging to the closest, she thumbed through a couple of her dresses before deciding that she would wait to prepare for the day. There was no need to go outside quite yet, so she was content wearing her undergarments for now. After all, she had opted to wear one of her most modest outfits to bed last night, the traditional option covering her entire upper and lower torso down to her knees. The cotton fabric was soft and comfortable, helping her to avoid the discomfort she often felt from the blanket.

Of course, her hair was too unruly not to fix.

Running both her hands up along her forehead, she focused magical energy into her fingertips. With a mild, clear light, she ran this energy down into each strand of her hair, releasing it to her control. Pulling her hands back behind her head, the hair followed with ease. Flicking her fingers out, she fluffed the hair and held it in place. With a faint smile on her face, she walked towards the door. She wondered, as she did occasionally, how any elf could control long hair without magic.

Putting this thought aside, she pushed through the door and entered the main room to the house. She performed a quick scan, looking for any signs of her husband. Fresh wood was stacked in front of the stove, so it appeared she would not find him inside. She couldn't hear any chopping from outside though, so that might mean that he was doing some other preparations.

It appeared that the rest of the kitchen area was left untouched, the counter clear and the cabinets shut tight. After discovering Artimus was awake, part of her was hoping he might have a breakfast prepared. But, since the table over in the southwest corner was also empty, she knew that wasn't happening. Now that she thought of it, there was a good wheel of cheese and a nice assortment of berries in the pantry.

Before jumping on that idea though, she decided it would be prudent to make sure Artimus wasn't out getting something else. Walking past the stove and the pantry, she approached the door to the west of the house. The home was arranged as almost a perfect mirror image, the front door leading to the stove in the center, the bedchambers to east, and a similar-sized room to the west.

As per his original plans, Artimus moved his fletching materials into this room the day after they had gotten married. He setup a work area where he could care for his arrows, sharpen his knives, and perform a variety of other "essential" tasks. To Savannah's delight, he also had a bookshelf erected in that room when the house was built. This shelf stored some files he used and it also stored some of Savannah's own collection. Though she didn't build one yet, she also planned to create a workstation of her own in that room.

Skipping to the door, she stopped just outside and knocked.

"Artimus are you in there?" she asked, her voice timid.

After waiting for just a few seconds, she pushed the door open to confirm he wasn't. Scanning the room, she noted it was a bit more disheveled than she remembered. Other than that, there was nothing out of the ordinary.

Shaking her head, she pulled the door shut and walked back towards the stove. She paced around for a few minutes, pondering what her best course of action would be. Perhaps it would make sense to change into a more fitting outfit for the day, but she was really comfortable as she was. Tending the garden without getting dressed wouldn't be a good idea though.

Maybe she would be better off taking out that cheese and berries and preparing a breakfast. After all, it was inconsiderate of Artimus not to wake her when he did. Even if he was going to fetch something else, it was his fault, not hers. There was no sense in waiting around if she didn't know when to expect him back.

There was no way he had gone to the castle, was there? What if there was some problem early in the morning that required his attention? Though Cabal had promised them they could take this day off while he negotiated with the humans, who was to say that something hadn't happened?

Deciding she could not wait around to find out, Savannah stomped back towards the bed chamber, shoving the door aside and walking straight for the closest. She pulled out her favorite green top and long green skirt before remembering that she would need to change into less bulky undergarments.

Tossing her outerwear onto the bed, she proceeded to her dresser and opened the bottom drawer. She pulled out a slim, satin brassiere and a matching pair of underwear. Untying her current top, she pulled it out from behind, careful not to upset her hair. She also loosened the knot on her trunks and dropped those to the ground. Kicking aside her old undergarments, she put on the new ones.

Without delay, she hopped to the bed and retrieved her clothes. Stepping into the top, she pulled it up over her thighs, past her stomach, and used it to cover up her breasts. Cinching it around, she was careful to cover up her breasts and position it so that it rested just a few centimeters above her belly button. She proceeded to grab the skirt and slide into that next.

The reason she liked this outfit so much was that it left her completely unrestricted. The top and bottom were both made from spider silk and dyed in a gorgeous shade of green to match her eyes. This material was tough on its own, but she had enchanted the top with a little extra something, which is what allowed it to tighten over her brassiere and offer secure coverage despite its lack of straps. Combined with the loose skirt, she had full range of motion in her arms and was able to easily move about with her legs.

Pausing for a moment, she considered her next move. Would she be better off eating now or tending to the garden?

It would have to be the garden.

With a pep in her step, Savannah proceeded out of the bed chambers and shut the door behind her. Jaunting to the front door, she continued outside. She held her hands up above her head, the full force of the sunlight causing her to squint. Though it was still early in the morning, the sun was high enough that it was peaking over both sides of the house, leaving her nowhere to turn for shade. Then again, her garden needed no shortage of sunlight, so it was probably better that way.

Lowering her hands to her side, she stepped along the short walkway and off to her right. The front of the house looked a little bare, reminding her that she still had to plant some berry bushes to fill in the gaps. If she just had more time to tend to the regular garden, perhaps she could go out and procure some seeds to get started. Right now, she just barely had enough time to tend to her herbs, so adding anything else to the equation was not something she much looked forward to.

As she rounded the house, she took note of some tracks along the ground. While she might not share her husband's hunting abilities, she was observant in her own right. These tracks likely belonged to a rabbit, or perhaps two. For their sake, she hoped they didn't return, or they were liable to end up on her dinner table when Artimus caught sight of them.

Continuing her path, she arrived around the rear of the house. While she had less time than she liked, she really had done a good job with the setup thus far. She had marked the border of the garden with a half circle. It measured ten meters wide, bordering the back of the house and lined up right along the foundation. At its widest point, it measured out to be five meters long, offering her plenty of space to work with.

So far, she had planted an array of wildflowers along the edge of this path, sowing a thin layer of seeds that would complement the stone border. In the center, at the farthest point, she left a path open and designated that path with two, smooth stones placed less than a meter apart. Each of these stones was about the size of her hand and had a symbol carved into it.

While most visitors would just think it was decorative, the symbol was not random; instead, it was imbued with a particular magic that would help deter unwelcome guests from entering. Stepping around to this entryway, Savannah wiggled her fingers around, allowing her to enter without disturbing the enchantment.

Beyond the wildflowers, which were just now starting to peak out of the ground, she had transplanted some of the herbs from her old hut. Her verbena had handled the move nicely, both the pink and purple flowers flourishing in their new home along the left side of the garden. The garlic was also growing strong, some of the bulbs less than a week away from harvest. Meanwhile, her marjoram was just starting to sprout up around the right end of the garden, the green leaves barely peeking out of the soil. Her moonflowers still hadn't appeared, but with some extra magical coaxing she was expected to see them show up soon.

Of course, the first plant she needed to tend to was her prized Yggdril tree. One of her few possessions that she really cared for from her old tribe, this tree was at the center of the garden. It had an extra level of protection around it, four stones positioned at all four cardinal directions, each marked with a different symbol. Unlike the basic protection spell placed around the rest of the garden, this one was more specialized.

Kneeling before the tree, Savannah leaned in and inspected each individual leaf. She took care as she touched them, releasing the tinniest bit of magic into each one in turn. The flowers were blossoming just fine; in fact, she spotted a new bulb on one of the smaller branches. Its gray petals were starting to shine a dull silver, indicating that it would likely make the transformation within the next day or so and start to blossom. Then it would glimmer like the other ones, offering a brilliant silver shine to reflect the latent magic within the tree.

The leaves looked strong as well, deep green and filled with vibrant life. Finishing her inspection, she got to one knee, closed her eyes, and took a deep breath. There was nothing more calming than the smell of a well-cared for garden. While hers was still young, she could still feel all the magical energy around her, giving her the extra vigor she needed to really start her day.

Rising to her feet, she scanned the herbs in her garden. None of them really needed special attention yet. Extending her palm towards the Yggdril tree, she focused some of her energy into her hand. Closing her eyes again, she felt the life force from the tree. It was thirsty.

Snapping her eyes open, she walked over towards the back of the house where she left her water pail. She had fashioned this pail when she first moved to the city years ago and it served as another sentimental reminder. It marked her new life in Erathal, which is what led her to her husband.

The pail was a simple construct. After clearing out some trees from her plot, she had used some of the leftover scraps and worked her magic. Employing a funneled design, she had created a shape that was round on the bottom, tapered out in the middle, and then narrowed up at the top. It also had a convenient spout built into the side and positioned at a thirty-degree angle to allow for easy pouring of the water.

Using the handles on either side, she lifted the unique bucket and tucked it under her right arm. Walking back around the Yggdril tree and out of the garden, she swung her left hand up as an afterthought, ensuring the protection spell was ready to go.

She strode confidently to the east, heading towards a thick formation of oaks. Pushing aside some extended branches, she stepped through the apparent coverage and into the small enclave within. It was always enchanting to take that step through the trees, the area buzzing with life and magical energy.

There was a menagerie of flowers to enjoy: water lilies, marigolds, alyssum, lilac, daisies, dragonsbreath, and so many more. Butterflies fluttered from flower to flower, frolicking through the air and filling it with even more colors. The magic of Evorath was at its strongest here and stepping onto the fertile soil Savannah felt full of vitality. This was a goal to strive for. Letting that energy fill her up, she continued forward to the reason she was here in the first place.

At the center of all this life sat a simple spring. It was no more than a meter in diameter and less than thirty centimeters deep. Despite this, it offered an endless supply of water, which offered the convenience Savannah needed. When she came here before sunset, she would usually run into some other savvy elves who were looking for clear water. This time, no one else was there.

Taking advantage of this, she proceeded straight for the water and took her bucket in hand. Dipping it into the running spring, she carefully filled it up. The water was clearer than anywhere else around, even the river to the east.

Once it was full, she lifted the jug back up by both handles. It was much heavier now, and though she wanted to dilly dally and enjoy the solitude, she figured it was best to move on. Holding the bucket tight, she pushed back through the thicket and out into the clearing of the city.

Continuing back to her garden, she kept her eyes wide, looking for any signs that Artimus would soon return. She saw nothing.

As she reached the edge of her garden, she set the pail down and waved her hands in front of the path. Squatting, she lifted the bucket and continued into her garden.

Keeping to the edges, she began stepping around the outer ring, tilting the bucket and letting the water drip out. She started to her left with this, continuing around at a steady pace and gradually tilting the bucket more and more. As she reached the end of the half circle, she continued along the back of the house. The moonflowers didn't need quite as much water as the wildflowers, so she pulled back to slow down the flow.

Reaching the other end of the circle, she resumed the generous pour, ensuring that the wildflowers got all the water they needed. Regarding the water, she smiled and moved on to the verbena, where she let a small amount of water trickle down. Ignoring the garlic, she moved to the Yggdril tree at last. Taking her time, she tilted the bucket over at 90 degrees and poured the rest of the contents onto the tree.

Skipping back over to the house, she replaced the bucket in its proper place before walking back to the center of the garden. Closing her eyes, she lifted her hand hands to get a feel for the soil. Satisfied that everything had received enough water, she focused on pulling out some of the magical energy she gathered from the enclave.

She felt the verdant force welling up in her body and focused it through her hands. Releasing it out in waves, she bombarded the entire garden. Maintaining this transfer of magic, she opened her eyes and watched as it took effect. The verbena peaked up some more, new flowers opening as they received the energy. The wildflowers each lifted more, new seedlings pushing through the soil and up for a chance at life. Even the garlic appeared to grow plumper, getting ready for the upcoming harvest. While she still couldn't see the moonflowers yet, she knew those were getting ready to sprout as well.

Satisfied she had done enough for one day, she lowered her hands and capped the flow of magic. As she turned to exit the garden, she caught an unexpected sight in her peripherals and jumped back.

"You startled me!" she shrieked.

"Sorry," Artimus apologized stepping into the garden. He held a burlap sack in his hands, the bottom stained in crimson.

"I know you aren't trying to bring a dead animal into our garden," Savannah said regarding the bag.

Artimus stopped dead in his tracks and offered a nervous smile.

"Of course not," he said turning around. "I'll just meet you inside. If you care to help get breakfast ready, you know where to find me."

Savannah chuckled as he walked away, and back around the garden, his head tilted down towards the ground. Shaking her head, she regarded the garden one last time before following.

Chapter 18

Dumner Village
29 Zerrum, 1087 MT

Irontail was as still as a tree, glued to the central guard hut in anticipation of more news. The sun was climbing in the sky, noon approaching and offering a taste of the upcoming summer heat. A brief gust of wind swept through the village, providing a moment of relief against Irontail's sweaty fur.

After assuming his role last year, Irontail had to make some difficult decisions. A few months into the position, he began to realize not all his fellow centaur thought the same way he did. For many, being told what to do had become so normal that the concept of not being led by elders was too unfamiliar to adopt. It was this fact that made finding good leaders so difficult, but he had managed. He had a vision for what this tribe could become, and he intended to fulfill that vision.

Since the Avatar's visit, that vision was a bit less clear. Erathal was a big place, with lots of races and plenty of villages and cities, but now it didn't feel quite so large anymore. If there were other worlds out there, where was his tiny tribe of Dumner in the grand scheme of thing? Did Evorath really care so much for such a small society of centaur? If Yezurkstal did make a move soon, how would Dumner be able to survive?

As a gentler breeze swept through the village, Irontail adjusted his stance. He swung up and swatted a fly from the air before resuming his stance. Just as impatience started rearing its head, he could hear hooves coming from the south.

"Sir, I have a report," the sentry barked, trotting towards him.

"Proceed."

"There is no human activity to the south, but there are some elves approaching from Erathal. It appears two messengers are nearing the village," the sentry finished with a slight bow.

"Alright," said Irontail scratching behind his head. "You may return to your post."

The sentry nodded and turned back around, trotting back through the tree line and to his post at the south.

A few seconds after he had vanished behind the foliage, Irontail could hear another sound from the southwest. Leaning over and grasping his trusty club, he looked in this direction expectantly.

In a flurry of leaves, an agile figure darted through the coverage and landed just a meter away. Lifting the club up to swing, Irontail stopped himself short as he recognized the unexpected visitor.

"Tel' Shira" he exclaimed in surprise. "What are you doing here?"

"From Erathal, I have come. A dozen humans, the elves have found. To rescue more, they hope. Behind me, messengers are. Request, I believe they will, help."

Tel' Shira said all this without rising from her runner's stance her knees in a deep bend, back tilted forward, and arms hanging down like she might crawl on all fours. As she finished, she rose and looked up towards Irontail. Judging by the sweat of her brow, she had run the entire distance from Erathal. Despite this, it appeared she was not fatigued in the least.

"Did you just run here to tell me this?" Irontail asked. "If there are elvish messengers coming, why did you feel this was important?" Irontail rested his club against the nearest post.

"Myself, to warn you, I wanted. Uneasy, this situation makes me. To my people, go, I must. My friend, you are. On guard, you should be."

Irontail nodded.

"Thank you, Tel' Shira. I appreciate you sharing your concerns. I too am uneasy about these humans. Please be careful on your journey home."

Tel' Shira nodded and smiled.

"Farewell," she said before crouching and sprinting off to the east.

Hearing her concern had Irontail doubting himself even more. If she was coming from Erathal, she purposely took an indirect path going home by coming through Dumner. Or maybe she didn't want to use the road. Whatever the reason, her fears put Irontail on edge.

Before he could really sort his thoughts, he heard more rustling, this time from the bushes to the north. Since the northern watch had already reported in, Irontail grasped his club again, resting it on his shoulder and spinning around.

The northern sentry burst through the bush. He stared intently at Irontail and spoke.

"Sir, we just caught sight of some humans to the north. But...well -they are being attacked."

"What is attacking them?" Irontail asked without hesitation.

"Demons, sir."

"How many?"

"At least half of a dozen," the sentry replied.

"Follow me. Now."

Resting his club over his shoulder, Irontail started forth. Galloping to the north, he positioned his club out in front to act as a wedge. Bursting through out-hanging branches, he quickly arrived at the northern watch. The other sentry, Woodenbrow, was standing watch.

"Move aside Woodenbrow," Irontail commanded as he slowed to a halt, his hooves digging deep into the dirt.

For once in his life, Woodenbrow responded quickly, stepping back and over to the right. Irontail jumped forward and looked ahead. It appeared that his sentry was right.

From this vantage point, Irontail could count seven demons. They were circling around a small contingent of human troops, slowly moving in and pushing through their defense. The humans did have a number advantage, at least eight of their numbers wielding sword and shield, two with a bow, and five more with a polearm. This had to be the largest organized group of humans he had seen.

"We must help them," Irontail instructed backing away. "Both of you follow me."

Without waiting for his sentries to respond, Irontail darted off again, this time heading towards the skirmish ahead. With deft precision, he ducked under some large branches and kept his club held horizontal to deal with any foliage at his sides. As he ran, he felt smaller twigs and branches scratching at his arms.

Leaning hard to his right, he maneuvered around a towering oak. Ducking down, he felt the wind overhead as he avoided a low-handing willow branch. Jumping to the left, he dodged a large knot of roots.

The trees were spread further apart at this point, which meant the humans were only a little further. Tightening his grip on his club, he prepared himself for what lied ahead. It occurred to him in the moment that a year ago he would have never been able to respond so quickly.

In that next moment, he was upon the enemy. Tramping through a thick bush, he charged with his front hooves up and kicked the nearest demon. Letting out a battle cry, he followed through with the charge and took the demon down to the ground. His enemy immediately tried pushing, spreading its wings wide and causing Irontail to falter. Not giving him the chance, Irontail lifted his club overhead with both hands, slamming it down with enough force to shatter a boulder. With the resounding crack and yellow ooze that followed, it was time to move on.

Now Irontail found himself in a pickle, as the nearest two demons both recognized him as the biggest threat. Shifting his focus from one to the other, he quickly evaluated which one would be the better prey. Recognizing that the one on his left was closer, he opted for that one first.

This demon had leathery flesh the color of charcoal. Crimson streaks ran across its chest and part of its abdomen, matching closely the color of blood. Its forearms were equipped with sporadic spikes about the size of bear claws and its wings were as dark as the night. With two dagger-sized horns atop its head, it certainly had its share of defenses.

The demon darted forward in an instant, its wings flapping back to propel it towards Irontail with haste. Pulling down with his left, Irontail punched towards the demon with his right. This motion allowed him to jerk the club from the fallen demons and target it on his new attacker. With a minor adjustment mid-swing, he connected the thickest part of his club with the demon's face.

There was another loud crack and more yellow ooze as the demon fell harmlessly to the ground, its body seizing as it hit the dirt lifeless. Craning his neck back around to check on the other nearby demon, Irontail was relieved to see that his support had arrived. He watched for only a second, which was long enough to see Woodenbrow charge shoulder first and knock the demon off its flight path. The other sentry followed up right behind and grappled the creature by its wings. It looked remarkably like the first one he killed; in fact, all of them did.

Refocusing on the rest of the field, Irontail got a glimpse of the humans, who looked to be just as afraid of him as they were of the demons. He hadn't even thought about this possibility, but for now it would have to wait. So far, the swordsmen were all focusing on one of the larger demons to the rear. Meanwhile, those wielding polearms were protecting the archers -whose arrows had no doubt proven ineffective- by swatting away at another demon as it approached.

Of course, that left two other demons to deal with and one of them was taking the opportunity to flank around and attack the swordsman from the rear. Realizing his intentions, Irontail decided to go for this one next. Unfortunately, he did not account for the fact that there might be other demons lurking above.

Just as he galloped around towards this next demon, he felt an impact from behind. The force from this blow caused his knees to buckle and fold in on themselves. Realizing there was no way to prevent his fall, he released his club and let it drop to the ground. Tucking his arms, he pulled back away to avoid injury.

Landing with a thud, he struggled to put his arms under him. His right shoulder exploded in pain, a hot sensation filling the spot as his arm went numb. With his adrenaline, he pushed through the pain, swinging his left elbow around with all the force he could muster.

His elbow impacted the surprise attacker and knocked the demon off his back. He could feel the flesh tearing from his own shoulder as the demon was dislodged. Ignoring the pulsing pain, he continued to push off the ground and get back on all four. Just as the demon worked to regain its footing, Irontail stomped down, forcing it back to the ground. Rising once more, he let out a primal roar and slammed down, his front left crushing the demon's throat.

He looked up just in time, one of the remaining demons choosing this moment to pounce.

"Protect the humans!" Irontail exclaimed as he threw up his arms defensively, palms open.

This new demon aggressively worked to break his guard, coming in with a powerful hook. Irontail kept his left up high, blocking the attack and reaching in for the creature's throat with his right. As anticipated, the demon intercepted his attack, giving Irontail the opportunity to grab its arm in a vice. As he squeezed its wrist tightly, he blocked another right hook. This time, he was able to hook his hand around the demon's arm.

With this leverage, he pulled the demon close and thrust forward to deliver a powerful headbutt. This dazed the demon just long enough. Leaning back, he adjusted his position and grabbed both the demon's arms. With all the force he could muster, he jerked his body around, throwing the beast to the ground. From this position, he dropped onto his knees and pinned it in place. Delivering a swift punch to the throat, Irontail eliminated yet another threat.

There must have been another demon that swooped down from above, because upon reassessing the field he found there were still four more to go. Fortunately, one of these four was engaged with his two sentries, struggling to block as they advanced through his defenses. The other had joined its ally against the swordsman, which had effectively broken them into two groups; it didn't look promising for the humans.

One of the swordsmen swung his blade, just missing the demon. As he followed through, the hell spawn took the opportunity to grab his arm and jerk him forward. With an earsplitting tear, it punched straight into the human's throat. Blood poured out and Irontail cringed.

Without hesitating, he leaped up from the demon he had just slain and ran to retrieve his club. Grasping it mid-stride, he pulled it off the ground and assumed a two-handed grip. Seeing his approach, the demon disengaged from the humans and turned to intercept.

Irontail swung his club around, once again aiming for the head. This time, the demon seemed better prepared. It threw up its arms and intercepted the club. With outstretched hands, it grasped onto the club and prevented Irontail's follow-through. Pushing forward, he attempted to end the stalemate, but the demon wouldn't falter. This one was stronger than the others.

Channeling his rage, Irontail shifted his weight back and yanked on the club. The sudden shift of weight and jerking motion caused the demon to lose its footing. As it stumbled towards Irontail, the savvy centaur released hold of his club and threw a haymaker. The powerful punch landed square against the demon's jaw, causing it to pop out of place.

Shifting his weight forward, Irontail wrapped his right arm around the back of the demon's neck, putting it into a headlock. With a sharp twist, he snapped the creature's neck, clean.

Letting this new victim fall to the ground, he looked up towards the next demon in line. It finally seemed that the humans were getting the upper hand. The remaining seven swordsman must have taken advantage of a weakness in the demon's form as two of the members burst in to break its guard and thrust their swords into his chest. The demon attempted to counter, but the human on the left held up his shield, deflecting the blow.

With the demon held by two blades, the other five soldiers fanned out and moved in for the kill, stabbing the beast repeatedly. Satisfied they didn't need his help, Irontail moved his attention to the final demon.

Of course, it seemed that this demon was getting a sense of the battlefield too. Swatting away one of the human's weapons, it looked around and backpedaled. Not giving anyone a chance to follow, it spread its wings, bent at the knees, and jumped into the sky. Flapping its bat-like wings quickly, it took off towards the top of the tree line.

Irontail scanned the battlefield again to ensure that he wasn't missing anything. His sentries had eliminated the last demon they were struggling with, leaving a host of these foul creatures dead on the battlefield. Though one human had lost his life, the other fourteen appeared unharmed. If he wasn't careful though, Irontail realized he and his men might not share this fortune.

Also realizing that the demons had been eliminated, the humans looked around in confusion. Their faces were still red hot from the battle and Irontail could tell they were not at ease. This was a crucial moment if he hoped to calm them down.

"I know this all must feel like a strange place, but we are not your enemy," Irontail said holding up his hands. He kept his palms facing forward, hoping that the sign was universal.

The humans all exchanged glances, some of them lowering their weapons while others kept them held high. As they looked to one-another, they seemed to falter in their resolve. One with a lowered weapon would look to his ally in a defensive stance and they would both switch positions. Others simply shifted stance between Irontail and his sentries, holding their weapon's up defensively but apparently unsure of which was the biggest threat. It appeared that they had no organized leadership.

"Please, allow me to further explain. Surely, you realize that we helped you fight off those demons. My name is Irontail, and I know there are no centaur where you come from, but here we are quite common. Is there a leader among you?"

The humans continued to look around in confusion, each one seemingly hoping the next would provide some form of guidance. Finally, one of the swordsmen stepped forward, his shield held close but his sword hanging down by his side.

"What is this strange land?" he asked, shifting his gaze between Irontail and his sentries.

Irontail took a small step forward, keeping his hands held up submissively. He bent slightly at the knees as he spoke, hoping his lower position would help convey some form of surrender. Though he acknowledged his own diplomatic flaws, this was the perfect opportunity to practice.

"You are in a land called Evorath," he began without moving. "These creatures that attacked you are demons, and I am afraid they serve the same master who brought you here."

The armored human looked to his left and then his right, pausing for a few moments between. He appeared to be contemplating the situation, his eyes focused up and away from the action.

Though he did not have the wrinkles of a truly wizened individual, he did have some wear on his face. Judging by the looks he exchanged with his fellow soldiers, he was no stranger to the battlefield. His face was tanned, darkened by continued exposure to the elements. His eyes were hardened, baring the burden that can only come from seeing an excess of death on the battlefield. Despite their apparent differences, Irontail held some hope that he might relate.

"Judging by what we have seen since our arrival, I am willing to consider anything."

The human relaxed, his shield falling to his side. He lifted his sword arm and spun the weapon around, quickly sheathing it at his side. Standing up tall, he balled his fist, lifted it up, and gave a nod.

Apparently, this was a signal for his soldiers to follow, as all the swordsmen took this opportunity to sheath their blades. Those baring polearms followed suit as well, assuming an upright posture and holding their weapons with the spearhead facing upward. Now that he had a moment to really observe them, he noted that the blades on these weapons were single-edged facing forward. The shape was like an inverted tear drop, the top curving back towards the soldiers as they stood in place.

"Thank you," started Irontail with a deep bow. "I understand that you must be frightened by our land, but I hope you find Evorath to be a welcoming environment for your people. If you accompany me back to our village, I believe we can help you."

Keeping his hands up submissively, he stood firm in place. The last thing he wanted was to save these humans only to kill them himself. Eyeing both of his sentries, he was happy to see them both standing passively by. Woodenbrow had even joined his leader by holding up his hands with palms open.

Though the human did not make any aggressive movements, he shifted his gaze around. His shoulders were still tense and though his breathing was relaxed he still appeared somewhat suspicious.

"I must say, while we are grateful for thy help, we are uneasy about obliging. In our realm, a creature like thyself would be considered a monster. That you speak our language is unsettling." The human's tone was guarded, his strange accent making it difficult to read into his intentions. Irontail also noted that his hand drifted towards the hilt of his sword as he spoke.

"How about I offer an alternative?" Irontail continued in a soft tone. "I can lead you to a city to the west where there are creatures more like yourself. They are called elves, and they more closely resemble you."

"Elves? You would compare us to some queer forest sprites? I see not how man might resemble a fairy." The human wore a look of disgust as he spat these words.

"I apologize. I was not aware you had any sort of elves where you came from. I assure you, here they do not resemble fairies. They are bipedal creatures like you in stature. I assure you; I meant no offense. Some of my greatest friends are elves."

"Pfft. A man-horse like you is friends with a creature that you say resembles us in stature. Don't jest!" The man wore a grin, letting his hand fall by his side as he spoke.

Though Irontail was trying to be diplomatic, it seemed this human lacked the same respect. Gritting his teeth, Irontail pushed away the anger.

"Sentries," he commanded turning towards his men. "Please return to the village and let one of the elders know where I am. Have them send the elves to our location when they arrive."

The humans shifted their formation, the archers falling to the back of the group and keeping their bows at the ready. The spear-wielders formed around on either side, keeping their weapons at the ready. Though none of the swordsman drew their blades, they all held up their shields and closed ranks. Irontail didn't budge.

"Please," Irontail pleaded, the pain in his shoulder flaring up as he kept his hands held high, "wait here with me for their return. Once these elves arrive, they can help explain the situation."

"How shall we trust thou are not setting a trap?"

"Consider my position. I am the Chieftain of my village. If it seems that I am setting a trap, then you can kill me. I assure you, I have nothing to gain from doing you harm."

The lead human cast his glance downward, shifting his stance and rubbing his chin in thought. After a few moments, he looked back to Irontail with piercing eyes. He held this stare for a few moments more, and then finally relaxed his stance.

"We shall wait."

Chapter 19

Outside Yezurkstal's Cave
1 Neglur, 1087 MT

This was perhaps the most pleasant sensory experience Yezurkstal could have imagined.

The looks of abject horror and despair, the smells of iron, the sounds crying women and shouting men, and the taste of salt in the air. All of it added up to a beautiful symphony of anguish.

When he had tasked his demons to retrieve these humans, he never imagined they would have so much success. His ritual had brought forth much more than the dozens he had seen in the mountains. Instead, it seemed that they were spread out in groups throughout the continent -perhaps even the world. For now, these would serve his purposes nicely.

While he was down overseeing the planning of his new home, his demons had built an effective prison for these humans. The valley was closed in with downed trees and rocks, building up a sheer wall to keep them from leaving. This wall was at least four meters tall at the lowest point and was held together by potent magic. There was little room to move within this enclosure, which would make the work that much easier.

As expected, the demons had done a phenomenal job of bringing back the humans alive. While many of them had broken limbs or bloodied bodies, at least three quarters of their ranks were still breathing. Regardless of their physical condition, they were all thrown in the prison like the animals they were. If he could always have subjects gathered like this, he would have figured out how to access the ether years ago.

Now that he had these humans here, he would put them to good use. Remembering how he had accidentally killed one of them upon his arrival, Yezurkstal was taking no chances. He was at full strength now, and even had a little extra juice thanks to his most recent victims. Reaching into the satchel he wore at his side, he felt the still warm heart of the dryad. Stepping forward to look down on the subjects, he projected his voice.

"Fear not, for today you get to make the ultimate sacrifice for the betterment of Evorath. I have released you from your strife and now offer you a meaningful future. Soon, you will have no more struggles."

His speech did little to calm the subjects. Those who were able-bodied continued to struggle for a way to get through the walls. The injured continued to cry and scream in pain. Women clung to their children and looked upon him in fear.

Yezurkstal paused.

Perhaps it should have been apparent, but somehow he had not figured there would be children. Scanning the crowd more thoroughly, he counted four of them scattered among the hundreds. Not many, but it would be enough.

With a smile spread across his face, Yezurkstal extended his hand towards the humans. Pouring forth a surge of magical energy, he sent four streams of concentrated necrotic energy into the crowd. Each stream impacted one of the children, the energy coalescing around their bodies and throwing them like rag dolls away from the others.

Yezurkstal was thrilled to hear their shrieks of pain rise above the chorus of anguish. He watched with sheer delight as they writhed in agony. The color faded from their skin and wounds festered around their bodies. As they continued the transformation, one of them even reached up and tore out a chunk of her own hair.

All the humans around these children backed away. Even their mothers appeared too shocked to move, one standing there like a statue, her mouth left agape. Another fell to her knees, clasping her hands together and crying out some gibberish -a prayer to her god.

Shifting his attention back to the children, he felt the anticipation build as each fell to the ground, lifeless. He stared daggers at their fallen bodies, waiting for the magic to take effect.

Then he felt their consciousness.

It was an influx of new sensory information. One by one he felt them. He could see what they saw, hear what they heard, feel what they felt. Willing them all to rise, Yezurkstal kept his eyes open and watched as the four corpses pulled themselves from the ground. Each was a shadow of what they once were, a shambling bag of bones and dead tissue.

Not wasting a moment, he commanded one of the boys to charge forward and attack its mother. The zombified creature charged forth without hesitation, bringing its mother to the ground and biting into her neck. Blood poured out from the wound as it yanked away with a chunk of flesh.

Commanding another boy, he decided to take a different approach. There was a group of soldiers nearby, two men wearing matching plate mail and a third in heavy leather. Though the demons had removed their weapons, they still appeared to have some fight in them. In fact, they were calm and collected compared to the other subjects. They would reveal the extent of his zombie's power.

While his other new minions stood unmoving, he compelled this one towards the soldiers. The boy closed the distance in an instant, sprinting up behind the nearest soldier and swinging for his legs. Taken by surprise, the man had no time to react and he fell with a thud to the ground. His heavy armor appeared to hinder his movement, but the other two soldiers didn't waste any time reacting.

The other plate mail soldier tackled the zombie boy, bringing him to the ground. His leather-clad counterpart followed up right behind him, rushing to his fallen comrade's side to help him up. Yezurkstal could feel the boy's arms. They were clasped tightly by the man, but not tightly enough.

Letting out a moan, the boy yanked his arms from the man's grasp. Pushing at the man's chest, he dented the armor and caused the man to stumble backwards. With his assailant staggering, the boy jumped back to his feet and charged. This time, he lunged up and tackled the man himself. Slamming his fists down on the dented spot of the armor, he unleashed a barrage of punches.

Yezurkstal laughed as the man garbled on his own blood, the armor caving in his chest and crushing him. His other two allies were not taking any chances though.

Both men ran to the zombie boy in a pincer formation. With the leather-clad man on the left and the plate-mail soldier on the right, each grabbed the boy's corresponding arm. Yezurkstal tried to have the boy wriggle free again, but this time their strength seemed too much. Dragging the boy to the ground, the man on the right threw a powerful punch.

Yezurkstal could feel the dull sting of the attack, but it did not impact his lifeless little soldier. The man punched a second time, a third time, a forth...none of it mattered. With the boy's face bloodied and shattered the two soldiers loosened their hold. The man on the right was the first to let go, rising to one knee to get up.

Using this opportunity, Yezurkstal commanded the boy to attack. Even with his face mutilated, the blind zombie lurched up and grasped the man's throat. With a violent squeeze and a forceful pull, he crushed the man's windpipe and tore out a chunk of his throat. Like the first man, this one fell bloody to the floor.

The third man wore a look of absolute horror, his eyes widening and his mouth hanging open in shock. Though he had not released his hold, his grip loosened just enough for the boy to wrench his arm away. With both hands free, the boy grabbed the final victim's head and plunged his fingers into its eyes. The man shrieked as blood rushed out. With a diabolical smile, Yezurkstal ordered the kill, and the zombie obliged, snapping the man's neck.

While this boy did his work, the other zombies continued their rampage as well. The two other boys had stacked up five corpses between them and the little girl had taken down four all on her own. Yezurkstal controlled it all, compartmentalizing their collective consciousness in his head and unleashing his fury. These zombies would make for the perfect pawns in his army.

Of course, this meant that there was no need for further experimentation. The undead were clearly stronger than the living and unquestionably obedient. They were, after all, a part of him now.

Still, there was no sense in wasting the opportunity to experiment. Calling for the zombies to stop their onslaught, he had them slowly walk towards the center of the cage. Everyone around them backed away in fear. Some of the able-bodied dragged those who were injured, but others were left crying in their spot, unable to escape. It didn't matter.

As the zombie children took their place in the center of the prison, Yezurkstal gathered up more energy.

The only question that remained: which spell should he try next?

-=-=-=-=-=-=-=-=-

Somewhere in Central Erathal
1 Neglur, 1087 MT

Rubbing his hands together to force off some of the dirt, Zelag pulled himself up to one knee. Sweat dripped down his face, a solid bead impacting his hand and staining it with a spot of mud. Every sensation in this form was still so unfamiliar and adapting to the clumsy shape seemed ineffective.

"I do not understand," he blurted in his frustration.

He looked towards Casandra, who stood before him. She grinned at his remark.

"What don't you understand?"

"Why does the Avatar insist I practice like this? I would be much better off as the dingo. Or maybe I could learn how to change into an elephant, like my progenitor."

Casandra shrugged and slithered closer to him.

"*Sometimess*, you just need to accept that the Avatar knows what he is doing. Have a little faith in your *masster*. I don't usually understand why he has me do the *thingss* he does, but I know it is for the *besst*."

"How do you know it is for the best?" Zelag asked, placing his hands on his knees for stability as he stood upright.

"I have faith in Evorath. The Avatar is of Her, so I trust *hisss* word."

"Like I trusted my progenitor..." Zelag muttered, casting his gaze towards the ground.

Casandra reached out and touched Zelag's face, running her fingers through his scruffy beard and lifting his chin up. She offered a radiant smile, her blue eyes glistening like the morning sun rise on the ocean.

"I know what it is like to lose everyone you hold dear. There is not a day that *goess* by when I do not think about my family. Because of their *ssacrifice*, I am still alive today and now I get to *sserve* Evorath directly by following Her Avatar. It might take a while to realize, but you can find this *ssame* clarity."

Zelag held her stare. He felt a strange tingling feeling along the back of his neck and up into his head. Though it felt pleasant, the unfamiliarity made him uncomfortable. Pulling away, he directed his eyes towards the trees behind her.

"There is just too much for me to process," he blurted out. With his progenitor, Zelag had known nothing but honesty. This made it difficult to communicate in his current form. All these strange sensations, new emotions, and the thoughts of his fellow Preajin left him vulnerable. This left his body stiff and his posture rigid.

"Try to trust in Evorath and it will work out. *Thiss iss* all I can offer." Her voice was softer now. Somehow the hushed tone had a calming effect. Despite this, processing these emotions was too much. It left his eyes shaking and his stomach nauseous.

"Let us go back to the camp. Maybe the Avatar has returned and can provide us with further instructions."

Zelag hoped this would end the conversation and they could return in silence. Without waiting for a response, he turned around and started forward. He pumped his legs fast, not turning to see if Casandra followed. After a few seconds, he could hear her slithering to catch up.

He felt something for Casandra. It wasn't the same connection he felt with his progenitor, but it was similar. The Avatar and she were all he had. Trying to focus on other matters, he wiped a tear from his eye and continued forward through the foliage. He could hear voices up ahead.

Without turning to Casandra, he took off into a sprint, running towards the camp to see who it was. He recognized the Avatar's voice among them. Breaking through the clearing, he looked around to see who else was speaking.

A grotesque creature stood nearest to them; his back towards Zelag. He was taller than the Avatar, his skin gray and covered in blisters. Though he wore some sort of animal hide around his waist, his butt stuck out at the top. A necklace of some kind hung around his neck, made from the bones of another animal; or perhaps the same one that provided the hide. While he had some patches of hair on his body, his head was topped with just a few, long, loose strands.

Zelag wasn't certain, but by what he had learned, he guessed it was a troll. Turning his attention over to the left, he noticed a creature he was more familiar with. This participant was also larger than the Avatar, but shorter and wider than the presumed troll. He was covered from head to toe in brown fur and his snout opened to reveal sharp teeth. He also wore a bone necklace and complemented this jewelry with red warpaint on his face. He was a barghest.

Right now, it was a third stranger who was speaking, her voice high-pitched and gentle. She was a sylphid, whom Zelag had always found to be calm and peaceful. Now, her voice cracked as she spoke, resembling his own voice in this form when he felt anger or sadness.

"I told you, they will not listen. He took my sister and still they refuse to meet with you. You have to do something!"

The sylphid flailed her arms as she spoke, her aura flaring out with her words. She wore a plain, white dress, hanging loosely about her. On her back, her orange and black wings flapped vigorously. Though hovering a good half-meter above the ground, she was just barely at eye level with the Avatar.

"She is right," the barghest added, his voice gruff like most of his kind, but much calmer than expected. "I'm afraid my people are just one snagged nail away from pledging their loyalty to this hájje. I may have no home to return to if you do not take care of him quickly."

Casandra slithered up next to Zelag and he turned to regard her for a moment. She looked just as surprised as he, her eyes wide as she motioned back towards those gathered. No one seemed to notice them.

"Do you not think I am aware of how dire the situation is?" Zelag had never heard the Avatar take such a tone before. His voice boomed through the camp, echoing off the trees. His own aura was vibrating quicker than ever before, his green energy becoming darker as he spoke.

"You are all my children and I feel every needless loss of life. Aeria, I understand that your sister's death is not easy, but do you know where Yezurkstal has gone? He has been a tumor on this land for too long, but if I cannot find him, I cannot vanquish him."

The Avatar turned and looked to each of those gathered. "Do any of you know where he is?"

The assumed troll spoke up, his voice raspy and wizened.

"I have not seen Yezurkstal, but my fellow tribe members have reported seeing demons roaming the forests. They seem to be corralling these humans that you are so keen on saving. Perhaps it has some-"

"I know where he is," the barghest interrupted stepping forward. "At least, I have heard rumors."

Zelag noticed the energy around the group darken with this news.

"Why are you just now telling us this?" Aeria shrieked. She stepped forward and shook her fist. Her eyes flared with anger, the light green turning almost yellow.

"Calm yourself," the Avatar stepped forward and placed himself between the two. "Please, tell us what you know," he instructed stepping back. Aeria followed suit.

"Over the past year, Yezurkstal has been strategically wiping out my kind. Every time he destroys one of our tribes, you show up too late. Finally, I was able to parlay with some of the other leaders and we have formed a stronghold to the south."

"We already know this" the troll interrupted.

"What you don't know" the barghest continued without pause, "is that not all the tribes have joined us at the stronghold.

Instead, some of them have been converted to serve Yezurkstal in his evil army. He twists their souls, turning them into mindless juggernauts of destruction. According to reports, many of these barghest roam the Marta Plains. Some have even reported seeing demons there, and others claim Yezurkstal himself has chosen this as his new home."

All the participants seemed preoccupied with additional thoughts. The sylphid looked like she wanted to say something, but her lips remained pursed, her hands hanging by her side. Meanwhile, the troll scratched his forehead, his dull aura indicating deep thought. Even the Avatar stood silent, his powerful aura matching his stance -strong and statuesque.

To Zelag's surprise, Casandra stepped into the conversation.

"That would be a fitting place for him. We all know that the Marta Plains are avoided for a reason. The souls of the dead still roam that land, remnants of The War. No one dares enter that area, not if they wish to live."

"She is right," the sylphid affirmed, her face pale and aura fading. "Only dark spirits dare venture there. It is a haven for all sorts of foul creatures."

The Avatar regarded Zelag and then looked around to the others gathered.

"If your information is true, then it is time we put an end to this plague. Casandra, Zelag," he said turning back towards Zelag and his training partner, "it looks like I may have a job for you both after all."

Chapter 20

Erathal News Article 101:89
The Kingdom Is Safe
By, General Zeidrich

As the General in charge of Erathal's entire army, it is my number one priority to ensure that all citizens of our Republic are safe from harm. Recently, you have read some articles by Guildpac and other agitators that there is some strange new threat you need to worry about. I am writing to tell you this is not true.

Here are the facts as they now stand:

First, Yezurkstal has used some powerful new magic. This magic has reached through the ether and pulled a new species out from the other side. This species, humans, are not all that dissimilar to us, but they come from a realm without magic. They are not demons and they are definitely not a threat to our Republic.

Second, we are actively searching for any humans we find throughout the forest. Coming from a realm without magic, they are scared. Our Chancellor believes that allying ourselves with these humans will make for a great alliance to help fight Yezurkstal.

Finally, we are devoting a great many resources to find these humans. We have already received aid from the centaur and have sent out word to the felite as well. Our goal is to make sure none of these humans can be captured and forced into Yezurkstal's forces.

Contrary to popular belief, we have not kept this a secret because of some horrible threat. Instead, we wanted to accurately assess the situation. Humans are not our enemies.

If you are reading this, we ask that you keep an eye out for humans in your travels. Unlike elves, they have small, rounded ears and many of the males in the species have facial hair not that dissimilar to a dwarf. On average, we have found them to be larger in stature than elves.

Rather than engage these humans yourselves, we ask that you immediately report any sightings to your nearest city guard or local ambassador. This is to ensure we do not frighten the humans and provides for your safety.

If you have any concerns about this, please report to your nearest ambassador for guidance. Your safety is our number one concern.

-=-=-=-=-=-=-=-=-

Erathal City, Castle Hall
2 Neglur, 1087 MT

Forty-seven.

Counting those Cabal had originally brought in, those the scouts had added, and those Irontail had most recently introduced into the fold, this marked the entirety of the human population thus far.

From the buzz around the forest, this was well under 10% of the total population that had been brought over, and that number was not acceptable.

"I shouldn't have to repeat myself," Cabal declared, slamming his fist on the table. "I put you in charge of bringing in more humans and so far, you aren't delivering. Zeidrich told me I could count on you to get the job done, and now you are making him look bad as well."

Artimus was seated opposite Viviko at the table, doing his best to avoid eye contact with the Captain. Though he was not present when the original conversation took place, he imagined Cabal was getting more worked up than necessary. Irontail had revealed these humans were being snatched up by flying demons. Unless the Chancellor had somehow given Viviko the tools to fly, it seemed unrealistic to expect fast results. But this was not something Artimus cared to weigh in on.

"I'm sorry. The last thing I want is for this to reflect poorly on the General." He sounded sincere, his tone filled with remorse, voice cracking as he spoke. Through their limited interactions, Artimus had never heard Viviko sound anything less than cheerful and often sarcastic. Now he sounded miserable and dejected.

"Your apologies are not going to fix this situation. Tell me what you are doing to correct this." Cabal commanded. There was less anger in his voice, but he was still speaking louder than usual.

"I have all my troops out looking and they are instructed to send word through our scouting network as soon as they find anything. They were originally being sent out in units of five, but with the news about these demons I have had them recalled and reassigned. Now they are searching in full units, but I'm afraid they just can't cover enough ground. You only gave me command of four mixed units, so-"

"*I* did what now?" Cabal interrupted indignantly. "Are you saying *I* am somehow responsible for *your* failure. Are you not a Captain in the service of the Erathal Republic? Do you not have the authority to request more troops? *I* stressed the importance of finding these humans before Yezurkstal. *I* told you to use whatever resources you needed. Explain to me how a shortage of troops is anyone's blunder but your own."

Artimus glanced up as Viviko shifted in his chair. His eyes were wide, a hint of terror showing, but his face held firm.

"You seemed clear at our initial meeting that I only had the four units at my disposal. I expressed then that this would not be enough, but you told me figure it out. General Zeidrich was there. He can-"

Cabal slammed his fists on the table once more. His eyes looked like they might burst into flames as he yelled.

"Get out of my hall. You are relieved until further notice."

Viviko stood up on command, not even hesitating for a moment as he walked towards the exit. His hands were shaking as he pushed open the double doors and exited the hall.

Artimus looked around the room to see if anyone else was uncomfortable. Cabal stood at the head of the table, his face tight and eyes hard; it looked like an expression of malice. Meanwhile, both the Military and Trade senators sat on his right and left, respectively. Both elves had been with Cabal since before the revolution, and it seemed they were more accustomed to this sort of meeting. They both wore stone expressions, their pale, green eyes blank.

General Zeidrich sat next to the Military Senator, and he seemed to share Artimus's concerns. His gaze was down on the table, perhaps a bit of disappointment involved, but Artimus sensed more discomfort than anything else. This seemed to be supported by his posture, his right hand on his forehead as if to shield his face, his shoulders pulled back, and seated towards the back of his chair.

Across from Zeidrich, General Ollerus appeared to have mixed emotions. His lips were curled down in a frown, but his eyes seemed attentive, and his focus rested exclusively on the Chancellor. Since taking over as the lead general of the archer unit, he always seemed to be looking for ways to impress Cabal, so perhaps his discomfort was outweighed by his position.

Artimus was next in line, and now the empty seat across from him. Moving to his left, Artimus regarded the other two generals -magic and spear- as well as the six captains who had been gathered. Both the generals seemed to have mixed emotions, but the captains had a harder time hiding their feelings. It seemed that every one of them emitted a palpable discomfort over the situation. At least Artimus wasn't the only one who felt this was wrong.

Since the other head of the table was left empty, Artimus turned his attention back to Cabal.

"Alright," Cabal continued, apparently oblivious to the discomfort in the room. "Let's take care of this then. Zeidrich, I want you to reevaluate the approach. Four mixed units is clearly not going to be able to cover enough ground to get results. After this meeting adjures, I want you to organize all off-duty personnel. Get together as many units as we can spare without compromising city security and send them out to join the hunt.

"General Ollerus, I want you to work with Zeidrich. First, speak with the humans and see if you can get some willing participants from their ranks. Have at least one man accompany each unit we send out. This might smooth out or initial relations and ensure we aren't met with too much resistance. Speaking of those humans we have already corralled, what is your report General?"

Ollerus cleared his throat, shifting in his chair and laying his hands down on the table before speaking.

"They are getting a bit anxious. The west dining hall is easily able to accommodate their ranks, but apparently, we have brought in members of various nations into the fold. Though none have taken violent action yet, there is definitely a tension that needs to be addressed."

Cabal shook his head.

"Don't worry yourself with this. I will go and speak to them personally when we conclude our business here. I'm sure I can convince them to put aside their conflict." Cabal continued without pause, looking past Artimus to the other generals.

"General Veles, how are defenses looking on your end? Have the mages completed their expansion of the walls to ensure there are no potential weaknesses to be exploited?"

"They will be completed before nightfall. In the meantime, I have posted the extra sentries as per your request. Though not all the mages were enthusiastic to work extra, the monetary incentive seemed to do the trick." His voice was nasally and high pitched. Though he seemed better than his predecessor, Artimus never felt comfortable around him and the fact that he was so thin and sickly didn't help matters either. If a weasel were to get magically transformed into an elf, it would look like Veles.

"That is acceptable. General Lugus, what about our spear units? Do they stand ready to defend the gates should we find ourselves besieged?"

"Yes sir," Lugus affirmed, his voice deep and confident. He was the elf whom Artimus knew least about but judging by his terse response he wasn't one to mince words. Speaking straight like this was a good quality to have.

"Good, good. Captains, are there any issues within your ranks you need to report? Any apprehension about a potential conflict, or civil unrest your sentries have noticed? If it's a military matter, report it to the appropriate general, but if it has to do with the general population, I want to hear it now."

Cabal paused, leaving the room in silence for a good five seconds.

"Alright, I will take your silence as a confirmation that everything is going smoothly. If anything changes, make sure to let your general know. Now, we turn to the final order of business for this meeting."

Artimus clenched his fists under the table, adjusting his posture to sit perfectly upright. Pulling his shoulders back and chest out, he looked towards Cabal and put on the sternest expression he could. His hands remained just out of sight below the table, allowing him to nervously tap his legs as he listened.

"In all likelihood, we could have another attack on the city before the next segment of the wall is completed. This leaves a few hundred families to the southwest exposed during a potential attack. I met with Lieutenant Atyrmirid earlier about establishing a more effective plan of defense, as his experience with these demons and general expertise give him a special skill-set that could come in handy in this environment. So, Lieutenant, how are preparations coming on the outskirts of the city?"

Taking a deep inhale, Artimus did his best to stay calm and speak slowly.

"As you instructed, I spent the better part of the day studying the lay of the land. That district of the city is perfectly flat, which precludes the possibility of assuming the high ground and preparing traps in that fashion. Fortunately, it does have its share of trees spread throughout, which opens up some possibilities for traps to be laid. These traps will give our soldiers on the ground an element of surprise and could help slow down or dispose of some of our flying foes.

"In addition to these traps, I also have some magical forces standing by to add their own little touch. As we speak, some of the lab mages are working on deploying special runes throughout the area. These are meant to ward specifically against demons, and while an elf can walk through them harmlessly, any demon caught in their wake will not be so lucky."

Artimus shifted in his chair and rubbed his hands together as he continued.

"On a practical level, I also have my Royal Rangers at the ready for a fight. They can supplement whatever troops our generals deploy. Thanks to the training drills we have been conducting using felite battle tactics, they should be more than ready to handle battle in a wooded area like this.

"Tomorrow, I intend to continue my survey and develop a more detailed plan. In the event of offensive movement from any direction, I can have the rangers implement this plan and we can set a net of traps that will slow down the attackers. If you would like more details, I could elaborate."

"No, that is quite enough for now," Cabal said, raising up his right hand dismissively. He glanced down as he said this, his voice inflection conveying disinterest. Artimus wasn't sure if he was really that boring or if Cabal just trusted him that much. Either way, it didn't feel right.

The entire room waited in silence for another ten seconds.

"Well, if there is nothing else, I'd say our business here is concluded," Cabal offered after the long pause. "General Zeidrich, please remain behind so we can discuss our outreach with these humans. The rest of you, return to your respective duties. Until this threat has passed, remember to remain accessible for any emergency meetings."

Not wanting to delay even a moment, Artimus took this opportunity and rose to his feet. Casting a quick glance towards Zeidrich, he could read the dread on the General's face. Glad he was not in that position, Artimus pushed his chair back in and walked to the exit. He was the first to arrive, hesitating for a moment and fighting the temptation to turn back around and look at the others. Successfully winning that fight, he pushed on the heavy door and proceeded through the exit.

-=-=-=-=-=-=-=-

The smell of burning incense assaulted her nostrils, smoke stinging her eyes. Sitting cross-legged wasn't helping matters. Tel' Shira shifted her position, trying to focus through the uncomfortable sensory experiences. So far, it was not working.

She clenched her jaw, squeezing her eyes shut and forcing extra air out her nostrils. Her whiskers let her pick up movement from behind, and her keen ears heard rustling from outside her tent. How did the elders do this?

Adjusting her legs, she moved into a kneeling position. Ignoring the sounds from outside, she breathed in through her nose and held the air in her lungs.

Three. Two. One.

Pursing her lips, she blew the air out at a slow ten-count. She let her eyes relax, opening them up so she could see the flames flickering from the fire. As she continued her breathing, she focused on relaxing every muscle in her body. Visualizing herself floating, her eyes sagged. They felt heavy, and she let them close again, continuing her metered breathing.

She focused on the crackling of the fire, the calming smell of the incense. With each breath she took, she thought about Evorath's grace. Each time she exhaled, she imagined all negative energy leaving her body.

A twig snapped just outside her tent.

Her eyes darted open, and she swung around to face the entrance. She blew air out of her nostrils like an angry bull and rose to her feet. How could anyone be expected to concentrate with so many distractions?

Stepping outside the tent, she squinted her eyes and observed. There was no one in sight. Taking a breath of fresh air, she could smell the faint odor of an animal nearby. Was another felite out this far from the city as well? Standing perfectly still, she listened for any indication.

All she could hear now was the fire in her tent. Perhaps it was just her nerves. Judging by the light trickling through the trees, the sun had reached its midpoint in the sky. She had been trying for a vision since it rose that morning. Maybe it was time to take a break and eat something. With this thought, she turned around stepped back into the tent.

Snap!

It was another twig. With lightning speed, she flung back around and looked with wide eyes. This time, she caught a glimpse of something moving behind the trees. Whatever it was, it disappeared as soon as she saw it, leaving nothing behind but a gray streak.

Though her better judgment told her to proceed with caution, she couldn't fight her instincts. She lunged into pursuit. Keeping her base low, she pushed through the foliage. Relying on her intuition, she sprinted towards the creature's assumed destination. Breaking branches to clear a path, Tel' Shira focused on her sixth sense to guide her.

After a few minutes of sustained running, the forest opened into a clearing. Tel' Shira stumbled out, swatting aside some stray leaves and fixing her gaze ahead. She couldn't believe her eyes.

It was a lynx.

Her four-legged feline cousin stood in the clearing. Its regal gray fur accented with sporadic dark stripes. Its ears were magnificent, long hair reaching out past the lobes and spiked back. With a slender frame, it stood perfectly still, not even its breath causing any noticeable movement. Its long whiskers twitched as it stared into Tel' Shira's eyes.

Tel' Shira held the creature's gaze.

Its deep verdant eyes were endless, precious pools of potent power. She could feel the energy radiating from the creature, its life force calling for her. After what felt like an eternity, it finally moved. As it relaxed its tail, it began to purr.

Accepting the invitation, Tel' Shira crept forward, pausing after a few steps. Seeing that it was still inviting, she continued forward with more confidence. Arriving by its side, she reached down and touched its soft fur. The lynx tilted its head, rubbing against her outstretched hand. She felt a jolt of energy as she touched it.

Visions flashed through her head faster than she could keep up. There were demons -fire and destruction. An injured barghest. Panicked lamia. A pale figure, and…

Tel' Shira pulled away at the last sight, shuddering and closing her eyes.

It was a vision of Yezurkstal.

Taking a deep breath, she opened her eyes to approach the lynx again.

It was gone.

Chapter 21

Barghest Stronghold
2 Neglur, 1087 MT

Yezurkstal surveyed the stronghold walls, using magic to
enhance his vision. There were only two sentries guarding the
wall, one on either side in makeshift watchtowers. The wall itself
was poorly made, built around the jagged mountain terrain, and
formed using loose stones and poorly cut wood. With no apparent
defense mechanisms in place, Naberius would breach it without
breaking a sweat.

Of course, he didn't want to send his most powerful ally
into a stronghold without knowing what to expect from inside.
Squinting his eyes, he was able to focus his gaze on top of the
primitive gate. Behind the sporadic pikes positioned along the
top, he was able to make out two more guards, but still no other
obstacles. That would be the easiest way in.

Opening his eyes wide, he flicked his hand away and
returned his vision to normal.

In an example of fortunate timing, Yezurkstal heard
rustling through the bushes up ahead. This was followed by a
painful bark, and the snapping of some branches. Smiling ear to
ear, he watched as the captured barghest tumbled into the
clearing, two demons following right behind.

Not in the mood for chitchat, Yezurkstal glanced down
and extended his hand. Releasing his dark energy, he took hold of
the dog and watched as it squirmed. It was helpless against his
powers, writhing in pain as it fell to the ground and howled. As

the darkness overtook it, the foul beast's muscles bulged. Its eyes turned red, and its teeth and fangs extended. The fur on its body darkened and grew. Within seconds, the transformation was complete, and the creature rose to full height.

Yezurkstal felt his consciousness flow in, but unlike the smarter creatures of the forest, these barghest were feral. Over the past year, he had learned they were valuable soldiers, but not the easiest to gather intelligence from. Sorting through the images was a headache.

"How many of your kind live within the stronghold?"

"There are more than one hundred of us," his new servant growled.

Yezurkstal cursed under his breath. He was hoping for much fewer, and with a species like the barghest such numbers might prove insurmountable for his new forces. It would be less of a test and more of a slaughter. Perhaps he would be better saving those troops for an attack against the lizock or lamia.

"Very well," he began contemplating aloud. "You are to accompany me servant. You two!" he turned his attention to the demons.

"Report back to the camp and bring me as many able-bodied warriors as you can, including Naberius. Let the mages continue construction on our new city. I expect you back here within the hour."

Both demons nodded, neither saying a word. Spreading their wings wide, they took off into the sky. Yezurkstal shielded his eyes from the dust as they flew west and returned his attention to the barghest.

"Follow me."

-=-=-=-=-=-=-=-=-

Watching Naberius work had to be the most satisfying aspect of consorting with demons. Yes, these creatures were imperfect and had no proper place in his future kingdom. But, maybe he would keep creatures like Naberius around for sport.

The massive demon overlord crashed into the stronghold wall, the structure splintering around his girth like an axe chopping through wood. Yezurkstal watched the two barghest atop stumble and fall, neither able to make it to safety before plummeting to their demise. As they struck the ground, Yezurkstal took immediate advantage of their position, casting his hands forward and releasing necrotic energy. After a few moments, they both rose again, ready to join his ranks of reanimated soldiers.

Meanwhile, Naberius continued forward, bringing his massive fists down on a barghest shaman and swatting him like a bug. While the massive demon continued his march forward, Yezurkstal refocused on the rest of his army.

The other demons were following behind their commander, dozens of them spilling through the opening Naberius had created. Now, it was time to send in the rest of the troops. Holding his hand to the sky, he focused on all the bodies he had gained control of. With nearly one hundred different zombified humans, some of them in better shape than others, he needed to keep his head clear.

Focusing his magic, he swung his arm down, pointing towards the city. Each marched forward, charging in after his demons. It was a new sensory experience for him, an overwhelming barrage of input from so many different vantage points.

This was the power of the gods.

His zombies sprinted through the shattered gates, following up behind the demons and charging forward. It was a beautiful bedlam of flesh, each of his pawns moving with abandon as they sought out the barghest inside. By the time they broke into the city, the streets were already riddled with corpses, evidence of the demon's efficiency.

As expected, there were still some survivors ready to put up a fight. Two barghest warriors charged out of a crude wooden structure. They pushed through the doorway with axes held high and poised to strike.

Yezurkstal smiled, willing the nearest troops to respond. A handful of these zombies met the barghest head-on, rushing in for the kill. The nearest barghest attempted to defend himself, swinging down his crude weapon and chopping straight through one of the woman's arms. Yezurkstal felt a slight tingle, watching as the arm fell harmlessly to the side.

The woman didn't flinch, ignoring her missing arm and continuing forward. As the barghest raised his axe to strike again, she moved in and bit down on his neck. Another zombie followed suit, a lightly armored male. A third continued forward, an even larger male. He grabbed the axe and bit into the barghest's arm.

While these three zombies wrestled to take the first warrior down, a dozen more followed suit. This second mutt managed to chop off an arm from one and a hand from another, but it didn't matter. Within seconds, he was taken to the ground, the mindless mob tearing into him like the other.

Once he was sure they were dead, Yezurkstal willed the zombies to continue forward. He commanded them to enter the structure, the nearest zombie pushing through and stumbling forward. Using their ears, Yezurkstal could hear whimpering from inside. With multiple sets of eyes to see from, he scanned the room and identified the source.

The whimpering came from behind a crude dresser in the west corner. Without delay, the zombies charged forward and threw the dresser aside. A small barghest child sat in the corner, cupping its face and shaking in fear. Yezurkstal chuckled and let his zombies do the rest.

The horde continued its march forward, Yezurkstal commanding them from his safe position outside the gates. Though he kept a magical ward up to alert him of danger, he couldn't even see the area around his body. Instead, he could see and feel everything these creatures felt.

Leaving the child behind in pieces, his soldiers rejoined the ranks outside and continue their assault. The sheer amount of sensory input was awesome, perhaps as much so as when he had reached through the ether and brought back these humans. With

each action his soldiers took, the input became easier to sort
through. Instead of just one being, it was as if he was there within
each of these zombies. His power would soon rival those of the
gods.

The mindless soldiers continued their rampage, tearing
into the stronghold without resistance. Much of their path was
clear thanks to the demons, but every few huts they entered had
at least one or two of those helpless dogs ripe for the slaughter. It
was hard to describe what this felt like, but one thing was for sure
-it was intoxicating.

They marched forward, merciless in their slaughter.
Yezurkstal was in control the entire way, relishing in every
victim they claimed. After ransacking a couple dozen structures,
they finally arrived. Until recently, this had been the inner
defensive perimeter. Now, it was a bloody melee, demons and
barghest, tearing into one another with abandon.

This poor excuse for a city was laid out in a peculiar
fashion. The initial walls were just the first line of defense,
offering a scouting position and initial deterrent. Each of the
structures up to this point served as houses or communal
gathering places, where people could live their daily life. When
they received notice of an attack, the plan was to evacuate into
the inner wall and fight as a unified whole.

Thanks to Naberius, the swift attack left them without any
advanced notice. Still, it appeared a modest force had bolstered
up the inner walls and was putting up a fight. With stones
crumbled around him, Naberius rampaged within these inner

walls. He swatted aside a warrior barghest, the creatures over-sized club cast aside like a small stick.

As his zombies came into visual range, Yezurkstal noted three spear-wielding barghest up in one of the remaining spires. Across the way, another two wielding spiked maces stood at the ready. They were organizing an attack against his commander.

With determined ferocity, they lunged from their perches towards the demon overlord. Yezurkstal laughed, watching in joy as two demons soared up on either side. Their wings spread wide, they intercepted this coordinated attack and tore four of the barghest away. Still, one of the spear-wielders made it through, landing on the archdemon's right shoulder.

Naberius reached around with his left hand, grabbing for the mutt. Demonstrating surprising agility, the barghest ducked under the demon's hand, letting himself slide down and plunging his spear into Naberius's left wing. The archdemon howled in pain and spread his wings to dislodge the assailant. Showing determination of its own, the barghest held fast.

Digging its claws into the demon's wings, he yanked down on the spear, tearing through more flesh. Naberius let out another shriek of pain, spinning around and swatting aside three barghest on the ground. Even this sudden motion was not enough to remove the pesky attacker, the dog clinging tightly to the wing. None of the zombies was equipped with a bow or arrow, which meant they could not help. Fortunately, another demon decided to step in.

Swooping up from below, one of the warrior demons plucked the barghest out of its commander's wing. Tearing the barghest off and into the ground, he tore out the creature's throat. Meanwhile, the barghest were still putting up a respectable defense. One of the larger warriors squared off against another demon, swinging its mace overhead and catching Yezurkstal's troop off guard. Not five meters away from this action, two club-baring barghest were beating down one of the demon mages.

Why wasn't this working out like he planned?

Yezurkstal commanded his zombies forward in anger, the mindless pawns rushing to join the melee. The initial wave took the barghest by surprise, tearing into those that had gotten the upper hand over some demons and bringing them down in short order. Other than debris from the fallen wall, the area was an open field, leaving them free reign to rip through the unsuspecting dogs.

The two mace-wielding barghest that had tried to attack Naberius were overtaking the demons who had brought them down. Letting out primal battle cries, the duo caved in one demon's skull and continued to smash the other in its legs. Just as they went for the kill, a half dozen zombies interrupted the fray.

Four latched on to the nearest barghest and the other two jumped in front of the further one's mace. The mace tore through the first, crushing his left half and causing him to fall helpless on the demon. The other was able to latch onto the dog's arm. Biting into the creature, he held on tight. As the first four finished with the closer barghest, they joined as well, jumping on the other's back.

They ripped away at fur and bit into flesh, taking the creature down. As the life seeped from his body, the barghest made one final move, latching onto a zombie at his throat and ripping its head clean off. Blood soaked the spot and the surviving zombies moved on.

Despite Naberius's injuries, he continued to devastate the opposing army. Then something unexpected occurred.

The fallen stones from the wall began shaking. In a flash of green light, the ground opened between them, sucking the stones towards it. Soil and grass ripped up around this, forming a large mass of ground. These rocks floated into the sky, tumbling into each other and expanding outward. In an instant, they took on a humanoid shape -a gigantic golem.

This giant creature was nearly as tall as Naberius. Taking the demon lord by surprise, it threw its weight forward. With a powerful shove, it sent Naberius reeling back. The archdemon stumbled over zombies and dead barghest alike as he struggled to regain his footing. Not giving him time to do so, the giant golem threw a punch, landing it square on the demon's jaw.

The sheer force of this attack was enough to knock him off balance, causing him to fall like a downed erath tree. He landed with a thud, killing some of his own kind on the way down.

Yezurkstal focused to expand his reach, looking through the eyes of his zombies to find who was controlling this massive creature. He spotted a small hut still standing across from a mass of his zombies. Four barghest stood fast in front of the hut, spears extended, and eyes trained forward. With his nearest troops, Yezurkstal could spot movement inside the hut through gaps in the wall. There had to be a powerful shaman inside.

Ignoring the rest of the battlefield, Yezurkstal ordered the entire force of zombies towards the hut.

They took off with vigor, ignoring the few remaining barghest soldiers still fighting. With dozens of zombies still at his command, these dogs wouldn't stand a chance. Still, the four defenders stood like statues, spears at the ready and eyes trained forward. The first wave of zombies crashed straight through, running headlong into the spears. Yezurkstal felt a faint sting in his side as they pushed forward. Though the spear bisected their bodies, they grabbed onto the shaft and continued pulling themselves towards the foes.

Despite the shock clear in their eyes, the barghest remained determined. All of them loosened hold of their spears with one hand and kept firm with the other. As the zombies approached, they swiped out, keeping Yezurkstal's troops at bay. Then the second wave arrived. These soldiers also pushed into the spears, allowing themselves to be impaled in an effort to disarm the enemy.

Unable to maneuver, the barghest let go of their spears, taking an unarmed defensive stance. Without their weapons, the remaining zombies made short work, swarming over the dogs and taking them to the ground. Before they had even finished slaughtering these animals, more zombies charged for the doors of the hut.

Another snag.

The first zombie to reach the hut reached forward, pushing on the door. Yezurkstal felt a burning sensation run through his body and the link to this zombie was lost. After a brief flash of red, his vision cleared and seeing from another pawn's perspective he watched this first zombie melt away into ash. Cursing at his luck, he refocused his attention back to Naberius.

Though he still appeared to have some fight left in him, the archdemon was not faring well. The over-sized stone golem had him pinned to the ground. Naberius grasped one of the creature's arms with his left, straining to hold it at bay. With his right, he appeared to be angling for an escape.

Not giving him the chance, the golem threw another punch. It landed square on Naberius's jaw, the earsplitting pop echoing throughout the battlefield. This broke the archdemon's defense, his left arm collapsing under the pressure. The golem used this opportunity to grab Naberius's throat.

Yezurkstal cursed, his mind racing for a way to get around this defense. Perhaps the curse on the door was specific to foreigners. Regarding the bodies of the fallen barghest guards, he commanded his soldiers to gather round. The zombies took formation before the corpses and lifted them from the ground. They threw the bodies towards the hut with all their might.

The dead weight of these creatures was enough to shake the hut, but it didn't leave an opening. Still, they seemed unaffected by whatever magical barrier was protecting the shaman.

This left him little choice. With a final consideration for Naberius, he watched the demon lord unleash one final attack. He spat a torrent of fire towards the golem, the flames engulfing the primal creation. But, it wasn't enough. As Naberius ceased the attack, the golem still held firm, pinning him to the ground and choking him with a firm hold.

Sending a mental command to his griffin, he gave an order to the rest of his pawns.

"Take out any stragglers. Avoid the hut."

He let his consciousness shift back to his own body, the transition causing him to falter and lose balance. Shaking his head, he turned to await his mount.

The mangled griffin swooped down after a few moments wait, landing just beside him and lowering for him to mount. Leaping up, he landed on the creature's back and commanded it forward. Flapping its wings, the beast blew up some loose soil and took off into the sky.

Yezurkstal held tight and squinted up at the battlefield ahead, channeling magic into his eyes. He could already see the golem and Naberius up ahead. Each second they traveled, his vision became clearer. Some of the lesser demons had joined in the struggle, attacking the great golem, presumably looking for a weakness. No matter where they struck, the creature wouldn't stop. The life was draining from Naberius.

Urging his griffin to travel faster, he felt the limitations on the creature's speed. He needed a faster way to get around.

Closing his eyes, he refocused the energy, pumping magic into his mount and providing the creature with some extra energy. This gave it the boost it needed. Yezurkstal felt the wind beating against him, the resistance increasing as he gained speed. He was nearing the outer walls.

Soaring through the ruins, he focused straight ahead on the inner defenses. The griffin dove as it made the approach, leveling out a few hundred meters before the hut. Seeing a few zombies in his path, he reestablished the mental connection and commanded them move. Each ran out to clear a path, allowing his griffin to make a swift landing.

As it set down, it slowed to a trot and stopped just a few meters from the hut. Yezurkstal was off before it even made a complete stop, jumping to the side and drawing his adamantium blade. Funneling magic into the weapon, he held it out towards the hut. With a shout, he released a large bolt of dark energy. His attack exploded on impact, tearing through the magical barrier, and breaking the walls wide open.

Yezurkstal strode forward, his sword poised in front for an attack. As the smoke cleared, he noted three barghest inside, all funneling their magic into one central sphere. Shifting his glance over to Naberius, he had to push aside a brief flash of anger.

His general was dead.

The golem rose above the fallen demon, ready to turn its attention to the smaller ones. Yezurkstal didn't break stride, turning his gaze back to the shaman. They must have been engrossed in their spell because none of them reacted as he approached.

With a smile upon his face, Yezurkstal swung the blade, releasing a slash of dark energy towards the three shaman. It sliced through like a knife through butter.

The magical sphere turned dark, fading to nothing as the trio fell dead to the floor. Turning back around, Yezurkstal watched as the golem did the same, crumbling to the ground. Rocks and dirt showered the battlefield, most of them too small to cause any damage.

Looking around the battlefield, he considered the results. At least half of his zombies were mangled beyond use. Dozens of demons had died as well, much more than he had figured on. Adding to that Naberius, this seemed a hallow victory.

Or maybe it was a new opportunity.

Re-sheathing his blade, he turned back towards the griffin, considering the chunk of flesh missing from its side. He then looked to some zombies nearby, each of them standing like a statue as they awaited command.

It was time for another test.

Chapter 22

Marta Plains
3 Neglur, 1087 MT

Zelag was not sure how much more he could walk.

His shoulders hurt. His legs burned. His back ached. Parts of this form he could not even identify were in pain.

Of course, it was not the pain that got to him.

Learning to shapeshift was a painful business, so he was no stranger to uncomfortable and downright excruciating situations. No, the thing that bothered him was all this sweat and the constant need to replenish his energy.

Having never spent this long in a single form, he had never experienced how much of a chore this was. His stomach would ache, and he would have to eat. His mouth would go dry, and he would need to drink. Traveling all these kilometers, it felt like he needed to do both of these entirely too often.

As they journeyed through dense woods and uneven paths, he wished he could be back in the open fields of his birth. He longed for the progenitor's guidance, and it brought on a new wave of sadness. He had to fight the tears welling up in his eyes.

He glanced over at Casandra, who somehow seemed perfectly content. Her life force was strong and full of vitality and beholding it somehow gave him energy. Perhaps her lamia body was better equipped for such travel. Then again, the barghest, troll, sylph, and Avatar all appeared free from fatigue as well.

"What troubles you?"

Zelag turned his attention to the Avatar, who had slowed down and marched just a few paces ahead. He looked back at Zelag, his aura soft and face tight. Perhaps an expression of concern?

"Why did you ask me to come along?" Zelag asked.

The Avatar smiled. He glanced over to Casandra just ahead and then turned back to Zelag.

"You were growing tired of staying in the camp, were you not? I know you are still uncomfortable with your current form, but if you are going to have a life in this world, you will need to adapt. I promised to teach you how to hone your abilities, but with that you also need to learn how to utilize the forms you are in. How does your body feel now?"

"I do not know how to describe it," Zelag started looking down at his hands. "It is painful, but nothing like the pain of shifting. My body aches. My throat is dry. My stomach hungers. I have never held a single form so long; these sensations are all so new and I feel like I am slowing everyone else down."

The Avatar nodded, his aura remaining constant. He turned back around and stopped his march.

"Everyone else keep going. Stop when you have reached the edge of the forest. Zelag and I will catch up."

Zelag continued walking until he reached the Avatar, staring at his new teacher with a look of disapproval.

"I don't need to rest. I can keep going," he offered, perhaps trying to convince himself as much as the Avatar.

"I didn't suggest you needed to stop. But, I believe you underestimate your own power. Zelag, your people are a primal force. When Evorath created this realm, she designed each species with an aspect of herself. This was intentional to promote unity within the world. People were meant to fight together using their strengths, building a thriving society. But she did something special with the Preajin. You are not like the flesh and blood creatures you imitate. Your limitations are of your own design."

Zelag shook his head.

"What do you mean? You speak in riddles even more than my Progenitor did, but at least I understood what he meant. You just go in circles. Every day I have spent with you, you continue to talk about my potential. But, what is that potential? This body is tired. Why can't I transform into something else? It looks like Casandra's body is well-equipped to handle this travel. Why don't I mimic her?"

The Avatar placed his hand on Zelag's shoulder, his aura becoming a deeper green. He looked Zelag in the eyes, power emanating from his body. Underneath the well of immeasurable power, Zelag could still feel compassion.

"You are not to attempt this transformation yet." His aura became lighter again, the air brightening around him. "Besides, you need to conserve your energy for when we reach the Marta Plains. I am uncertain if we will find Yezurkstal there, but I am sure that the journey will be worthwhile for you. These plains are a strange place, much different than the forest or the flat lands you grew up in.

"These plains have aberrations of nature. The land has been blighted ever since The Demon Wars and it has spawned creatures that you will not find elsewhere. Predators lurk in the tall grass and unseen creatures hide away underground. It is also home to some of the most malevolent fairies and even darker spirits. Whether Yezurkstal is using this spot for his new hideout or not, I brought you along for this very reason."

Zelag looked past the Avatar. The others had disappeared through the foliage ahead. He looked to his teacher, still unsure of what he was suggesting. Running his hands through his hair, he closed his eyes and shook his head.

"And what do I have to do with these dark creatures?" he shouted, throwing his hands out and opening his eyes.

"You are to observe. Every life force in Evorath is unique. Growing up, you spent time exposed to a very select area of the continent. Over the past week, you have been exposed to many new creatures of the forest. Through the coming years, this exposure will continue. Now, you will get a glimpse of just how many other creatures there are."

"So, you want me to transform into one of the creatures we find in the plains?"

The Avatar shook his head.

"I want you to realize the power at your disposal. You are not to transform into anything we see unless I specifically instruct you to. But you are to study the aura of everything we encounter. Commit them to memory. Once we return to the camp, then you can start trying your hand at some of the transformations."

Zelag nodded, a frown on his face.

"So, you wanted me along just so I could observe."

"Observation is the first step to learning. Now, stop trying to get yourself down, and let us join the others. They are waiting for us right through those trees ahead," he finished pointing to the south.

Reaching down to his side, the Avatar grabbed a water skin and handed it to Zelag. Without another word, he turned around and walked towards the indicated trees.

Zelag untied the waterskin and took a few sips. Holding it in hand, he followed behind his teacher.

Though he had just rested for a few minutes, his heart had time to relax and his muscles felt some relief. As he pushed through the underbrush, he thought about this conversation. If the Avatar wanted him to try out different forms, then why didn't he just have him explore more of the forest? After all, he had spent every night and a good part of the day in this human form. When he did practice shifting, the Avatar had him stick to a dingo, squirrel, or a rock.

Swatting aside a branch, he trudged through a pile of leaves and continued forward. He kept his eyes downcast, avoiding all the obstacles strewn about the forest floor. Navigating around the uneven ground, he used a tree for balance and stepped over a few loose rocks. Looking up to get his baring, he saw the entire party waiting for him up ahead.

Looking back down, he continued forward, hoping over a branch and running through some open grass to reach them. He looked up at Casandra, who offered a smile. The others seemed less patient, especially the sylph, who was emitting a red aura.

The Avatar took his place in front of the group.

"There is a clearing straight ahead and some oaks lying just outside the reach of the forest. As we pass from the cover of tree, we will be entering into a place where few dare to venture. Do not fear. If you follow me, we will make it through safely. So far, I do not feel Yezurkstal's dark presence, but if we do find he has a base out here, our task is not to engage. This is a scouting mission only. Once we know, we can prepare an appropriate response."

"I will not leave him alone if we find him. My sister must be avenged." the sylph's aura darkened, her eyes burning as she spoke.

The barghest chuckled at her comment and the troll planted his face in his hands. Casandra looked to the Avatar, so Zelag followed suit.

"You cannot beat him alone and you gain nothing from revenge. More important, he will not be alone. But, if he is, I will be the one who deals with him."

"Fine, but if you don't deliver the killing blow, I will." The sylph clenched her fists, her aura changing shade to a near-orange color.

"We get it. Let us just go already," Zelag blurted before thinking.

Everyone turned towards him in surprise, their auras changing color to convey their confused emotion. Casandra grinned ear to ear, her eyes glowing. Even the Avatar looked like he was fighting back a grin, though his aura did not change to reflect it.

"He is correct," the Avatar continued. "Let us get moving. Keep quiet and do not stray too far behind."

Reaching out, the Avatar pushed aside some of the branches blocking the way. The sylph followed behind him, and the barghest next. The troll waited and motioned ahead, pointing with his blistered arm towards the others.

"I will guard the rear. You two go."

Casandra put her hand on Zelag's back and willed him forward. Pushing through the underbrush, he heard her following close behind.

As the Avatar had indicated, this opened into a clearing. The open field was filled with green grass and a handful of trees scattered about. Usually, Zelag could spot a steady green energy coming from trees of this size. Instead, these let out a dull brown glow, a sign they were barely clinging to life. Looking ahead, he noted the grass further away from the trees was dull as well, fading to a yellow-brown.

Stepping into the open, he felt the sun beating down on his skin, the warmth causing some comfort. Continuing behind the barghest, he could feel the life energy of the forest fading away. As they walked past the dying trees, this energy was replaced with a darker force. The hair of his arms stood on end as they walked. He felt a strange tingling down his spine.

Walking past one of the last trees, his skin became cold, the sun's warmth fading away. Looking up, he was unsure what to make of it. It was mid-afternoon and the sun was still high in the sky. But it looked dull, as if someone had thrown a black sheet over it.

No one broke stride as they stepped forward, but Zelag could see that the barghest was unsettled by the change. His aura darkened, gaining a hint of purple. Glancing back at Casandra, he noticed that she had crossed both her arms over her chest. As she slithered behind, her aura faded as well. With the troll following close after, it appeared he was unaffected, maintaining a stern face and steady aura -just like the sylph.

Getting used to the camp his teacher housed him in was easy enough. Like the land of his birth, it was tranquil, calm, and full of life. These plains, on the other hand, were a place of death. But, despite the uneasiness this human form felt, there was a change occurring in his own life force. Zelag could feel himself adapting to these new surroundings.

Aside from dying grass and the foreboding atmosphere, Zelag was noticing much more than expected. One of the first things he noticed were the unnatural placement of rocks about the field. Looking around, it looked like these large stones had been placed intentionally, like the remnants of structures. While the grass they walked through now was dying, he also noted a thick brush up ahead, with grass that looked as tall as his own head.

Unfamiliar flowers bloomed in the tall grass, giving off a deathly aura.

They resembled a flower Zelag had seen before, but he could not remember their name. It was a reddish-orange flower that he was familiar with, the blooms overlapping and spreading around one-another to create a beautiful menagerie of color. But these ones were not reddish-orange. Instead, they were jet black, with light shades of gray. At their center, each bloom had a pointed barb.

Zelag noticed various mushrooms on the ground as well. One stuck out, a red and yellow variety. Its top was almost as wide as the palm of his hand. Reaching down, he plucked it up to inspect more closely. The stem was at least 10 centimeters long and the large growth had a squishy texture. Though he found the sense of smell in this form to be lacking, he could even detect a strange odor -similar to mildew on a rotting, wet log. Since it did not have an aura of its own, he could not quite pinpoint what the odor might indicate.

"I wouldn't mess with those," the troll warned.

Zelag turned around, still holding the fungus.

"Why not?"

"Those are piscoshrooms. They are deadly to us warm-blooded creatures. It's not a pleasant death either."

Zelag dropped the mushroom, stepping away from it as he turned around and continued forward. Looking ahead, he noticed they were nearing the tall grass. The Avatar paused just as he reached it, turning around to face everyone.

"Remember, follow in my footsteps and we shall arrive. There are malevolent forces in this grass, but I sense something more sinister straight ahead."

Turning back towards the grass he stepped through. The grass almost reached his chin as he stepped forward, but he was still visible. The sylph and barghest both followed without hesitation. Zelag paused before entering, glancing back at Casandra as if looking for reassurance. She looked a bit nervous, her aura weaker and smile wavering. Still, her eyes were steeled, burning with the fires of determination.

Using this to give himself some hope, he stepped into the grass after the barghest. Though the grass was at eye level, the barghest was large enough that he displaced it as he walked. Following behind this large lump of fur, he did not have to worry about straying from the path.

As they walked, he noticed the sun faded even more. The strange veil that blocked the sunlight seemed thicker here, somehow enhanced by the grass. There was still enough light to see the barghest though, so he did not worry about it too much. Instead, he just followed without question, gingerly pushing aside any barbed flowers and following in line. They proceeded for a few minutes in silence, but then his ears started to pick something up.

Someone whispered, but he could not make out what it was saying. He heard rustling to his right, but could not see any movement. The whispering got louder, but it was still hazy. Something flashed in front of him, zipping by before he could identify it. He heard rustling from his left.

"You shouldn't be here."

The voice was clear now, but still incredibly quiet. It sounded feminine, but he could not be sure.

"Does anyone else hear that?" he asked without breaking stride.

"Hear what?" the barghest mocked. "All I hear are your noisy footsteps and the rustling of all this pesky grass."

"What do you think you hear?" Casandra asked.

Zelag glanced back, noting a frown on her face and uneasiness in her eyes.

"I thought I heard someone say we should not be here."

The barghest laughed.

"You're so scared that you'll make up strange voices? You're greener than a new-born pup."

Just as he said this, Zelag saw something else zip by.

The barghest yelped and turned around. He raised his hand above his head and growled at Zelag.

"What do you think you are doing?"

Zelag backpedaled, stumbling and bumping into Casandra.

"I did nothing," he blurted, fearful the barghest might strike.

"What are you on about?" Casandra asked, putting out her arm to help Zelag stabilize. "What exactly do you think Zelag did?"

"He just tugged on my tail!"

"I did not touch you."

"Yes, you did!"

"No, he didn't," Casandra interrupted. "His hands have been by his side this whole time."

The barghest growled, lowering his hand. With eyes narrowed, he glared at Zelag. The troll pushed Zelag aside, stepping between the two.

"That's enough. We're falling behind The Avatar and if you fall behind, I'm not going to be there to protect you. If the boy says he didn't touch you, he didn't touch you. Let's keep moving."

With a snort and a low growl, the barghest turned. Offering no apology, he continued forward, pushing through the grass. The troll glanced down at Zelag, motioning for him to continue. Just as he took a step forward, the barghest let out another yelp.

The barghest must have been struggling with something. He barked, the grass ahead shaking violently. Stepping back in front of Zelag, the troll pushed forward.

"Stay close."

Zelag followed right after the troll, trusting Casandra would do the same. After lunging forward through the grass, it took just a few moments to arrive at the scene. The barghest was on the ground, rolling around and swinging his arms up as if to swat away a bug. He was flattening the grass, leaving a small clearing for them to gather.

Standing to the side, the troll looked down and scratched his head. Zelag exchanged a look with Casandra, who appeared just as confused as the troll. Then he spotted it again. It was a brief flash, and something zipped by.

For a split second, a swarm of bugs flashed into his own vision. Then they were gone.

The barghest flailed for a few more seconds before ceasing. He looked up and growled. Seeing the others around him, he jumped to his feet and brushed himself off.

"What was that about?" the troll asked.

"I don't know, but I don't think any of them stung me."

"Any of what stung you?" Casandra asked.

With a low growl, the barghest glared at her.

"What do you mean, 'any of what?' The bees of course! There were hundreds of them."

"What kind of mushrooms did you eat?" the troll asked. "There were no bees."

The barghest growled. "What are you-"

"I saw them too." Zelag interrupted.

Everyone turned to face him, their collection stares causing him discomfort.

"I mean, I saw something, but I don't know that it was bees. It moved much too fast."

"It wasn't bees."

This time, the Avatar interrupted, stepping back through the grass.

"I told you to stay behind me. Please, follow me and I will explain. We are almost through the grass."

Everyone hesitated for a moment, but it seemed they knew well enough not to question the wisdom of the Avatar. The barghest followed right behind him, and both Zelag and Casandra pushed through the grass side by side. She smiled at him as they moved forward but looking closer, he noticed that her aura had hints of yellow, a sign of clear nervousness. Not even looking to see if the troll was behind, they continued through the rest of the grass.

After a few more minutes, they made it through to the edge, pushing out the grass and into a new clearing. As he pushed the last bit of grass aside, Zelag caught another flash to his left. Ignoring this one, he made sure Casandra and the troll made it through before turning to face the Avatar.

He noticed that it was even darker on this side of the grass, the sun almost invisible in the sky. If they went much further, he feared this form's vision would not be enough to see.

"OK, so what was that?" the barghest asked.

The sylph flew down from above, floating just before the barghest.

"I'm afraid we caught the attention of some of my less-than-friendly cousins. Though you'll still find some enclaves in the forest, many of them have found these plains to be a more suitable home. They won't typically cause you any harm, but they have a nasty sense of humor."

"You don't mean-" the barghest started, pivoting around and clutching the necklace around his neck.

"Fairies." The Avatar finished his thought, stepping next to the sylph.

"Upon our return, you are all to stay close to me. None of them will dare get near me. For now, everyone remain behind me. I sense a darkness ahead."

Zelag looked out on the open field. The ground was filled with various types of grass and fungus, as well as some downed wood and scattered rocks. Looking southeast, it appeared the ground was flooded, which was supported by the mangroves off in the distance. The southwest looked like an empty void, a few small bushes scattered about alongside the fungus.

Upon closer examination, he could sense various insects crawling about, many of them unfamiliar. Remembering what the Avatar had instructed, he tried to imprint their life force on his memory. Turning straight south, he was able to tell what the Avatar meant by "darkness." In fact, he could see several dark auras about.

Whatever emitted this darkness was concealed from sight. Just at the edge of his visual range, Zelag could see a formation of dead trees. They were barren and dry, the branches casting a shadow in the dim sunlight. The dark energy was past these trees.

"Remind me again why we are out here?" the troll started, taking a step towards the Avatar. "You know I have faith in your leadership, but is this really safe for us to venture out this far? I mean, your students don't have experience out these ways, and it doesn't seem like we are going to find Yezurkstal."

"If you had faith, you would not need to ask." The Avatar squared up with the troll, giving him a severe look. Despite his shorter height, he somehow appeared larger than the troll.

"I just mean -I think maybe- perhaps we should consider that our friend barghest might be wrong."

"What do you mean I might be wrong? I told you that my people spotted mutated barghest out this way. I never guaranteed this was where Yezurkstal was."

The barghest growled and stomped towards the troll. Zelag backed away, putting his arm out in front of Casandra instinctively.

"Enough." The Avatar's voice boomed.

"We're being watched."

Zelag flashed his eyes across the plains, looking for any sign of movement. With the dim light the movement from the others, he did not spot anything at first. Still, he remembered his training from youth. If he wanted to detect anything, he needed to stay focused on their energy rather than rely on his eyes.

The Avatar had taken a position to the south, walking towards the dead trees in the distance. With a fluctuating red and yellow aura, the sylphid stayed close behind. Pivoting around in place, the troll grasped his staff, a short branch wrapped in leather and adorned with more animal bones. His aura turned a solid orange. Casandra slithered around behind him, looking in all directions for any threat. She kept her hands free in front, her aura a mixture of yellow and purple.

Zelag followed behind Casandra, keeping his hands held up in a defensive position. He continued to scan the area. The barghest had moved to the east of the group, creeping back at a steady pace. His aura was blue, demonstrating a surprising calm despite the situation. Or maybe it was because of the situation.

Looking past the barghest, Zelag caught sight of some newcomers. Dark auras filled his sight and the sound of footsteps followed. With his focus on these auras, he caught a glimpse of something else to his left. Turning towards it, Zelag could spot more dark auras, these ones mixed with crimson red. Zelag was not the only one who saw them.

"It looks like they were expecting us," the sylphid exclaimed shaking her head between the two groups.

"So it appears," the Avatar remained calm, his voice unwavering as he held up his right, palm exposed. A beam of light shot from each of his fingers, circling overhead and growing in intensity. The light continued to brighten, extending around the party and still expanding. After a few moments, it washed over the dark auras, revealing just what they were up against.

By Zelag's count, four demons approached from the south, but they were joined by seven other creatures. Three of them must have been mutated barghest, their black fur and massive claws betraying what they once were. The other four were of an unfamiliar race. Each of these creatures was tall and lanky; unlike the barghest and demons they were armed and armored. They wore leather and wood plates and wielded short spears. Despite his trepidation, Zelag made sure to focus on the barghest and this new race, taking in all their features.

He felt the large sinewy muscles of the barghest, their sharp claws and teeth, their broad shoulders, enlarged hearts, and thick rib cage. The other four creatures were skinny and frail, with gray flesh like the troll. Looking beyond this, he saw their fast-beating heart, their nocturnal eyes, their sharp teeth, and the unusual amount of tendons and ligaments that reinforced their musculature. Whatever these creatures were, they were made for fighting.

Refocusing on the barghest, he watched five other dark auras arrive from the east. Each of these belonged to another mutated barghest. Though his inclination was to yell for the barghest to watch out, he realized in this moment why this shaman maintained a calm aura. The five mutated creatures walked right up to him and stopped, gnashing their teeth at Zelag and the rest of the party.

"To be honest, I was hoping there wouldn't be so much collateral, but I had little choice," the barghest spat out his words with contempt.

"You betrayed us?" though the Avatar phrased this as a question, he seemed somehow unsurprised.

"I betrayed no one. I merely am looking out for myself. Yezurkstal is the future of Evorath and if the barghest want to survive we need to unite behind him. When I tried to convince the other members of the stronghold to join me, I couldn't. Instead, I was given a more important task -to kill you.

"But, you are my only target. So, I implore the rest of you to leave. Leave the Avatar to his fate and you can live another day. Submit to me, and maybe Yezurkstal will let you join his ranks as well."

"No one else will fall victim to your folly."

The Avatar seemed confident of this and when a quick scan of the others, Zelag believed his confidence was well-placed. The sylphid and troll both squared up against the barghest and his five minions to the east. Casandra slithered up beside the Avatar, facing the creatures to the south. Zelag was not sure where he should go.

"You see," the Avatar continued. "My followers will never be led astray as you have been."

Hushing his voice, he glanced at Casandra and then back to Zelag.

"Casandra, fight with the others but stay to the rear. Attack with your magic from a distance as you have practiced. Zelag, you follow my lead. Watch what I do and don't engage unless I tell you to."

Zelag wanted to object, but he did not have the chance. As soon as Casandra refocused her attention to the east, the demons charged. As the Avatar had instructed, Zelag kept his attention glued forward, his eyes locked on the Avatar.

The four skinny creatures charged first, followed in line by the three barghest. For the moment, the four demons stayed behind.

With a simple extension of his hand, the Avatar gathered up magical energy. Zelag had never seen anything quite like it. Despite the darkness and decay that surrounded them, he seemed to be accessing an almost endless reserve. Green magic flowed into him from every direction, enveloping him in a layer of energy. As it gathered around his body, vines shot up from the soil.

The lanky creatures were nimble, dodging the first few attacks by weaving around them. But, they could only hold off for so long before the dozens of vines took hold. Each grabbed on and wrapped around these creatures, pulling them to the ground. Within moments, all four were overwhelmed by the unexpected attack. Of course, the barghest were not going to submit so easily. Despite the barrage of vines, these three beasts continued forward, tearing away at them with a complete disregard for the thorns cutting into their skin.

Still, it slowed them down, which must have been the Avatar's intention. Without regard to the other creatures, he charged, running faster than Zelag could even track. By the time he caught up to him, the Avatar had one of the barghest in hand. He restrained both the creature's arms, letting some of the green energy flow outward. The two other barghest were closing in though, making Zelag wonder if he should intervene.

Then, the first barghest collapsed, falling still on the floor. Just as the two others leapt for the Avatar, he threw up a magical barrier. Zelag watched them collide with the invisible energy and smiled. The one on the left was seized with vines, covering it from head to toe while the Avatar moved to his right. This time, he just touched the creature on the chest. It looked like he gave him a light tap and the barghest fell still like the first.

By that time, the final barghest was ripping through the vines. Before he could stand back up, the Avatar bent over and tapped him on the snout, causing him to fall lifeless as well.

No, they were not dead. Zelag could still detect their life force; they were sleeping.

Of course, keeping his eyes on the Avatar made him forget about the demons, which had taken this opportunity to strike. None of these four monsters had wings, but their leathery red and black skin was accented with various horns and spikes. One of them had a set of six horns lining the top of his head, surrounding it like a halo. Another had horns like those of a ram. Still another had spikes protruding from his elbows, wrists, and shoulders. The final one had no visible horns or spikes, but he stood at least twice as tall as the Avatar.

As the Avatar stood back at full height, this massive demon slammed into him, wrapping its arms around Him and holding on tight. The ram horn and halo horn demons followed behind, grabbing for the Avatar's wrists to make sure they remained restrained. The spiked demon looked ready to finish things off, stepping up to the Avatar's head and raising up his hands.

With hands held overhead, he pulled in magic of his own, the dark energy forming into a large axe. Zelag had to do something. But he was paralyzed with fear.

Just as the demon went to drop his axe, Zelag noticed the area fell dark again. His eyes were drawn upward, where the light magic the Avatar had used was coalescing. The demon swung and the light flew like lightning. It split apart, striking all four demons and disintegrating them in an instant.

Their life energy had completely vanished. Zelag blinked and refocused, thinking he must be imagining things. They were gone, obliterated by the light.

The Avatar did not take a moment to recover, pushing up to his feet and sprinting to the other side of the battlefield. Zelag turned quicker this time, shifting his attention to the six remaining barghest and his other allies. By now, those numbers had changed.

Two of the black barghest were already dead on the ground, their guts spilled out by what looked to be large claws. Two of the surviving barghest were circling around the sylphid, snarling as they approached from a flanking position. Both the barghest and troll shaman wrestled on the ground. Right now, it looked like the troll had the advantage, maneuvering behind his canine opponent and locking up one of his arms.

This left Casandra, who was in the process of fighting the final barghest. With both her hands aimed forward, she fired a stream of water towards this creature, the pressure enough to keep it at bay. But, as Zelag focused on her, the mutant made its move, ducking down and stepping to the side. Casandra readjusted her stream, but the canine creature dodged on all four.

Zelag ran towards her, knowing he could not make it in time.

With arms outstretched, the Avatar did make it.

He charged in and tackled the barghest straight into the stream of water. Casandra stopped her assault, but Zelag kept running. She looked tired, drained from exerting so much energy.

As he ran, Zelag refocused on the Avatar, who had put this barghest to sleep like the others. His teacher then focused on the two engaged with the sylph, walking with a purpose towards these final foes. From his vantage, Zelag figured the barghest noticed the Avatar approaching, for as he moved, they lunged. Both flew straight for the sylphid, but instead of hitting her they hit one another. The one of the left slashed with his claws, slicing through the right's chest. The right one bit down on the left's arm, tearing into muscle before pulling away.

"I can't believe that worked again," the sylphid giggled as she reappeared above the two mutants.

"Enough." The Avatar arrived between the two injured barghest, touching them both and causing them to collapse.

"No innocent blood needs to be shed."

Zelag arrived next to Casandra. Captured her gaze and gave her a nod. In this form, something told him that would be a reassuring gesture. She nodded in return, confirming that inclination.

Turning towards the traitor and the troll, he saw the latter still had the upper hand. Pulling the barghest up from behind, the troll had both his arms underneath the traitor's armpits and rested against the back of his skull. As the traitor struggled, he applied pressure.

The Avatar stepped in front of the duo, looking up at them without saying a word. Seeing him, the traitor gave up his struggles, his aura turning yellow in fear.

"I had to look out for the interest of my people."

"No, you were looking out for the interest of yourself. Unfortunately, you were misguided. Yezurkstal has no room for barghest in his world and you should be wise enough to know that. Your creator cared for you, but you have betrayed Her trust."

"Let me make up for it. I can be your loyal servant again. I will do whatever it takes. I will kill all of Evorath's enemies."

The barghest whimpered, his aura darkening. Shaking his head, the Avatar stepped closer to the barghest.

"Evorath never wanted blood to be shed."

Reaching up, the Avatar touched the barghest on the nose, sending a jolt of energy into him. Like his mutated cousins, the traitor fell limp -sleeping. After a brief delay, the troll let go, allowing him to drop to the ground.

Floating over to the Avatar, the sylphid spoke up.

"It looks like none of our numbers were injured. Let us press on and find Yezurkstal."

The Avatar shook his head. "He was never here."

Chapter 23

Erathal City
4 Neglur, 1087 MT

Artimus sat at his workbench, squinting as he lined up the fletching on his next arrow. He focused on keeping the half-feather flush with the shaft, pulling down as he secured it with string. He continued around the shaft, twisting the arrow, and wrapping the string around the next feather. Pausing for a moment, he made sure to keep the tension and twisted around to the final feather half. With a slight tug, he pulled down on this one as well, keeping it flush as he finished the wrap. With all three in place, he spun the shaft more quickly, tightening the string around the fletching.

As he came to an end, he tucked the string under itself and placed the finished arrow in a bin on the floor to his right. Though he had been taught to work on one arrow at a time, Artimus had learned over the decades that he could work faster this way. For now, he was just securing the fletching in place. After he finished this batch, he would then move onto the next step. Reaching to his left, he picked up another arrow.

Knock, knock, knock.

He put the arrow down on the workbench and turned around. Looking through the crack in the door, he could see his wife on the other side. Since she wasn't in the habit of interrupting him, it must have been important.

"Come in."

She pushed open the door, smiling as she stepped into the small workshop.

"We just got a carrier pigeon," she said, holding up the small scroll in her hand.

"From whom?"

Savannah's face become stern, the smile evening out and eyes filled with concern.

"Tel' Shira."

Artimus waited a few seconds for his wife to continue. Since she didn't, he asked.

"And judging by your facial expression it is important. What does it say?"

"To paraphrase, she had a vision and wants us to meet her in Dumner. Apparently, her elders wouldn't do anything about it but she claims it's important that we act. She says she is heading there straight away to meet with Irontail. She also asked that we bring along as many military units as we can."

Artimus stood up, holding his hands out in confusion.

"Does she not understand that we oversee the protection of this district from outside attack? How does she expect us to bring along any military support? I'm not a general. Does she even say what this vision entailed?"

Savannah shook her head and shrugged.

"No, but she insists that it's urgent. She says it concerns the safety of both our people."

Artimus rubbed his temples, glancing back at his unfinished arrows before returning to the conversation.

"If we do go, we need to stress the importance of details for future communications."

"Agreed. But we can't just ignore her. She is our friend."

Savannah held the letter out, offering it to Artimus.

"No, I don't need to read it myself. Since when are Tel' Shira and Irontail on cordial terms? I didn't know they kept in touch."

He reached down and grabbed his dagger from the table, sheathing it behind his back and walking to the door. Savannah proceeded out, allowing him to pull the door shut.

"I think she has been unofficially meeting with him to discuss a treaty with the centaur for months now."

Artimus retrieved the key from his pocket and locked the workshop door. Savannah continued towards the exit to the house and he followed close behind. With the front door left open, they stepped outside and Artimus pulled it shut behind him. Reaching into his other pocket for the key he locked this door as well.

Savannah chanted something under her breath, touching the door and leaving behind some extra magical protection.

"What do you think the chance is that Cabal will actually let us take any soldiers with us?" Savannah asked as they proceeded down the steps and along the short walkway.

"I'm not even sure he is going to let us go," Artimus replied offering his hand.

Savannah smiled and took a hold of his hand, interlocking her fingers around his as they walked.

"Well, good thing he isn't our king."

-=-=-=-=-=-=-=-=-

Savannah held her hands behind her back, twiddling her thumbs as she waited.

Artimus and she stood outside the door to the Chancellor's chambers, waiting for him to answer their request for an audience. The attendant, Falahar, had informed the Chancellor of their presence.

"He will allow you in once he has finished with his thoughts," Falahar had instructed after shutting the door.

That was more than five minutes ago, and Savannah was growing impatient. Judging by the way Artimus tapped his left foot, it seemed he was losing the battle with patience as well. Prior to him taking over as Chancellor, Cabal had always been accessible. While she understood he had a lot on his plate right now, she still expected better treatment considering the role she and her husband had played in bringing him to power.

As she stood there, she went over some of the recent events in her head. The story Artimus had shared about the strategy meeting just days before was startling, but it wasn't the only strange situation. Cabal had been acting different since taking power. And for some reason, he always seemed to have an easy time getting his way without debate. She wasn't sure how long she continued along the thought when the door finally creaked open.

Artimus had taken to leaning against the wall. He darted upright as Cabal stepped into the hallway.

"Please, come in. I was just going through some proposed changes to how merchants operate on the streets. Apparently, some of the elderly elves insist that they are causing travel issues as they take up too much room. But so are the burdens of leadership!"

As he spoke, he stepped back into his chambers, motioning Artimus and Savannah to follow. Though he had been working from these chambers for months now, Savannah realized this was her first visit. Artimus had been in here a few times already, but she still caught him surveying the room as they entered.

The room was modest in size, offering only the basic conveniences. For her own curiosity, she took a quick inventory. The wall to the right was covered in bookshelves, each a good half-meter taller than she was. She recognized some of the tomes, such as *Innap's Collective Works*, *The Demon War Chronology*, and a few books by her favorite philosopher, Artur Aurelius. The rest were unfamiliar.

At the base of this shelf, he kept a small, wooden ladder, which he must have needed for those books higher up. The floor featured a woven carpet with a simple pattern design featuring red, blue, and green. On the left, the wall featured a painting of the castle as well as a small table with some goblets and a decanter. The Chancellor continued around the middle of the room to his desk.

It was made of a heavy mahogany and featured a dark brown finish. Piles of parchment were organized on the right and left side of the desk, as well as a few sparse decorations, such as a ceremonial dagger. In the center of the desk, he had a rolled scroll, some loose parchment, and a quill and ink well. Looking past the desk, Savannah also noticed a portrait of Artur Aurelius and a plaque featuring a gnarled wand.

"Please, let's discuss your news. The attendant said it was quite urgent."

The Chancellor stepped behind his ornate wooden chair, leaning against the backrest, and smiling.

Artimus stood in front of the desk, looking at the Chancellor and then turning to Savannah. She nodded in response.

"Savannah and I received an unexpected communication from Tel' Shira. According to her intelligence, Yezurkstal is planning another major attack. She has requested that we lend aid with as many units as we might have to spare."

The Chancellor eyed Savannah and then looked back to Artimus.

"And why aren't the elders reaching out with this request? The ink on our treaty has dried. If they need help, then they should request it as per our agreement."

"Which is what I thought at first," Artimus continued. "Unfortunately, the elders are not interested in lending aid because the attack is not on the felite village."

The Chancellor pulled out his chair and stepped to the left of it.

"Then where is this attack to take place?"

"I'm afraid she didn't specify," Artimus said looking down. "But she received a vision of this attack and wants us to join her at Dumner so we can mobilize."

"She had a vision and didn't specify where the attack would be? Does she even know where the attack will be? Even if her vision is true, what if the attack is here?"

"Knowing her as I do, that wouldn't add up," Artimus continued without breaking stride. "If the attack were here, she would have warned me to mobilize at home. The attack may be targeting Dumner though; Yezurkstal did do a number on it last year. Perhaps he wants to return to finish the job."

The Chancellor ran his hand along the back of his chair and looked down. After a few seconds, he looked back up and pulled the chair out further. Taking a seat, he looked straight at Artimus.

"And she wants how many units? As many as we can spare? I'm afraid right now we cannot spare any units."

"You're right," Artimus replied immediately.

Savannah turned to him in shock. Why was he agreeing so easily?

"Perhaps you would allow Savannah and I to go there and get more information? If the threat is real, then maybe we can convince the Confederacy to send aid at least?"

"No, you and Savannah are better off staying here and completing your work. Our borders need to be secure."

Artimus nodded.

Savannah could no longer hold her tongue.

"I'm sorry Chancellor, but that is unacceptable. You are not our king and we are not your subjects. Artimus and I are going to help our friend. If she says she had a vision about Yezurkstal, then she did. It would be irresponsible to ignore that."

The Chancellor refocused his gaze, looking into Savannah's eyes with a piercing stare.

"No, it would be irresponsible for you to go. You must stay here and continue defensive preparations for the exposed portion of our city. Now, both of you go back home and continue your work."

Savannah nodded. The Chancellor was right. They should go back to their more important work.

"Well, thank you for your time and advice," Artimus said as he turned towards Savannah.

"Of course. I am always willing to lend an ear."

Her husband motioned for her to leave first, so Savannah stepped out the door. By the sounds of his footsteps, Artimus followed right behind. She heard the door shut as she continued down the hall.

"Well, I am glad Cabal keeps a level head about these things. We are better offer defending Erathal rather than chasing after untested visions."

Savannah turned to her husband and offered a smile. "Yes, he has always been a wise man. We can just focus on-"

She stopped mid step, a strange sensation overtaking her. Chills went down her spine and she felt a tingling sensation in the back of her skull. She must have been frowning too.

"What's wrong?" Artimus asked putting his hand on the small of her back. "You look like someone just killed one of your plants."

"What are we doing?" she asked.

"What do you mean? We are returning home to continue our work. We must make sure our city has the proper defense should Yezurkstal attack."

"But why are we doing that? Our friend asked for our help and before meeting with the Chancellor we had every intention of going to Dumner. Why do we suddenly just want to obey his edicts?"

"Because it would be irresponsible for us to go. We need to stay here and-" Artimus's face scrunched together. His eyes darted back and forth and assumed a confused expression. It was as if he just had a major realization.

"Do you understand what I am asking now?" Savannah asked placing her hand on his left arm.

He looked down at her and they locked eyes.

"I do." he started, lifting his right and clasping her hand. "But I don't know the answer. Why are we listening to Cabal? We should be going to Tel' Shira anyways, shouldn't we?"

"Yes."

Savannah looked around the hall, making sure no one else was around.

"But let's discuss this outside of these walls."

Holding Artimus's hand, she led him down the corridor and around the corner, heading back towards the main hall. As they stepped into the next walkway, they passed by a couple of attendants. Savannah merely offered a smile and nod.

Arriving back at the main hall, she smiled to the guard who stood watch there and turned left towards the castle entrance.

She walked at a brisk pace, Artimus staying by her side the entire time. Just as they approached the exit, a familiar voice came from behind.

"Lieutenant, sir!"

Savannah closed her eyes and cursed silently. She recognized that grating voice anywhere and it seemed Artimus did as well. Squeezing her hand, he continued forward.

"Leave your report at my desk Constable Dunder," Artimus shouted without turning around.

Savannah smirked, but as she expected, Dunder didn't give up that easily.

"But sir. I wanted to run a new theory-"

"Write it down and leave it on my desk. I have urgent business to handle for the Chancellor."

Stifling a giggle, Savannah continued forward and glanced at Artimus. He wore a stern expression but shifting his gaze to her he hinted a smile.

The two guards watching the double-doors remained emotionless as they pushed the doors open and allowed the couple to pass through.

"Thank you," Savannah offered, maintaining her grin.

Of course, as they stepped outside the castle, she let herself return to thoughts about the Chancellor. Was he using some kind of magic? In all her decades of experience with magic, she had never encountered anything that could manipulate people like this. But, reflecting on the past few months, it was all starting to make sense: he was controlling them.

Both she and Artimus remained silent as they walked down the steps and passed a group of soldiers. Though she did her best to keep a smile on her face, she knew that her discomfort had to show through. Artimus must have been experiencing similar thoughts, breaking the silence as they approached the castle walls.

"We'll gather what we need at home and then head out. We can discuss this situation more once we are outside the city."

Savannah regarded him for a moment and nodded.

"Agreed."

Chapter 24

Road between Erathal City and Dumner Village
5 Neglur, 1087 MT

Artimus pulled down on his quiver strap, adjusting its
position and considering his wife. She marched to his left, seated
atop a chestnut courser with eyes cast ahead. Unlike his trusted
Thoron, Savannah never had a horse of her own, which made
getting one from the stable master a bit of a chore. Since the
appearance of the humans, military resources were under tight
guard. This meant getting a horse was reserved for official
matters. Though he was tempted to lie and claim it was for
investigative use, he went with the more honest choice -a couple
silver coins.

Other than his exchange with the stable master, he and
Savannah hadn't spoken since leaving the castle. They gathered
the necessary gear from home, stopped by the stables, and now
trotted along the road to Dumner. Having passed the last guards
on the road a good three minutes before, he felt it was time to
break that silence.

"Thank you."

Savannah turned his way and squinted.

"Thank…for what?"

"For keeping a clearer head than I. We would be at our
house blindly obeying Cabal if you hadn't snapped some sense
into me."

Shaking her head, Savannah cast her gaze down.

"I don't think you should be thanking me. Do you realize what this means?"

"No, well, yes. Maybe. It means Cabal has been using some sort of magic to manipulate us."

"No," Savannah started, her voice labored with sadness. "I mean, yes, but not just that. How long do you think he has been doing this? This is much more than the two of us. I helped bring him to power. I introduced you and got you involved. Whatever magic Cabal is using, I helped get him into a position where he is poised to benefit from it."

Artimus looked down at Thoron, considering her words and formulating the proper response.

"Your culpability is no greater than my own. Yes, you introduced me, but I introduced others. We can beat ourselves up over this, or we can start considering the greater implications. I thanked you for good reason -you are the one who broke through his spell. How did you do it?"

"What do you mean? I don't know. It just all makes so much sense now."

Her voice trailed off and she kept her gaze down. Her horse slowed as she did, leaving Artimus to loosen his legs around Thoron and match her pace.

"As I said, there is no need to beat ourselves up. It's water under the bridge at this point. But there must be some reason you were able to overpower his spell. What changed?"

Savannah shifted her gaze ahead, her face tight and pensive. Artimus had to squeeze Thoron to keep up as she increased her pace. She kept her attention forward for a good minute, but he knew better than to interrupt her thoughts.

"It has been bothering me for a few weeks now," she blurted. "Why did I always agree with him on every important decision? Why would I go into a debate firm in my beliefs and then come out with a completely different outlook? Sure, he made me feel important by asking for my opinion at times, but when decisions were to be made, he always made them."

Artimus nodded.

"I noticed that too, but that doesn't change the fact that I just kept going along with it. The biggest anomaly was when we first encountered the humans. I couldn't believe how easily he won them over. But now everything is making more sense. Again though, I still couldn't break free until you pointed it out. So, how did you do it? How did you even know he was controlling us?"

"I'm not sure. I have been trying to figure that out and I can only come up with one theory. While we were waiting to meet with him, all I could think about were some of the recent decisions he has made. I thought about all the unilateral choices and the times where I completely caved to his way of things. It made me angry.

"Going over it in my head, I wonder if perhaps I built up a sort of magical barrier. I was impatient and I felt this sort of ephemeral sensation as I focused on these events. Whatever spell he was using, I must have somehow countered it with one of my own. In the moment, I agreed with him 100%, but as we walked out of his office, I had that same feeling rise from my stomach. But, even if I did counter his magic, I'm not sure I can do it again, nor do I know how to protect you."

She shook her head, looking back down at her horse in thought.

"I can only imagine your frustration." Artimus steered Thoron a bit closer to her as he spoke. "But you should also take some pride in what you did. Considering what we just experienced, it's safe to say Cabal has been using this strange magic for some time now. You could be the first person to see through his spell, which is not a small feat."

Reaching out, he ran his hand through her hair. She looked up at him and smiled, bringing her own hand up and grasping his for a moment.

"Now," Artimus continued, "the important thing is that we consider what we can do going forward. If you are uncertain about your ability to counter his magic, then we need to consult with someone who can help. What kind of magic would allow him to control people like that and who do you know who can help us counter it?"

Savannah pulled her hand back and looked ahead.

"I've also been trying to come up with an answer for that. I recall reading about magic like this in a tome years ago. It mentioned that merfolk often rely on magic like this to trick land-dwelling creatures into doing their bidding Alternatively, it mentioned a sort of fox-creature on the Eastern continent."

She kept her eyes trained ahead, guiding the horse around a slight bend in the road. After waiting to make sure she was done, Artimus replied.

"So, all we have are a couple of myths to go on?"

"Myths," Savannah's voice raised in pitch as she cast him a confused gaze. "Hardly. While I can't verify whatever the fox-creature is, I can say that merfolk are anything but a myth. Unfortunately, I'm not on good terms with any of the ones I've met."

Artimus craned his neck to look back at Savannah.

"You're joking right? So, not only are merfolk real, but you are telling me that you have met some. As in, you have spoken to them?"

"That's really not important now dear. What matters is that I don't have a resource to consult."

"What about the tome you read about these spells in? Doesn't it talk about a way to counter the effects?"

"I don't remember. But it really doesn't matter. I don't have it. I read it when I was at my old village."

Artimus hesitated for a moment, letting a few moments of silence pass, and considering his words.

"I know how much you hate the idea of-"

"Don't you dare suggest what I think you are going to suggest! We are not going back to that village. Even if you could convince me it was worth it, I can't say for sure they are still there. For all we know, Yezurkstal wiped it out this past year. And frankly, I don't care to know."

Frowning, Artimus considered alternatives, but he was drawing a blank. Like usual, talk of her old village seemed to stir up nothing but pain. She took off, her horse galloping ahead. Fighting the urge to yell after her, Artimus tightened his legs around Thoron and followed suit.

They wrapped around a slight bend and continued at a brisk pace, charging down the road as if possessed. Artimus tightened his legs even more, willing Thoron forward. He sped up, overtaking Savannah, and focusing on the road ahead. Glancing back, he noticed she was keeping pace. With a smirk on his face, he squeezed just a bit harder, steering Thoron left to block Savannah's path.

He heard a loud neigh from behind and turned to see her veering right. She galloped past, shooting him a quick smile. Artimus shook his head and squeezed Thoron even harder. It still amazed him Savannah could refocus her attention so quickly, but this was a matter of pride. There was no way he would let Thoron lose a race.

Holding the reins tight, Artimus concentrated on the road ahead. Thoron picked up speed, galloping to catch up with Savannah's horse. Though he could never explain the connection, Artimus knew that Thoron understood the stakes. Within a few seconds, they closed the distance and were right alongside his wife.

Savannah turned his way again and smirked. Shifting her attention ahead, she looked determined as her horse edged just ahead. Artimus laughed.

"I have you beat!"

With another burst of speed, Thoron overtook his challenger. Pulling ahead, Artimus turned back to see Savannah admitting defeat. She held up her right hand and loosened her hold on the reins. As her horse slowed to a trot, Artimus ordered Thoron to do the same. He let his legs relax and loosened his hold on the reins, patting Thoron on the side as they slowed.

Seeing he was still a few meters ahead of his wife, Artimus pulled the reins and led Thoron to double back. As they met up, Artimus took a deep breath.

"You had me worried for a second there," he offered. "But Thoron and I have been doing this for too long to be beaten so easily."

Savannah let out a loud exhale and breathed back in through her nose.

"Believe what you want honey. I just didn't want to hurt your pride."

She winked, coming up alongside him and trotting forward.

"Pfft. Yes, I'm sure it had nothing to do with your lack of familiarity with that horse."

"All horses love me," Savannah countered with a big smile.

"I'm sure that's true." Thoron snorted as if agreeing.

"Of course, it is." Savannah paused for a few moments, her smile diminishing as she looked at the road ahead.

"What is it?" Artimus asked, pushing Thoron to speed up and take the lead. He surveyed the road and noticed no indication of trouble.

"Just returning to reality. Tel' Shira is summoning us because she had a vision about Yezurkstal -one that she believes is important enough to include us and go around her own tribal leadership. Of course, it is bad enough that we can't get approval to lend official aid, but that's not the end of it. Now we find that our trusted leader has been manipulating us. It makes you question the will of Evorath."

Artimus nodded, waiting a few seconds to allow Savannah more time to speak. She cast her gaze down, her horse still trotting forward.

"I prayed to Her you know." Savannah continued. "I thought maybe Evorath would send the Avatar to help us out, but here we are marching along and there is no response."

"Maybe we'll have better luck after we meet with Irontail and Tel' Shira." Artimus started.

"After all, the Avatar has been on a mission to stop Yezurkstal, right? If Tel' Shira's vision is true, he will want to help us prevent the attack. When he comes, we can ask about Cabal."

"I just hope it's that easy," Savannah replied looking into his eyes. "At any rate, we should probably pick up our pace. If there is an imminent attack, we want to have time to prepare."

"As usual, your beauty is outmatched only by your wisdom."

Savannah smirked and shook her head.

"You need new lines."

"Perhaps, but-" Artimus paused, his ears perking up as he heard rustling from the brush up ahead. The road was straight at this point, trees overhead creating a canopy over the path. On either side, there was a dense cover of bushes and trees, making it hard to see anything more than a meter off the road. He listened intently and held up his right palm towards Savannah, pointing towards the sound with his left.

The rustling continued. Artimus pulled back on the reins and whispered in for Thoron to stop. Dismounting his horse, he walked towards the noise and drew his bow. Notching an arrow, he kept his eyes and ears focused on that point.

There was another sound, this one high-pitched. It was coming from an animal. Taking one step at a time, he was able to get a better idea of what it might be. It was crying.

"Who goes there? You have no need to hide from me. Please, come out and we can help you."

The bushes shook and the voice sniffled. He could hear hushed murmurs but couldn't make out what was said.

Dropping his arrow back in the quiver, he slid his bow over his back. He could see movement through the foliage. It looked like there were two of them. He held his hands out, palms open.

"Are you lost? I can bring you to safety. Please, let me help you."

Glancing back, he noticed Savannah had taken a position behind him. She was still seated on her horse. Shifting his gaze back ahead, he watched the bushes part. A small boy pushed his way through, followed behind by a little girl.

They wore dirty tunics made from simple, brown fabric and torn, cloth shoes. Their skin was tan, smudged with dirt on their arms, legs, and face. Both had brown hair and rounded ears -they were humans and by the looks of it they had been wandering the forest since their arrival.

More than their physical distress, they both looked terrified. The boy had brown eyes and the girl hazel. Both looked to be kilometers away, a deep longing in their face as they stared up towards Artimus. He could sense their fear and he imagined his ears didn't help things much.

"It is going to be alright," he offered, keeping his palms visible. "I know how scared you must be, but I can help you. Why don't you two come with us so we can bring you to safety?"

The girl's face softened, and she took a step forward. The boy seemed less receptive. He pointed at Artimus and took a step back.

"E-e-ears! De-demon!"

"No demons. I am an elf. We have already helped many of your kind. I promise we can help bring you to safety."

The girl hesitated now, and the boy backed away some more. Artimus heard Savannah dismount her horse and take her place by his side.

"He might look scary, but he is telling the truth," Savannah offered. She stepped forward and crouched, lowering to match the children's gaze.

"My name is Savannah," she said touching her chest. "And this is Artimus." She motioned back to him. "What are your names?"

The boy stopped, looking up with wide eyes. The girl took another step forward, extending her hand towards Savannah.

"My name is Elizabeth," the little girl offered, her voice timid. "And this is me little bwother, David."

Savannah knelt and extended her hand, leaving it just centimeters from the girl's.

"Elizabeth. That is such an exotic name. And David; that sounds like the name of a very brave warrior. Are you brave, David?"

Artimus watched in amazement as the boy shuffled forward, turn his gaze towards the ground as he approached

Savannah. If they were anything like elvish children, the girl had to be no more than eight or nine years old and the boy perhaps five or six. Yet, Savannah was handling them like she was their nanny.

"I want to be bwave," the boy offered, his voice coated with a great deal of sadness. "But, we lost our pear-wents."

Savannah smiled and offered her other hand.

"Well, I think you are doing a great job. I also think we can help you find your parents. How about you come with Artimus and me? We may know where your parents are."

The little girl stumbled forward, running into Savannah, and embracing her. The boy sniffled and stepped forward to follow his sister. He folded his arms around Savannah and nuzzled his head into her shoulder.

"It's alright," Savannah offered, patting them both on the back. She looked up at Artimus with a mixed expression. Her mouth was curled in a semi-smile but her eyes were tight and burdened. He hadn't seen that look very often from her, but he recognized it as sympathy.

Artimus knelt next to them and laid his hand upon the boy's arm.

"You two are familiar to horses, right?" He wore a wide smile, trying to convey his friendly intentions.

Both children stepped out of the embrace and looked at him. They looked at one another nervously and then nodded.

"Good. How about we see if we can find your parents?"

Chapter 25

Dumner Village
5 Neglur, 1087 MT

Tel' Shira stood watching the road, wondering what delays might be keeping the elves. They should have arrived by now. The sun had passed its highest point hours ago, and though it was obscured by the tree cover here, she guessed that it had less than two hours before it set for the night.

"Are you sure they got your message?" Irontail asked, creeping up from behind her. Concentrating on her vision, she had almost forgotten he was there.

"Sure, I cannot be. Sent early this morning, I did. Arrived by now, they should have."

Irontail scratched the back of his head, looking ahead and releasing a loud sigh.

"Perhaps the bird never made it. Or maybe they aren't able to come. Your letter wasn't exactly detailed. Maybe we should discuss your vision with the other elders and just fill them in when they get here."

Tel' Shira shook her head, keeping her eyes trained on the road. While she considered Irontail a friend, she also found him quite annoying at times. He should understand why she didn't want to discuss it before they arrived; she hated repeating herself.

Trying to come up with an appropriate response, she almost leapt with joy as she caught sight of the couple turning the corner. They were still a couple hundred meters away, but with her keen vision she could see two figures on horseback winding their way towards the village. Squinting for a clearer view, she confirmed that it was Artimus and Savannah.

"Wait anymore, we need not. Here, they almost are." She pointed at the pair.

Irontail stepped forward and held his hand over his eyes.

"I don't see them yet, but I'll take your word for it. Oh -I see something! You sure that's them?"

"Sure, I am."

"Well then, I will make sure the others are assembled."

Irontail turned, trotting back through the trees and towards his village. Tel' Shira closed her eyes and inhaled through her nose. She held the breath for a count of four and released it through her pursed lips. Focusing on the lynx from a few days before, she ran through the vision again in her mind. Observing every detail, she focused on making sense of it.

The truth was she still couldn't be sure when or where this vision was to unfold. Despite that, she got a tingling in her spine thinking about it -the same feeling she got to warn her of imminent danger. But how would she explain this to the others?

She opened her eyes, letting out another long exhale. Artimus and Savannah were drawing near. The ranger waved to Tel' Shira, wearing a thin smile as they approached. Savannah shook her head and waved.

"Greetings," Artimus shouted as they moved closer.

Just a few meters away, both of their horses slowed to a halt, allowing them to dismount. Both elves grabbed their horses' reins and led them forward.

"Greetings," Tel' Shira replied as they made it to arm's length. She took a slight bow, her hands hanging loose by her side.

Artimus and Savannah both returned the bow.

"We are sorry for not arriving sooner." Artimus said proceeding past Tel' Shira. "Our day has been one unexpected development after another."

"See, I do. Bring reinforcements, you were unable to?"

Artimus shook his head and glanced back at Tel' Shira.

"I'm afraid not. One of the unexpected obstacles involved our own Chancellor Cabal. I won't go into it, but let's just say we are questioning our support for his leadership."

"Jeopardize your positions, I hope I did not." Tel' Shira looked between the two elves, trying to get a better feel for their disposition.

"No, it's not your fault," Savannah replied. "In fact, we should probably thank you. If not for your request, who knows if or when we would have realized Cabal's dishonesty. Though that explains our lack of any military support, it doesn't explain our delay. We actually ran across a different surprise."

Savannah continued forward, leading her horse alongside Artimus. Since she did not continue her explanation, Tel' Shira pried.

"Surprise?"

Artimus nodded, but it was Savannah who replied.

"Yes. We came across a couple of human children on the way here. It seems that they were separated from their parents. I think Artimus almost scared them away, but fortunately I was able to calm them down."

"Hey, it was the guards who they were really afraid of, not me."

Savannah giggled.

"He's not entirely wrong. Naturally, we took them back to Erathal and when we arrived the children were afraid of being left behind. We had one of the guards summon a castle attendant whom I know, and we were finally able to convince the children to go with him. It took no shortage of coaxing though. Hopefully, their parents are at the castle."

Savannah's voice trailed off as she looked ahead.

Tel' Shira turned her attention this direction as well. They were nearing the inner part of the village. Passing a couple cabins on either side, she could see the central mound ahead. A few centaurs wandered through the clearing, but no one of note. That is, no one beside Irontail, who stood at the entrance to the central mound.

"Great timing," he said stepping forward.

"I have gathered a few of the elders as well as my lead general, Nickelear, and my trusted commander, Silvertoe. They are waiting in the first meeting hall on the left."

He turned around and shouted to a nearby centaur -a warrior judging by his simple attire.

"Cedarback! Take our guests' horses to the field so they can graze. Make sure they are both comfortable."

The centaur ran over without delay, offering a slight bow to the elves before extending his hands.

"Yes, sir." he exclaimed, his voice deep and powerful. "Please, allow me."

Artimus nodded and handed over the reins. Savannah followed suit, offering a "thank you" and a polite bow.

As Cedarback led the two horses away, Artimus and Savannah proceeded ahead of Tel' Shira. All three walked to the mound and joined Irontail. The chieftain offered a smile and turned around, causing the mound to open.

"Follow me."

He led the two elves inside and Tel' Shira followed right behind. The hall was a bit darker than last time she was here, but the meeting hall was just ahead. Irontail touched the wall and it opened to allow passage. Motioning inside, he let Artimus and Savannah go in first. Tel' Shira stopped outside the entrance.

"Go ahead," he instructed. She nodded and proceeded inside.

The room expanded out for some distance, leaving enough space for at least one hundred centaur, if not more. Despite the width of the room, the ceiling was lower than most meeting halls, and as Irontail entered Tel' Shira noted his head was less than half a meter from touching the ceiling. Like most of her previous experiences in this mound, she noted the room was almost empty.

A candle lined the wall every meter, emitting enough light for everyone to see. In the center of the room, a table had been prepared, which included a map of the forest and some loose parchment. Artimus and Savannah walked towards the table to join the gathered centaur, so Tel' Shira followed.

Aside from the two elves and the two centaur warriors, there were three other centaur in the room. All were old, two of them with more gray fur than brown and one of them who appeared emaciated. His skin was taut to his face, all four legs skinny and shaky, as if he struggled to stay upright.

Tel' Shira made it a point to stay behind the two elves, watching as they took up a position to the right of Silvertoe, whom she had met before. The other warrior, Nickelear as she figured through the process of elimination, was to the left of Silvertoe. Not wanting to be near the rickety old centaur, she circled around to take her place on Nickelear's left. She glanced over to the elder centaur for only a moment before turning her attention back to Irontail.

He made his way around and took his place at the table next to the three elders. Shuffling aside the loose parchment, he allowed an unobstructed view of the map. Looking down at it, Tel' Shira found herself impressed. Either Irontail was hiding his cartography skills or someone else in the tribe was keeping incredibly detailed tabs on the recent events.

Aside from major locations like Dumner, Erathal, the Confederacy, and the Runeturk Mountains, this map had different color markers spread about. Red flags marked what Tel' Shira recognized as confirmed skirmishes between Yezurkstal and various forest tribes. There were also yellow, green, and blue flags scattered about. Tel' Shira even noted a few other villages marked on the map that she didn't know about.

"Alright," Irontail began. "I have gathered you all here at the request of our guest, Tel' Shira. Before she shares her startling news, let us ensure everyone is familiar here. Beside Tel' Shira, we have Nickelear and Silvertoe, two brave warriors of our tribe. Next in line, our two other guests are Artimus and Savannah, influential elves within the Republic of Erathal. Joining us, we have the three oldest elders of our tribe. This is Stonehair on the far left, Oakleg in the middle, and Quartzhand on the right."

Irontail motioned to each person as he spoke and Tel' Shira caught Artimus's smile upon the mention of Oakleg. The irony was not lost on her either.

"Now, rather than trying to explain anything, I'll let Tel' Shira share her experience with everyone. Please let us try not to interrupt her and allow her to give us the full story before we discuss." He looked at the elders as he said this, a certain severity in his face.

Being a warrior all her life, Tel' Shira was not comfortable with this. Having to explain the vision to her own elders was tough enough.

"Know, you do already, of foresight abilities felite possess. These abilities, just now learning, I am. Vision quest, three days ago, I was on. To hone these abilities, I intended. Spotted a lynx, I did."

She looked around to make sure everyone was following. Out of all those gathered, Savannah was the only one who really showed interest. Artimus was looking at her mouth, but she could tell his mind was elsewhere.

"Visions, lynx are said to offer. Touched the lynx I did. Visions, it gave me. Yezurkstal, I saw, and an army. Many demons he has. Defiled creatures, dark and rotting, he also commands. Across Erathal, march he will. Begun his campaign, he has already. Warned about, I was, a major attack."

She paused for a moment, trying to think of the best way to explain her vision to them. Apparently, Oakleg mistook this as a sign that she was finished.

"I don't get it," he began, his voice dull and raspy. It was a perfect match for his wrinkled face. "What are you asking us to do? If Yezurkstal is waging war with such an army, our little tribe can do little to turn the tide."

"I second that notion," Stonehair jumped in, his voice a bit more tolerable, but still dry and cracked. "What are your people doing to prepare? How large is his army? All you've told us is that he will attack, but you've left out all the details."

"I too would like an answer to these questions. And, if this is your first vision, can we even trust in its accuracy?" At least Quartzhand sounded like he was still in good health.

"Why don't you let her give us more details then," Savannah interjected, staring daggers at the three elders. Her voice was resolute, a certain fire in her eyes.

"Well, if she has more detail-" Stonehair started, but was cut off by Irontail.

"Yes, we understand. More details are necessary. Perhaps we can let her continue then." He gave the elders a stern look and turned back to Tel' Shira.

"Please, continue."

Tel' Shira nodded, casting Savannah a quick look of gratitude before continuing.

"More details, I have. Though, exact location, I do not know. Hundreds strong, his army is. Follows them, death does. Attacked barghest, they have. Lamia, I also saw."

Distracted by a noise from just beyond the walls, she turned towards the entrance just in time to see it open. Another centaur stepped inside.

"I thought I told you not to interrupt us," Irontail shouted.

"Yes, sir, but…"

"But," a gentle and powerful voice continued, "I thought you might want to know of my presence."

The Avatar stepped inside from behind the centaur, followed by a familiar lamia and…a human?

Tel' Shira jerked her body around, looking the unknown creature over with cautious eyes. Yes, it appeared to be human, but she got a strange sensation there was more to him than she could tell. As he cleared the entryway, another followed behind - a troll.

"Avatar?" Irontail stepped forward, his voice conveying clear surprise. "We were not expecting you."

"No, but I have many eyes and ears. I knew you could benefit from my presence. My companions and I return from a false lead regarding Yezurkstal. To my understanding, you have a more substantial idea of where he might be."

Not sure how to respond, Tel' Shira remained silent.

"Return to your post," Irontail commanded, continuing towards the Avatar.

The other centaur looked to the Avatar then back to his chieftain before nodding and exiting the room. Tel' Shira noted both the lamia and human seemed uncomfortable, remaining close to one-another and standing to the left of the entry. The troll looked more relaxed, even though he was ducking down to avoid brushing his head on the ceiling.

Savannah moved towards the Avatar as well, a certain urgency in her step.

"Tel' Shira had a vision. She was just explaining how she saw Yezurkstal building an army. According to her vision, there is another attack happening soon, but she is unsure where. Perhaps you can help her sort it out and we can prepare a defense?"

The Avatar nodded and looked around the room. After a few seconds, he looked right at Tel' Shira.

Taking a gulp of air, Tel' Shira stood perfectly still. She hated the attention as it was, but the Avatar was a being of Evorath herself. Last year, she had been comfortable keeping her distance when possible. Now she was expected to share her vision with Him?

He walked towards her, each step a resounding thud. His presence was overwhelming, the full power of the forest at his disposal. With all that power wrapped in such a humble body, it gave Tel' Shira a greater appreciation for hidden strength. She held her breath as he took that last step and stood before her.

"If you would allow me," he began, his voice mighty but gentle, "I would like to see your vision for myself."

She stood silent; her throat constricted. After a few moments, she was able to push her voice through.

"Possible, is that?"

"Indeed. I will lay my hand upon the base of your skull and see what you see. Close your eyes, relax, and think about the vision. Focus on every detail. Even the smallest one is important."

Tel' Shira took a deep breath and closed her eyes, trying to tune out everything around her. She had learned how to focus on the battlefield many decades ago. Tapping into that experience, she tried to tune everything else out. Through her focus, she almost didn't notice the Avatar placing his hand on her head.

She thought about the vision she had, of Yezurkstal, the demons, and city they attacked. It flashed through her mind, like she was experiencing it all again. There was pain, destruction, death. Then it all came to an end.

She opened her eyes, that feeling of discomfort gone from her body. Lifting his hand from her head, the Avatar wore a stoic expression. Tel' Shira had to imagine she had a look of horror on her own face, but somehow this manifestation of Evorath was able to remain calm.

"Well," Oakleg barked. "What did you see? When and where will the attack be?"

The Avatar turned towards the old centaur, maintaining the same blank expression.

"I believe your presence here is no longer required."

It felt like a mountain was pushing down on the room, the air growing dense as everyone stood in silence. Tel' Shira didn't move, using her eyes to glance between the Avatar, Oakleg, and Irontail. It looked like neither of the centaur knew how to respond. The Avatar didn't seem to care.

"Please, the three of you can leave," he said still facing the elders. "We need to plan our next move, and none of you have anything to contribute."

Quartzhand stomped his front legs, stepping forward to look down at the Avatar.

"Now listen here boy. I will not be spoken to by some creature in that way. You will not tell us what to do in our own tribe. We run this place, not you."

In a flash, Irontail charged in front of the elder and shoved him back. The older centaur flared his nostrils as he regained his footing.

"I am in charge here actually. And how dare you speak to the Avatar of Evorath in such a way? We are all supposed to be followers of Her will and here you are, actively questioning it! As he commanded, depart from my hall!"

Irontail stomped forward with these last words, pointing towards the door, and staring at the three elders. Tel' Shira took a step away from everything, using her peripheral vision to see that both Artimus and Savannah had stepped back as well.

The elders all looked to one another in fear. Oakleg wobbled even more as he started for the door and the other two followed behind. As before, the exit opened to allow them passage through and closed as they left.

With the elders out of the room, the tension seemed less pronounced. The Avatar continued to the table, examining the map. Tel' Shira looked around, exchanging glances with Irontail and the two elves. After a few moments' hesitation, they all proceeded to the table. The troll joined them as well, hunched over to avoid brushing the ceiling.

As the Avatar examined the map, everyone remained silent. Tel' Shira tried to tune out the noise of everyone's breathing, shifting her stance, and looking at the map as if she had any idea where the Avatar was looking. Everyone else seemed trapped in the awkward silence, so why should she try to break it?

After about a minute, the Avatar broke that silence.

"The next target will be here," he said pointing to an unmarked area to the south of Lake Algarath. "Over the past year, both the barghest and lamia have built up strongholds to the south. Your vision showed the destruction of the barghest, which has already occurred. It also showed an attack on this lamia stronghold."

The Avatar looked up from the map, glancing back at the lamia in his party for a moment before looking at all those gathered around.

"We must make haste. Barghest in Erathal are on the brink of extinction. If we don't stop this, the lamia will be too."

Tel' Shira cursed silently.

She knew her vision was important. If her people had just trusted her, they would have some real chance at stopping this. But how could this small group stand against the legions she had witnessed in her vision? Irontail had the same concern.

"What are we supposed to do?" he asked holding his arms wide. "Even if I could spare the entire might of Dumner, I have but a few dozen warriors and druids. Tel' Shira mentioned that there were hundreds of demons and other dark creatures. How can we make a dent in that?"

The Avatar nodded.

"Alone, you cannot. But Evorath gives strength to those who trust her."

Silence again.

Artimus decided to break it.

"OK, but what does that even mean? We have zero support from our government, zero support from the Felite Confederacy, and just a small number of usable soldiers from Dumner. I understand how powerful you are and I trust Evorath knows what she is doing, but what do you expect from us? Against a few dozen foes, maybe we can mount a defense. But, hundreds? Unless that lamia village is full of able-bodied fighters, I don't see things going too well."

"Trust me and we will know victory."

Once again, no one seemed sure how to respond. Tel' Shira even had her doubts. Yes, she trusted the Avatar and his might, but even he could not best an army of that size, could he?

The Avatar turned and walked towards the exit. He glanced back at the lamia and strange humanoid, shaking his head.

"Prepare yourselves for battle and wait for me in Dumner. Watch over my disciples. I will return soon with answers."

Stepping into the wall, he vanished.

Chapter 26

Dumner Village
5 Neglur, 1087 MT

Irontail picked up another carrot, looking it over and pondering about all the turbulence of late. The elders had questioned his takeover as Chieftain enough as it was, but these last couple of weeks had raised tensions higher than ever. There was a divide within him between the old centaur traditions and his own ways of leadership.

The Dumner tribe had a history of leadership that ruled by power first. Warriors like Goldenchest put the fear of Evorath in the rest of the tribe, suggesting their rule was somehow predestined by heavenly power. Since Irontail could never accept this concept, he approached leadership differently. He invited people to question his commands and make suggestions. And why shouldn't he?

None of the elders would have been willing to seek out outcast centaur and invite them into the tribe as Irontail had. Without his rule over this past year, Dumner would be one of the smallest tribes in all the forest. He demonstrated there was power outside brute force and believed this sort of leadership would help the centaur survive.

Of course, the old ways always seemed to show up in times of trouble. Getting the elders to first accept new tribe members from the outside was a challenge. Now, he had to get the elders to appreciate the authority of the Avatar. With humans being sucked into the picture and Yezurkstal building up an army, it seemed this would become another one of those pivotal moments. Without the elders' support, he would have trouble keeping order in the tribe.

"So, what do think Irontail?"

Irontail looked up, shifting his glance around the table to figure out who has asked the question. It was a masculine voice that dragged him from his thoughts, so perhaps Artimus?

"What do I think about what?" he asked, looking at the elf.

"I was saying that the elders seem a bit testy. Do you think you have your tribe's support if you travel with the Avatar or will they cause more trouble?"

Placing the carrot back on the table, he shook his head.

"I can't say for sure, but I don't think they will cause too much trouble. Most of Dumner believes the Avatar to be Evorath's champion. If I am following him into battle, they will support my move. The elders are just stuck in the past and they miss the lie that their edicts are somehow infallible."

"Trust your judgment, do the other centaur?" Tel' Shira interjected from across the table before sipping from her goblet of water.

"If you mean my best warriors, then yes. That much, I can be sure of. Also, considering the fact that we have more new members in the past year than we do old ones, I think we are on the right path. I am confident that Dumner will continue to grow under my leadership."

He lied about this last part.

"Good, that is. Wise, your leadership must be. Significantly grown, the village has."

"Yes," Savannah added in between bites of a pepper. "Dumner is hardly recognizable since you took over. I wish all leaders could follow your example."

Irontail nodded, accepting the compliment with pride. He took a bite of the carrot, but as he chewed, he thought more on Savannah's words. Once again, he failed to pay attention to the conversation. The troll, Oogmut, was saying something.

"...but I just wish they could follow your example."

Irontail turned to Oogmut and forced a smile. Assuming he was talking about his own people, Irontail nodded.

"Yes, that would be helpful. I hope to unify the rest of the centaur tribes someday. I think everyone would benefit from the idea that we are better together. Maybe one day, we will all be unified in one big city without the racial divides."

Oogmut laughed. "That would seem an impossibility in the current climate, but it would be most welcome by me."

"But," Irontail continued turning back to Savannah, "what do you mean about leaders following my example? Aren't you happy with the direction Erathal is going? You helped teach me the value of cooperation and it seemed that your Chancellor was very much on board with that leadership strategy. Has something changed?"

Artimus shifted in his chair, picking up a peach and biting into it. Savannah sat upright and crossed her arms.

"Just remember, honesty is an integral part of leadership. Sometimes, the reasons you do something are as important as what you do. Recently, Artimus and I discovered some startling news about the Chancellor. We'll leave it at that for now."

She put on a smile and put her hands on the table. Turning to Casandra, she shifted the conversation.

"So, Casandra, it's been over a month since I saw you last. How are your studies going?"

Casandra smiled.

"Things have been great. The Avatar is the perfect teacher. I mean, don't get me wrong. You were definitely a great friend and teacher, but training with the Avatar is like getting direct access to Evorath herself. He's helping me to really understand the extent of my powers. I still have a lot to learn, but I am really happy with my progress."

She turned towards the strange human-looking fellow, Zelag.

"I've also gotten to meet some really unique and interesting people. Like Zelag here. I'm afraid his story is tragic, but you wouldn't believe the gifts he possesses."

Zelag hunched over, keeping his eyes pointed towards the floor and arms crossed.

"I think we'd all be lying if we didn't admit some curiosity towards you Zelag," Artimus said after finishing a bite of his peach. "Are you one of the humans who Yezurkstal summoned here?"

Irontail pondered this question as well. But he could tell there was more to this being. Zelag was no human. He had a sort of primal energy about him. Since he didn't seem interested in responding himself, Irontail decided to cut in.

"You're not human, are you Zelag? I think you are something of Evorath. Perhaps that gift of yours will tell us more. What is it that Casandra suggests is so impressive?"

Zelag kept his gaze down and mumbled under his breath.

"What was that?" Irontail asked.

Casandra reached over and patted Zelag on the shoulder.

"Come on. These are the Avatar's friends. You see Artimus there?" She pointed to Artimus.

"He rescued me after Yezurkstal burned down my village. And his wife, Savannah," she continued pointing to Savannah.

"She is a powerful druid and helped restore me to health. After the big battle last year, I also spent some time studying with her while the Avatar was busy. And Irontail," she finished pointing back at Irontail.

"He is one of few leaders that the Avatar ever communicates with directly. We're all friends here and everyone wants you to be comfortable."

Zelag looked around the room. Though Irontail was still a bit unsure, he was willing to give this man the benefit of the doubt. If the Avatar took him on as a student, there had to be something special about him. Still, Irontail's warrior upbringing couldn't help but cringe at this apparent weakness. What kind of person just hunched over and mumbled the answer to a question?

After a few more seconds, Zelag finally loosened his arms and looked at Irontail. He still avoided eye contact.

"You are right. I have nothing to do with those horrible humans. They destroyed my world and took away everything I had. They are monsters. I just wear the face of one of those monsters because the Avatar insists I continue training in this form."

His voice was pitiful. It was deep pitched, but hoarse, as if something was blocking his throat. As Zelag sniffled and looked down, Irontail realized it was because he was on the verge of tears. How pathetic.

No, not pathetic. Irontail paused for a moment and pushed this thought aside. This creature was showing great strength. Irontail thought of the pain he felt when Dumner was attacked last year. Then he imagined how much more painful that would have been if he had been the only survivor. Holding back his tears was perhaps the best way for Zelag to demonstrate the strength he had within him. But that couldn't possibly be the "gift" Casandra had referred to.

"Wear the face. Meant by this, what is?" Tel' Shira leaned forward with this question, a hint of real intrigue visible on her face.

Zelag sniffled, keeping his gaze downward. Casandra must have taken this as an invitation to speak on his behalf.

"He can change his form to match anything in nature. He takes on both the shape and physical qualities of whatever he transforms into. Apparently, it's a trait reserved to his people, the Preajin."

Irontail didn't know how to respond. He had never heard tales of such a species, and he couldn't figure out why it was such a special gift. If he could take on any form, why would he choose to maintain the form of a human -especially after they massacred his village?

"I've read about the Preajin in one of the ancient texts," Savannah said after a mere second of silence. She wore a pensive expression, twirling her hair with her left and tapping her fingers on the table.

"But, that was one I accepted as a myth. According to what I read, your people were born alongside the dryads."

Irontail heard the door creek open, drawing his attention away from the conversation. A strange female floated in, her orange and black butterfly wings revealing her as some sort of sprite or other woodland spirit.

Irontail began to turn, dropping a carrot and clenching his fist. Just as he prepared to attack, another figure followed her in - the Avatar.

-=-=-=-=-=-=-=-=-

Zelag hated this.

Why did the Avatar have to leave him behind with all these people? The centaur smelled funny, the felite talked funny, and the elves' auras looked funny. The different energies swirling around them made it impossible to know what they were feeling. Then there was Oogmut, who Zelag still did not fully trust. At least Casandra was here.

Still hunched over, Zelag recognized the centaur's voice.

"You're not human, are you Zelag? I think you are something of Evorath. Perhaps that gift of yours will tell us more. What is it that Casandra suggests is so impressive?"

Keeping his eyes downcast, he muttered under his breath.

"More of Evorath than you are for sure."

"What was that?" the centaur pressed.

Zelag felt Casandra's hand fall on his shoulder.

"Come on. These are the Avatar's friends. You see…"

Casandra kept talking, but he was not interested in listening. He did not know why conversing with these creatures was important. But, if Casandra wanted him to interact, he would interact. Zelag lifted his head and glanced around the room. All eyes were on him.

"You are right. I have nothing to do with those horrible humans. They destroyed my world and took away everything I had. They are monsters. I just wear the face of one of those monsters because the Avatar insists I continue training in this form."

Zelag looked back down and hunched over, trying to push memories of the slaughter out of his head. He sniffled, the urge to cry rearing its head once more. Did the Avatar expect him to become friends with this strange group?

Casandra responded to one of the felite's questions. Perhaps this was just another strange lesson. Maybe he ought to pay better attention. The elf was speaking now, so he glanced up towards her, keeping his shoulders hunched.

"But that was one I accepted as a myth. According to what I read, your people were born alongside the dryads."

As she said this, Zelag felt a familiar presence from just outside. Rubbing his nose and stifling another sniffle, he turned towards the source. Immediately recognizing the auras, Zelag jumped to his feet.

The sylphid floated into the room, followed by the Avatar. The usual splendor of the Avatar shone through with a bright green aura, but the sylphid appeared troubled, a dull gray glow emanating from her skin.

"We are glad you have returned," the centaur exclaimed, trotting towards the Avatar.

Zelag shot him a quick glare and then turned his attention back to the Avatar. He walked over beside the sylphid and stood, his arms hanging by his side. The Avatar took a moment to speak, looking around at everyone first.

"Continue eating if you must. I have troubling news to share. First, let me introduce Aeria. She has been performing reconnaissance for me. Aeria, please tell them what you have found."

Zelag glanced over at Casandra, who had joined him in the corner. Her eyes were bright, but she had a certain dread in her aura, a dark tint blocking her eagerness.

"The monster has already wiped out the last barghest stronghold. I went there this morning to find the place in ruin. The walls were destroyed, buildings damaged, and blood stains lining the streets. But, whatever he did, he didn't leave anything else behind. There were no dead there at all. No demons, no barghest, no nothing. Aside from the destruction and the blood, one might think that all of the barghest simply abandoned the place."

"What do you mean there were no bodies?" the troll asked standing up. "What could Yezurkstal have possibly done with the dead?"

"That's the more troubling part," the sylphid continued. "It seems he is using some sort of necromancy to control them. I followed a trail of blood and body parts out of the city and was able to track them west. It seems this blight has tapped into profane powers and is bringing corpses back from the dead. But that is still not the worst of it.

"We continued to the west and found an entire settlement being built. It seems that he is building up a city just south of Lake Algarath. He already has various buildings constructed and a substantial wall. Of course, I didn't expect that to be trouble for our Avatar. Apparently, I was wrong about that."

Zelag could feel the tension building in the room. Looking around, he could see this fear showing through in everyone's aura. But he still had a question he needed answered.

"What of the humans? Does he control them too?"

The sylphid turned to Zelag and shook her head. "Not any more than he controls the barghest. They are his undead servants."

Before anyone could ask another question, the Avatar spoke up.

"Worry about this later. For now, I must tell you this. I cannot enter Yezurkstal's city. There is a special barrier around it that prevents me from getting too close or from seeing inside. I believe he is serving a goddess of his own now, Frogatha."

How could that be possible? Were there really beings as powerful as Evorath herself? Zelag's progenitor had always taught him that Evorath was the creator of everything. But, if that was not true, then why would the Avatar say otherwise?

"Hold on," Savannah shouted. "Frogatha is just a myth! A story told to little elf children to scare them into behaving. You're telling me that she is real, and she can overpower Evorath?"

"Yes, and no. She is real, but she could never overpower Evorath. Evorath is a bringer of life and verdant growth. Frogatha is a bringer of death and decay. Life always wins. But, I cannot enter into Frogatha's domain."

Artimus slapped his hand down on the table.

"So, we know where Yezurkstal is making camp, but you cannot help us? Great! We cannot hope to overpower him at his own home. Even if we could get all the felite, elvish, and centaur armies to unite, we still wouldn't be able to take him down, especially not if he has the defensive position."

"The lamia, what about?" Tel' Shira asked stepping forward. Despite the apprehension in the room, she kept a stable aura, a soft white glow emanating from around her form. It was quite surprising.

"Their village is south of Yezurkstal's camp," the Avatar replied. "Since we cannot pass through without alerting Yezurkstal, I have arranged other travel options. Your top priority is to relocate the lamia. I will be traveling alone to stop Yezurkstal."

"But you just said you couldn't enter his camp. How are you going to stop him?" Casandra asked.

The Avatar looked to Zelag and gave him a slight grin. He then turned to the rest of those gathered.

"If he wants to keep me out, I will keep him in."

Chapter 27

Lamia Village
6 Neglur, 1087 MT

Irontail squeezed his eyes tight. Ignoring the embarrassment of this situation was bad enough but ignoring the discomfort in his stomach was almost impossible. When the Avatar had suggested an alternative means of transportation to expediate the journey, he should have known it was not centaur friendly. While the others were able to ride on the back of these wild roc, he was stuck being carried like helpless prey.

It was humiliating to be sure, but not as bad as the wind beating against his face. His stomach turned over as he forced himself to open one eyes and look down. There was a field of blue, which meant they were still over the ocean. Clasping his eyes shut again, he tried to think about something else.

It wasn't working.

The wind stung his face. It felt like he was running through a never-ending squall. As he started to descend, the unpleasant smell of sea life entered his nostrils. This only made the nausea worse. Clenching his fist, he focused on the end goal.

"We will stop him," he kept repeating in his mind.

Curious about how close they were to landing, he peaked open his eyes again. This time, he got a clear look at an open field. Green grass stretched out ahead and the hills in the distance looked to be about at the right height. Glancing down, he watched the approach.

He fought the urge to close his eyes again, preparing for the landing by taking a deep breath. His hooves were a few centimeters from the ground when he started timing his steps, hoping to make the landing as smooth as possible.

The roc let out a shriek, releasing its talons and letting Irontail fall. Pumping his legs fast, he set down in a run. With a long exhale, he slowed to a trot and came to a stop.

His eyes couldn't adapt fast enough. He stumbled; his vision blurred. Shaking his head and clenching his fists, he took a few steps before looking up and clenching his stomach. For a moment, he thought he would lose it. With another breath, he was able to hold it in.

Looking back up, he watched the other roc touch down with the rest of the party. Zelag and Casandra had ridden together on one of the larger ones, its wingspan easily 12 meters wide. The next two roc set down just behind this first one, letting Artimus and Savannah off. Tel' Shira's was the smallest of the bunch, followed by Oogmut's, which was also quite large. Last in line, the sylph touched down, her orange eyes a bit dull from the flight.

"I think I'll just walk on the way back," Irontail joked walking towards the rest of the group -his stomach still uneasy.

The others were dismounting their rides, sliding down the side as the birds kept low to the ground. As each roc was relieved of its load, they flapped their wings and took off. They were majestic creatures, launching into the air and back towards the ocean.

"All of you will be walking back," the sylph exclaimed floating forward. "Roc are not as abundant as they once were. The Avatar offered them for this, but they won't be able to carry all the lamia. We'll likely be hitching a ride on the water to cross over to safe land."

"So, the Avatar can command roc and also has some great sea creatures on his side too?" Irontail asked.

"Actually, the sea creature is a friend of mine" Oogmut interjected. "One of my good friends. He'll be thrilled to meet you all."

Irontail was ready to question this, but Savannah interrupted his thoughts.

"Shouldn't we worry about getting the lamia to safety before talking about our exit strategy?"

"Yes, I think that would be prudent," Casandra added. Her face was flushed, and voice unsteady.

She must have been a bit apprehensive about this whole mission and Irontail couldn't much blame her. If there was only one remaining centaur tribe and he had the opportunity to get them out of harm's way, he would feel the same.

"What are we waiting for then?" Artimus asked, stepping ahead of the group. "Let's get moving."

Irontail looked to the others. All of them seemed ready to follow Artimus. He paused for a moment, a bit peeved that they were not looking to him for direction. Perhaps his position as Chieftain was going to his head.

Pushing aside the annoyance, he started forward.

If Yezurkstal got to the village before they did, he would have to find a weapon. Unlike the others, he did not bring his club along. It would have been cumbersome and heavy, especially for the roc carrying him. Of course, if they were up against as large a force as the Avatar suggested, retreat would be the only option anyway.

Irontail stumbled again, tripping himself over an uneven tuft of grass. He looked around, hoping no one noticed his clumsiness. Fortunately, they all seemed engaged in their own conversations.

Artimus, Savannah, and Tel' Shira were at the front of the group. They appeared to be in conversation, but Irontail could not hear what they were discussing. Cassandra followed close behind, with Zelag jogging after her. She seemed to be in a hurry, and he didn't seem willing to talk with anyone else. Irontail was next in line, pausing to regain his footing and brush some dirt from his arms.

Oogmut and Aeria passed him, having their own conversation.

"We are certain the barghest have no remaining cities. If they are dispersed, it is unlikely they will survive on Evorath for much longer."

Oogmut nodded, bringing his right hand up to his chin.

"I suppose you are right. It's really a shame."

"They have always been a foolish species," Aeria countered, contempt clear in her voice.

"That's a bit harsh, isn't it?"

Irontail continued behind them, trotting at a steady pace so he didn't appear to be butting into the conversation.

"Just as they did millennia ago, they seem destined to side with evil. Evorath is better off without their bestial impulses."

"Evorath put the barghest in her world for a reason. I would think one of your kind would accept this. I just hope this doesn't upset the balance of nature."

The sylph cackled, her high-pitched tone causing Irontail's hair to stand on end.

"Evorath should have stopped creation with my kind, or at the latest stopped with the kitsune of the east."

Rubbing his chin, Oogmut turned and looked at Irontail. "What do you think Chieftain? Do you trust Evorath?"

Irontail averted his eyes, looking down and noting the ground's gradual incline as they continued forward. He thought about his feelings on the subject, but he found more uncertainty than anything.

"I don't think I'm the best to ask," he started, still trying to come up with an intelligent answer. "I uh, I do believe Evorath had a plan, but I leave spiritual matters to the druids. I guess though, well -I trust the Avatar. And I believe he represents Evorath."

He felt extremely uncomfortable and kept his eyes downcast to avoid further scrutiny. Leading his tribe was one thing. Questioning his God was another. It just didn't seem right to express his doubts out loud. He really did trust the Avatar though, so that had to be enough, right?

"You can follow Her blindly if you like, but it is not my way. Your shaman and druids might have learned to manipulate nature, but I am a force of nature. If Evorath, as you seem to believe, is perfect, then She created me this way for a reason. So, I am meant to question Her choices."

The troll snorted, and Irontail had to hold his tongue. That sounded too much like something Goldenchest or one of the previous Dumner elders would have asserted. There was a flaw in Aria's reasoning. Though he wanted to point it out, Irontail decided to exercise his better judgment and keep his mouth shut. The troll didn't seem as worried.

"That's nonsense. Why are you following the Avatar if you don't trust him?"

"So long as we have a common interest, I will support the Avatar. You know what I have lost." Her voice cracked, her tone becoming dull and distant. "I will get revenge and I trust that the Avatar is the only one powerful enough to ensure I get it."

"Heh," Oogmut shook his head. "You may be an ancient force of nature, but your outlook is absurd. You do know that the Avatar would risk his own existence for you?"

"Yes, I do." Her voice was firm, laced with confidence.

Her response seemed to bring the conversation to a close and Irontail wasn't going to try and make it otherwise. He found this entire topic made him uncomfortable. Since they were making their way up a substantial hill, it seemed that he wouldn't need to worry about it for much longer.

Irontail had to focus to ensure his balance remained stable. Having lived his entire life in Erathal forest, he was used to flat land. This hilly terrain was not well-suited to someone of his species. He envied Aeria, who floated effortlessly up the hill as if she noticed no difference.

"Disagreements aside, it seems we are drawing near," observed Oogmut.

"That is correct," Aeria replied. "The village is located just beyond this hill."

Irontail nodded, focusing on every step he took. He hoped that traveling downhill would be easier.

-=-=-=-=-=-=-=-=-

Artimus kept his weight forward, working to ensure his balance was stable as the hill grew steeper. In his time as a hunter, he had occasionally traveled through hills, but it was never quite this steep. The incline was enough that he could feel a burn in his legs. Glancing back, he could tell Irontail was struggling to make the trek. Considering how difficult it was for a horse to make this steep a climb, he was not surprised.

His wife seemed to fall more in the middle of spectrum. Artimus could tell by her face that she was not enjoying the extra strain, but as usual she seemed content ignoring the discomfort. On the other hand, Tel' Shira looked like she was enjoying this journey. Her eyes had a certain youthful energy in them as she climbed.

"Obviously, I prefer the flat terrain of the forest, but I do appreciate the beauty of this hill. I mean, did you notice those snapdragons on the way up? They are absolutely gorgeous. In fact," Savannah continued, pointing ahead, "there's another plant worth noting. I could use some of that trillium for my garden."

She pushed ahead, a smile forming on her face as she passed Artimus.

He grinned and regarded Tel' Shira.

"What about you?" he asked. "You seem to be enjoying our hill-climbing endeavors as well."

Tel' Shira looked at him and smiled. Though she had joined Savannah and him on more than a few leisure adventures over the past year, he was quite certain this was the happiest he had ever seen her.

"Climb mountains, as a child, I used to. To the eastern Runeturks, my mother would take me. Remember fondly, the terrain, I do."

Artimus smiled.

"It's nice to see you can appreciate that, even with the imminent danger. I guess we all could use a change of scenery from the forest. But I must agree with my wife. I wouldn't want to live anywhere with such terrain."

"Little things, time to appreciate, we must all take."

Artimus nodded and looked back towards his wife, who was returning with a handful of white flowers.

"I'm afraid I came ill-equipped for foraging," she exclaimed holding them out. "Would you please hold onto these for me?"

Artimus extended his hand and accepted the flowers. Reaching to his left, he unlatched a small satchel and deposited them. Clasping it shut, he focused back ahead.

They were nearing the top of the hill and the terrain leveled out. The grass was a deeper green at this height, but there were far fewer flowers. As they approached the peak, Artimus listened for any signs of activity. Like the rest of the climb, there was a strange absence of any animal life. In fact, he realized he hadn't even noticed one insect or bird on the way up.

Looking back, he waited for the others to arrive. Savannah and Tel' Shira joined him first, followed by Cassandra and Zelag. Oogmut, Irontail, and Aeria all trailed a few meters behind. As they neared, he turned back and surveyed the area ahead.

It looked like the journey downhill was a bit more gradual. Like the climb up, he could spot various flower and limited plant life. But, it was what he couldn't spot that was peculiar. According to the Avatar, this was where the lamia village was supposed to be. Could the Avatar have been mistaken?

"I don't mean to raise the alarm, but are we sure this is where the attack is supposed to take place?"

Artimus pointed towards the empty valley, looking to those who were gathered for confirmation. Tel' Shira looked the most confused, her cheerful energy fading faster than one of Artimus's arrows soaring through the sky. Cassandra shared a similar expression of shock. Savannah wore a different expression, one that Artimus recognized as contemplative.

"What are you thinking?"

She twirled her fingers through her hair and kept glaring at the valley. After a few seconds of silence, she looked up.

"Dumner uses a special spell that cloaks it from those unwelcome there. Perhaps the lamia use a similar spell."

"Of course they do," Aeria floated between them interrupting. "Likely a much more effective barrier too. As far as *mortal species* go, the lamia are some of the most adept with their magic."

Artimus didn't much care for her tone. She seemed to stress "mortal species" as if that was some sort of handicap. From his peripherals, he detected both Irontail and Oogmut caught the inflection as well.

"Be careful talking too much to us mortals," Oogmut started, confirming at least half of Artimus's suspicion. "We might infect you with our simple ways."

"Hmph." Aeria floated ahead of the group, levitating a few meters out and looking down at the valley.

She pivoted left and right, casting her gaze across the empty valley. The rolling hills seemed barren, the stretch of grassland an unnatural green. In fact, Artimus registered as he looked closely that it seemed there was nothing down there but grass -perhaps their cloak was not as well-designed as he first thought.

Regardless of the detail the lamia took in concealing their village, Artimus was more concerned with Aeria, who had closed her eyes and began to mutter words under her breath. Even with his acute hearing, Artimus couldn't make out what she spoke. He guessed it was an ancient language anyways, so he didn't bother trying too hard.

Instead, he paid attention to the movement of her hands. Aeria swayed at the hips, her arms moving rhythmically, as if in tune to some unheard music. They flowed fluidly around her, wrists slack and fingers alternating up and down. For a moment, Artimus could feel a palpable sensation, his hair standing on end as the power from her spell pulsed outward.

In an instant, a flash of light.

Artimus held up his left, shielding his eyes. As he squinted and opened his eyes back up, he looked down upon the valley. Where there was once an empty field, there were now huts, quite like those he saw last year in Casandra's village. He also spotted gardens, the vibrant color of many flowers. Looking further, he spotted some crudely built palisades. In fact, there was even a creek running through the center of the valley.

"I suspect they will know we can see them," Aeria said lowering her arms and floating still in the air. "Perhaps Casandra should lead introductions to avoid any hostilities."

-=-=-=-=-=-=-=-=-

Casandra looked around, first to Zelag and then panning past the others in the party.

Lead the introductions? Sure, this was a village of Lamia, but she was no diplomat. Like most of her kind, Casandra was far from a social butterfly. In fact, she much preferred to keep to herself and her small community. Since losing her village, that just meant Zelag in this situation. How was she supposed to make an impression on an entire village?

As if feeling her concern, Savannah placed a hand on her shoulder.

"I think that's a wonderful idea," she began. "Casandra, I know you can do this. And, if you do need any help, I'm here with you."

Casandra smiled and looked around. Everyone seemed to be focused on her. It was an odd sensation -as if the back of her neck was abuzz. Embracing this tingling sensation, she looked ahead towards the village and locked her eyes.

She opened her mouth to say something encouraging, but the words escaped her. Uncertain what she had intended to say, she started forward. Slithering down the hill, she kept her gaze ahead. It was like the world around her faded, her eyes focused only on the village in the valley. Uncertain if the others kept up with her, she proceeded.

The descent was smooth, her body easily maneuvering down the hill and through the grass. While the village had defensive palisades surrounding its borders, she spotted a crude gate ahead. Slithering towards this gate, she glanced back to spot the others following not far behind.

Still a good ten meters out, she spotted movement from behind the gate and began to slow her approach. The wooden doors parted and two lamia passed through the slim opening. Like all her kind, these guards had ruby red hair, the sunlight bouncing across their porcelain skin and glimmering across their scaly bodies.

They were both taller than Casandra, the one on the left broad-shouldered and the one on the right slender. Both held ceremonial spears, wooden shafts imbued with various gemstones and topped with an iron point. While instinct kept her focused on the visual, she focused on her breathing and thought back to training with the Avatar.

Closing her eyes, she flared her nostrils as she exhaled. Taking a deep breath through the mouth, she stopped dead in her tracks, arms spread wide.

"Stop!" she uttered without thought. She felt it creep down her spine through her body. As the strange energy flowed through her, she recognized just how correct Aeria was. This was a much more effective barrier than the one around Dumner.

After ensuring her party has stopped, she looked ahead and locked eyes with the broad-shouldered Lamia to the left of the gate. While still about five meters out, she was well within earshot.

"My friends and I mean your village no harm. I request you allow us passage to visit with your elder."

The broad-shouldered lamia smiled, her top teeth coming through and crossing her crimson lips.

"We were uncertain whether your strange company might cloud your senses. It seems I won this bet," she muttered, glancing at her slender counterpart.

"But you mussst know; we do not abide outsiders in our village. You may enter, but your companions are not welcomed to continue forward. I trust you can explain the consequences if they insist on imposing."

She looked back to the others, confused looks on everyone's face, including Aeria.

With her arcane training, Casandra realized the Sylph likely weren't affected by the protection spell around this village, which could explain why she seemed undeterred. But, she looked to Oogmut and Savannah, the two magic users who might be a bit more in tune with these arcane powers.

Both wore blank expressions; seemingly unaware how close they were to imminent danger. Casandra hesitated for only a moment, glancing back to her companions.

"There is an invisible protection spell still in place. You should uh -" she paused for a moment, hesitant how to best explain it. "Just wait there. It's not safe for anyone but Lamia to move through this barrier."

The slenderer of the two Lamia hissed. "You're more observant than I antisssipated," she murmured.

Turning back ahead, Casandra forced a slim smile. She took a few more moments to choose her words and fought through the nervousness.

"There's no easy way to say it," she began. "A great evil is at your doorstep. And, we have come to seek audience with your elders. If you hope to survive, you'll need all the help you can get."

The two guards exchanged a quick glance before the larger one spoke. "We supposes you refer to the necromancer. We haven't felt magic like hisss ever before."

"Yes," Casandra nodded, her eyes watering. "He has destroyed many lives, including my entire village. My companion Zelag," she continued motioning to him, "also had his entire village destroyed. We've all felt great loss."

The guards once again exchanged a look, but this time they held it for a few moments. Casandra opened her mouth to continue, but the larger guard held out her hand.

"We will confer with our elders. Wait here while we do."

Without allowing her a moment to respond, the two guards slithered away.

Chapter 28

Lamia Village
6 Neglur, 1087 MT

Savannah was no stranger to discomfort, but she preferred to limit that discomfort to more arcane endeavors. Sure, she had learned to be diplomatic, but she never enjoyed being the center of attention.

Yes, she was happy to be there for Casandra, but as they proceeded through the village towards the meeting, she couldn't contain her apprehension.

It didn't take a profound sense of observation to know that everyone in the village had eyes on them. And, despite the lamia allowing them all to enter, it felt as if she could cut the tension with a knife.

Of course, it occurred to her as they walked that now was an opportune time to practice observing. In recent months, it really had become apparent that Artimus was right -most people never learned to observe. Often, taking a moment to look at the details could reveal much more about a situation than initially meets the eye.

For instance, the fact that the two original guards were joined by three others. This, coupled with the fact that all five were escorting the group suggested the lamia still did not fully trust them. In fact, as she considered this, she noted the lamia to her immediate left kept her hand hovered around her waist. Knowing that lamia favored magic over anything else, it might suggest the satchels they carried held some sort of magical implements. Either way, the way her hand hovered over the satchel had to be a sign of readiness.

Looking further around, she noted Casandra was keeping herself positioned between Zelag and another one of the lamia guards. Zelag, accordingly, seemed to be walking as close as he could behind Casandra. Whether they realized it or it was subconscious, Savannah couldn't be sure. But, those two had definitely formed a connection.

Away from the immediate party, she also observed the apparent civilians within this village. By the looks of it, this lamia settlement was considerably larger than most. There were dozens of onlookers as they made their way through the village and many of them appeared young. Keeping her eyes wide, Savannah also observed a crude system of roads and many more structures than she initially expected.

When it was all said and done, this had to be the largest settlement she had visited, aside of course from Erathal.

While she continued to look about, her thoughts were interrupted by a pleasant voice.

"Seeing anything interesting?" her husband asked.

She turned to her left with a smile. "Nothing you hadn't noticed already, I'm sure. Just surprised at how many lamia live in this village."

Artimus nodded. "I'm surprised myself. This must be one of the largest settlements on this side of the lake."

"I wouldn't be surprised if it's the absolute largest," Savannah suggested. "I've seen smaller lizock villages."

Artimus nodded and one of the lamia guards interjected.

"We've been able to grow this large because we haven't allowed outsiders to interfere. Let's hope you're ready to convince us about this necromancer, or you'll sssoon see why we have thrived so completely."

Savannah turned and forced a smile.

"I think you'll find we're not exaggerating the threat."

The lamia hissed and nodded ahead. Redirecting her attention forward, Savannah observed the large structure ahead. It was at least six meters wide -probably eight. And, from the size of the logs, this longhouse must have taken much of the village to construct. While most of the structures so far seemed to meld into their surroundings, this central structure was built more like an elf's log home.

The thatched roof had green growth coming around the sides, but aside from this the structure was clearly dead. Despite this, Savannah couldn't help but feel a bit small looking on. And, it occurred as they approached, that she hadn't considered the full politics of this village.

Would they be meeting with a single leader, or with an assembly? Were there any other cultural considerations she should look to observe? It was too late to worry about this now.

The two original guards went to either side of the structure's entrance, the one on the right pulling on the door to allow for entry. Aeria continued forward, followed by the rest of the party.

Not wanting to be near the front, Savannah made sure to pause and allow everyone else but Artimus to enter. With a brief glance and quick nod from her husband, she proceeded forward and allowed him to take the rear.

Entering the longhouse, Savannah did her best to capture all her surroundings. It seemed the primary method of lighting came from torches along the walls. Otherwise, the walls were sparsely decorated, the simple log construction left bare. The floors were left bare, while notably flatter and uniform, the feel of dirt must have been easier for the lamia to navigate than more traditional wood flooring.

She noted across the entrance on the right that a couple lamia stood talking. Judging by the size and position of this longhouse, she assumed it served as some sort of governmental office. But, the layout was certainly unlike any elvish design.

A long table stretched nearly the entire width of the room, no chairs in sight. It appeared this structure was even longer than wide, with a good three meters between the table and the entrance and another four or five meters before the back wall. And, this wall appeared to connect to another wing, with the three doorways. Both the left and right doors were closed, with the center left open and leading to a hallway. The party continued to follow the guards around the table and towards the left door.

No one spoke as they proceeded forward, but Savannah caught the conversing lamia glancing their way as they moved forward. As they reached the doorway, the guards stopped and turned to the party.

"Please wait here. The council will see you momentarily," spoke the guard on the left.

Without delay, she opened the door and slithered inside.

Savannah looked to her husband to speak, but as she opened her mouth, she heard the door creak back open.

"The counsel will receive you now."

Artimus motioned for Savannah to continue forward, and she nodded in appreciation. Once again, she stayed behind the rest of the party and continued into the final room.

As she passed the threshold to this room, she was immediately reminded of Erathal's own throne room. Rather than the simple log exterior, this room had the walls covered over with some sort of mortar. This gave the walls a surprisingly smooth appearance and after looking for a few moments, it reminded Savannah of the outside of an eggshell.

Beyond this smooth, painted wall, the room was also adorned with its share of decorations. Tapestries hung along the left wall, with an intricately carved window allowing natural light to enter the structure. The window itself was made from stained glass, the design resembling a lamia holding a scepter and wearing a crown. Glancing up, Savannah spotted more posh decorating, with a golden chandelier providing additional light for the area.

Up ahead, the room had marble steps leading to an elevated platform. This platform was arranged with a center pedestal elevated above and two shorter pedestals on either side. It was here that Savannah got a better sense of the village's hierarchy.

Three lamia stood at the top of these pedestals, but it was clear the idea of a counsel was more of a platitude. The center pedestal itself was more generously decorated, with garnets set running along the entire exterior. The floor of this center stage appeared to be made from an animal fur of some variety, dyed red. Meanwhile, the pedestals on either side had but a single garnet in the center of them. And it was made from the same marble as the steps leading up to them.

If this delineation weren't enough, the three lamia standing on these pedestals reinforced the clear hierarchy. Both lamia on the left and right wore basic tiaras and simple, green gowns. The center lamia wore a full crown -the center garnet inset had to be the largest Savannah had ever seen. She also wore a flowing red cloak.

The two guards had taken their position on either side of the chamber. And, bringing her attention to her party, Savannah noted the others had taken a staggered approach and formed a half circle before the stairs. Before moving to join them, Savannah cast a glance to her husband.

He smiled and nodded, giving her the reassurance she needed. Standing side-by-side with her husband, she remained behind the rest of the party as Aeria spoke up.

"Greetings great Mistress. We are honored to be granted entry into your abode. If I may introduce myself and my allies. I am Aeria, renowned Sylphid, the Lightbringer of Erathal, and trusted advisor to Evorath's living Avatar. I have brought with me Oogmut of the trolls, Irontail of the centaur, Tel' Shira of the felite, Artimus and Savannah of the elves, Casandra of the lamia, and Zelag of the Preajin. They represent their respective tribes and have banded together to fight the evil of Death."

Savannah couldn't quite put into words the expression on her husband's face as these words were spoken. What happened to the inferiority of mere mortals? Apparently Aeria was capable of tact when the occasion required it.

The lamia Mistress seemed to be gathering a response, her face pensive. She cast her gaze across the party before responding.

"We welcome your presence great Sylphid Aeria. We are Mistress Pellera. Any friend of yours is also welcome within our hall. The threat of Death, however, we do not recognize."

She paused for a moment, her tongue darting forth as she shook her head.

"Our borders are protected by more powerful magic than any of your tribesss. Even if He knew where our village was, Death would stand no chance of breaching our defensesss."

Savannah looked around, holding her tongue in the hopes that someone else would reply first. Seeing none of her party taking the initiative, she opened her mouth to speak. But, as she did, Casandra slithered towards the steps and spoke.

"Mistress Pellera. Please permit me to speak."

She paused until Pellera nodded, her face stoic.

"You must have heard storiesss of the destruction Yezurkstal has wrought. He laid waste to my entire village, decimated the Dumner tribe to the north, destroyed most of the major barghest villages, and who knowsss what other damage he has caused. Where he goes, death followsss. There is a reason the storiesss aren't of a Hájje leading an army. He is the embodiment of Death. If he comes for your village and you are not prepared, you will not survive the encounter."

Savannah could feel the tension in the room building, as if she could cut the air with a knife. After what seemed like an eternity of silence, Pellera's lips curled into a faint smile and she nodded.

"You speak boldly for such a young one. We feel the passion in your words and sense your belief in them. While we are not convinced, we will heed your warnings. Accepting Death is inevitable, what is it your party suggestsss?"

The whole party exchanged glances, the air losing its weight. Casandra pressed closer to the stage.

"We mussst take the fight to him."

Chapter 29

Hájje Settlement
6 Neglur, 1087 MT

Every time he used a new spell, Yezurkstal could feel his power expanding. Though many of these spells tested his limits, he found a little practice made things easier and easier. Despite his usual aptitude, getting used to controlling so many undead was still a bit foreign.

But he couldn't deny the thrill he got from having control over so many live- rather, over so many undead creatures. If he could exercise his will this completely over his wives and children, he could truly make the changes in Evorath that it so desperately needed. But alas, as loyal as they may be, undead were not suitable in the grand scheme of things. They were just pawns. Regardless, he couldn't deny the allure of it -the pure control over another creature. Evorath needed more of this.

The sensation of seeing through so many eyes at once was more than he ever imagined. He could almost feel the ground each of them walked on. Hundreds of these so-called "humans," dozens of barghest, and an array of miscellaneous creatures he had reanimated along the way. Each added to the might of his army, and each would prove an asset as he continued his conquest.

Sitting in his new southeastern watchtower, Yezurkstal led his legion through the hills. His gaze was fixed on the village ahead. Using a seeing spell, he had located a sizeable lamia village on his doorstep. And, if he was going to create a kingdom worthy of his rule, his borders would need to expand.

With only a few lamia already in his undead army, he couldn't help but be excited about the prospect of adding more. Of course, if he were to really expand his reach across Evorath, he would need more than his own might. Or even the might of many hundreds of soldiers. And that's what made this next conquest so exciting.

To fully realize his necromancy, he would need to test himself. Could he win a battle without even being on the battlefield?

Absolutely!

Today would be the day he made a massive shift in his approach to conquest. The reality -he could not possibly lead every advance. But, with a reanimated army and competent commanders, he could shape the world.

The images started to flash through his mind.

Once his children reached the right age, he'd start teaching them all his craft. Each of them would be loyal to a fault -obeying his every command. They would lead his armies beyond the shores of Erathal and throughout all the continents of Evorath.

He'd wipe out the centaur from the forest, the dwarves from the mountains, and the merfolk from the sea. And this was just the beginning.

His whole body vibrated with excitement, a sense of accomplishment and contentment filling his soul. But, as he gazed ahead with his third eye, beyond the sight line of his undead army, this feeling quickly faded.

It seemed the lamia were aware of his approach.

There they were, well outside the borders of their village. Not only were there well over 100 lamia headed his way, but it seemed the same pesky elves were getting involved again. He recognized the ranger and the druid from last time year, along with a troll, felite, centaur and…was that another sylph?

Those evil elves and their rotten interference. How they found out about his attack, he could not be sure. But, without the element of surprise he might lose the advantage.

His army still outnumbered this approaching force, but they were unproven. Perhaps his best move would be to take some demons and lead the charge himself.

Yes, that was the only solution.

Sending out a command to stop the undead legion's advance, Yezurkstal stood up. It took him a moment to reorient to his surroundings, a wave of dizziness sweeping through. It faded as quickly as it came and cracking his knuckles he turned towards the ladder.

Yezurkstal slid down the length of the ladder, landing with a thud on the floor beneath. Perhaps he could have softened the landing a bit more. Ignoring the modicum of pain in his knees, he started back towards the barracks. With fist clenched about the hilt of his sword, his march was interrupted by a bell that rang out.

In constructing the walls for his new city, he had three watchtowers set into the outer east wall. In the short time since construction, only one of the towers had a bell installed. Which meant this was coming from the central tower.

Without delay, Yezurkstal turned and sprinted towards the tower. What else could possibly go wrong?

Halfway to the tower, a demon swooped down and landed just a few paces ahead.

"Report!" Yezurkstal barked.

"Someone is approaching the gates. By his appearance, we believe it is the Avatar you warned us about." The demon's voice was raspy and Yezurkstal noted his voice falter as he mentioned 'Avatar'.

Yezurkstal's skin felt as if it was on fire, his mind racing as he clenched his jaw.

Taking a deep breath, he sent out a final command to his zombie army: *stand your ground and destroy anything living that comes your way.*

"Get all available demons to the eastern gate," Yezurkstal spat at the demon as he sprinted towards the gate.

He couldn't hear if the demon had responded. Everything around him seemed to be muted. There was nothing in that moment but the pounding of his chest and the heat of his skin. He seethed with anger and contempt.

Nearing the gate, he flung his right hand forward. Propelling a bolt of black energy to the portcullis control, he willed the gate open. A few seconds more, the wind rushing through his hair…he slipped through just under portcullis as it rose.

There he was, the Avatar. And what audacity he had.

The Avatar stood less than ten meters outside the gate, his arms spread wide and head tilted back. What a fool.

Yezurkstal didn't slow his approach, continuing in a headlong sprint and drawing his sword to strike the abomination.

Infusing the blade with necrotic energy, he swung the blade overhead.

Yezurkstal shrieked as his stroke fell. But, it didn't hit it's mark. It was like striking solid stone. A green field of energy coalesced around the Avatar, his blade bouncing off harmlessly.

The air left his lungs as he staggered back. His hands vibrated in pain as he barely kept his grip on the sword. While he attempted to regain his balance, the Avatar cast his gaze down.

Yezurkstal felt frozen in place as he locked eyes with the Avatar. He held his sword overhead, unable to redirect the blade back at his foe. All the heat of his anger and rage was replaced with a cold tingling.

"You have been a blight on this land for too long," the Avatar spoke, his eyes locked on Yezurkstal's.

Yezurkstal attempted to move, but it seemed as if his entire body were stuck in place by some invisible force. He couldn't even close his eyes. Trying his best to pull in magic from around him, he realized even this ability was stifled.

"How are you doing this?" Yezurkstal asked, his voice raspy.

"Death has no power over Life. I come with a mission from Evorath herself. While I may not excise you from this land, I can keep you contained. Without life to take, you will wither away."

As he spoke these words, it seemed the hold on Yezurkstal loosened. He could see green energy seeping from every pore of the Avatar. This energy flowed as a river, running both left and right and wrapping around the walls of Yezurkstal's new settlement.

Just a little more.

Yezurkstal pulled from his power reserves, calling upon the dark energy within his heart and soul. With all his willpower, he was able to close to his eyes and focus this power.

Letting out a primal scream, Yezurkstal forced himself to move. He pulled the blade away and opened his eyes to attempt another strike.

It was hopeless.

Both hands grasping the sword tightly, he made a forward slash. But, before the blade could strike its mark, the Avatar thrust his right hand forward. He struck Yezurkstal palm-first in the chest.

Once again, Yezurkstal gasped as he was thrust back. His feet dragging through the ground, he found himself back within the gates of his settlement.

"Your living body will never step foot outside these walls," the Avatar stated plainly.

He held his arms wide once again. The green energy had formed a barrier for as far as Yezurkstal could see. It even rose overhead, coating the sky above.

How could this be happening?

Opening his mouth to protest, Yezurkstal watched in defeat as the portcullis closed, landing with a thud before him.

The green energy seemed to dissipate as the Avatar lowered his arms. He held Yezurkstal's gaze for just a moment more.

Without another word, the Avatar turned and walked away.

-=-=-=-=-=-=-=-

East of Lake Algarath
6 Neglur, 1087 MT

Zelag glanced back, still in awe by the number of lamia warriors the village had produced. It was like gazing into a sea of crimson, an entire people united for a single cause.

If things went according to plan, Zelag understood he would not have to face Death himself. But there was a pit in his stomach, a palpable biproduct of his fear. It was Yezurkstal's fault -all of it.

And while he was getting used to movement in this human form, Zelag shifted his gaze to his own feet. This form was a constant reminder of those who slaughtered his people. He was alone in the world because of them. If not for Yezurkstal bringing this evil into the world, he would be back at home training under his progenitor.

Still, as he marched forth with this party, there was another feeling. He just couldn't quite place it.

No one could replace his fellow Preajin, his progenitor most of all. And yet…he was no longer alone.

Just like him, Casandra had lost her village to Death. She was his new family. Tel' Shira, Irontail, Artimus, and Savannah. They treated her as family too.

That must have been what this sensation was telling him. The slight tingling in his neck and the tightening in his chest.

Everyone was united under the cause of Life. He was part of the family of Evorath and together with his allies he would get revenge for his fallen Preajin.

Continuing his march alongside his new family, Zelag knew in that moment that he still had purpose.

-=-=-=-=-=-=-=-=-

Artimus strode forward, trailing just a few feet behind Irontail, Tel' Shira, and Oogmut. He and Savannah marched in stride, occasionally exchanging a glance or nervous smile as they made their way. Behind them, Casandra, Zelag, and Aria marched, followed in the rear by a force of nearly 200 lamia mages.

They had marched in relative silence for the last twenty minutes, putting a good couple kilometers between them and the village. Having passed up the hill and through some lightly wooded ground, they continued to move into more open terrain. The trees becoming more infrequent and opening into flatland.

Despite his position, Artimus kept his eyes trained forward, looking for any sign of the enemy. He squinted towards the horizon. Was that just another hill in the distance, or?

"Approach the enemy, we do," spoke Tel' Shira breaking the silence.

Artimus turned to Savannah and exchanged a nod. She returned the gesture and slowed her stride as he trotted to catch up with the leading three members.

Slipping in between Irontail and Tel' Shira, Artimus kept his gaze forward.

"Well, I'll concede that bet. It looks like you can see farther than I can." Artimus smiled and looked to Tel' Shira.

"Disadvantage, you were always at. Best eyesight in Evorath, the felite have."

Irontail snorted. "You two are about to engage in battle with an undead army that outnumbers us two to one and you're betting on who can see further ahead? May Evorath help us."

Oogmut shook his head and pointed forward.

"If the Avatar did his part, we're just fighting a few hundred mindless zombies. I reckon a bit of levity prior to that fight is warranted."

"Odd, this is," Tel' Shira stated, tilting her head to the right and slowing her stride. "Stopped, the enemy has."

"How can you tell?" Irontail asked.

"Still, they have become," Tel' Shira replied.

Artimus locked eyes with Savannah and exchanged a nod. Holding up his right fist and pivoting towards the rest of the army, he shouted.

"Halt the advance!"

The three leading members stopped and turned about.

"It makes sense to hold back until we can scout ahead and get a sense of what's happening," Artimus began.

Oogmut opened his mouth, but Savannah spoke up first.

"It's possible this means the Avatar succeeded. Perhaps in containing Yezurkstal, he's also cut off the connection to his army."

Artimus nodded, looking to Oogmut to confirm whether he had something else to add. As he did, he noticed Tel' Shira grab for her knives and jump around.

Reaching for an arrow, Artimus turned and watched as the ground before them split apart. Dirt fell aside as the figure of the Avatar rose from the soil. Taking shape, Artimus noted the smile he wore on his face.

"It seems your mission was a success," Oogmut began.

"Perhaps you can explain what is happening with the undead we were all prepared to fight?"

The Avatar surveyed the group, looking back to the lamia and to each of the front party members in turn.

After a notable pause, he finally spoke.

"Yezurkstal has been contained, yes."

There was something unusual about the Avatar's tone as he turned and glanced back towards Yezurkstal's undead army. Artimus couldn't put his finger on what it was, but his tone was more somber and metered than usual. Perhaps even more subtle, his smile faded as he gazed at the now frozen enemies.

"And the undead army," Artimus started. "Are they still a threat?"

The Avatar appeared perfectly still, his face hardened as he kept his gaze ahead. The air felt as thick as butter as there was once again a pause. After a solid six seconds of silence, the Avatar finally spoke.

"They are nothing but empty vessels now. The profane magic Yezurkstal used to reanimate them will leave a permanent blight upon this land. But you need not concern yourself with that now. Return home. I will ensure they find rest."

Irontail approached the Avatar, twisting his grip on his club.

"We could assist you in disp-"

"No." The Avatar's voice boomed through the valley.

"These humans don't deserve the fate they met with. Only I am equipped to properly handle this."

Artimus turned to Savannah and the rest of the part in turn. He was met with wide eyes, closed mouths, and a mixture of fear, dread, and confusion. There was something primal inside him that indicated the 'no' alone was all they needed to hear.

It was a command, and no one present was going to disobey a command from the Avatar of Evorath.

Chapter 30

Outskirts of Erathal City
7 Neglur, 1087 MT

Artimus shook his head, looking down at the cabin floor in disbelief. He wanted to get lost in the pattern of the wood grain, forget about the troubles of the world. But, here he sat with an elf he never really respected or cared to work alongside.

In fact, he had never trusted the company of Guildpac. Yet here he sat with Savannah, ready to reveal this secret. It felt like a betrayal, but then again, it couldn't compare to the level of betrayal Cabal had executed.

"You must understand, I was quite surprised that you summoned me here," Guildpac began after an uncomfortable silence.

"I hope that this is not some elaborate ruse to further damage my reputation, or that of our King Ulagret."

Artimus looked up, focusing, and locking eyes with Guildpac.

"I promise you Guildpac, we have no such agenda. In fact, we come to you penitent, realizing we made a grave mistake with Cabal. But Savannah would be better suited to explain."

Guildpac seemed unable to hide his amusement. His lips curled into a wide smile, his teeth showing through. Artimus wondered if it was intentional. He wanted to stand up and punch the bureaucratic windbag directly in the jaw.

"Penitent, you say" he smirked and leaned back, loosening his arms.

"Don't get too comfortable," Savannah interjected. "We still don't think highly of you, but perhaps our judgment of Ulagret was a bit harsh."

Artimus couldn't hold back a smile of his own as he considered Savannah's words. And, seeing the color drain back out of Guildpac's face made it all the better. As the windbag opened his mouth to pipe in again, Savannah continued.

"I'm sure even you want to stay quiet long enough to hear this. We've learned something unsettling -no, not just unsettling. We've learned something terrifying about Cabal. What do you know about neuromagic?"

Guildpac opened his mouth and raised his right eyebrow. Just as he exhaled to begin talking, Savannah interrupted.

"And, I don't want some bureaucratic garbage," she started. "I mean, what experience do you have dealing with neuromagic?"

Exhaling, Guildpac slowly lowered his hand as his smile leveled out.

"Well…I guess no direct experience. But, I do kn-"

"Let her continue," Artimus jumped in.

Slumping down in his chair, Guildpac nodded.

"So, here's the deal," Savannah began. She glanced back to Artimus, her eyes heavy. That single glance seemed to convey the burden of what she was about to explain. Artimus nodded, knowing how difficult it was to admit.

"We've been hoodwinked," she said turning back and looking Guildpac in the eyes.

"Cabal is using an advanced form of neuromagic. My old mentor told me stories of sea witches who could exercise complete control of their victims through neuromagic. And, while his mastery doesn't seem quite that complete, I have come to realize that in the past few years, Cabal has garnered his support thanks to this magic."

For the first time since he had known him, Artimus watched Guildpac sit up straight, a stern look coming over his face. His eyes met Savannah's glare and for a moment it almost seemed as if he conveyed a sense of humility.

"Please, go on," he requested.

And, as Savannah explained Cabal's treachery, Artimus couldn't help but feel his entire world was crumbling in. What would the future hold, and would he be prepared?

With Savannah at his side, he felt some comfort knowing they would survive.

-=-=-=-=-=-=-=-=-

Erathal News Article 101:96
Your Chancellor Lies
By, High Wizard Guildpac

Previously serving as the right hand for your King Ulagret, many of you recognize my grand magical abilities as some of the greatest in all the realms. Over the years, I have earned the trust of many. Despite this, it seems that our true leader, King Ulagret is not garnering the support of Chancellor Cabal. With a heavy heart, I write today to explain why.

While I want what is best for this Republic, it pains me to know that its citizens have been hoodwinked. For the news I have today is of the most disturbing variety. It is a betrayal that cannot be ignored.

I have learned from a reputable source within Cabal's inner circle that, despite all appearances, his motives are much more sinister than we have been led to believe. According to these sources, Cabal has quite the magical prowess, and over the course of the past few years he has been building his following using manipulative measures.

With my accomplishments as a wizard, it pains me to admit that I had not previously noticed such maneuvers, but upon hearing this magic described, I do believe I have an explanation.

As some of you are aware, there are fables of sirens, mermaids, and other folks of the ocean that employ a sort of neuromagic. That is, a magic that attacks the mind of its victim. This can be used for a variety of applications. Whether to cause someone undo anger, make them forget something of importance, or even to downright control the mind of others.

These creatures are said to have the ability to employ such magic to enslave the minds of their foes. Apparently, it seems that your current Chancellor has studied the lore and even gotten his hand on a spell book that gives him access to these powers.

I fear that his manipulative and controlling magic may prevent this news from being released. If his forces learn of my discovery, my life will no doubt be in grave danger. In fact, I suspect that by writing this I paint a target on myself. But, should it go through, I know that my life is but a small price to pay.

Your free-will is essential to your life as an elf. For someone to employ such dishonest and manipulative magic to steal away power is a terrifying proposition. Despite this, I can assure you all that it is very real. Your very will is being manipulated each time Cabal speaks, and with the election only one week away, it is essential we vote accordingly.

We must take a stand and let him know that we will not put up with this. Perhaps more importantly, when our true leader, Ulagret is appointed as the new chancellor, we must act. Cabal must be brought to justice for this affront.

If you are reading this, make sure to vote with your conscious. Make sure Cabal is not around to destroy our Republic.

-=-=-=-=-=-=-=-=-

Yezurkstal won't remain imprisoned forever. Read book 3, *The Battle for Erathal* and learn the fate of your favorite heroes.

The Rise of Yezurkstal is the second book in the Evorath trilogy. Visit us online for free access to additional stories, and to sign up for notifications about future releases. The third book, *Erathal's United Stand,* is due for release in February 2024, so get ready to join the adventure as the next chapter unfolds.

If you enjoyed this book, please help other readers find that same enjoyment by returning to where you purchased it and leaving a positive review. Your voice matters. Leave a review on Amazon.

Appendices I - Map of Evorath, continent of Erathal

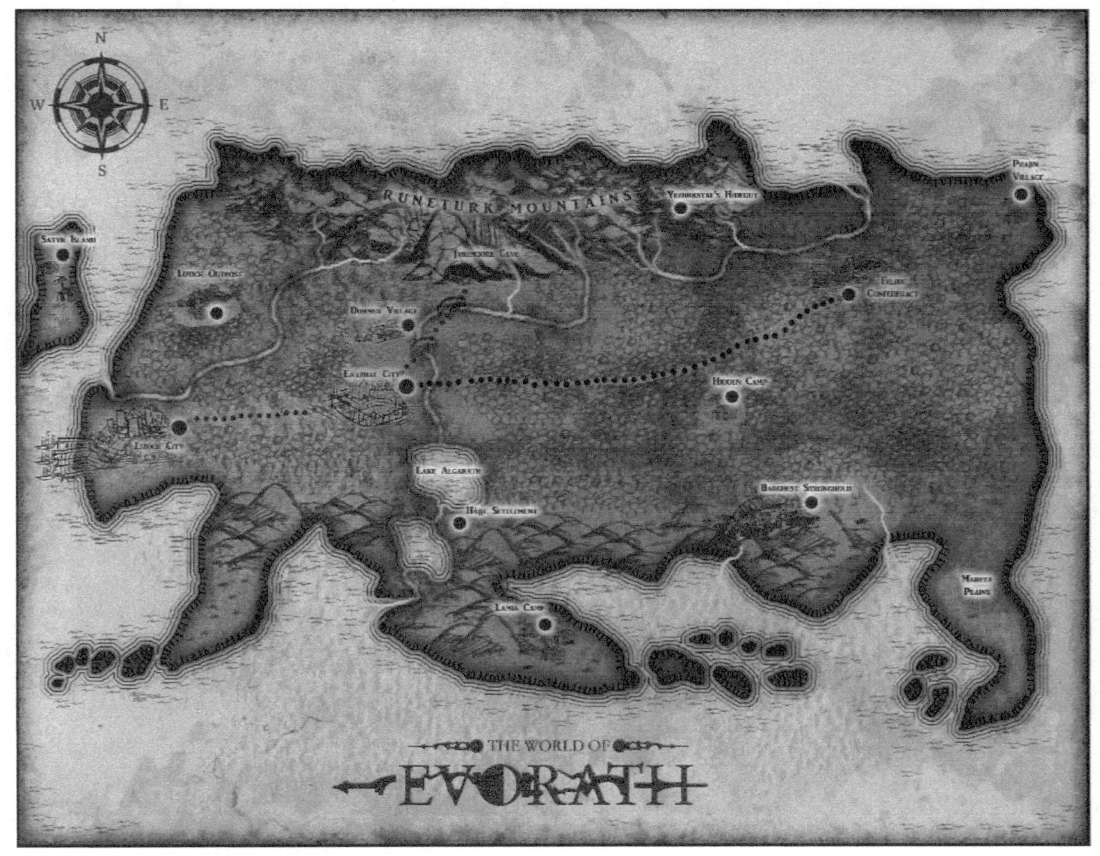

Appendices II - Glossary of Select Terms

- Adamantium - Also known as Admantite, Adamantine, or Adamant. Strongest metal in existence, yet weighs no more than steel. This natural metal is light green in color and can be found in some of the deepest, darkest, caves.

- Barghest - A broad-shouldered and wide-chested species of bipedal canines. They make up some of the strongest warriors in Evorath but are nearing extinction due to their warrior nature.

- Centaur - Half-horse and half-man, this sentient species has many tribes scattered throughout the continent of Erathal..

- Demons - Not native to Evorath, demons are summoned from another realm. These creatures come in all shapes and sizes, but usually have dark, leathery skin.

- Destrier - A special breed of horse raised for war. They are bred to be hardy and stout, giving them great stamina and favoring strength over speed.

- Dryad - Guardians of the forest, there is one dryad for each type of tree on Evorath. They have untold powers over the forest and work to maintain balance in the forest.

- Dumner - This centaur village is located near the Elvish Kingdom of Erathal and is home to a great warrior tribe.

- Elf - Similar in stature to the humans of Earth, Elves are the most abundant sentient species in Evorath. They have pointy ears and almost exclusively have light features.

- Erathal - Name of the continent this adventure takes place in. Also the name of the major Elvish city. It is inhabited by many sentient creatures.

- Ether - The space between different worlds. Reaching through the ether requires great magical abilities and allows a mage to summon creatures from one of these other worlds.

- Felite - One of the most populous species on the continent of Erathal, felite are a bipedal feline species that resemble their four-legged cousins. While many felite roam in small tribes, most are members of the Felite Confederacy, which sits to the northeast of the forest.

- Hájje - Elvish word for a dark elf. It comes from the elvish word Haijja, which means 'dark', or 'evil'.

- Jyrimoore Caves - An abandoned dwarven mine initially prospected for adamantium deposits. It is now the notorious site of heinous experiments conducted by a misguided elvish researcher.

- Lamia - A sentient race that still maintains a tribal nature. Their lower half resembles a snake and their upper half is that of an elf. Females greatly outnumber the males of the species, which is why their population is diminishing.

- Lizock - One of the most populous sentient species on the continent of Erathal, lizock are a bipedal reptilian race that resembles the common lizard. Though they can vary in size, shape, and color, the race is most well-known for its warriors and merchants.

- Lynx - A medium-sized wild cat with a short tail. Folklore indicates that these elusive felines have latent magical abilities.

- Mythril - A silverish-blue metal used primarily by elves and sometimes by dwarves. It is as light as aluminum and stronger than steel, making it a great option for the battlefield.

- Roc - A large, eagle-like bird with light brown feathers. Though wild roc can have wingspans over 15 meters, some species use these tamed birds as mounts for their aerial units. These tamed variety typically have a wingspan under 10 meters.

- Runeturk Mountains - Major mountain range bordering Erathal to the north. This range is populated by thousands of dwarves, some gnomes, and less civilized creatures like ogres, orcs, goblins, and wild animals.

- Satyr - A sentient species of Evorath once known for great works of art and music, they are now known more for their proclivity towards alcoholism. These bipedal creatures are half-elf, half-goat, with their upper half being the former and their lower half resembling the latter.

- Troll - A sentient species of Evorath. Nomadic in nature, trolls are both tall and menacing in their physical features, with many blemishes on their skin and a crude language.

- Urgo - An elvish word of affirmation. Essentially equivalent to saying "yes, sir" or "understood."

9 780099 788324